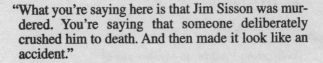
—————————— ★ ——————————

"What you're saying here is that Jim Sisson was murdered. You're saying that someone deliberately crushed him to death. And then made it look like an accident."

"It appears that way."

"That means whoever it was would have had to clout him on the head or something first...overpower him in some way. He wouldn't just lie still, waiting to be crushed."

"Exactly," I said. "Maybe the autopsy will show something. But if it was something as simple as a blow to the back of the head, that's not going to show up. Not with his skull crushed the way it was."

"Give me a photo. At least give me that much," he pleaded. "It's not often I get to scoop the big-city dailies."

"One one condition," I said. "On one condition, we'll fix you right up."

"What's that?"

"Don't use the word *homicide* yet."

—————————— ★ ——————————

Previously published Worldwide Mystery title by
STEVEN F. HAVILL

OUT OF SEASON

Forthcoming Worldwide Mystery title by
STEVEN F. HAVILL

BAG LIMIT

STEVEN F. HAVILL
DEAD
WEIGHT

WORLDWIDE.

TORONTO • NEW YORK • LONDON
AMSTERDAM • PARIS • SYDNEY • HAMBURG
STOCKHOLM • ATHENS • TOKYO • MILAN
MADRID • WARSAW • BUDAPEST • AUCKLAND

For Kathleen

DEAD WEIGHT

A Worldwide Mystery/January 2002

First published by St. Martin's Press, Incorporated.

ISBN 0-373-26408-9

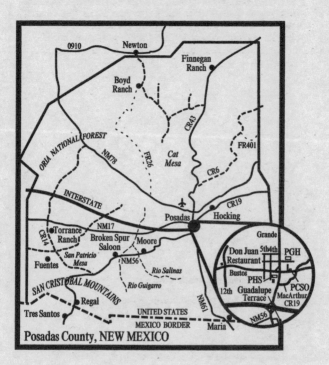

Posadas County, NEW MEXICO

ONE

THE AIR CONDITIONING in car 310 worked so well that my knees ached from the arctic blast out of the vents. The rest of me simmered. The tinted windows were marginal help as the afternoon July sun baked the car's paint, the vinyl inside, and me.

I had tried opening all four windows, but the effect was like putting a fan inside an oven that was set to broil and then standing in front of the stove's open door. It would have been a good afternoon to sit in my office and work on the budget. I had returned from lunch with exactly that plan when I found the Post-it on my door from Gayle Torrez, our chief dispatcher and wife of Undersheriff Robert Torrez.

I held the note out at arm's length so I could read Gayle's neat, precise printing. The message was clear enough: *Carla Champlin asked that you stop by her house this afternoon.* There wasn't much there that needed clarification, but a dodge was still worth trying. I walked the half-dozen steps that would put me within easy talking distance of where Gayle sat by the dispatch console.

"Gayle, ask one of the two Toms to swing by and talk to the old battle-ax," I said, referring to Deputies Tom Mears and Tom Pasquale. "Or—"

"Ms. Champlin asked specifically that you stop by, sir," Gayle said without looking up from her computer keyboard.

"I'm sure she did," I said. I crumpled the note and tossed it in the trash can.

"And it's probably very important, too," Gayle added, and glanced up at me with a grin. "She didn't want to talk on the phone."

"Oh, yes," I said. "I'm sure." There was no point in arguing. I was in no mood to talk to Carla Champlin. Facing her took patience in any weather, and the sweat that trickled down my back had eroded my marginally good humor. But I suppose I felt just a touch guilty. I hadn't seen the woman in months. The village of Posadas didn't include a multitude of souls or a multitude of streets. Still, our paths hadn't crossed recently, and I hadn't made much of an effort.

Miss Champlin—and she insisted on that Miss rather than a Ms.—had retired from the post office three years before at age seventy. Either the postal service didn't enforce the sixty-five-and-out rule, or she had lied to them all these years. The latter was entirely possible.

She was three years and some odd months older than me, and at the time of her retirement she still had been rake-thin and agile. She'd been blessed with the sort of good health that kept the arthritis out of her joints and the stiffness out of her back.

During the decades that I'd known her, our conversations were the comfortable sort that took place with her on one side of the postal service window and me on the other, leaning on the worn and polished wood of the customer window shelf. She was one of the village fixtures, a woman who knew everyone and everyone's business.

For years, we'd exchanged at the very least a grunted pleasantry every day except Sundays and legal holidays. More often than not, it was just the voice that I heard, with the woman hidden by the rank and file of postal boxes as she rammed bills, circulars, and catalogs into the five hundred and sixty postal patron slots.

In retirement, Carla Champlin had retreated to the comfort of her small, neat home and the gardens that filled her lot, one of the few showplaces in Posadas. I'd driven by on numerous occasions and never stopped. Several times I'd heard secondhand versions of disputes she'd had with neighbors who didn't know quack grass from cholla, but what was a neighborhood without a rumor or dispute or two?

And so that afternoon I drove west on Bustos Avenue, past Pershing Park where Black Jack's old tank, too hot today to touch, rested on its concrete pedestal, waiting all these years for Pancho Villa to spring another attack across the border. A few blocks beyond the park, I turned right onto 6th Street. As far ahead as I could see, until the macadam of 6th turned to dirt and the horizon faded into the heat waves, not a soul stirred...no kids on bikes, no health nuts striding out their daily mileage, not even a dog sniffing a tire.

Posadas baked, and anyone with any sense stayed inside where air conditioners or thick, cool adobe made the midday heat bearable.

The retired postmistress lived two houses from the north end of 6th Street in the house that she'd purchased new in 1974. When she'd moved in, the lot was level sand, a nicely uniform, blemish-free canvas for her to attack. And attack it she had. Whatever she planted thrived, whether or not the garden catalogs or the experts said it would survive our blast-furnace summers. Carla Champlin didn't just give in to the climate and plant cacti and rocks like her neighbors did.

Maybe Carla Champlin had a water bill in quadruple digits. My theory was that she simply told the plants that they'd damn well better grow, or else. And grow they did, a riot of color and texture that packed every square inch from curb to front door and then skirted the house to the backyard with its huge grape arbor and vegetable garden.

I parked 310 at the curb and took a deep breath before getting out, taking in the incredible show. Carla could have won every class in every county fair flower show if that's what she had wanted. Apparently she left the competition to others.

Judging from the drape of the grapevines in the arbor, she was going to have a bumper crop—of raisins if nothing else. The arbor served a dual purpose, though. Parked in its shade was a medium-sized self-contained RV, one of those big stub-nosed beasts that folks in the North buy to flee southward come winter.

I hadn't realized Carla Champlin was the traveling type, but whether she was or not, the colors of the RV meshed perfectly with the rest of the display.

With a sigh, I got out of the car. Not a breath of air stirred, and the sky was a blank and featureless, like a fine piece of stainless steel with a light spray coat of blue paint.

Two strides put me between the first rows of daylilies, dahlias, and delphiniums. Although I was sure it was my imagination, the yard felt cooler and a little more friendly.

I reached the front step just as the front door opened.

"Good," Miss Champlin said. "You got my note." That sufficed as a greeting, and she pushed open the aluminum storm door and beckoned.

The first wash of cool air from deep inside the house was wonderful as I stepped inside. I took off my straw Bailey and dropped it on a handy chair. With one smooth motion, Carla Champlin closed the front door behind me, stepped around and picked up my hat, and hung it properly on the rack beside the dark wood-framed mirror. Having thus established that she, by God, was in control, she beckoned me to follow.

"Let's go to the kitchen," she said over her shoulder. "It's cooler there, and I'm sure you'd like some iced tea or some such."

"How are you doing, Carla?" I said. "Your flowers look great." If she replied I didn't hear it. As I made my way toward the kitchen, I scanned the photos that lined the hallway. They weren't of family or famous politicians or snowcapped mountains. Each was an identically framed photo of Carla Champlin kneeling beside a show dog, the ribbons—mostly blue—prominently-displayed. The champions were without exception boxers, each as flat-faced, stub-tailed, and bulging with muscles as the next. They all looked like clones of the same dog.

I stopped beside one photo whose background included a large sign that announced the PAWTUCKET NATIONAL TRIALS. The dog in that portrait was gazing off into the distance as if deep in thought— probably an impossibility. The ribbon Carla Champlin held was enormous, and beside her on the floor stood a trophy that must have been three feet tall. Capping the chrome monument was a cast figure that I assumed was a boxer.

The Carla Champlin in the photo was decades, perhaps even centuries, younger than the one currently clanking glasses in the kitchen.

"When did you do show dogs?" I asked.

"A long, long time ago," she said, and appeared in the kitchen door holding a dish towel. "That's Blake."

"Blake?"

"It's short for what's on his papers, which is even more asinine," Carla said without offering further explanation. "He was the first national champion I ever had."

"But not the last."

"Not the last."

"I didn't know you even owned a dog, Carla."

"I don't. Not anymore. As I said, that was all a long, long time ago. Come have some tea."

I moved into the kitchen and she handed me a tall, elegant glass already sweating from the ice and topped with three slices of lemon. "As I remember, you don't use sugar," she said.

"No, thanks." I had no idea why she would know anything about my tea habits, but thirty years in a small town supplied lots of ancillary, and most often useless, information if you chose to take notice and remember. Maybe she'd just noticed my ample girth and made a lucky guess that I was trying to do something about it.

"Why did you give the dogs up?"

"Allergies," she snapped with considerable venom. "And a reversal of fortune. All about the time I turned forty." She smiled without much humor. "Such a delight life can be, sometimes."

"I suppose." I knew that she had been married at one point in her life, but I didn't suppose that discussing her early life with the dogs was why she had summoned me to her home on a broiling summer's day. "This is the first time I've ever noticed your camper out back."

"Oh, that thing," she said. "Now listen," she added, as if I hadn't been. "You know my sister." The blank look on my face stopped her. "Elaine Doyle?" she prompted.

I frowned and shook my head. "I didn't know you had a sister, Carla."

"Well, she's my sister-in-law, really, but that's just a technicality. You know Bobby Doyle."

"He ran the drive-in theater," I said, remembering a small, quick-moving man who smelled of buttered popcorn. "He died some time ago. I didn't know he was your brother."

"He wasn't," Carla said. "Elaine's first husband, Scott Champlin, was my brother."

I chuckled. "I didn't know Scott, either."

Carla waved a hand. "He lived in Terre Haute, of all places. Never visited here. But that's neither here nor there. Listen. Elaine's not wired just right, if you know what I mean. I love her like a real sister, but sometimes she just goes off the deep end. When she's into the bottle...well, you know how that goes. Anyway, about five years ago, when they moved away, I purchased that little house of theirs over on Third Street. Two Twenty-one Third Street, just behind the Salazar funeral home. And by the way, that was their RV, too. I bought it as a favor, thinking maybe I'd do a little traveling, like I used to do on the show circuit."

"That might be fun."

"Well, not traveling alone it isn't. If you hear of anyone who wants to buy the thing, let me know. It's in perfect condition. It just sits there."

All of that was delivered with the rapidity of a machine gun. Carla Champlin's voice had lost none of its metallic bark.

"So, what's the problem?"

"The problem, Sheriff, is that I purchased the house on Third Street as something of an investment. I know it's not all that much, just five rooms, but it was just such a dollhouse. I rented it to the McClaines for almost four years, and they were just perfect tenants. Just perfect. You remember them, of course." She paused for a moment to let that sink in. I knew that the McClaines no longer lived at 221 3rd Street, but I knew better than to interrupt Carla just when she was spooling up.

"A beautiful yard, everything. The two of them had one small child, but then Mr. McClaine took work out of town, and they had to move."

"Uh-huh," I said, and sipped the tea.

"And now, I'm just worried sick."

I pulled out a chair from the white kitchen table and sat down carefully. "Start from the beginning," I suggested, knowing exactly what was coming. "You're unhappy with a tenant?"

"Unhappy is an understatement," Carla Champlin said, sounding pleased that I had cut to the chase in such fine fashion. "I wish I had thought to take a photograph of the place when the McClaines left. What a picture."

"And now it's a mess," I said.

"You've seen it?"

"At a distance. I know the renter."

"Of course you do. It's one of your deputies." Her expression said, *And that's why I called you.* When I didn't respond instantly, she added, "I know it's none of your affair, except something has to be done. I'm not going to stand by and watch my investment just go frittering out the window."

"Have you talked to Deputy Pasquale?"

"I've driven by there endless times. He's either not there or makes these grand, endless promises that he never keeps. He can be a charmer, that's for sure. Have you seen the front lawn?"

"Not recently, ma'am."

"Well, you should go look. It's just such a shame. And everything else. If it's green, he kills it."

I tried my best not to smile. "Let me talk to Tom," I said. "I'm not sure what I can do, but let me talk to him first."

"I wish you'd do that. Perhaps he'll be reasonable. You know, I even tried calling Judge Hobart's office. I've left messages, but he hasn't seen fit to respond. I don't have the time, or inclination, or the money to go to a lawyer, Mr. Gastner. But if you can convince that young man to be reasonable, that would be such a help."

Reasonable wasn't the first adjective that came to my mind when someone mentioned Deputy Thomas Pasquale, but I nodded agreement, certain that the whole problem was just one of those petty things that festered in hot weather until it blistered out of all proportion.

I drained the last of the tea and stood up. "I'll see about it," I said, as if that were the first thing on my afternoon's agenda.

TWO

THAT WAS THE FIRST TIME that Deputy Thomas Pasquale's name was mentioned to me that day. I could put up with once. It was the nature of law enforcement that complaints were a hundred times more common than compliments. Few people enjoyed being drawn up short, whether for a routine traffic ticket or something worse. Reprimands, tickets, and jail were all ego bruisers, and lots of folks who crossed our paths in an official capacity didn't much enjoy the experience.

It was human nature to blame the cop. If we wrote a speeding ticket to a local, we were called hard-nosed, unreasonable, and then accused of making it impossible for honest law-abiding citizens to earn their livings. If we wrote tickets to out-of-towners, we were making Posadas a speed trap, harassing the tourists and truckers, ruining the local economy.

And domestic disputes were the worst, no matter whether it was a spouse pounding on his better half or a mindless dispute over a flower bed that encroached six inches over a property line. Tempers flared, especially if they were alcohol-fueled. That's what made me uneasy when I heard complaints like Carla Champlin's.

Deputy Thomas Pasquale, one of our department's youngest officers and certainly our foremost hot rod, had garnered his share of scathing mention by citizens, despite a couple of well-publicized occasions when he'd been nothing short of a goddamn hero. It all went with the turf.

More than once I had given him a dressing-down reminiscent of the recruit ass-chewings I had delivered countless times during twenty years in the marines. To his credit, young Pasquale took the corrections in stride and learned from them, after a fashion.

Regardless of what he did on duty, his living habits were none of my business, and I had no intention, despite what I had told Carla Champlin, of placing myself in any formal fashion between Thomas Pasquale and his landlady. I had told Carla that I would talk with Thomas, and that was a promise easy enough to keep.

After the cool of Carla Champlin's house and tea, the heat inside the car was enough to take my breath away. The patrol car started, hesitated, and then settled into a rough idle as the air conditioner compressor kicked in. I winked a trickle of sweat away from my left eye and jotted a quick entry in my log, then tossed the clipboard on the seat and pulled 310 into gear. It promptly stalled.

I cursed a string of abuses as the engine cranked rapidly with that high-pitched, jingling sound of a motor well past its prime. With the windows buzzed down, I waited for a few seconds and tried again with the air conditioner off, and this time was rewarded as the engine caught.

Three blocks later, at the intersection of 6th and Bustos, a small yellow idiot light on the dash flickered on, the temperature needle hovered in the red, and the engine sighed into silence once again. I drifted the car over to the curb and stopped. Several abortive efforts to start the damn thing produced only an additional sheen of sweat on my forehead.

As if she'd been listening, Gayle Torrez's mellow, cool voice said, "Three ten, Posadas. Ten-twenty."

"Three ten is disabled at the corner of Bustos and Sixth," I snapped into the mike, and then took a deep breath before I added, "Call Manny at the county yard and tell 'em that he's got a dead one that needs the wrecker."

"Ten-four. And, three ten, there's a gentleman here who'd like to speak with you."

"Ten-four," I said, and rummaged through the litter on my front seat to find my cellular phone. I punched in the number and Gayle answered on the first ring.

"Just a moment, sir," she said to me, and I could hear voices in the background. I heard Gayle say to someone else, "No, sir, this is fine. He won't mind," and then another voice said, "Sheriff?"

"This is Gastner." I wondered what it was that I wouldn't mind.

"Sheriff, this is Arny Gray. Did I catch you at a bad time?"

I laughed. "That depends, Doc. What can I do for you?"

"I'd sure like to talk with you for a bit," Arnold Gray said, and his voice dropped a couple of decibels.

"Well, I'm a captive audience at the moment," I said, and wiped a trickle of sweat off the end of my nose. If I didn't make a move soon, I was going to be a puddle. The nearest business was just a few steps away, and I knew that Kealey's Kleaners and Laundry was air-conditioned. I started to heave myself out of the car.

"I heard your radio call," Gray said. "Let me swing by there and pick you up. Then we can have a glass of iced-tea or something at the Don Juan."

Dr. Arnold Gray, a chiropractor whom I had always thought to be the smartest of the five county commissioners, leaped several notches upward in my estimation.

"That is, if you've got the time," he added.

"I've got the time. I'm right at the intersection of Sixth and Bustos, beside the dry cleaner's. I'll be looking for you. And I appreciate this, believe me."

"Won't be but a minute," Gray said, and switched off. I took the phone and locked the car, the sun hard on my back, as if someone inside Kealey's were holding the pressing table to my shoulders.

The young lady behind the counter at the cleaner's looked teary-eyed, as if she might have been sniffing the cleaning fluid. Maybe it was just midsummer allergies or a wrenching romance novel that she'd been reading. She smiled brightly and nodded at me.

"Can I help you, sir?"

"I've got a ride coming to pick me up," I said, and waved at 310. She looked out the window, puzzled. "It broke down," I added. "If you see anyone trying to steal it before the wrecker gets here, wish 'em luck for me."

"Oh," she said.

I didn't know her name, and although her name tag said *Judy,* that didn't ring any bells. Royce Kealey had owned the place for all of the thirty years I'd been bringing my weekly load of shirts there, and I knew Judy wasn't family. Trying to know every living soul in a tiny village became an occupational hazard after a while. If I worked at it hard enough, I could be a walking gazetteer of who was who in Posadas County, New Mexico. Not that it all mattered much in the great scheme of things.

"Would you like a drink of ice water or something?" Judy asked, and I shook my head.

"You're a sweetheart for asking, though," I said.

In less than two minutes, a white Continental slid to the curb. I turned to the girl as I headed toward the door. "Thanks."

"You have a nice day, Sheriff. Come back and see us." She sounded as if she really knew who I was, and that puzzled me even more.

Arnold Gray touched the electric door lock button of the Continental just as I reached the curb.

"Hot, eh?" he said when I opened the door.

"It's a dry heat," I replied as I slid into the cool leather. I slammed the door, and the armrest cracked my elbow hard enough to make me wince.

"So's the Sahara," Gray said, and pulled the Continental away from the curb. "Patrol car broke, eh? Just like you said it would."

I grinned. "You've got a good memory," I said.

Two meetings previous, I'd given the county commission hell for not allowing adequate funding for four new vehicles beyond the one already in the budget. Somehow, the concept of police cars actually wearing out was a novel idea, even though every county in the United States went through the identical process on a routine basis.

Two of the commissioners, Gray and Janelle Waters, had been in favor of spending whatever it took to buy the new units. They were a minority.

"How many miles on that thing now?" Gray asked cheerfully.

"A hundred and eighty-seven thousand," I said, and reached out a hand for support as we wafted into the parking lot of the Don Juan de Oñate Restaurant, just six blocks west of Kealey's Kleaners. "I'm the only one who drives it," I added. "I don't let any of the road deputies use it." We pulled into a parking place in the shade of the building. "I move slowly enough that it can keep up with me...most of the time. But you didn't take time out from cracking bones to talk about old cars. What can I do for you?"

Arnold Gray frowned and shoved the car into park. "Let's go inside and find a quiet corner."

In midafternoon of a July Tuesday in Posadas, that wasn't hard to do, even in the most popular restaurant in town.

The place was cool as a refrigerator, and the bright yellow plastic booth benches were downright cold. I slid in until I could turn sideways and lean against the dark wood wainscoting.

Even as I came to a comfortable halt with one arm stretched out across the back of the booth, JanaLynn Torrez appeared around the partition.

My undersheriff's cousin grinned but otherwise refrained from mentioning that I'd left that very spot not an hour before.

"What can I get you gentlemen?"

"Two iced teas?" Gray said, glancing at me. I nodded.

She disappeared, and Arnold Gray leaned both forearms on the table. He had either hemorrhoids, gas, or something serious nagging at his insides. I pulled my arm down from the booth and straightened up, attentive and serious.

"So what gives?" I asked.

"God, I hate this," Gray said, and grimaced. He looked off to the right at the empty tables surrounding us.

I shrugged. "Just say it, then."

Gray regarded me thoughtfully. "This is between us," he said, and I frowned impatiently. We hadn't gone out of our way to make it a public meeting, unless we invited JanaLynn to sit in when she returned with the tea. She arrived and set the two extra-large, perspiring glasses in front of us.

"Anything else, sir?"

I waved a hand. "No, nothing. We just need some peace and quiet for a while." I grinned at her, and she touched my shoulder.

"I'll be out front if you need me."

The two of us were left in vinyl-padded silence. I sipped the tea, and it was wonderful, as usual.

"So," I said.

Gray took a deep breath, leaving his tea untouched in front of him. "How well do you know Thomas Pasquale?"

"Uh," I groaned, and sat back hard enough that I thumped against the seat. "Now what?"

"I'm serious. What kind of fellow is he? I don't know him except to say hello."

"He's a local boy," I said. "Worked the village PD for a while as a part-timer. Applied to our department a handful of times and each time was refused, mainly on my say-so."

"And why was that?"

"Way too immature."

"But you eventually hired him."

"Yes. It's been three years, going on four. He's grown up a lot. Still eager, sometimes way too eager."

"Ambitions?"

"What do you mean by that?"

"What's he want out of life? FBI? Some big department?"

"As far as I know, Posadas is his life. His family's here, and he's never mentioned anything else to me. Not that I pry much. He seems content working here. There are always surprises, of course."

"Huh," Gray mused. He looked down at the tea for a long minute and I let him think uninterrupted. I had all day. I knew the commissioner would get where he wanted to go eventually. "You ever hear anything about his finances?"

"His finances are none of my business. Or yours," I said.

Gray grinned. "I appreciate that. But if Deputy Pasquale were in some kind of financial trouble, you'd know about it, probably."

It wasn't a question, and I didn't respond. Gray finally took a sip of his tea, grimaced, and reached for the sugar. "This is what I got," he said, but made no move other than letting the sugar slide smoothly out of three packets. He swirled the tea, pulled out the spoon, and placed it on the table—all little preparatory gestures as he wound up to tell me what was on his mind.

"This is what I got," he repeated, and reached in his pocket. He handed the white number 10 envelope to me, holding it by one corner. There was no stamp, just the name Dr. Arnold Gray typed in the address spot. It had been zipped open with either a letter opener or a knife. I looked inside and saw the neatly folded message. Laying the envelope to one side, I spread the message out, well away from my sweating glass of tea. It was typed, just a few lines:

Commissioner: you need to know that one of the Posadas Deputies Thomas Pasquale is hitting up on Mexican nationales when he stops them for routine traffic checks. In five instances that we have documented, he has collected an average of $100.00 each.

A concerned citizen

"Christ," I muttered, and read the thing twice more, then adjusted my glasses and peered more closely at the typing. "Single-strike typewriter, or word processor," I said. I looked across at Arnold Gray. His expression was pained. "This didn't come in the mail."

"No. Under the door of my office when I got there this morning."

"Just this envelope?"

He nodded.

"Huh," I said, for want of anything better.

"Do you believe it?" Gray asked.

I almost snapped out an unthinking response, then stopped. "Do you?"

"I'm not much for anonymous notes," Gray said. "What worries me is why that note was written in the first place, and written to me, of all people."

"You're a county commissioner."

"But why not to you? You're sheriff. You're Tom Pasquale's boss, not me."

"The implication there is pretty clear," I said more offhandedly than I felt. "Obviously whoever wrote this note thinks that I'm in on the deal."

"Oh, sure," Gray laughed and sat back, some of the strain going out of his face. "I can see that. You don't speak enough Spanish to make yourself understood beyond *'I'll have a burrito.'*"

"That's cruel," I said.

"I can just see you, standing out in the dark, negotiating with a vanload of Mexican nationals," Gray said.

"I don't see Tom Pasquale doing that, either," I retorted. "But they claim documentation. Either they have it, or they don't. If they have it, why the hell not come forward with it?"

"I don't know."

"You trust me with this?" I picked up the note. What I really felt like doing was crumpling it up and sticking it in the Don Juan's trash with all the uneaten refried beans and rice.

"Of course."

"Did you make yourself a copy?"

Arnold Gray gave me a look as if I'd stuck a fork in the back of his hand. He didn't dignify the question with an answer, and I moved his name even farther up the list to "favorite people" status.

THREE

DR. ARNOLD GRAY dropped me back at the modest flat-roofed two-story structure that Posadas grandly called its Public Safety Building. As I walked inside, a trash can by the pay phone reminded me that my first inclination, to tear the anonymous note into shreds before it could do any damage, was probably a good one. The whole idea of someone sanctimoniously tapping out a little message that could ruin either a career or a life made my stomach churn.

But I wasn't naive, either. In a department with a dozen employees, there was always an off-chance that one of them wasn't as pure as the driven snow.

When I walked in, Gayle Torrez glanced up from her desk. Hell, I'd known her since she was a skinny twelve-year-old. She'd started working for the Sheriff's Department when she was eighteen, had been with us for a decade, and was now married to Undersheriff Robert Torrez. If the note rang true, was she in on the scam? Was he?

I dropped the white envelope in my center desk drawer and slammed it shut until I could figure out what to do about the damn thing. After taking a minute to straighten my face so the anger wouldn't show, I strolled out to Dispatch. Gayle was on the phone, the pencil in her right hand doodling little spirals on the scratch pad. Every once in a while, she'd stop spiraling and the pencil point would tap a few times on the pad as she listened.

"Sure," she said. I leaned against one of the black filing cabinets and waited. The pencil tapped another series. "Sure." She nodded. "I know it does." I took a deep breath and looked off into the distance. "Let me pass it on to the village for you. Maybe they'll listen to me." Gayle sat patiently through another long string and nodded as if the nod were carried over the wires. After a few more noncommittal pleasantries, she hung up.

"Another dog," she said, jotting in the big logbook by her elbow. "You'd think it would be too hot to bark." She looked up at me. "What's wrong, sir?"

"Wrong?" I asked.

"You looked peeved," Gayle said.

"The damn car, I suppose," I replied, and she accepted that with an understanding nod. I pushed myself away from the filing cabinet. "I need the dispatch logs for last month."

"Just June's?" She reached across to the steel bookcase under the window and pulled a slender black volume off the shelf. I took it and started back to my office.

"No calls for a while, all right? And when Bob comes in, I'd like to chat with him."

"He's home right now if you need him," Gayle said.

"No," I answered quickly and shook my head. "Just whenever he comes in this afternoon is fine." Gayle didn't ask what I wanted with the dispatch logs, my privacy, or her husband, and I felt better. Gayle Torrez worked hard at being the best dispatcher I'd ever met, making her a perfect match for her husband. Undersheriff Torrez worked the four-to-midnight shift, as well as twenty or thirty other odd hours during an average week. He avoided the boredom of working the day shift whenever he could.

Back in my office, I slumped back in the cool of my old leather chair, swung my feet up on the corner of my desk, and browsed through the logs. The volume included April, May, and June, and I concentrated on the last month, assuming that if there was any validity to the charge against Pasquale, the incident that had precipitated the note would be a recent one, not something from the distant past.

The logs were simple, black-on-white abbreviations of any activity that included radio conversations with the patrol officers. But their nebulous character could be frustrating. On June 3, for example, an entry read: *18:36, 303, 10-10.* That was followed by *18:59, 303, 10-8.*

Deputy Thomas Pasquale's vehicle was 303, and at 6:36 p.m. civilian time, he had announced that he was out of service, at home, no doubt engaged in something as exciting as eating a sandwich. Twenty-three minutes later, he was back in service—and there was no way to determine from the log where he was or what he was doing.

After studying the log for half an hour, I looked at my legal pad jottings. During the twenty-two days that he had worked in June, Deputy Pasquale had called in one hundred and thirty-seven requests for vehicle registration checks...the sort of routine action a deputy took when he stopped an unfamiliar vehicle for a traffic infraction or because something in the driver's manner had piqued his attention.

A rate of six or seven registration checks a night was average. On one extreme was Undersheriff Torrez, who might request one check a week; on the other, rookie Deputy Brent Sutherland, with us for three months, whose idea of a good time was running routine checks at three in the morning on cars parked in the Posadas Inn parking lot, down by the interstate.

Of Pasquale's one hundred and thirty-seven registration checks, one hundred and two were on vehicles stopped on one of the four state highways that cut up Posadas County like a little, withered pizza. That was logical, too, since the state highways carried the most traffic.

I frowned. If my numbers were right and my bifocals didn't lie, eighty-four of the traffic stops were logged on New Mexico 56. That particular ribbon of asphalt, at the moment damn near liquid under the fierce sun, wound southwest from Posadas across the two dry washes that New Mexicans loved to call rivers, up through the San Cristobal Mountains, to plunge south through the tiny village of Regal and then into Mexico.

My frown deepened, even though State 56 was the logical route for traffic stops. The snowbirds flocked up and down that route, either headed for who knows what in rural Mexico or turning westward at Regal, headed to Arizona. The only highway to carry heavier traffic was the interstate, but for the most part, deputies stayed off that artery, leaving it to the state police.

The anonymous note claimed that Pasquale was shaking down Mexican nationals, and at first blush State 56 would be the logical highway for that activity, were it not for the border crossing a mile south of the hamlet of Regal. That crossing was open from 6:00 a.m. to 8:00 p.m., with the stout gate securely locked the rest of the night. Foot traffic was no problem, if travelers didn't mind a little barbed wire. Vehicular traffic was out of the question.

If the Mexicans were crossing in Arizona, then ducking east through the mountains, 56 might be a logical route. I ran the numbers for April and May and found comparisons that differed by insignificant percentage points. Deputy Pasquale was consistent, if nothing else.

"And so what?" I said aloud.

I tossed the yellow pad on my desk, dropped the log on top of it, and leaned back, eyes closed. After a moment I picked up the log again. Deputy Tony Abeyta shared the swing shift with Pasquale and Torrez. Ten minutes later, I knew that Abeyta made forty-six traffic stops in June, barely two a night. Only eight of them had been on State 56.

There were explanations for that, too, but trying to crunch numbers only made me impatient. I was no statistician—and on top of that, I didn't believe that statistics would give me the kind of answer I wanted.

FOUR

THE CONUNDRUM was simple. If Tom Pasquale was innocent of the charges spelled out in the note, he deserved kid-glove handling. He would need all the help I could give him. He didn't deserve to lose sleep over the charges; he didn't deserve the beginnings of an ulcer.... In short, he didn't deserve what some slimeball was trying to do to him.

If, however, Tom Pasquale was guilty of using his badge, uniform, and gun as magic wands to create pocket money, then he deserved every ounce of the world that would come crashing down around his ears. And I'd be the one to kick the globe off its pedestal.

I left the office before Undersheriff Torrez came in, assuring Gayle that what I wanted wasn't important and that I'd catch him sometime later in the evening. I took the unmarked car and drove home, drenched with sweat by the time I pulled into the driveway.

Inside, I sighed as the silent coolness of the old adobe seeped into my bones. No thundering swamp cooler, no whining refrigerated air—just musty coolness seeping out of the old twenty-four-inch-thick walls that rested in the shade of enormous spread-limbed cottonwoods.

While a fresh pot of coffee dripped, I leafed through the mail that I'd picked up earlier in the day and then ignored. All of it could remain ignored for a while longer. For several minutes I sat with elbows on the counter, chin propped in my hands, staring out across the dark sunken living room while the coffee trickled into the urn.

Whoever had written the goddamned note had already accomplished part of his goal. Without any hints of ownership, the note just sort of floated there in the ether, generic typing on generic paper. All I knew for sure was that the author wasn't the world's hottest speller or grammarian.

But the young deputy's name had been mentioned, and I found myself trying to imagine whom Deputy Pasquale would stop and when he'd make the decision that the driver was an easy target, how he might twist the screws, and what he might do with the money.

If I drove over to his house, the one about which Carla Champlin was building a head of steam, would I find a flashy new boat in the yard, a fancy new truck parked in the driveway, and Deputy Pasquale sitting there on the porch sipping imported beer and wearing a new pair of snake-hide boots? Maybe he'd make enough scam money to pay for some water, at least making his landlady happy.

With disgust I bit off a curse and poured myself a cup of powerful coffee. With that in one hand, I juggled the telephone off the cradle and punched the auto dialer for the office. Gayle Torrez answered.

"I'm going to be occupied for most of the evening, Gayle, but I'll have my phone with me, if you need anything."

"Yes, sir. Did you need to talk to Robert? He's right here."

"No, that's all right. Ernie's on Dispatch tonight, right?"

"Yes, sir. He's here, too, if you need to talk with him."

I almost said, *"I don't need to talk to anybody,"* but instead bit it off and settled for, "No, that's fine. Just pass the message along. Have a good evening."

I refilled my cup, snapped off the coffeemaker, and ambled through the cool maze of rooms to the inside door leading to the garage. The Blazer was tucked in between towering piles of junk that I'd never gotten around to sorting, and I grunted into it, careful not to nick the door against the aluminum stepladder.

As the garage door spooled open behind me, the engine kicked into velvety life, and I felt better. By the time I had enjoyed a massive burrito dinner at the Don Juan de Oñate Restaurant, the sun would be on its way toward the back side of the San Cristobal Mountains. Things would start to cool down.

I could drop the windows and idle around the county in the cool of the night, listening and watching. If I was really lucky, I wouldn't find a damn thing.

I backed out carefully, made sure the garage door lowered solidly into place, and turned out on Escondido, past the trailer park by the interstate, and then northbound on Grande. I hadn't driven more than four blocks before I saw the white-and-blue Posadas County patrol car coming in the opposite direction.

It flashed by, already well over the posted speed limit. Under-sheriff Robert Torrez was behind the wheel, and he glanced my way at the same time the radio in the Blazer barked twice. I lifted a hand in salute, wondering why I had been expecting that it would be Deputy Thomas Pasquale, heading south toward State 56.

The Don Juan was quiet, and I slid into my favorite booth, the one whose window looked out across the parking lot toward the San Cristobals to the southwest. The blinds were turned to ward off the evening sun, and I could feel the heat through the glass. Bustos Avenue stretched flat and hot east-west, bordering the restaurant's parking lot. Traffic was light.

I picked at my food, my irritation growing by the minute. I had time to dig my way through about a third of the Burrito Grande when my privacy vanished as Sam Carter appeared around the service island.

"Damn, he was right," he said, and advanced until he was staring down at my burrito plate.

"Hello, Sam. Who was right?"

"Your dispatcher. Ernie Wheeler. He said odds were good that you'd be here."

"And sure enough," I said. "Pull up a chair."

He slid into the booth, hands clasped in front of him, just like Dr. Arnold Gray a few hours earlier. It wasn't yet six, and Carter's Family SuperMarket hadn't closed for the day. I was surprised to see Sam out and about, mingling with the public. He ducked his head, his prominent Adam's apple bobbing, and glanced back the way he'd come.

"You being followed?" I said, but he didn't take it as the joke I'd intended. His eyes widened for just a second, and he leaned forward. The waitress appeared by the service cart, hand reaching for the coffeepot. I caught her eye and shook my head. She nodded and vanished.

"What's the problem, Sam?" I said. "Two county commissioners in one day in this same booth...that's something of a record for me.''

Sam Carter's narrow face crumpled up in a grimace, as if he was genuinely sorry to have to talk to me in public...or in private, either, for that matter.

"Somebody sent me an anonymous letter,'' he blurted out, and his hand darted for the inside pocket of his limp blue seersucker jacket.

With anyone else, I could have made a wisecrack about the man cheating on his wife or not paying mounting gambling debts or something of the sort. But Sam Carter's life was a mess, and both he and I knew it. His senior cashier had filled a complaint against him a couple of months before, charging him with making obscene phone calls to her home after she'd refused his amorous advances at the store.

I knew the woman and somehow found it hard to imagine the weasel-thin Sam Carter, semibalding, with a mouthful of perfect false teeth, bending the stout, frizzy-haired matron backward over the sour cream display while he attempted a quick, passionate smooch.

Taffy Hines had complained and even been brassy enough to sign her name. Estelle Reyes-Guzman, my chief of detectives at the time, and I had talked to old Sam and pointed out to him the error of his ways...and made it clear to him what a field day the *Posadas Register* would have if the story ever went public—which it would do if he didn't button his mental trousers.

As far as I knew, he'd behaved himself since then, but our relationship had turned a touch chilly. When the previous sheriff had died in a plane crash, Carter had talked me into taking the post until after elections—but that was not because of any love for me on his part. Next in line was Estelle Reyes-Guzman, and the county fathers weren't about to accept a young Mexican as the first woman sheriff of Posadas County. They needn't have worried, since that's not the way the cards were stacked, anyway.

Still, there was no trace of gloat in his expression when Sam Carter pulled the white piece of typing paper out of his pocket. I knew what it was before he handed it to me but took it nonetheless, looking at it as carefully as I had at the first one.

I read it through, wondering how many copies the author had printed.

"What do you think?" Carter asked.

I took a deep breath and pushed my plate off to one side. "It's enough to give me gas, I'll tell you that much."

"You don't seem surprised."

I looked at him for a long minute, then said, "I don't guess I am. One of your brethren got a copy and shared it with me earlier in the day."

"You mean one of the other commissioners?" he asked, and I nodded. "Which one?"

"It probably doesn't matter," I said. "I wouldn't be surprised if all five of you got the same thing. Photocopies are cheap. You have the envelope?"

"Envelope?" he said.

"I assume it came to you in an envelope?"

"No...well, yes. It did. I didn't even think about that. I'll look for it."

"That would be helpful." I scanned the message again, and if my memory served me correctly, it was identical to Gray's.

"Well," Carter said, and watched as I carefully refolded the letter and placed it on top of my hat. "What do you think?"

I shrugged, hoping I looked far more casual than I felt. "It's always welcome when concerned citizens give us these nice little tips," I said, and smiled.

"This is serious, though," Sam Carter said.

"Of course it is."

"If this got out, it'd be a real mess."

"Yes, it would. Did you show this to anyone else?"

He shook his head vehemently.

"But I tell you," I said, and then stopped to take a deep drink of my iced tea, "it's going to be all over the front page before we're through, no matter which way it goes. The last thing we're going to tolerate is a crooked cop...or someone writing libel about honest cops. We'll find out which way it falls, and then you watch the headlines."

Sam Carter leaned forward a bit. "You can't just sort of..." and his voice trailed off as he made little chopping motions with his right hand. I didn't have a clue what he was trying to suggest, and I didn't want to pursue it.

"No," I said. "I can't. That's not the way I work." I smiled again, without much humor.

Sam reared back as if he'd seen an apparition seated across from him, maybe Don Juan in person. "You think someone would..." He stopped in midthought.

"Maybe they would, and maybe they wouldn't," I said. I pushed myself out of the booth, dropped a ten-dollar bill beside my plate, and patted Sam Carter on the shoulder as I stepped past him. "I try not to think too much at all these days, Sam. You take care."

FIVE

POUNDED INTO FRAGRANCE by the heat during the day, the prairie collected back its vapors when the sun set and the air lost its heat. I breathed deeply, savoring it all. The Blazer ticked gently as it cooled, parked with engine off, windows open, and police radio turned to a whisper.

About five miles southwest of Posadas, New Mexico 56 passed by the remains of Moore—a couple old wooden buildings long since wilted into disuse, an abandoned truck or two, the remains of a 1924 Moline tractor with steel wheels that I had once considered salvaging for restoration.

Just west of Moore, the highway bridged the Rio Salinas, a broad dry wash that in thirty years I'd never seen carry water. The grandly named arroyo formed the western border of Arturo Mesa, and I had bumped the truck up an abandoned two-track on the flank of the mesa until I had a view of the highway below.

To the northeast, the village lights shimmered in the last haze of the dwindling summer heat. To the southwest, the San Cristobals formed a massive featureless block against the darkening sky. Lights from a few ranches were sprinkled in between. Traffic on the interstate coalesced into a Morse code of lights running east-west, with few drivers bothering to swing off the highway at the Posadas interchange.

Arturo Mesa was a grand place to sit and watch, listen, and think. As the evening passed, I could no longer see the state highway below me. It remained yawning, featureless black until a set of headlights meandered through the curves east of Moore and then vanished southwestward, followed by amber taillights.

The restaurant's Burrito Grande worked its wonders, and I shifted position, leaning heavily on the center console. A cigarette and a cup of coffee would have tasted good. I hadn't bothered to bring the remains of the pot I'd brewed, and I hadn't smoked a cigarette in six years.

With comfortable drowsy detachment I watched a pair of headlights approach Moore from the northeast. The vehicle slowed and its lights swept across the broad black front of the Moore Mercantile building. A spotlight beam lanced out, darting down the flank of the building toward an old stone barn favored by high school kids for an occasional beer party.

The spotlight winked out and the car idled around and then backed in beside the mercantile. Headlights switched off. Odds were good the vehicle was one of ours. The state police didn't spend much time on our county's low-profit roads, preferring instead the bustle of the interstate with its high-speed traffic. If it was just some jack-lighter with a spotlight unit screwed to the windshield frame of his car, then he'd picked a poor place for nighttime game.

From where he was parked, the deputy had a commanding view of State 56 in both directions, a clean sweep for radar. My undersheriff, Robert Torrez, rarely ran traffic unless it was within line of sight with a bar where he could nail drunks, his personal passion. The only other deputy on duty was Thomas Pasquale.

"All right," I said aloud. The highway was a pretty good route for whatever fishing the deputy was trying. By taking NM56 rather than the interstate, truckers could cut some time on their runs to some of the communities in eastern Arizona. The road was fast except for the pass through the mountains down through Regal. And for the heavy loads, there weren't any of those pesky weigh stations where logbooks could take a beating.

For the tandem car business, those Mexican used car dealers who purchased units in the United States. and towed them across the border, 56 was a convenient route in the daytime if they wanted to cross into Mexico at Regal or at night, when the towing was cooler and easier on high-mileage engines, heading into Arizona for a morning crossing at Douglas.

As I waited, old-fat-dog comfortable with the night breeze starting to take a chill, the first set of headlights was local. Even from a mile away, I could hear the jingle and rattle of the empty stock trailer, towed behind a big diesel pickup truck with running lights across the top of the cab.

The truck wasn't speeding, and the patrol car parked in the shadows never stirred. In the next ten minutes, three more vehicles drove by, all well under the speed limit. Not a murmur broke radio silence.

I frowned. Sitting there in the dark was fine with me. I was two months away from seventy years old, well fed, just about devoid of ambition, and lacked any significant hobbies that might draw my attention away from watching for shooting stars or smelling the fringe sage as its soft tips roasted against the Blazer's catalytic converter. It made sense that I'd plunk down and watch the world go by for want of anything better to do.

On the other end of the scale, Thomas Pasquale was twenty-six years old and as close to a perpetual motion machine as a human could be. From his hero, Undersheriff Robert Torrez, he'd adopted the habit of prowling the county's nethermost reaches, never content to orbit the village for the easy pickings. He had put the department four-wheel-drive Broncos in some of the damnedest places, more than once walking back.

Parking in the lee of an abandoned building beside a dull state highway didn't sound like the Thomas Pasquale I had come to know...at least not if he was parked there for long.

I picked up the cell phone and pressed the auto dialer.

"Posadas County Sheriff's Office, Deputy Wheeler."

"Ernie, what's Pasquale's twenty?"

"Hang on, Sheriff."

I reached out and turned the radio up just a bit.

"Three oh three, Posadas, ten-twenty."

The reply was immediate, and if I'd been a few hundred yards closer, I probably could have heard it directly.

"Posadas, three oh three is ten-eight on Fifty-six, at Moore."

"Ten-four. PCS two five one."

Wheeler came back on the phone. "Sir..."

"I heard," I said. "Thanks. Everything quiet?"

"Except for the Sissons, I guess so."

"The Sissons?"

"Jim and Grace Sisson. They're at each other again. The undersheriff's been out there a bunch today, the last time just a few minutes ago."

"Wonderful," I said. "Talk to you later."

I dropped the phone on the seat and watched a double set of headlights coming up from the south. One of the lights turned off about where the Broken Spur Saloon sat in the dust, and the second set continued on toward us.

In a few moments I could see the running lights on top, marking the hulk of a tractor trailer rig. The exhaust note was that of a big diesel wound tight, and it burped only slightly as the truck dived down across the Rio Guigarro just two miles west. The truck hit the flat, laser-straight stretch between the two rivers, the reports of its exhaust bouncing off the hills.

"Not a mile under seventy," I muttered. If Pasquale was running radar, the trucker was dead meat. In a blast of sound, the rig flashed through Moore, and I heard the exhaust note change just a touch— the right timing as the trucker's headlights picked up the sheriff's star on the door of the patrol unit. The trucker evidently wasn't impressed, because he swept on by without even a tentative touch of the brakes. Maybe the driver figured what the hell, he'd been nailed and that was that.

No red lights blossomed, and the patrol unit remained locked in the darkness beside the old building.

"Huh," I grunted. For another ten minutes both of us sat in the stillness. Then the lights down below flicked on, and I watched the patrol car pull out onto the highway and cruise southwest for no more than a hundred yards before turning north on the narrow, rough two-track that cut across the rugged prairie. I'd driven that two-track myself a number of times and had gotten myself stuck on it once. Other than a couple of ranches, there wasn't much to see.

After two miles of skirting the Rio Salinas, the two-track would fork, with one track angled west again, eventually emerging behind the Broken Spur Saloon. The other track continued north until it was sliced to a stop by the interstate right-of-way fence.

From my perch high on the mesa I watched the lights of Pasquale's unit dip and bob. They vanished at a spot where I knew the two-track crossed the Salinas and then emerged on the other side, sweeping a yellow fan across the open prairie. At that point, he punched them off, and the vehicle disappeared as if it'd been levitated off the planet.

"Huh," I said, and started the Blazer.

Picking my way in the dark wasn't something that my bifocaled eyes were good at any longer. Between the starlight and a sliver of moon, I could creep down the rock-strewn incline off the mesa. Four or five more vehicles passed by on the highway before the Blazer thumped down the last few yards and drove across the bunchgrass south of the pavement.

Once on the highway, I turned left and idled toward the Broken Spur. I'd covered no more than a mile when a set of headlights blasted up behind me like a ballistic missile. First the night was dark except for my own lights, and then I was illuminated without warning...as if the driver had come up from behind with his lights off and then, a few yards behind my vehicle, snapped them on.

Just as quickly, the driver backed off half a dozen car lengths, and I could see the boxy silhouette of the Bronco. I reached out and squeezed the mike's transmit button a couple of times and after a second or two got two barks of squelch in return.

Picking up the mike, I said, "Three oh three, three ten on channel three." That put us on car-to-car, and I added, "I'd like to talk to you a minute. The parking lot of the Broken Spur will be just fine."

The saloon was remote but a favorite watering hole for local ranchers and anyone else who wanted weathered wood and crushed black velvet ambiance. The owner, Victor Sanchez, and I had enjoyed an uneasy truce since the night Victor's oldest son had died from a bullet through the heart, fired by Victor himself.

A few minutes later Pasquale and I pulled into the parking lot of the Broken Spur, surrounded by a swirling cloud of dust. Three pickup trucks, including one with an empty stock trailer, were parked in the lot, along with a large camper with Michigan plates.

Pasquale turned around so his vehicle was pointed at the highway, parking window-to-window with mine.

"Quiet night," I said. He grinned a little sheepishly, a handsome kid with an easy smile and a broad, open face. The small scar over his right eye was a persistent reminder that I'd been his roadblock to joining the sheriff's department. He'd earned the scar by flipping his village patrol car over in the middle of Bustos Avenue, flying low to beat the deputies to a routine call. At the time he'd been a part-timer with the village, and he'd been trying hard to redeem himself ever since.

He'd done a pretty good job. Only once in a while did I wish that I could wave a magic wand and age him through his long-lasting adolescence to a good, solid forty or so.

"What are you hunting?" I asked.

"Well, sir, I saw your vehicle up on the side of the mesa and wondered who it was and what they were doing."

"Sharp eyes," I said.

He shrugged. "I saw the moonlight glint on your vehicle, and so I pulled into Moore and sat for a little bit, like maybe I was running radar. I just kinda sat there and watched for a few minutes."

"I see."

"None of the ranchers are workin' that area up there, so..." He let it trail off. If he was curious about what I had been up to, sitting out in the dark by myself, he didn't let it show.

"How many Mexican tandems go through here in a week?" I asked. "You care to guess?"

"You mean the used cars going to Mexico?" He puffed out his cheeks. "Dozens, I'd guess. I see 'em all the time."

"Their paperwork always in order?"

Pasquale looked nonplussed. "I guess so, sir. About the most often I talk to 'em is when they're broke down at the side of the road. And that happens a lot. I figured they'll be checked pretty close at the border, so I don't mess with 'em. Should I be on 'em?"

I shook my head. "Just something that came to mind," I said. I watched a rancher emerge from the Broken Spur Saloon, walking with the exaggerated care of someone just this side of blind, staggering drunk. He looked over, saw the two county cars, and lurched to a stop, then turned around and retreated back inside.

I figured we had about two minutes before Victor Sanchez roared out to chase us off his property with his predictable "bad for business" diatribe.

I pulled the Blazer into gear. "When you circle back through Posadas, stop by the office. I want to show you something."

"You want me to come in now?" he asked, and a tinge of worry crept into his voice.

I waved a hand in dismissal. "No. Later. Just when it's convenient. I'll be there most of the night. I've got a bunch of paperwork I need to do."

That was true. I had paperwork, and I needed to do it. But I had not the slightest intention of spending the night staring at budget figures.

SIX

No MATTER WHAT my intentions might have been, they flew out the window when I was still five miles southwest of Posadas. My phone chirped, and I damn near drove off the road before I found the thing. The little cellular unit had been in my hand not more than ten minutes before, but when released it tended to dive to the depths of whatever pile of junk covered my car seat at the time.

A trace of urgency had crept into Dispatcher Ernie Wheeler's voice.

"Sir, Bob's responding to a call over at Sisson Plumbing and Heating. He said to have you meet him there."

"Domestic dispute?" I asked.

"Uh, he's not sure. But it looks like there's a fatality. Emergency is over there now."

"I'm on my way." I tossed the phone on the seat and concentrated on the winding dark road.

There wasn't any point in tying up the air waves with more questions. I couldn't do any good from five miles away. But before I'd traveled two of them, I saw the red lights behind me, and in a few seconds Deputy Pasquale's Bronco passed me, wound up tight.

His spotlight beam lanced out ahead, probing the side of the highway for sets of eyes that might wander into his vehicle's ballistic path. I eased off and let the youngster charge on ahead. If we were responding to a fatality, the victim would patiently wait for us all.

I drove back into the village of Posadas from the south, ducking under the interstate. The lights of travelers flashed overhead, on their way to points east and west, oblivious of our emergency. A mile farther, the first significant street off Grande to the right was MacArthur.

Despite what tourists might think after viewing Pershing Park, assuming that MacArthur was yet another tribute to military might, the street was named for Peter MacArthur, the second mayor of Posadas. The first mayor, Fred Pino, had been shot before he'd managed to accomplish enough to earn a street name.

MacArthur wound in a wide loop around the southeast quadrant of the village, encompassing a residential area of aging mobile homes, a neighborhood that blended into a scattering of businesses as it approached Bustos Avenue, the major artery running east-west through Posadas.

Sprawled on the southeast corner of MacArthur's intersection with Bustos was Sisson Plumbing and Heating. Jim Sisson had lived in the county his entire life, the son of Granger and Mary Sisson, ranchers who'd tried their best to run a successful cow-calf operation in the middle of the sage, creosote bush, and cacti. They'd managed after a fashion until 1967, when their pickup truck hadn't rolled out of the way fast enough and a southbound Union Pacific freight train had pounded it to tangled junk at a crossing near Alamogordo.

Their son, Jim, hadn't thought much of the ranching life and had opened his business in the village about the time I'd started with the Sheriff's Department in 1966. He'd married Grace Stevenson, rescuing her from her fate as the only daughter of the local Methodist minister and his wife. Only Jim and Grace knew what they saw in each other. They'd been festering along for more than three decades.

Grace was blessed with a razor tongue and an astonishing lack of tact. Like the one step forward, two steps back dance, the Sissons' list of customers pulsed up and down, first because they were attracted by the mild-mannered, courtly Jim and then repelled by Grace when it came time for billing or complaint.

Over the years the "Jim and Grace Show" had become something of a department joke. Their scraps were legend. When it came to Grace, Jim put his courtly manners to one side. He could swing a calloused hand as fast as anyone, and Grace retaliated just as promptly.

About the time their relationship would deteriorate to the hurling-hard-and-heavy-objects stage, or maybe when one of them was thinking of reaching for a shotgun, they'd solve their problems by having another kid. That would cool things down for a while, and Sisson Plumbing and Heating would flourish and grow.

Their prefab home looked across the street at Burger Heaven and diagonally across the intersection at the Chavez Chevy-Olds dealership—a hell of a view.

The house was surrounded by various outbuildings and shops and a mammoth collection of junk—at least it all looked like junk to a nonplumber like me. Jim Sisson had purchased his first backhoe in 1968, and the worn-out carcass of that machine and of every other he'd ever owned since then were parked along the back of the largest shop building.

I was sure that when Sisson replaced someone's swamp cooler he always kept the corroded shell of the old one, probably "just in case." Just in case what, I didn't know.

The board fence around Sisson's enclave was six feet high, but I could see the emergency lights winking from two blocks away. A fair-sized crowd of rubberneckers had assembled, all of them standing in the middle of the street gawking toward the Sissons' property, spectators to an event that everyone in town had known would come one day or another.

Deputy Tony Abeyta, who wasn't on the duty roster for the evening but had jumped in response to the call anyway, had parked his patrol unit across the Sissons' driveway, beside a yellow ribbon that stretched from the corner downspout of the house across to the high wooden fence.

One of the village's part-time patrolmen, Chad Beuler, detached himself from a group of half a dozen gawkers and waved a flashlight at me. Chief Eduardo Martinez hadn't arrived, but at 9:30 we were well past his bedtime. Beuler, a beanpole with a receding chin who kept twitching his shoulders as if his undershirt was binding his armpits, shook his head in deep frustration as he stepped to the curb and intercepted me.

"We got us a hell of a mess," he said, and waved the flashlight again. The beam caught me in the eyes, and I lifted a hand to ward it off. "Now you-all just step on back," he barked toward the gathering of folks on the sidewalk. None of them appeared to be moving in any direction, forward or back, but Beuler liked to make sure. He walked ahead of me toward the ribbon.

He turned to face me, still walking—not a bad feat. If I'd tried it, I'd have been flat on my back. "The undersheriff is in there," he said, indicating the narrow driveway that ran between a slab of fence and the side of the house. "It's a hell of a mess."

"Thank you," I said, and slipped past, ignoring the four people who tried to talk to me at once.

"And I think a couple of the bigwigs are inside the house," Beuler called after me.

I walked along the dark side of the house toward the artificial daylight of the well-lighted backyard and shop area. As I passed under a frosted window, I could hear voices inside, one of them tight and distraught and trying to piece a sentence together around sobbing gulps of air.

At the back corner of the house, Tom Pasquale's Bronco was parked bumper-to-bumper with one of Bob Torrez's personal pickup trucks, a faded red-and-black hulk with two spare tires chained in the back to the ornate iron racks.

I could hear the heavy, clattering idle of a diesel engine, and as I made my way past the vehicles I caught a glimpse of Torrez's towering bulk as he walked around the back of a large yellow backhoe. In the instant that my attention was diverted, my toe caught something hard, sharp, and immovable, and I stumbled hard, landing on one knee, driving the palm of my left hand into the sharp gravel that covered the driveway.

With a string of colorful curses, I pushed myself to my feet, the shock of the fall hammering my joints and making the lights dance. I stopped, brushed myself off, and took several deep breaths, realizing that I wasn't looking at just one machine. There were two, the backhoe parked butt-to-butt with a huge front loader, like a beetle backed up against a scorpion. With no breeze, the cloying sweet odor of diesel exhaust hung thick as it chuffed out of the rear tractor's stack.

"Sir?" Deputy Pasquale appeared from out of nowhere at my elbow.

"What have you got?" I asked. Once out of the tangle of shadows cast by the house and the vehicles I could see just fine, and I snapped my flashlight off and thrust it in my back pocket.

"Over here," he said, and almost made contact as he reached out toward my elbow. It was a simple-enough gesture of assistance, the sort of thing I'd do if I saw a little old lady startled to a standstill by the sudden rush of the automatic doors at the supermarket.

I stepped around the large yellow bucket of the front loader and stopped short. "Jesus," I said.

Jim Sisson appeared to have managed one of those incomprehensible accidents that would be difficult for Hollywood stuntmen to reproduce. And like most accidents, it had probably started simple.

The left back tire and wheel had been taken off the disabled front loader, and the machine's axle was supported by a terrifying collection of wooden blocks and old boards, along with the single hydraulic jack. The tire and wheel were lying several feet away, the cleated tread just inches from the wall of the shop. The backhoe bucket of the second machine was poised overhead, a length of heavy chain hanging from its teeth. Underneath the tire, head scrunched up against the building at an unnatural angle, one leg grotesquely kicked out, was Jim Sisson.

Robert Torrez had been kneeling beside the building, near Sisson's head, in company with two EMTs. He pushed himself to his feet. "Don't touch that," he snapped as Tom Pasquale bent down as if to poke at the huge rubber tire.

The undersheriff stepped gingerly around the machinery and approached me. "It looks like he was lifting the rear wheel off one machine with the backhoe of the other, sir. Somehow the chain slipped. He's dead, for sure. Skull's crushed, and his neck must have snapped like a twig."

"Did you call Linda?"

Torrez nodded. "She'll be here in a minute." He beckoned. "So will Perrone," he added, referring to Posadas County Coroner Alan Perrone. "Step around this way."

I did, catching a glimpse of a figure in the partially open back door of the house. It was Deputy Abeyta, and he no doubt had his hands full keeping the stream of people from flooding out into the yard. At the same time, I heard a serious of deep, heavy barks. The family dog, eager to leap out into the backyard with the rest of us, tried to shove his broad head between Abeyta's legs. The deputy reached out and swung the solid back door shut.

I stood with my hands in my pockets, looking at what was left of Jim Sisson. "Christ almighty," I murmured. "Why the hell don't you get him out of there?" But a closer look made it clear why there was no frantic activity to free Jim from his predicament. The man's skull had been pulped.

"If he hadn't swung it so close to the wall, he might have had a chance," Torrez said.

The wheel and tire, complete with bolt-on weights for added traction and probably loaded inside with calcium chloride for even more weight, had struck the wall of the shop and then slid down, crushing Sisson in between. His skull had slammed against the corrugated steel of the shop siding until it cracked like an eggshell, and then he'd been pushed downward, his neck bent so that his chin was driven down into the hollow behind his collarbone.

Dark rubber streaks marked the steel siding, tracing the tire's path as it slid downward. Blood puddled on the cement under Sisson's head.

"Look here, sir," Torrez said, and he knelt beside the tire. He beckoned me close and dropped his voice. "Right there." He played his flashlight under the tire, illuminating what little space remained.

"What am I looking at?"

Torrez reached out and touched the smooth concrete of the shop apron with a ballpoint pen. "Rubber marks. From the tire tread. Between these and the marks on the wall, I'm thinking we can backtrack and pretty much tell just what happened."

"What happened was that the goddamn tire fell on him and crushed him," I said. "He was working by himself?"

"Apparently so."

"Jesus," I muttered, wondering what spat had driven Jim out of the house at that hour to seek the comfort of his machines. "Is Mrs. Sisson inside?"

"Her and a mob," Torrez said. "Half the neighborhood, I guess. Tony tried getting a preliminary statement, but it's rough going.

We're going to have to talk to her after a bit, when things calm down. It's a zoo in there right now.''

"I can imagine. Does anyone have a clue about what Jim was trying to do? Was he just trying to change a goddamn tire or work on the brakes or what?"

Torrez reached out with his boot and touched the front loader's tire. "This one is flat, so I assume he wanted to work on it. We don't know for sure. Neither does his wife. She said initially that she was watching television. Jim was out back, working in his shop. According to one of the neighbors, they'd had a rough day. I'll vouch for that. I was over here three times. Lots of shouting. Tom Mears is working on that angle."

"So what else is new," I grunted. "Where would we all be without nosy neighbors? And Grace said that Jim was alone out here?"

Torrez hesitated, and I looked up at him. His response wasn't much more than a whisper. "That's what she said."

"You don't sound convinced."

Torrez reached out and lightly tapped the big tire with the toe of his boot again. "This doesn't look like a one-man job, sir."

I gazed at the two machines. "Stranger things have happened, Robert," I said. "It's jury-rigged, that's for sure. He wanted to lift the tire, so he tried to do it with the backhoe. Something slipped, like where he had the chain hooked, and he got down to work on it. The damn thing nailed him. In fact, that's exactly what it looks like—one man trying to do something by himself that he shouldn't have been. And he was in a foul mood to begin with."

"You'll be at the office later?" The way he said it sounded like he'd dismissed my logical scenario.

I nodded. "I'm just in the way here. Let me know if you need anything." I indicated the idling tractor. "And you might as well shut that thing down. Make it easier to hear and breathe both."

Torrez glanced at his watch. "Dr. Perrone will be here in a minute. Then we'll clear things up. There's no hurry."

SEVEN

BRENT SUTHERLAND SAT in front of the dispatcher's console with both elbows on the table and his head supported in his hands. His unruly red hair was about an inch longer than I would have liked, but what the hell. If that was the only concession I had to make as the millennium clicked over, I was lucky.

Whether Sutherland was reading the *New Mexico Criminal and Traffic Law Manual* that rested open between his elbows or sleeping was hard to tell.

If the deputy was studying, he certainly had peace and quiet. The persistent exhaling of the building's circulation system as it moved stale air, summer dust, and range country pollen from one room to the other was all the excitement the Public Safety Building had to offer at 3:15 that morning.

In four weeks Sutherland would attend the Academy, and until then the weekday graveyard dispatcher's shift was just the right time and place to whittle away at his inexperience. Once in a while, Bob Torrez assigned Sutherland to double up on patrol with one of the deputies. We didn't have the manpower to do that often, though, and Sutherland had to content himself with the bottom rung on the duty ladder.

Tom Mears, a veteran who preferred the midnight-to-eight shift so that he had time to race his beloved stock cars on summer weekends, was the only deputy on the road at the moment. Undersheriff Torrez and one or two others who were supposed to be off-duty were still over at the Sissons', probing and photographing, oblivious to whatever else might be going on elsewhere in the county.

Mears and Sutherland had the place to themselves, and I trusted that Mears could keep the rookie out of trouble.

Whether the sound of my boots on the polished tile floor woke him up or it was just coincidence, Sutherland's right hand drifted down from his chin and picked up the pencil on the table. He jotted a note in the margin of the book, replaced the pencil, and glanced at the digital clock in front of him.

"Fascinating stuff, eh?" I said, and Sutherland started, cranking his head around so fast I thought I heard a vertebra crack. "Sorry about that." I stepped closer and looked at the log. Since the Sisson emergency, things had drifted to tomblike peace and quiet.

Thirty-one minutes before, Deputy Mears had radioed in that the side door of the tiny Catholic church in Regal was open, not an unusual state of affairs, and that he was going to check it. Three minutes later, logged at 02:47, Mears had radioed 10-08, the numerical mumbo-jumbo that meant he was back in service.

"No sleep-overs this time," I said, and Sutherland looked puzzled.

"Sir?"

"Sleep-overs. The church in Regal is never locked. I don't think there's even a lockable hasp on the door. It's a favorite place for Mexican nationals to spend the night."

"That's why the three minutes, then," Sutherland said.

"That's why. And that's why you need to be on your toes, even when you're bored to death and you've committed that book to memory and you're counting the ticks on the clock. Where's the nearest officer who can provide backup to Mears?"

Sutherland frowned and I saw his back straighten and one hand move an inch or two in the direction of the transmit bar on the radio.

"No matter who you find," I said, "odds are that they aren't going to be close to Regal. So Mears is on his own. If he walks into that church and there are about eight illegals snoozing on the pews and two of them happen to be armed with something more than an attitude, the night can get exciting. So when someone goes in to check a place like that, you give him three or four minutes, no more. If he isn't on the air ten-eight by then, you remind him."

I leaned across and pushed the bar. "Three oh seven, PCS. Ten-thirty-nine."

Three seconds later, Tom Mears's matter-of-fact voice responded, "Three oh seven is ten-eight."

"Ten-four. PCS two five one."

I straightened up. "You know his status now, and he knows you're not asleep." I grinned. "And that's all the weird folks who spend the night listening to scanners need to know, too. That's why you don't spend your shift asking the deputies where they are. There's only one of him and a big, empty county. He's got little-enough edge as it is without someone being able to plot his course every minute."

"That's what Ernie Wheeler said."

"Listen to him." I nodded. "On a night like this, when you've got deputies and civilians both edgy after the mess over at the Sissons', somebody needs to be paying attention to the little things. Don't let yourself be distracted. Pay attention." I grinned. "End of sermon."

"Yes, sir," Sutherland said, nodding his head in appreciation. I wasn't sure if he was glad to have such monumental erudition bestowed on him by the sheriff of Posadas County or glad that I had finally shut up.

I checked my mailbox and retrieved a yellow WHILE YOU WERE OUT note. I recognized Ernie Wheeler's angular printing—just the name Frank Dayan, time recorded as 21:05, and a check through the please-return-call box. I turned it so that Sutherland could see it. "Were you here when Dayan called?"

"No, sir."

"Huh," I said. Dayan had called before the Sisson tragedy, so there was the possibility he wouldn't even remember what he had wanted. Not that a call from the publisher of the *Posadas Register* was unusual at any hour. He was either an insomniac like myself or a twenty-hour-a-day workaholic—I wasn't sure which. The *Register* came out on Fridays, reduced from its heyday as a twice-a-week rag, and most of the time Dayan and his staff of three did a pretty fair job selling ads and sandwiching a little news in what space was left.

I folded the note into a wad and tossed it in the trash. "Huh," I muttered again, the nagging feeling that some creep had sent Dayan the same anonymous note that had been dispatched to at least two of the county commissioners sinking to the pit of my stomach. That was all we needed.

"If Linda Real comes in, I need to talk to her," I said over my shoulder.

"She's downstairs with Tom Pasquale," Sutherland replied, and I stopped in my tracks. My reaction flustered him, and he stammered, "At least I think they are. Linda said that she wanted to finish printing the photos."

"Nothing wrong with that," I said. I couldn't imagine there being enough room in the small darkroom for both Linda Real and Thomas Pasquale. Maybe that was the point of the whole exercise.

The door downstairs was beyond the drinking fountain and conference room. I opened it and then stopped, groping for the buzzer button below the light switch. The wiring was one of Bob Torrez's brainstorms and more than once had saved a valuable piece of film from someone inadvertently opening the wrong door and letting in a blast of light.

I tapped the button twice lightly, hearing its bray down in the bowels of the basement. In a couple of seconds, the stairwell light snapped on and the doorway at the bottom unlatched with the sharp, quick *snick* of an electric dead bolt, activated when the folks in the darkroom knew that any unexposed film or paper was safely stowed.

I made my way down and pushed open the door at the bottom of the stairs. The darkroom shared the basement with the heating/cooling plant and the concrete fireproof evidence locker that had been built a couple years before during the renovation. A dozen steps ahead, the darkroom's black doorway was partially obscured by the corner of the furnace. The door was open and the light on. Thomas Pasquale was bent over the counter examining a display of photos.

Linda Real, about half his size, stood beside him, and she was using Pasquale's broad back as a leaning post, her elbow comfortable on his shoulder, her head supported by her fist.

"How do they look?" I said.

Linda jerked her arm off Tom's back. I didn't know who she had been expecting, but evidently it wasn't me.

"Really good, sir," she said, and traded places with the deputy. Pasquale made for the door and I stood to one side to let him pass.

"Are you going to be around for a while, or are you going home?" I asked him.

"I can stay as long as needed, sir."

I waved a hand, wishing sometimes that he didn't have to be so goddamn formal when he talked to me. "I just need to talk to you a minute. But it can wait if you have something you need to do." To Linda I added, "Let's see what you've got here."

"Nasty, nasty," Linda said.

I didn't share her enthusiasm for watching crime scene photos appear under the magic of the darkroom safelight. Corpses in their natural habitat were bad enough without special effects.

A live Jim Sisson may have been photogenic, but he certainly had made a mess of himself this time. "These were taken after Sisson's body was moved by the medical examiner," Linda explained needlessly, indicating the set on the right. "And this is what Bob was trying to understand." She positioned half a dozen eight-by-tens in front of me. I could smell her perfume or shampoo or whatever the source of the fragrance was—light, fresh, appealing even at that hour and in that morbid place of red lights, chemicals, and time-frozen tragedy.

"This is a tread mark on the outside wall of the shop." She touched a photo with the tip of her pen. "The way the siding's dented, that might be the point of first impact."

"It would have to be," I said. "It's the farthest point up on the wall."

Linda nodded. "From there to this mark on the concrete apron is fifty-four inches, give or take."

"And that would be the height of the tire," I said, and turned to Tom. "Did you measure it yet?"

"Yes, sir. It matches that."

"So the tire dropped off the chain, or whatever, and crashed against the side of the building. Jim Sisson happened to be there, for what reason we don't know. If the chain had started to slip, I would have thought he would have just lowered the thing to the ground."

"It caught him somehow," Linda said. "And I guess they're pretty heavy?"

"Loaded, with weights and all, I would guess close to a ton," I said. "Somewhere in that ballpark, anyway. More than he could manage, that's for sure."

I looked at the photo. "And these?"

Linda pointed. "You can see where the tread slid down the wall. In order to do that, the bottom has to kick out, too."

"Sure. That's not surprising. And it looks like it did." The black marks on the concrete scrubbed away from the building as the tire slid down, with Jim Sisson pinned underneath.

I frowned and leaned close, trying to bring the marks into the right portion of my bifocals. "On that concrete, though, I would have predicted that the tire would just have leaned against the building and stayed there. Or maybe rolled off to one side. It'd have to hit it absolutely square."

"Sir?"

"I'm surprised that it slid down in the first place. That's all I'm saying. The concrete isn't slick, and the rubber tire would have had a pretty good grip. It must have dropped hard, maybe with even a little bounce to it."

"And then there's this," Linda said, "and you have to look close. But I made an enlargement." She pulled another photo closer. "See the last set of black marks on the concrete? They're the farthest out from the building, right?"

"Right."

"The tire would have been almost horizontal by then, propped up by Jim's body."

"Yep."

"Now look at this."

I folded my arms on the counter to act as a brace, relieving my protesting back. Linda bent the goosenecked drafting lamp closer. "What am I seeing?" I asked.

"The scrub marks are darker, more pronounced, and abruptly change direction. They look like a comma, with the tail off to the left."

"Huh."

"The tire had to jig sideways," Tom said.

"I can see that." I looked at the marks for a long time, then turned my head to gaze at Linda. She was a fetching kid, a little heavy from too much fast food at odd hours, but with raven black hair that she kept cut short, framing a wide, intelligent face. She looked like she could be Tom Pasquale's younger sister.

"You do good work," I said, and she grinned. The late hour was costing her, though. When the fatigue started to win, her left eye wandered a bit. She had been blinded in that eye during a shotgun assault a couple years before that also had taken the life of one of our deputies.

The harsh light from the table lamp played on her features, and the scars on the left side of her face were just faint pale tracks against her olive skin. She could have covered them with makeup if she had been the sort to worry about such things.

"So tell me what you think," I said to them both.

"The tire had to kick sideways some," Tom replied. He reached across and tapped the enlargement. "That sideways mark is about six inches long."

"So the tire fell against the wall and then slid down, and just as it stopped sliding downward, it kicked sideways. All right. Maybe. I can think of several explanations for that." I reached across for the other photos. "What do these tell us?"

"The most instructive set are these," Linda said. The first was a grisly photo of Jim Sisson crushed under the tire. The weight of the tire had smashed him into the small space beside the wall, his skull crushed against the metal flange that made up the frame for the massive overhead door. The tire was resting diagonally across his back.

Linda took a second copy of the same print and with a grease pencil circled the portion of the photo that included all that could be seen of the actual contact point between the tire tread and Sisson's back.

"See these tire treads?"

"Cleats, I think they're called."

"Yes. Now, they're about four inches apart, and each one is roughly two inches wide. That's what Tom measured. Here's one resting on Sisson's right shoulder, digging into his neck and head.

Going to the left, here's another, just past his spine and down a little bit."

"OK," I said, feeling uneasy.

"Now this." Linda slid one of the photos of Sisson's corpse across for me to look at.

Sisson had been a wiry little guy, the sort who could work ten or fifteen hours without a pause. That he hadn't been able to scramble out of the way indicated that the chain had snapped loose so fast he hadn't had time to even say, "Oh, shit."

"Here's a bruise, here's the second, and here's a third," Linda said. "One, two, three, in an arc that we could extend from top right shoulder down to lower left flank."

I blinked and straightened up, grimacing at the kinks in my back. I took off my glasses, pulled a lens-cleaning tissue from the box by the enlarger, and polished them. Tom and Linda waited for me to mull whatever it was that didn't click.

"There's no way that we can predict with one hundred percent certainty how that tire struck him," I said finally. "But he had to have been crouching down when that tire hit him...maybe groping for a bolt or something—some tool maybe. That tire's big, but it's not like it's off one of those giant earthmovers or something."

"But there's a clear match between how the tire is resting on Mr. Sisson in this photo," she pulled the first enlargement out of the pile and put it beside the photo of the corpse, "and the two upper bruises here and here."

"True."

"In this photo, the tire isn't in contact with his body at this point, where the lower, third bruise is."

"Also true." I didn't add that there could be several explanations for that, because I couldn't think of a single one. "Anything else?"

Linda shook her head. "Bob's out there now. I guess Mrs. Sisson went to Las Cruces with the kids to stay with some relatives. He wasn't too happy about that, but..." She shrugged. "He said he was going to hang around until light. He wants me back out there then."

"All right. Get some rest before that." I looked at the photos again and frowned. "It doesn't quite add up, does it?" I said.

As I turned to go, Tom Pasquale asked, "Did you want to talk to me about something, sir?"

I stopped short and frowned. "If I did, I'm damned if I remember what it was. Couldn't have been too important." I grinned at both of them. "You guys keep after this."

I had no doubt that Undersheriff Robert Torrez was sitting over at the Sissons', deep in thought, the same thing bothering him that now bothered me. Somehow, a heavy tire had fallen on Jim Sisson, crushed him to death, and then been jerked sideways.

Maybe Sisson's death throes had been enough to do that, even with a two-thousand-pound, fifty-four-inch-diameter, nineteen-inch-wide tractor tire on top of him. If there had been a spark of life in him, it had been crushed out during the hour that he'd been pinned before his wife finally stuck her head out the back door to see when he was going to shut off the damn machine and come to bed.

EIGHT

FOR AN HOUR I poked here and there without particular rhyme or reason. The events of the evening jumbled in my mind, and I couldn't see a well-defined path of action. I didn't want to end up stumbling all over Undersheriff Robert Torrez's trail, getting in his way, slowing him down. I idled 310 east on a deserted Bustos Avenue shortly after 4:00 a.m., not breaking fifteen miles an hour.

A mechanic at the Ford garage had replaced some part deep in the car's guts, and it was almost eager. Still, fifteen miles an hour was just fine, a perfect match for my mood.

By habit, I drove with the windows open and the two-way radio turned low, listening to and smelling the night. In the past, that had always accomplished one of two things: It either cleared my mind or made me drowsy enough that I could go home and grab an hour's sleep. This time I couldn't even make myself hungry.

Turning south at the intersection with MacArthur, I cruised past the Sissons' driveway. Bob Torrez's old pickup truck squatted in the driveway, well back from the street. He'd been using that oil-burning, huge-engined heap since earlier in the day, his idea of an unmarked car.

Farther south on MacArthur, I passed the neighborhood where the undersheriff lived with his wife, Gayle. It was a scattering of squat, old adobe houses that sat helter-skelter with a spiderweb of dirt streets. The oldest neighborhood in the village, it had once been called *La Placita* and nestled right up to the banks of Posadas Creek. The creek became a dry arroyo, mines opened, Posadas bloomed, and MacArthur sliced through *La Placita's* vitals and killed it.

A couple dozen families lived in that part of town, and Bob Torrez was related in one way or another to most of them.

As I drove past, I caught a glimpse of 308, his county car, parked under the big elm tree in his front yard.

Reaching Grande, I turned north and a few minutes later completed the short loop by crossing Bustos. Salazar and Sons Funeral Home loomed, the lights in the manicured front yard washing up the white marble facade. The place was garish and prosperous. A black Cadillac hearse was parked under the wrought-iron portico, no doubt waiting to be polished and prepped in anticipation of Jim Sisson's last ride.

The lights were on at 221 Third Street. The streetlight half a block away cast vague shadows, but even in the poor light I could see that Carla Champlin would disapprove. While she lived in a manicured terrarium, this place was as desolate as the day it was built thirty years before as low-rent housing for copper miners. She may have been right—perhaps at one time the tiny yard had bloomed as a showplace, with a putting-green lawn. I couldn't remember.

The front yard was dirt, basically a parking lot. A single scraggly, thirsting elm managed a few green leaves in the postage-stamp backyard. If the house was more than eight hundred square feet I would be surprised—not much larger than my kitchen and living room combined.

Linda Real's Honda station wagon was parked in the narrow driveway, and pulled in beside it was Deputy Pasquale's old Jeep Wrangler.

"Huh," I said aloud.

Beyond the casual arm-on-shoulder I'd seen in the darkroom, there had been few other hints that indicated any particular relationship between Linda and Tom—although they had known each other back when he was still flipping cars as a part-timer for the village PD and she was a reporter for the *Posadas Register*. It was as a reporter that she'd been riding with one of our deputies when he'd stopped a suspect vehicle. A shotgun blast had killed the deputy and another had mangled Linda.

Her convalescence from long, complicated corrective surgery after the shooting had taken her out of Posadas, to live with her mother in Las Cruces.

Earlier in the spring, I'd hired Linda, despite her left eye blindness and left ear deafness. She could work wonders with a camera, was bright and quick, and had the potential to be the best dispatcher we had, next to Gayle Torrez.

In her complaint, Carla Champlin hadn't mentioned that 221 Third Street was no longer bachelor's quarters. I remembered her remark about the happily married McClaines and their one child and wondered if that had been a left-field way of voicing her disapproval of Linda and Tom's cohabitation, if that's, in fact, what was going on.

Parked to the right of the front door was a large motorcycle. I almost snapped on the spotlight but thought better of it. It was a Harley, but how new I couldn't tell.

"Huh," I said again. I hadn't known that Pasquale fancied motorcycles—and didn't know that he could afford a big, expensive road bike. If he was still making payments on the Jeep, that, coupled with his rent, would leave him just about enough from his meager county paycheck for one meal a week. No wonder he was prompt at the doughnut box when some kind soul brought them into the office.

I chuckled at myself. I was making the same kinds of assumptions for which I chided the deputies. The motorcycle might even belong to Linda. Who knew. Maybe she'd taken up black leather and small cigars during her off-hours. Tom might have inherited the Jeep from a rich uncle who had bought it to go hunting and then promptly dropped dead from a heart attack.

I idled 310 out of the neighborhood, leaving the kids to some short moments of peace and quiet.

Back on Bustos, I drove west. As I approached the Don Juan de Oñate Restaurant, still two hours from opening, my stomach twinged with conditioned reflex. Turning southbound, I slowed as I approached 410 South 12th, a neat brick-and-stucco place on a double lot. I felt a silly twinge of loss when I noticed that the for sale sign was missing. Somehow, as long as that sign had been up, the last connection hadn't been cut. Estelle Reyes-Guzman and her family had moved to the land of snow and *lutefisk,* but as long as they still owned 410 South 12th it seemed to me that there was a chance that Minnesota winters and summertime mosquitoes might chase them back to Posadas, where their home awaited.

A block south the pavement turned to dirt, and my car rumbled along toward the T intersection with State 17, the old highway that paralleled the interstate. Though it was once a major arterial across the country and even across the southern part of the state, only ranchers used it now, to reach their irrigation ditches on those rare occasions when there was enough water to bother.

"Three ten, Posadas."

The voice was so faint I almost didn't hear it over the crunching gravel. I turned up the volume and keyed the mike.

"Posadas, three ten."

"Three ten, ten-thirty-nine."

"I'm wandering," I said without keying the mike. "I'm without status." I pushed the button and said, "Three ten is ten-eight."

"Ten-four, three ten. Can you..."

There was a pause, and I could picture young Sutherland leaning forward, looking at the worn copy of the ten code taped to the cabinet beside the radio. Normal conversations over the new cell phone units, despite their limitations and other drawbacks, made the old-fashioned ten-code system seem pretty silly.

"...ten-nineteen."

"Ten-four," I said. "ETA about six minutes."

I reached a wide spot at Kenny Gallegos's driveway and turned around, and in less than five minutes I pulled into the parking lot of the Public Safety Building. Frank Dayan, the publisher of the *Register,* stood by the back door, smoking.

I glanced at the dashboard clock. Four twenty-six a.m. If Frank wanted to talk to me without interruptions, he'd picked a good time.

I swung around to the curb and stopped, leaving the engine idling. Frank crushed out his cigarette and took his time putting the butt in the trash can by the door. Dressed in his usual khaki trousers and short-sleeved sport shirt, he thrust his hands in his pockets and ambled out to my car. This was not the ballistic Frank Dayan that I knew, rushing from merchant to merchant, pushing those column inches of advertising space for every penny he could squeeze.

"This meeting of Insomniacs Anonymous is hereby called to order," I said, and he grinned, looking Irish as hell, more like a Frankie O'Rourke than a Dayan. He leaned both hands against the car door and regarded me with what I took for melancholy. "What's up? You about ready for breakfast?"

He freed one hand and looked at his watch.

"You've got time," I chided. "Don't give me this 'I'm busy' nonsense. The world's asleep." I nodded toward the passenger side. "Get in."

He did so, settling into the seat with a sigh. He regarded the stack of radios and other junk with interest. "I've never ridden with any of you folks before," he said.

"Well, then," I replied. "Let's lift your level of boredom to new levels. Put on your seat belt."

He struggled trying to find the buckle under all the crap in the middle of the seat but finally managed.

I jotted the time and Dayan's presence in my log, clicked the mike, and said, "Three ten is ten eight." Before Sutherland had completed half of his canned response, I had turned the volume down to a murmur.

"So," I said, heading 310 out of the parking lot. "Is there anywhere in particular you wanted to go, or are you just cruising?"

Dayan shrugged. "I just wanted to chat with you about a couple of things, if you're not too busy. Maybe get an update on the Sisson deal."

No one asks for an update on anything at 4:26 in the morning, and I laughed. I was willing to bet what he wanted, and so I said, "Oh...busy. As you can see, I am awesomely busy, Frank. Tell you what. I was going down toward Regal for a bit. Maybe bust some illegals." I glanced around toward the backseat, as if someone might be back there listening. "Maybe put the screws on some of them for a quick buck. Know what I mean?"

Frank Dayan's reaction was just as I had expected. His jaw dropped a fraction and his head jerked. Before he could answer, I added, "You got a note, too, eh?"

My stomach churned again, and not from early-morning hunger, when he didn't say, "What note?"

NINE

DAYAN REACHED INTO his pocket and pulled out a white envelope. From it he removed the now-familiar piece of white typing paper, folded neatly in thirds, just like the other two.

"This came to my office today. Plain envelope, just my name typed on it." He held it up as if I could read it in the darkness. I glanced his way, trying to work out in my mind how much I could trust him. "I gather you're familiar with the contents?" he asked.

"'Commissioner, you need to know that Tom Pasquale is a slimeball and is hitting up on nationals and tourists and God only knows who else, blah, blah, blah.' Is that the gist of it?"

"Yes." He folded the note, slipped it in the envelope, and extended it toward me. I took it and snapped it under the clip on my log. It lay there, on top of the junk pile, if Dayan wanted it back. "Except it was addressed to me, not a commissioner. You're saying that they all got one, too?"

"No." I paused as I cleared the intersection beyond the interstate and turned onto 56, heading toward Regal. "Sam Carter made a point of telling me that he got one. So did Arnold Gray. I haven't heard from the others yet."

"But you probably will."

"No doubt."

"Did you talk to the deputy yet?"

"No."

Dayan paused. He reached out and beat a short tattoo on the dashboard with his index fingers. Maybe it helped him think.

"I guess it's not anyone's business but yours how you handle it, but are you going to talk to him?"

"When the time comes...if it comes. The first thing that has to happen is that we move beyond the anonymous note stage. If someone wants to come forward with the 'documentation' that the note promises, and is willing to sign a formal complaint, then it'll be a different ball game. But a sleazy unsigned note, sent to all the right people? I don't think so.''

I knew it sounded as if I'd dismissed the contents of the note from my mind, continuing on as if it had never been delivered. If Frank Dayan thought that, it was fine with me. I trusted him as much as I trusted anyone associated with the media, but he didn't have to know the nagging little seeds of doubt that damn note had planted in my mind. In that respect, the writer had been successful.

"So you tell me, Frank. What are you going to do? Are you going to run a story about it in the *Register?*''

His reply was snappy. "Come on, Sheriff. We don't print rumors. We don't print letters to the editor unless they're signed and we can verify them. We don't even print 'name withheld' letters when they ask. No guts, no signature, no letter. It's that simple. And this kind of personal attack, even if it was signed? I don't think so.''

"Commendable," I said.

"I don't think the letter would have been written if it weren't an election year.''

"Oh? Not for me, it isn't an election year.''

Dayan turned as much sideways as his seat belt would allow and rested his left arm along the back of the seat. He laced his fingers through the grillwork of the security screen that separated the back-seat area from the front.

"Bob Torrez made a lot of people angry when he filed as an independent, Sheriff.''

"Whoopee.''

Dayan laughed. "I know, I know. You don't care. You were appointed when Sheriff Holman got killed last spring and agreed to serve until after the election. And the first thing you did was appoint Bob as undersheriff.''

"All that's public record," I said, shrugging. "So what?''

"If Estelle Reyes-Guzman hadn't moved out of town, you'd probably have appointed her, right?''

I looked over at Dayan, amused. "I did appoint her, Frank. I appointed her for the last week that she was here. If that gave the county fathers conniptions, so much the better. And then she and her family moved, as you said. Torrez was the next logical choice.''

"Sure he was. And then he files as an independent for the election, with probably as good a chance of winning as anyone, including Mike Rhodes, Sam Carter's brother-in-law, who just happens to be the only Republican candidate, and Leona Spears, who was unopposed in the Democratic primary, even though she doesn't stand a snowball's chance in hell.''

"And all of this means…''

"You're about as political as the amount of snow we get in the summertime, Sheriff.''

"Thank you,'' I laughed. "I try to lead a clean life.''

"Have you wondered yet why *you* didn't receive a letter?''

"The thought crossed my mind. But what good would it do to write to me? If there was some grand scheme to fleece the public, wouldn't I be just as suspect as my deputies? Hell, if it were true, I'd just cover it all up, wouldn't I? That's how things are done these days in what little of the political world I ever hear about.''

"You know what I think?''

"What do you think.''

"I think it's someone who knows you pretty well. They know that trying to get a rise, a reaction, out of you is probably a waste of time. Whoever it is knows that they can't smear you personally. You've been around too long. Too many people know you, know what kind of a hardheaded old…'' He paused, groping for just the right tone of insult that wouldn't leave him stranded by the side of the road.

"Son of a bitch,'' I prompted. "I'll take that as a compliment, I guess,'' I chuckled. "But I think you're blowing it out of proportion, Frank. If someone's got valid information on a crooked deputy, then why doesn't he just come forward and spill the beans? Go to the district attorney's office, or the attorney general. Sign a deposition. What's the point in all this anonymous shit?''

"The county sheriff can be a powerful position, Bill.''

"I'm overwhelmed with all the power I seem to have,'' I said.

He scoffed with amusement. "You're a cop. Not a politician. But besides the schools, the other wings of the county government, and the hospital, your department is one of the largest employers in the county. That's just for starters." He ticked off on his fingers. "Sheriff sales. Civil work. Bids to important vendors. You can make other politicians look good or bad, your choice. On and on and on. Even the little stuff. You can talk to any service club any time you want as a guest speaker, beating your own drum."

"That's something that's appealing, all right," I scoffed.

"Not to you, maybe, but it's all part of the package for someone who's interested. It's enough to make a regular citizen hesitate before going out on a limb against the county sheriff. There's probably some fear of retribution, a little bit of paranoia that if they try to stand alone without official support they're going to get squashed. It's just easier to have someone else fight the battle for you. Being a whistle blower is a lonely business. But an election." He rapped the dashboard again for emphasis. "That changes the whole formula."

"How so?"

"Hey, spread a little gossip, spread a little rumor, and pretty soon what happens? The rumor starts to take on a life of its own."

"And so I gather you think these moronic letters are the first stage in some kind of organized attempt to discredit us, discredit Bob, discredit the department, so someone else can win. A little nasty publicity just as the campaign gets under way."

"That's a good guess. Either side stands to gain."

"Why pick Tom Pasquale? He's just a kid."

"Assuming he's innocent? He's a good target, is why. He might have ruffled somebody's feathers sometime in the past. There might be a grudge there. If I remember my own newspaper's files, Pasquale has had his share of scrapes, and just enough heroics that when the story breaks in the newspapers, readers will say, 'Oh yeah, him...' "

"When the story breaks?"

Dayan waved a hand. "A figure of speech. Carter and Gray received letters. They're both Democrats. That leaves three to go. Tobe Ulibarri and Frank Weaver are Republicans. Janelle Waters is a Democrat. Care to bet who's going to contact you next?"

"So why are you betting on the Democrats? Why am I going to hear from Janelle Waters...not that she's such a bad dish to hear from, mind you."

Waters topped the list of Posadas's eligible singles. Her husband had been building a prosperous dental practice when cancer killed him at age thirty-eight. For reasons unknown to anyone but her, she had elected to remain in Posadas.

"Sheriff Martin Holman was a Republican, and an active one. You served as undersheriff for a long time before he took office and then nearly eight years as undersheriff for Holman afterward. Your department is a reflection of what he and you built as a team. Bob Torrez is a popular part of that. Hell, he's related to half the Hispanic population of the county."

"And if the Republicans jump on us, it'll look like they're turning on their own 'team,' as you put it. If they jump on Torrez, it'll make them look vindictive, even though he was never a registered Republican anyway."

"Something like that. All I'm saying is that to me, it explains why the one side is so quick to attack and the other side is holding back a little bit."

"So who's attacked? Neither Gray nor Carter wrote the note. They just apprised me of it."

"And lost no time, either."

"Why should they? If I was them, I'd give me the damn thing, too. And speaking of all that, you didn't lose any time, either, Frank."

"True enough. I hope that my motives are different, though."

I turned 310 onto the broad shoulder in front of the Moore Mercantile hulk and snapped on the spotlight.

"What are you looking for?"

"We just check," I said. "See that old stone building back there? It used to be a party spot. Sometimes folks from south of the border stop there, too. You never know." I looked over at him as I snapped off the spotlight. "We just check. That's what we do. We look a lot."

We pulled back out on the road and headed south.

"Tell me about Jim Sisson," Frank said.

"What's there to tell? You've heard the basics already. He was working on a big old front loader and had one of the back tires held up by a chain from another tractor. The chain slipped and the wheel and tire crushed him against the wall of his shop. That's it."

I glanced over at Dayan. "As the papers are fond of saying, 'he is survived by his widow, Grace, and six children.' "

"It was an accident?"

I hesitated only a fraction of a second, but that was long enough to tell Frank Dayan what he wanted to know. There was no point in being coy.

"Don't know," I muttered, thinking back to the photos Linda Real had taken.

"I saw the yellow ribbon across the Sissons' driveway, with the undersheriff's truck parked there."

"Yes."

"If it were a simple accident, I don't see much point in protecting the scene by having the undersheriff sit there all night."

I fell silent for a moment, not bothering to tell Dayan that I didn't have a clue about why my undersheriff was spending the night keeping two silent machines company when his young wife would have been a hell of a lot more cuddly. I said, "If I had any choice about what you print, I'd request that you said something vague like 'investigation is continuing.' "

"Fair enough. If something breaks, will you give either me or Pam a call?"

"Of course."

"How's Linda doing, by the way?"

"Linda is a treasure, Frank. Stealing her away from you folks was the best thing we ever did."

"And you're not forgiven yet, either, let me tell you."

We swept past the Broken Spur Saloon and in another couple of seconds passed the spot where the shooting of Linda Real and Deputy Paul Encinos had taken place two years before. As we started up the long, winding route through Regal Pass, I said, "After what she's been through, she deserves some happiness. She seems content now, and she's very good at what she does. And why she's so happy, only she knows."

Frank Dayan nodded, but I didn't add that the source of much of Linda Real's contentment was the human target of some creep with too much free time. That made me angry enough, but what was worse was the other side of the coin. If Tom Pasquale was a crooked cop, was Linda Real in on the scam, too?

"Shit," I said aloud, forgetting in the recoil from the thought that I had a passenger.

"What?" Frank Dayan asked.

"Nothing. I was just telling myself stories. It's an occupational hazard." I looked at the clock. "Let's circle through Regal, then head back and get some breakfast."

TEN

"LET ME GIVE YOU a tour," Undersheriff Robert Torrez said. The five of us stood near the back of Sisson's tractor—Torrez, Sgt. Howard Bishop, Tom Pasquale, Linda Real, and myself. The hub-bub of the night before was long gone.

Two cameras hung around Linda's neck, and a heavy camera bag with a plethora of gadgets rested on the gravel at her feet. Her right hand was poised on one of the cameras, index finger on the button as if she were covering an action sport.

"Jim is working right here, at the left rear hub. He wraps the chain from the backhoe's bucket around the wheel, so that when he takes off the lug nuts the wheel is supported. The front loader is jacked up, with all kinds of shit under the back axle for safety." Torrez looked at me and shook his head. "So far, so good. He's got the wheel and tire off, suspended from the chain. He wants to swing it around to the left, so that it's on the shop's concrete apron, and then lay it down flat."

He reached out and grabbed the chain that hung from the back-hoe's bucket. "When we arrived, the bucket that was doing the lifting, this one, was right where you see it now. And that's where it was when he was working. Then the tire was hanging right here, right above the apron. He figures there's no sense in taking it into the shop. He's going to break the tire loose right here, using the backhoe."

"I don't follow," I said.

"The tire's flat," Torrez continued. He thumped the rubber with his boot. "It doesn't look flat, because it's so stiff, but it is. In order to have it repaired, or put a new one on, he's got to break it off the rim. Most of the small shops around here can't do that. It's easier just to use the backhoe and break it that way. Push down on the tire, right beside the rim, with a couple of teeth. It'll pop it back from the rim."

"Otherwise you end up pounding on it forever with a sledge-hammer," Bishop said. He was a big, florid-faced man, almost as tall as the six-foot, four-inch Torrez, but with a gut that threatened to pop the buttons on his shirt. He squatted down beside the tire. "And there aren't any tooth marks along the rim, so he hadn't gotten that far yet."

"After we get some photos, we're going to do just what he did. If the wheel is suspended here, it makes sense that it was touching the ground, or close to it. If it's hanging right here, he's getting ready to lay it down."

"Why didn't he, then?" I said. "Why get off the tractor?"

"Maybe he needed to spin it around," Tom said. "If it's hanging from the chain, it might rotate some. He gets off to manhandle it around so that when he does lay it down, it goes the way he wants it to."

"Christ," I muttered. "This sounds like a two-man job, at least. What the hell was he doing out here all by himself?"

"Because he was royally pissed at his wife, is one reason. He spent the whole day being pissed. I talked to Bucky Randall for a few minutes last night. That was Jim's last job. Randall said one of the reasons this machine ended up in the shop is that Jim jammed it backward into a bunch of rebar and speared the tire. His mood wasn't the best. But this is actually pretty simple," Torrez said. "I mean, lifting it up is no trick and then swing it over. Maybe the tire nudged the lip of the concrete and turned some. If it starts to swing, to pendulum, then it's just easier to hop off and turn it by hand, then take a step and pull the lever to set it down. He wouldn't even need to be on the tractor to do that. It's careless, but operators do it all the time."

"So he's standing somehow between the suspended tire and the building. There's enough space there to lay the tire down. But it drops off the chain and he can't get out of the way? That doesn't make sense to me. That tire's not going to bounce like some crazy beach ball."

"No, sir, it's not," Torrez said. "And that's what's been both-ering me all night."

"He'd have had to lift it up a bunch for that to happen."

"And if the backhoe's boom is where he last put it, that wasn't the case. And there'd be no reason to lift it more than an inch or two...just enough to clear the concrete lip."

"All right," I said. "He lifts the wheel and tire. And then, he gets off the tractor." I held up my hands to mark an imaginary spot in the air. "The tire is hanging from the chain right about here." I turned and looked at the wall of the shop. An outline of Sisson's body had been marked on the concrete, behind where I stood. "He's got about six feet of space between the tire and the shop wall." I took a step back so that my boot was about where Sisson's had ended up. "If that tire comes off the chain, it'll drop, what, maybe a couple inches at most?"

"At most," Bishop said. "And it isn't going to bounce."

"So how's it going to catch me?" I asked. "Break my legs, maybe, knock me down. But how's it going to land on *top* of me?"

"It's not," Bob Torrez replied. "This can't be where the backhoe's boom was when the wheel dropped. It's that simple." He knelt down and pointed at a faint black rubber scuff mark on the concrete. "If you measure from this mark to the top one on the shop wall, you get a distance that's equal to the height of the tire."

"It hit that wall with more impact than just leaning over," I said.

"Indeed it did. Enough to scuff rubber and dent the siding. And then it slid down on top of Jim Sisson."

"I don't think so," I said, and Torrez nodded.

"I don't think so, either. For one thing, look at this." He stepped to the big tire. "We moved this tire up and over to the left just enough to remove Jim's body. If you look right here, you can see the imprints of the chain where it went around the tire."

I peered closely. The imprints were just faint, dark marks, with interruptions that corresponded to the end of each link. "Will this show up in a photo?"

"It should, sir," Linda said. She knelt beside me. "I took a whole bunch just a few minutes ago. With this morning light coming in at a strong angle, I think it'll work."

"You took plenty, to be sure?"

"Yes, sir."

I heard the clank of chain and looked up as Bob Torrez stretched out a section and laid it beside the marks. The match didn't take any imagination.

Linda said, "I took a series like that, for comparison."

"Good. So what else?"

Bob leaned over, moving the chain so that it crumpled into a tight *S,* just above the bright yellow rim, two feet from the first set of marks.

"The chain impacted the rubber here, too," he said. "If you look closely, you'll see that it actually scuffed the surface of the tire."

"Not with these eyes I can't," I said. "What are you telling me?"

"If I had to make a guess, I'd say that the chain was driven into the tire with a lot of force. And so was the reddish dirt."

"Reddish dirt?"

I bent over, shifting so that I wasn't blocking the wash of morning sunlight. The tire was clean, but even I could see the loose dirt on that section of the tire, some caught in the crevice between rim and tire, some ground into the rubber.

"I'll be damned," I said. "Did you get this?"

Linda nodded. "I've got a good close-up lens," she replied.

"I bagged a good sample," Torrez said. "And I'll bet a month's pay that it matches the dirt on the back side of that backhoe's bucket."

I turned and looked at the machine, its bucket poised seven feet above the concrete slab. The teeth were polished from the constant abrasion of the digging process, but soil clung here and there to the rest of it, the sort of thing I would expect after a session of digging beside someone's leaking water line.

"You got all that?" I said to Linda.

"Yes, sir."

"And you haven't moved the machine any?" I asked Robert Torrez.

"No. Nothing's been moved."

"What are you thinking, then?"

Torrez took a deep breath. "I think that after the tire was lying down—"

"On top of Sisson?"

"Yes, sir. After it was lying down, the operator, whoever it was, curled the bucket like this," and he curled his hand back toward the underside of his forearm, "and then set it down on the tire. The chain was still attached at the bucket, and a handful of links were caught between the bucket and the tire when he pushed down...." Torrez hesitated. "He pushed down hard enough to lift the backhoe off the ground."

Torrez walked back to the machine and beckoned. "Look here." The hydraulic outriggers of Sisson's backhoe were lowered into the gravel.

"Why would he bother to put the outriggers down just for a job like this?" I asked.

"Always," Bishop said. "The weight of that backhoe arm makes those big tires bounce like crazy. The stabilizers lock you in place. If the tractor bounces against the weight, then whatever you're swinging starts to bounce and pendulum, too."

"All right. So the outriggers are down, just like they're supposed to be."

Torrez knelt and touched the gravel with his index finger. "And you can see how they've dragged sideways in the gravel? I measured that gouge as almost six inches long."

Linda anticipated my glance and nodded.

"The machine moved?"

"There's only one way to do that," Bishop said. "You put down force on the boom, and if the bucket can't go down, the machine lifts itself up. Sideways force on the boom, and if the bucket can't move sideways, the machine does."

I squinted at Torrez. "I looked at all the photos that Linda has so far. The sideways scuffing of the tire mark?" I pointed over at the concrete apron. "That's a hell of a photo. I wouldn't see that scuff unless it was pointed out to me."

Torrez nodded. "The tire moved sideways. Not a whole lot, but a bit. Several inches."

"And when it did," I said, "there was a tremendous downward force on it."

"About as much as this machine weighs," Bishop said. "Old Jim might have survived the tire dropping on him, but not with the weight of a backhoe on top of it. That machine weighs about five tons. Crushed him like an insect."

ELEVEN

GRACE SISSON had wasted no time. The night her husband had been killed, she'd taken the three youngest children—twelve-year-old Todd, fourteen-year-old Melissa, and fifteen-year-old Jennifer—to her parents' house in Las Cruces. The older children had flown the nest years before, deciding that Posadas wasn't the answer to their every dream.

With the family gone, we had the place to ourselves. Still, I didn't want any legal complications. While Linda Real developed the film from her earlier sessions, I woke up Judge Lester Hobart, explained what I wanted to do, and walked out of his kitchen fifteen minutes later with a court order.

We could have impounded the machines and moved them all over to one of the county barns, but that seemed like a waste of time and money. Besides, I didn't want just an approximation of the episode that had ended with Jim Sisson's death.

Driving back on Bustos, I saw Frank Dayan unlocking the front door of the *Register,* and I swung over to the curb. He had a breakfast burrito in one hand and a steaming cup of coffee in the other, juggling his keys like a pro. It'd been more than an hour since we'd been the Don Juan's first customers, and the idea of a snack was appealing.

I buzzed down the window as he stepped to the curb. "If you've got time, drop by the Sissons'," I said.

"You mean right now?"

"Yep. Might be interesting."

"Well, neither MaryAnn nor Pam is here yet." Pam Gardiner was the reporter who'd taken Linda Real's place at the *Register,* a blubbery, much too cheerful person who apparently thought that most of the news would come to her if she sat on her butt long enough. Why Dayan put up with her lassitude I didn't know. Maybe he was working too hard to notice. MaryAnn Weaver, the wife of county commissioner Frank Weaver, had run the front desk of the *Register* for fifteen years.

"They've both got keys, don't they?" I grinned. "Come on." I reached over and opened the door.

"What the hell," Frank said, and got in. "You're going to tell me what's going on?"

"Of course not."

He laughed and sipped the coffee, grimacing. "Want some?"

"No, thanks. I'll take that burrito, though."

He hesitated and then actually extended the thing toward me. "Sure. Here."

I waved him off. "This is going to be a nasty one, Frank."

"You mean Sisson..."

I nodded.

He took a bite of the burrito. It smelled wonderful. "You know, Pam can cover this better than I can," he said between chews. "She's the reporter."

"It's an election year," I said. "Humor me."

HOWARD BISHOP pulled himself up into the seat of the backhoe with practiced ease. The machine cranked a couple of times and fired, belched a cloud of black smoke, and then settled into a clattering idle.

Torrez stood by one back tire, resting a forearm on it like a neighbor chatting over the fence. "I want to attach the chain over on the side, away from the original marks," he said to Bishop. "Swing the bucket to the left some, and I'll hook it up."

Bishop lowered the bucket and extended the arm so that the bucket's teeth hung over the left side of the tire, taking the heavy logging chain with it. Torrez threaded the free end of the chain through the wheel and around the tire near where it was supported by a short chunk of two-by-four, then hooked one of the links.

"You sure?" I asked, and Torrez nodded. I held out a hand. "That's not secure," I said. The chain hook had a scant hold on the link.

"I know, sir. That's what I want."

He turned to Bishop and gave him a thumbs-up, and the back-hoe's boom lifted until the slack was out of the chain. It slipped a little on the rubber, and then the tire eased off the ground as the backhoe took the weight.

"Nothing to it," Bob said.

"How high do you want it?" Bishop shouted.

"About a foot or two off the ground," Torrez replied. "There'd be no reason for Sisson to lift it higher than that." I glanced across at Linda Real. The red light on the video camera's snout was on. "And right over this spot," Torrez added, and he picked up a shovel that had been leaning against the building and touched the spot on the concrete where the tire had first impacted, close to the shop wall.

When he was satisfied, he nodded at Bishop. "Perfect," he said. The tire hung suspended about eighteen inches above the concrete apron. It drifted around in a lazy circle, stopping when the chain links tightened up. Then it started to drift back.

"Now what?" Frank Dayan asked.

"Now we drop it," Torrez said. "You guys back off some."

I stood near the rear wheel of the backhoe, and Dayan joined me. Torrez walked over to his pickup and rummaged in the back, finally returning with a six-foot length of one-inch galvanized pipe and a three-pound hammer. "This'll work," he said.

He walked altogether too close to the tire, stopped, and looked over at Linda. "You all set?"

"*World's Strangest Videos*, take one," she said.

Torrez grinned and lifted the steel pipe as if it were a toothpick. He rested one end against the tip of the chain's hook where it had a tenuous grip on the link. He struck the other end of the bar with the hammer, and it drove the tip of the hook out of the link with the first tap.

With a brief *rapppp* of sliding chain, the tire thumped to the concrete like a wet pillow, with just as much bounce. When he struck the bar, Bob Torrez was two paces from the tire, and even as it hit the concrete, he stepped forward and put a steadying hand on the tread. After a second or two, he took his hand away. The tire stood motionless, a fat bulge at the bottom.

"Don't turn it off yet," he said to Linda, and then looked at me with a raised eyebrow. "So much for it bouncing into the building."

Resting a hand on the top of the tire, he walked around on the other side. With a gentle nudge, the tire fell over, striking the side of the building with a crash. And there it leaned, refusing to slide down.

"I'll be damned," I said.

Torrez walked to one side and aimed a hearty kick at the tire. It thumped and refused to move.

"There's just no way," he said. Then he turned to Howard Bishop and beckoned. Bishop extended the boom, curling the bucket as he did so. Torrez pointed to the spot on the tire, and Bishop lowered the bucket until its back gently touched the rubber.

"Nail it!" the undersheriff shouted, and Bishop slammed the lever full forward.

The tire skidded down the wall, its bottom simultaneously kicking out on the concrete slab. When it thumped flat, I shivered, imagining Jim Sisson's final moments with that weight on top of him. Bishop kept the hydraulic force applied, and the backhoe lifted itself in the air, the outriggers clearing the ground by a foot.

Torrez held up a hand, and Bishop stopped, the machine frozen, bucket crushing the tire, outriggers up in the air. Bishop reduced the throttle as Torrez walked around and approached us.

"Now," he said to Bishop, "how do you jog it sideways?"

"It's easy to do," the sergeant replied. "If the operator gets excited, he can do it by accident. The sideways movement of the arm is on the same lever as down thrust." He pointed at the left of the two long central control levers.

"Do it," Torrez said. "Just drop her down. Try and make the same kind of marks."

"Move a little," Bishop said, and waited while we stepped away from the backhoe. Then he jammed the lever to the left and pulled back at the same time. The bucket jerked left; the tractor bucked right and dropped like a giant yellow stone, its outriggers crashing back in the gravel.

The tire had scrubbed a couple of inches to the left.

"And that's what I think happened," Torrez said. The tractor idled down and then died as Bishop pulled the manual throttle lever back.

"The tire clearly didn't drop and kill him," he said.

"Nope," Torrez agreed. "It had help."

Frank Dayan shook his head in wonder. "Wow. That's amazing."

I reached out a hand and put it on his shoulder. "And now you know that if you just print 'investigation is continuing' you'll be telling the absolute truth."

"But what you're saying here is that Jim Sisson was murdered," Dayan replied. "You're saying that someone deliberately crushed him to death. And then made it look like an accident."

"It appears that way."

"That means whoever it was would have had to clout him on the head or something first...overpower him in some way. He wouldn't just lie still, waiting to be crushed."

"Exactly," I said. "Maybe the autopsy will show something. But if it was something as simple as a blow to the back of the head, that's not going to show up. Not with his skull crushed the way it was."

"Give me a photo. At least give me that much," he pleaded. "It's not often I get to scoop the big-city dailies."

"On one condition," I said. "On one condition, we'll fix you right up."

"What's that?"

"Don't use the word *homicide* yet."

"Done deal," Dayan said. "And my paper doesn't come out until Friday morning, anyway. Maybe things will have changed by then."

"Maybe," I said.

Dayan bent down, looking at the tire marks on the concrete. "Do you suppose whoever did this figured you'd never look closely?"

"Maybe," I said. "And we can hope that's not the only mistake they made."

TWELVE

JIM SISSON'S DEATH hadn't attracted much press, to Frank Dayan's relief. His major competition, the Deming newspaper, stumbled across the incident in the course of their routine morning phone call to check the blotter.

The story didn't make the front page. The episode was tucked under several obits more local to Deming than Posadas. If it had been a hot news week, we wouldn't have made it at all.

The headline was artfully evasive across two columns:

Posadas Contractor Dies
Following Shop Incident

Most of the grim details were there, with the exception of any speculation about how the "incident" might have happened.

The fundamental conundrum—how a five-and-a-half-foot man managed to be crushed under a fifty-four-inch-tall tire and wheel assembly—was not mentioned, other than the cover-all expression that "investigation is continuing into the incident that claimed the life of James L. Sisson."

Apparently the use of the word *incident* rather than accident hadn't been lost on Posadas Chief of Police Eduardo D. Martinez, who waddled into the Public Safety Building with a copy of the Deming paper under his arm. He appeared in the door of my office shortly after 3:00, brow furrowed and mouth working either a wad of chewing tobacco or a rehearsal of what he wanted to say.

The chief was fifty-six, with about the same dimensions in the torso as a fifty-five-gallon oil drum. His large, square face, with dark eyebrows, wide, heavy-lipped mouth that winked gold, and enough chin for three people, would have made him perfect casting as the Mexican bartender in one of those grade-D spaghetti westerns.

I liked Eduardo, even though I'd never been sure just what purpose his tiny department served—especially since he made no effort to grab his share of the law enforcement turf. But state law was clear: Incorporated villages had to have a police department. A decade before, back when the copper mines were open and fat paychecks flowed directly from payroll office to bank to saloons, the police department had kept busy.

But that was before Eduardo's tenure as chief—back when he was still earning a living driving a road grader for the village street department. Now Chief Martinez and two part-time patrolmen kept themselves busy making sure that we had one of the best patrolled fifteen-mile-an-hour school zones in the state. Eduardo's philosophy seemed to be that if the kids could cross the street safely, what else mattered?

Chief Martinez was so adept at staying backstage that I sometimes forgot that he was there. If he took offense at that, he never let it show.

He ducked his head and smiled ruefully. "You busy?"

"No, no," I said quickly and got up, motioning toward one of the leather-backed chairs. "Come on in. Pull up a seat and rest the bones."

He did so and unfolded the newspaper. "This is sure something, eh?" he said, his soft voice carrying that wonderfully musical border cadence.

"Just about the goddamnedest thing I ever saw."

"You know," he said, looking up at me, "when Bobby answered that call, it was the third time yesterday." He frowned and tried again. "Three times he went out to that place."

"Out to the Sissons', you mean?"

"Yes." The chief nodded vigorously. "You know, there have been days when I went out there myself, three, four times."

"They put on quite a show from time to time, that's for sure."

He frowned again and scooted his chair forward. "What do you think happened?"

I leaned back in my chair and regarded Martinez with interest. The chief was adept at staying out of the way—he had never been the sort to weasel his way into an investigation that another agency was conducting, for limelight or any other reason. In fact, this was the first time that he'd ever taken the initiative to come to my office and ask to be brought up to speed.

The manila folder that included the set of photographs rested at my elbow, and I flopped it open. "Take a look," I said. "Tell me what you think." Like any of us, the chief enjoyed a little deference now and then, and instead of just handing him the folder, I selected several photos, reached across, and spread them out on my desk, facing him.

He leaned forward with his hands tightly clasped between his knees, as if afraid that touching the prints might smear the images.

"Linda shot this one before the tire was moved," I said. "And these were taken at the hospital."

Martinez grimaced. "Hm," he said, and blinked.

"Here's our problem," I continued. "See the way he's scrunched up against the wall? There just isn't very much space there. About four feet or so. And that's how tall the tire is, give or take."

"I don't get it," Martinez said.

"Me, neither. We picked up that tire with a chain, just the way Jim Sisson might have. We can't be sure, of course, but the chain marks on the tire," and I tapped another photo, "indicate that Sisson—or someone—lifted the tire with a chain that in turn was looped around the bucket teeth of a backhoe. From what we could pry out of Grace, old Jim was working alone out back. And that tire is flat, so it's logical to assume that's what Jim was doing."

"And the chain just slipped off?"

"So it would appear. We tried the same thing. Hoisted it up, knocked the chain loose, and let the tire drop. It hit the ground and stopped dead. No bounce. Bob stepped up to it and balanced it in place with one hand."

Martinez chewed his lip in thought. "He would have to be kneeling down or sitting or something to be caught like that."

"When we tipped the tire over, it just leaned against the wall. It didn't slide down. Not until we forced it with the bucket. And that explains the chain marks, there." I indicated one of the photos.

I leaned back and folded my hands over my stomach. "Bob went out there on three separate occasions yesterday. He never was able to determine what Jim and Grace were arguing about, but apparently it was a doozie. The first call came when a neighbor who happened to be walking by heard a screaming match and the sound of shattering glass. From what we can gather, a large mirror in the living room was the target of a flying object." I grinned. "And that was the first call. Right after lunch, they went at it again, apparently when Jim returned from a job he was doing at Bucky Randall's place. The third time was early in the evening, just before dark."

"When Jim came home again," the chief said.

"Probably. The interesting thing is that the Sissons wouldn't tell Bob what the argument was about. Grace still won't. She took the kids down to Las Cruces, and the city PD there confirms that all four of them are staying with her parents. The city cops are keeping an eye on her for us until we sound the all clear."

Reaching across the desk, I pulled the photo of the tire hanging from the chain. "We have a video of our little test, Chief. You might want to look at that, too. You asked me what I think happened, and I'm sure of this much: That tire didn't just drop off the chain and crush Jim Sisson to death. It had help."

For a long time Chief Martinez looked at the photo as if the still picture might come to life for him.

"Marjorie always gave them troubles," he said, and glanced up at me. "The oldest daughter."

"The blond bombshell," I said. "I remember an episode or two that involved her. But she's off in college somewhere."

"Over in California," the chief said. "But they had three at home, still."

"Todd, Melissa, and Jennifer," I offered.

"And when people argue," he said, "you can bet that it's about money or their kids. And if I had to bet, I'd find out a little more about that girl."

"Jennifer, you mean? Or Melissa?"

He nodded. "Jennifer. I see her around town, you know. All the time. Her tail...wag, wag, wag." He fluttered his hand back and forth but didn't crack a smile.

"And maybe the argument between Jim and Grace didn't have

a damn thing to do with Jim Sisson's death," I said. "There's always that. He might have been working back there, and someone came in without Grace hearing, without one of the kids looking outside and seeing who it was. We just don't know. They all say that they didn't see anything, didn't hear anything."

Eduardo Martinez settled back in the chair and folded his hands in his lap. "What did Tomas tell you?" he asked, and I didn't make the connection. Eduardo saw my puzzled expression and quickly added, "Deputy Pasquale."

"What do you mean, what did he tell me? What *should* he have told me?" Even before the question was out, I could feel my blood pressure starting to rise.

"A couple days ago—maybe it was Monday, I'm not sure—his unit was parked at Portillo's and he was talking to a group of kids. I stopped there just to pick up some things, you know. It was kinda late."

Portillo's Handy-Way, the convenience store a dusty field and one street east of the high school, was a popular hangout for youngsters—or at least the store's parking lot was. From there they could watch traffic cruising up and down Grande, an excitement that I somehow failed to appreciate.

"That doesn't surprise me," I said. "When Pasquale worked for you, Portillo's was one of his favorite haunts, if I remember correctly."

"Yes, it was. And one of the kids he was talking to the other night was Jennifer Sisson. I happened to notice her. The long blond hair, you know."

"Huh," I muttered, then took a deep breath. "Well, I'm sure that if she'd told him anything of significance, he would have mentioned it to me."

The chief reached out and tidied up the stack of photos, then pushed himself out of the chair. "At least you got one thing," he said. "Whoever done this is pretty good with a backhoe. To do that...that would never occur to just anyone, you know. They'd have to have some experience... They'd have to know how."

"So it would appear," I said. "I'll check with Pasquale about the Sisson girl. And I'll keep you posted. If you hear anything else, holler at me."

As soon as the chief left, I stepped into the dispatch room. Gayle Sedillos turned and raised an eyebrow at my expression.

"Find Deputy Pasquale for me," I said.

"I think he's at home," Gayle replied, and then, having correctly interpreted both the expression on my face and the tone of my voice, she added, "I'll call him in right away, sir."

"Send him to my office when he gets here," I said.

THIRTEEN

AFTER A FEW MINUTES, even the steady hum of the computer became a nuisance. The damn thing squatted on the corner of my desk, its screen-saver program presenting an endless series of twisting geometric patterns. Either the machine didn't have any of the answers that I wanted or I didn't know how to ask the right questions. The noise got on my nerves, and I shut the thing off and sat back, letting my head sag back against my chair's leather rest.

I leaned back and let my eyes wander around the room, wondering what the hell my next step should be. I didn't like not knowing. And I felt, with those damn anonymous notes piled on top of a messy homicide, as if someone was playing games with us.

With a start, I realized that there was one small mystery I could clear up. I leaned forward and picked up the phone book, rummaged for a moment, then dialed the number of Payson Realty. Maggie Payson picked it up on the third ring.

"Maggie, this is Bill Gastner," I said.

Her tone went up an octave with a pleasure that sounded genuine. "Well now, Sheriff, how are you? You know, I was just thinking about you."

I didn't pursue that, since with the way my luck had been running I was sure that, one way or another, her thoughts would end up as a complaint against someone in my department. Instead I asked, "How's your father?" George Payson had owned and operated a sporting goods store until a couple of months before, when a stroke had knocked him out of his chair while he was tying a difficult bass fly.

"Oh," Maggie said, "not good. It's so sad to see him slipping."

"I'm sorry to hear that." George and I had had a standing bet for almost two decades over which one of us would keel over first.

We'd both almost taken the trophy a couple of times, but at the moment I didn't feel like winning. "He's at home still, though, right?"

"Oh, yes," Maggie said quickly. "I tried to talk to him about a managed care place over in Deming, but that conversation lasted about ten seconds."

"He's stubborn," I said. "Maybe that will keep him going."

"We can only hope so."

I hesitated. "Look, the reason I called. It's none of my business, but I was wondering who bought the Guzmans' place over on Twelfth Street. I happened to be driving by there last night, and the sign was down."

Posadas wasn't the center of the world's real estate market, and Maggie Payson didn't have to consult a huge cross-referenced database to answer my question. She didn't even hesitate to shift mental gears.

"No, that didn't sell, Bill. Francis and Estelle took their place off the market."

"Off the market?"

"Uh-huh."

"I'll be damned. It's been a couple of weeks since I talked to her. She didn't mention anything about that."

"Well, this is a more recent thing. She called me Friday, I believe it was."

"Son of a gun. I guess I'll have to get on the ball and find out what's going on. We've been busy, and time slips away."

"Yes, you have," Maggie said, artfully dodging the opportunity to tell me what was on Estelle Reyes-Guzman's mind, if she knew in the first place. "That was awful about Jim Sisson, wasn't it? Such a tragic thing. I can't imagine what Grace's going to do now. Three kids still at home. I just can't imagine."

I heard murmuring voices out in the hall and glanced at my watch. "I'll leave you in peace, Maggie. Thanks for the information."

"My pleasure. And say, did you ever get those horses you were thinking about? Those wonderful draft horses?"

"I chickened out," I chuckled. "I came to the realization that my schedule would never fit theirs...at least not until I retire. Maybe then I'll rethink the whole idea."

"We've got a really good deal on a nice parcel of irrigated pasturage over west of town, if you need it. Just under eleven acres."

"I'm sure you do, Maggie. I'll keep it in mind. And give my regards to your dad."

We rang off, and the instant the light blinked out on my telephone, a set of knuckles rapped on my door.

"Come on in," I said, and Deputy Tom Pasquale appeared, one hand gripping the outside knob, the other drifting to the jamb, as if prepared to slam the door shut at an instant's notice.

"Gayle said you were off the phone," he began. "Did you want to see me, sir?"

"Yes. Come in. Close the door. Have a seat." I gathered up the photos that Chief Martinez and I had been examining, shoved them in the folder, and tossed it on the stack of papers to my right.

Pasquale sat down and carefully placed his straw Bailey on the floor and then shifted sideways a little so that the butt of his holstered automatic wouldn't dig the arm of the chair.

"There are about three things that I need to run by you," I said. "Chief Martinez said that you had the opportunity to talk with Jennifer Sisson a couple of nights ago."

Pasquale frowned and visibly seemed to relax. An intelligent kid, he was keenly aware of his past performance, and I knew that no one in the department tried more diligently to do the right thing— at least as long as I was watching.

He thought for a moment and then said, "Yes, sir. I did. I think it was Monday night, as a matter of fact. She was one of several kids messing around."

"Where was that?"

"Portillo's parking lot. It was pushing ten o'clock, and I thought it would be a good idea if I could sort of...move 'em on a little."

"Not a bad idea."

"Jennifer was the oldest in that group, sir. The others were just middle schoolers. And there were a couple of cars with older kids cruising around town, and I knew that the younger kids were waiting to be picked up.'' He shrugged. ''I figured that if I hung around, that might not happen. It was a quiet night, not much else to do.''

''And the PD?''

''Beuler was on, and he was tied up with a minor fender bender over at the Posadas Inn, sir.''

''Ah.'' I leaned my head back again and watched the fan idle in circles. Tom Pasquale waited. ''Did Jennifer Sisson happen to say anything to you at the time? Anything that, in retrospect, might fit in with the incident last night? Or with the fight between her parents?''

Pasquale frowned again and ran fingers through his sandy brown hair. ''No, sir. She didn't. But I really didn't get into it with them, either. The kids, I mean. I just figured that if I parked there for a few minutes, they'd move on.''

''And they did?''

''Yes, sir. We chatted for a bit, and then they headed toward the pizza place.''

''And this was all about ten o'clock, or thereabouts?''

''Yes, sir.''

I rested my chin in my left hand, elbow propped on the padded arm of the chair. ''Who were the older kids that were cruising around, do you know?''

Pasquale shook his head. ''No, sir. I caught a glimpse of one car that came out of the parking lot of the grocery store. There were a couple of kids in it, but they were behaving themselves, so I didn't check 'em out.''

''That was while you were parked at Portillo's?''

''Yes, sir. Kitty-corner across the street.''

''When you talked with Beuler last night, did he happen to mention anything? Anything at all that might tie into this mess? Any arguments that Jim Sisson had with anybody?''

''No, sir.'' Pasquale sighed. ''We haven't turned up a thing. Bob is convinced that someone else was there, and that Sisson's death wasn't an accident, and that maybe Grace knows more than she's ready to admit to. But that's it.'' He held up his hands. ''We haven't found a thing yet. No prints, no nothing.''

I grimaced. ''Maybe we're imagining things.''

''I don't think so, sir.''

"You agree with the undersheriff?" I knew that was a silly question, and Pasquale's answer was prompt.

"Yes, sir."

"Then it's footwork time, Thomas. We need to know who was on Jim's list of recent accounts—maybe some customer got bent out of shape. Who he's got debts with." I held out both hands. "Who his kids are seeing. Who Grace is having tea with, or who she's having an affair with. Whatever."

Deputy Pasquale nodded and started to reach for his hat.

"A couple other things," I said, and he relaxed back in the chair. "It's not my intent to pry into your personal life, Thomas, but..." I stopped. It would have helped if he'd just said, *"Well, then don't,"* but he sat there quietly, looking uncertain and apprehensive.

"I talked to Carla Champlin yesterday."

"Sir?"

"And Miss Champlin wants you evicted."

"Say what?"

I nodded. "She contends that the house you're renting has been damaged to a point where she's losing her investment."

"Sir, that's—"

I held up a hand to cut him off. "That's what Miss Champlin said. I pass it on to you for what it's worth. If there's a problem, it's between you and her."

"Why didn't she just come and talk with me?" Pasquale said. "I wouldn't think that's so hard."

"She said that she's tried, on several occasions." Pasquale looked puzzled, and I spread my hands. "That's what she says. I've known Carla Champlin for a good many years, Thomas. She's an...interesting...person. You happen to be her target of the month."

"What am I supposed to do, then?"

"I wouldn't presume to tell you, Thomas. Maybe plant some petunias. I don't know."

"It's the motorcycle," he said flatly.

"The Harley in the front yard?"

He nodded. "I'm trying to buy it from Mears. The other day I had it inside the house. It's got something wrong with one of the carbs, and I didn't want to get sand in it, so I rolled it inside and put it in the back bedroom. I put papers down and stuff.''

"And..."

"She happened to drive by when Linda and I were rolling it back outside.''

"I see," I said, and grinned. "Were you wearing your leather motorcycle gang jacket at the time?''

"Maybe I should have been," he muttered. "If I owned one.''

"Well, for what it's worth, I told Carla Champlin I'd mention it to you, and I have, so...''

Pasquale nodded and reached for his hat again.

"One more thing before you go," I said.

"Sir?''

I hesitated again. Maybe it was the wrong thing to do, but I knew I wasn't good at dissembling. Tom Pasquale would find out sooner or later, and I wanted it to be from me, not from an article in the newspaper or from someone on the street who couldn't wait to pass on juicy gossip. I opened the top drawer of my desk and took out the photocopies I'd made of the three letters received by the county commissioners and Frank Dayan.

I reached across and handed them to Pasquale. He read them one at a time with his lips forming the words silently. By the second one, his face had drained of color.

FOURTEEN

"DR. GRAY TRACKED down and gave me that," I said. Deputy Pasquale still hadn't found words, so I continued, "And then Sam Carter caught up with me while I was having dinner last night...or two nights ago. I lose track."

"All three are the same," Pasquale murmured. "Except for who they're sent to." He looked up. "What's Frank Dayan planning to do, did he say? Did he give this to you personally?"

"Yes. We spent a good deal of time together last night, wandering around the county and trying to figure out what the son of a bitch who wrote this had in mind. Frank said he has no intention of doing anything about the note." I managed a smile. "No front-page exposé in his paper. Not even the classifieds. And I think he'll keep his word."

"I don't understand, then."

I turned my chair sideways and hooked a boot up on the corner of my desk. "Neither do I, Tom. It interests me that the creep didn't just send the note to me in the first place." I spread my hands. "That would be logical, but a couple of reasons have occurred to me why he might not do that. Instead, he targets at least two of the five commissioners and the publisher of the local newspaper. That's who I've heard from so far."

"I never did any of this, sir," Tom Pasquale said.

"You don't have to convince me."

But the young deputy obviously felt that he did, and added, "I usually don't even stop cars with Mexican plates. Not unless they're doing something really wild and crazy. And every stop I make is logged, so there's a record."

I held up a hand. "Relax. This is the way I look at it. Either you've got yourself an enemy who's trying to make your life miserable, or the target is the department that you have the misfortune to work for. Someone's trying to make us look bad and happened to pick you as a good place to start." I shrugged and swung the other boot up.

"Who knows who we'll hear from next? Maybe we'll start getting cute little letters telling the world that I'm feathering my retirement bed by selling stuff out of the evidence locker over at the flea market in Las Cruces on the weekends." I paused and regarded Pasquale for a moment, just long enough that he started to twist in his seat again.

"Your landlady would like to crucify you at the moment, Tom, but this crap isn't the style of a crazy woman. And it's not the sort of thing some kid that you busted one too many times would do. My suspicion is that some damn fool has a grudge against this department and enjoys making some trouble. Somebody who understands the power of rumor."

Pasquale took a deep breath. "What should I do, sir?"

I put my feet down, swung around, and leaned forward, clasping my hands together in front of me as if I were about to begin a prayer session.

"My first inclination would be to ignore it, but I've been thinking about it some, and damned if I want to do that. What I really want to do is hang the son of a bitch who wrote these." I picked up the three letters and then let them fall to the desk. "Whoever it is thinks he's pretty slick. The thought occurs to me that if he'd written one of those notes to me, or to any member of this department, we could try to nail him for filing a false complaint."

"But he didn't do that," Pasquale said. "And those letters aren't signed."

"Nope, he didn't...and they aren't. There's a claim of documentation, but obviously we'll never see any of that." I leaned back. "And these aren't signed statements, as you point out. What I'd like to do is find out who wrote the notes—be able to prove it—and then go after 'em for libel. I've never sued anybody in my life, but this seems like a good opportunity to start."

"I don't have money for a lawyer," Pasquale said, his voice almost a whisper.

"No. But I do, and it'd give me immense satisfaction to make this bastard squirm."

"The only trouble is," Pasquale said, "even being in the right, even being able to prove it's just libel, some of the shit rubs off."

I grimaced in sympathy. "Yep. Welcome to the world, Thomas."

"What if someone really is stopping Mexican nationals?" Pasquale said. "What if someone else is doing it and blaming it on me?"

"Then we try our best to catch 'em at it." I grinned. "I'd enjoy that, too." I picked up the copies and slid them back inside the brown case folder.

"Maybe there's something we could pick up from those," Pasquale said. "Prints or something? Characteristic letter strikes, something like that?"

"That's being done," I replied. "These are copies. I sent the originals to Las Cruces. In a day or two, we'll know all there is to know. But in the meantime, don't hold your breath. I don't think we're going to find that they were printed on a 1936 Royal typewriter with half of its *e* missing. Life is never that simple. But speaking of little things..." I pushed back my chair and stood up with a crack of joints. "You spend a lot of time down on State 56." I looked down and regarded the yellow legal pad with my statistical computations.

"Of the one hundred and thirty-seven registration checks you requested through Dispatch last month, eighty-four were logged while you were working that particular stretch of highway."

I saw the flush creep up Thomas Pasquale's neck and cheeks and knew what he was thinking. He started to say something, but I held up a hand. "About the same the month before that, and ditto for May. What your logs show is that you cover that particular highway pretty thoroughly." I rested a finger on the logs as if marking my place. "What I want you to think about is anything you've noticed during that time. Anything that, thinking back now, is a little unusual."

"I don't follow, sir."

"This is what I think, Thomas," I said, and walked over to the window, hands thrust in my pockets. The sky to the west was dark, just enough to tantalize us into wishful thinking. "You're down that way a lot. I think someone else knows it." I turned and regarded him. "Seven or eight calls to Dispatch on any given evening. And each time, when you call in a license plate, you also give your location, don't you?"

"Yes, sir."

I held up both hands. "Well, then. Someone with a simple dime store scanner knows your habits. What happens if someone actually investigates? Let's say there's a complaint made that at twenty-oh-five hours on a Tuesday you stopped a motorist on Fifty-six and put the arm on them. The obvious thing to do is look at the dispatch log and see if you're working that area. Sure enough, you are. You're not dumb enough to log the vehicle that you stop for a little easy cash, but maybe the log will show that ten minutes before you stopped another vehicle...maybe just a tourist headed for Arizona."

"But there's no direct proof," Pasquale said.

"No, there's not. But the evidence shows that you're in the area, and what happens? There's some credence given to the rumor in people's minds." I shook my head. "Doesn't matter if it can be proved or not. The idea is planted."

"Christ," the young deputy muttered.

"We've got a little ammunition," I said. "We can guess that someone listens to our radio traffic. And it's somebody who's reasonably familiar with the county and the way traffic works. If the lab gets back to me with something interesting from the original letters, that's another piece."

Thomas Pasquale took a deep breath and held it for a long moment, finally exhaling with a loud sigh. "I hate this, sir," he said.

"I don't blame you. What I want you to do is start thinking, and researching. I've looked over the logs, and I don't see any consistency in the vehicles that you're stopping, except out-of-staters lead the pack, with the greatest share going to Texas plates." I shrugged. "That's reasonable. Now I want to know who you see when you're out and around. Don't change your patrol habits. Stay heavy on Fifty-six when you can, and stay on the air."

"Do you think somebody else is hitting up on Mexican nationals and blaming it on me?"

"It's possible, but it just doesn't make sense to me. Why not just keep it quiet? None of the Mexicans are going to say anything.... Hell, it's a way of life for most of them when it comes to government officials. Why bother drawing attention to the scam with a bunch of dumb letters?"

"It doesn't make sense."

"No, it doesn't. Just keep your eyes open. I'll talk to Bob Torrez about it and see what he thinks. And if you happen to see me parked off in the weeds when you're down that way, pretend I'm not there."

Deputy Pasquale gathered his hat and stood up. He was half a head taller than me and with the worry on his face no longer looked as if he were a twenty-year-old. "I guess I should ask, then," he said.

"Ask what?"

"Two nights ago, down on Fifty-six. You were parked up on the mesa? You'd already received one or two of those letters?"

"Yes."

"You thought there was something to them, sir?"

"I didn't know what to think." I reached out and gave him a paternal pat on the arm. "And when that happens, I go out and park in the dark somewhere, roll down the windows, and let great thoughts come to me." I didn't know if that answer satisfied him or not, but he nodded and settled the summer-weight uniform hat firmly on his head, the broad brim two fingers above the bridge of his nose.

"Keep your eyes and ears open," I said as he headed toward the door of my office.

"Yes, sir," he replied, and touched the brim of his hat. He opened the door, and at the same time a muffled drumroll of summer thunder murmured off to the west.

FIFTEEN

THE LATE AFTERNOON STORM, carrying the first promise of precipitation in more than a month, hung dark and broody over the western half of the county. I followed Deputy Pasquale outside, and we stood for a moment on the back steps of the Public Safety Building. The San Cristobal Mountains were obscured by long fingers of rain that curtained from ragged, torn scud clouds, while thunderheads built enormous billowing ranges whose tops anvilled out into wisps of ice.

A rich, prolonged rumble, like something from the gut of a colossal horse who'd eaten moldy hay, rolled across the prairie.

"The crazies are going to be out," Pasquale said. He hefted his briefcase. "A change in the weather is all the excuse they need." He grinned at me, the sort of expression that you paste on when you don't want others to know how rotten the world makes you feel. In no mood for small talk, the deputy turned and started down the steps.

"Don't worry about the letters," I said as he set off across the parking lot toward the gas pumps where 303, one of the department Broncos, was parked.

"That's going to be hard, sir," Pasquale said over his shoulder.

"Yes, it is," I muttered, and went back inside.

It was going to be a good evening to worry about a whole list of things. The lightning show out on the prairie might torch a grass fire. The resulting smoke could drift across the four lanes of the interstate, sending folks who didn't understand the function of the brake pedal into a colossal domino game of twisted metal. The rain might hang up there, never touching the ground, taunting us. And that was just the weather.

As I walked back into my office, I added to the worry list. Our resident heroic protector of the public trust might crawl out from under his rock and send another cute note to someone—this time, since there hadn't been any public reaction that I'd heard, to a blabbermouth who would get the job done.

And, most important, almost twenty-four hours had passed since a tractor tire served as a blunt instrument to crush Jim Sisson to death. We were no closer to knowing what had happened in that backyard.

I knew that the deputies were scouring MacArthur Avenue for any tidbit and that gradually Undersheriff Robert Torrez would put together a profile of what the neighborhood had looked like on Tuesday night.

My worry was that we probably knew that profile already. I had that nasty gut feeling that no one was going to jump out of the woodwork and say, *"Now let me tell you what I saw. I saw a 1989 yellow Mercury parked in front of the Sisson home, New Mexico license XYZ. I recognized one of the men who got out of it. He walked around behind the Sisson home, sure enough just about nine o'clock. I heard a heated argument, some machinery running, and then I saw him come running out a few minutes later and speed off."*

The longer I sat behind my desk staring at the blotter, the more skeptical I became. After a moment, I pulled a piece of paper out of the top right-hand drawer, picked up a pencil, and doodled a crude map. I was a rotten artist, but the map helped me focus my worries.

To the best of our knowledge, four people had been inside the Sisson home that Tuesday evening—Mom and three teenagers—while Daddy vented his frustration on a deflated front-loader tire out back.

Yes, the family inside the house could all have been absorbed with telephone gossip, video games, or raiding the fridge—whatever passed for evening activity in the Sisson household when Mom and Dad weren't throwing things at each other. They might have been so absorbed that they didn't hear an argument outside. Or they might have been arguing among themselves, that continuous nit-picking that scrubbed the nerve endings raw.

Outside, the gentle pulsing idle of the diesel backhoe could have blanketed any but the most strident sounds. Someone might have come in the driveway unbeknownst to the folks inside the house. Even if they heard the crunch of tires on the driveway gravel, they might not have cared one way or the other who the visitor was. Or the killer might have parked out at the curb, or down the street, or in the Burger Heaven parking lot, or in the back alley and sauntered through the back gate.

The opportunities for someone to slip in, murder Jim Sisson, and then slip out again, all unseen, were legion. The backhoe was the stumbling block. Jim Sisson wouldn't have crouched patiently while the killer fumbled with the machine's control levers. Whoever had killed the plumber would have had to immobilize him first, and a stout whack on the head would have done the trick—not that we'd find evidence of that, since the massive tire and rim had done a complete job of erasing any trace of a previous head wound.

The killer had to be someone who recognized the opportunity for a cover-up when it presented itself, coupled with a basic working knowledge of how to operate a backhoe. If we had a list of suspects, those two key factors would shorten it considerably.

What bothered me was that Jim and Grace Sisson had been at each other's throats all day—enough that neighbors had called in an official referee on three separate occasions to mediate. Why they were arguing no one seemed to know, and the Sissons never went public, even to the deputy.

I found it hard to believe that everyone suddenly, as the dusk of evening fell after a day from hell, returned to knitting or reading or the tube, conveniently unconscious of the comings and goings of their day-long adversary. Any compilation of crime statistics that I had ever bothered to read said that most homicides in the home were the handiwork of people well known to the victim. Family members led the list.

It didn't make sense that after a day of fascinating violence between husband and wife, someone else would slide in and whack Jim Sisson because of an unpaid bill or a copper pipe joint that still leaked.

I tossed the pencil down, crumpled up my doodled creation, and threw it toward the trash can. The shot missed, but I felt better. Knowing what I wanted to do prompted me out of my chair. In the outer office, life had come to a standstill. Ernie Wheeler sat in front of the dispatch console with his hands clasped in his lap, staring at the big chrome-plated microphone in front of him, trying to will it to squawk.

"Where's Linda?" I asked, and Ernie started. "Sorry," I added.

"I guess I was daydreaming," Wheeler said. "Linda went home, I think. She was downstairs for a while, but I think she left. You want me to call her in here?"

I waved a hand. "That's all right. I'll swing by."

Sure enough, Linda's Honda was parked at the curb on Third Street. I pulled 310 in behind it and left it idling when I got out. The front door of the house was open, ready to let in any cool breeze that the storm to the west might care to generate. I stopped in front of the screen door, noticing the long tear in the screen where something had snagged it—probably the handlebars of the Harley when Tom Pasquale wheeled the motorcycle inside.

Voices next door prompted me to turn my head, and I saw a kid about ten years old standing on the neighbor's front step, eyeing me with interest. Someone inside the house said something in rapid-fire Spanish, and the kid lifted a hand to me in greeting before ducking back inside.

"Knock, knock," I called through the screen, and rapped on the frame at the same time, the thin aluminum rattling against the jamb.

"Just a second!" Linda's voice floated out from somewhere inside. In a moment, she appeared, towel in hand, short black hair wild. "I smelled like basement," she said. "Come on in, sir."

"You spend much more time down in that darkroom, you'll turn into a mushroom," I said as I opened the screen door gently. The flimsy thing flexed on its hinges. Linda gave her hair a final drubbing with the towel and then ran her fingers through it to restore order. She was barefoot, wearing jeans and a T-shirt with "Property of the University of New Mexico Athletic Department" across the chest.

The little house was uncomfortably warm. With lousy insulation and cinder block construction, it was one of those places that would be cooled off nicely just about the time the sun rose...and by noon would be sweltering again.

I glanced into the tiny living room, and my first impression was of a welter of magazines on every flat surface. Beside one ratty chair was a pile of books, with one of them spread-eagled open across the arm of the chair.

"It's a mess," Linda said when she saw my glance.

If I had to clean a house, it would be in far worse shape, but I didn't comment. "I stopped by to ask you if you can break away for a bit to make a quick run to Las Cruces."

Linda stopped messing with her hair and looked at me, towel poised. "Cruces? Sure. When?"

"Right now. I want to talk with Grace Sisson, and it'd help if you went along."

She nodded. "Let me change real quick."

"What you're wearing is fine, if you've got a pair of shoes to go with it."

Linda grinned, the smile a little lopsided but fetching nevertheless. "I've got shoes. But I'd rather put on something a little more..." she pulled at her T-shirt, "a little more *something* than this. It'll only take a minute."

She disappeared into the back of the house, and I wandered into the living room. The book on the arm of the chair was Fulton's *A History of Forensic Science,* and being flopped over the furniture wasn't helping the old volume's spine any. I picked it up and saw that whoever was reading it was about to embark on chapter 7, a discussion of Daguerre's photography. A sample of his work, the familiar "mug shot" that was used for the first time as evidence in an 1843 trial, stared off the page. The suspect looked as if he had been forced to hold his breath for about a minute too long.

"Interesting stuff," I said when I heard Linda enter the room behind me.

"Tom's forcing himself to read that," she replied, and I glanced up at her. She had kept the jeans but donned a plain white blouse and a pair of running shoes.

"Forcing himself?" There was a mailer card from a magazine on the table, and I used it as a bookmark, closing the old volume carefully.

"Well," Linda said with a smile, "that's not how he'd describe it, but I get the impression that reading wasn't one of his strong suits in school. He works pretty hard at it."

"A little at a time," I said, and placed the book on the table. "You ready to go?"

She nodded, and we went back out into the blast furnace of the afternoon. The storm hadn't made much progress across the prairie and was still parked twenty miles west of the village. The sun peeked out beside one thunderhead, washing the cloud fringes in light.

Interstate 10 put the sun to our backs as we headed toward Las Cruces, and for the first five minutes or so we rode in comfortable silence—comfortable for me, anyway. As we flashed by a sign that promised DEMING, 12, she asked, "Have you heard anything from Estelle?"

"I keep meaning to call her," I said. "The house is off the market, whatever that means."

That was the prompting Linda needed, and for the next hour or so she chatted about this and that, a sort of bubbling overflow of information, most of which either I didn't hear or didn't require a response beyond an interested grunt.

As we started down the long hill west of Las Cruces, she asked, after spending five minutes talking about her mother's keen desire to run her daughter's life, "Do you think Tom is involved in anything?"

We were in the process of passing an oil tank truck at the moment, and I didn't answer until we'd pushed through the rig's bow wave and drifted back into the right lane.

"What do you mean by that?" I replied, knowing damn well exactly what she meant.

"He told me about the letters you received."

I looked at her sharply. "When was this?"

"The letters, you mean?"

"No.... When did he tell you?"

"This afternoon. In fact, it was just a few minutes before you came over."

"He didn't waste any time," I said, more to myself than to Linda Real.

"He said that he didn't want me finding out from someone else," she said.

I took a deep breath and sighed. "I don't know," I said. "I can't figure it out. The son of a bitch who's writing the notes obviously thinks that he'll accomplish something—damned if I know what.''

"Tom said that you hadn't actually gotten one directly."

"That's right. Two county commissioners and a newspaper publisher passed them along." I glanced over at her again. "I'm trusting you in this, Linda," I said.

"Sir?"

"You need to understand that whoever is writing those damned notes has a reason. It's not just a joke. You're an intelligent young woman, and you can figure out the possibilities just as well as I can. There's the possibility that the note writer was fed what he believes to be reliable information. That means someone else is in on it, too. Or there's the possibility that whoever is sending those notes just wants to make life hard for the department during an election year and picked Tom as an easy target. I'm sure you can add to the list of creative possibilities."

Linda gazed out the passenger side window in silence for a moment, then turned back and regarded me. "What makes you think that Tom *isn't* involved, sir?"

"I don't remember saying that I thought that."

"I guess I'm hoping," she said. "Tom got that impression from what you said to him."

"Well, then he's right. For two reasons. First is intuition, which I freely admit in my case isn't much to go on. But, for instance, my intuition tells me that I can trust you." I shrugged and smiled at Linda. "I've known you for a while, through some trying circumstances. I've watched you work, as the saying goes. The same is true for Thomas Pasquale." I chuckled at a sudden memory, and Linda looked puzzled.

"I'm sure he told you of his most famous stunt, when he flipped his village patrol car in the middle of the Twelfth Street intersection with Bustos. Before an audience, so to speak. What I remember most about that incident is that he never tried to make an excuse. He never tried to make the accident appear to be anything other than what it was—a young hot-rodder going altogether too fast in the wrong place."

I slowed 310 as we started the endless ramp that took us from

Interstate 10 to Interstate 25 northbound. "It's little things like that. They tend to collect over the years."

"You said there were two reasons, sir."

"The second is simpler. If Thomas Pasquale actually was putting the arm on traffic stops for some quick cash and an honest citizen found out about it and had proof, I find it hard to believe that the logical response would be to write little anonymous notes to politicians. The logical thing would be to give me a call. Or the district attorney. Or Judge Hobart. Or even the state police or the attorney general."

"Maybe they've already done that and we just don't know about it. Or maybe they haven't because they're just afraid of repercussions."

"Maybe. But you don't think so, and neither do I."

"I'm glad of that, sir."

We shot north, passing a large water tank with the history of the southwest painted on it, and then dived down Exit 1. "I'm sure you are. And for the time being, I'm going to ask that you keep all this to yourselves. I don't want you discussing those notes, or any possibilities about them, with anyone else." I glanced at her to make sure she was listening. "Not even with anyone in the department." I grinned. "Except the officer in question, of course. Not that it's any of my business, but I wasn't aware until today that you two were living together."

"We're sort of pooling our resources a little bit," Linda said. A light flush crept up the side of her neck.

"Well, as I said, it's none of my business. But you've got my best wishes. And you should know that Tom is going to need some help with all this before it's over."

She nodded. "He was pretty down earlier today."

"And it's going to get worse," I said. "As a born pessimist, I think I can pretty much guarantee that."

At the first stop sign, I pulled a small note out of my pocket that included the directions the Las Cruces PD had given me and handed it to Linda. "Navigate," I said. "I can't read the damn thing."

At ten minutes after six, we pulled into the driveway of 2121 Vista del Campo.

SIXTEEN

I SHUT THE ENGINE off and sat quietly for a moment. A block west, a large moving van was pulled into a driveway across the street, its tractor wedged sideways against the curb, out of traffic. Nearly hidden behind the truck, a Las Cruces Police patrol car was parked facing us.

Vista del Campo curved gracefully away from the main feeder street and the heavy stone wall that ran as far as the eye could see, undulating over what had once been the open valley. The housing project was surrounded by walls, like a vast, spreading fortress.

From the backyard of 2121, Grace Sisson's parents had a marvelous view of the interstate, and if they craned their necks, they could see the spread of development east of the interstate as well.

"You'd sure as hell have to like people to live here," I muttered, and Linda chuckled.

"Some people actually do, sir."

In a decade, Grace's parents, the Stevensons, would feel as if they lived downtown.

"Nice place," Linda said, regarding the house.

"Uh-huh." I guess it was, all bright and cheerful with its red-tile roof, manicured water-guzzling lawn, and tidy approach plantings. I was old-fashioned, preferring the dank insulation of old adobe in deep shade to the constant hum of a swamp cooler.

The sun was still hot as we got out of the car and so bright bouncing off the hood that I winced. A GMC Suburban with Posadas County plates was parked on the apron in front of the three-bay garage, and I walked up along the driver's side with Linda following. All three garage doors were down and snug.

"Two cars and a boat," I said.

"Sir?"

"That's my bet. The boat's in here." I rapped the first door, the one directly in front of the parked Suburban, with my knuckle as I squeezed past. "And they haven't had time to do much boating, either."

Somewhere inside the house a small dog started yapping, and as we walked across toward the tiled entryway I could hear him racing through the house, making his way toward the front door.

Before I touched the bell, the front door was opened by a doughy-looking man in tan Bermuda shorts and a tan knit golf shirt. He was shorter than me, perhaps five-six or so, with thinning gray hair that he combed in a wave upward from his right ear and across his round, balding dome. He grinned a perfectly benign smile of greeting, but nothing cracked from about the bridge of his nose upward. His eyes were watchful, shifting first from me to Linda and then back to me. In one arm he held the pooch, one of those tiny creatures with long fur that covered everything but the twitching black nose.

"Reverend Stevenson?" I said pleasantly. "I'm Sheriff Bill Gastner, from Posadas. I think we've met once or twice over the years. This is Deputy Linda Real."

"Sure, sure," he said, pushing open the screen door. He thrust out a hand to Linda. "Mel Stevenson," he said, and then shook my hand, his grip moist and limp, just a light squeeze of the ends of my fingers like a politician working the crowds. The dog squirmed in his grasp but stayed quiet.

"No one mentioned that you were stopping by, but I'm glad to see you just the same. What can I do for you folks?" he added, making no move to step out of the doorway. Before I could reply, he added, "This has been some sort of nightmare, I can tell you. Such a tragedy."

"We'd like to talk to Grace," I said, and Stevenson frowned as if taking offense that I might leave him out of the loop. "I realize it's inconvenient, but it's a lot easier than asking her to drive all the way over to Posadas."

"Boy," Stevenson said with a shake of his head. "She's been through the wringer, you know what I mean?"

"I'm sure she has," I said, knowing damn well that the good *padre* would rather that I'd said, *"Oh, some other time, then."* I let my hand fall on the handle of the screen door. "We'll make it as easy as possible. But we'd also like to talk with the children."

Stevenson nodded and stood to one side. "I would have thought you were about wrapped up with this," he said.

"Sometimes these things take us a while to sort out," I said, and ushered Linda inside ahead of me. The foyer included a small fountain that babbled water over a cascade of rocks more colorful than any that nature had ever managed, with two small koi swimming lazy circles in the collection pool.

I saw Linda glance at the fountain and the fish, frown ever so slightly, and then turn away, her gaze sweeping across the spacious pastel living room to the blue stone fireplace at the far end. As a visual surprise, one long wall of the room was floor-to-ceiling bookcases, broken only by a recess that included a floor lamp and comfortable leather recliner. Many of the books were old, their dark, musty bindings in sharp, welcome contrast to the rest of the room.

With the exception of the book wall, the living room's furnishings were standard stuff fresh out of *Tract House Decorating Ideas*—coffee table, wingback chairs, entertainment center, two lamps on gold swag chains, magazine stand...but the old recliner by the books said loudly on behalf of its owner, *This is where I sit.... Find your own chair.*

"My daughter has spent all day trying to find some rest," Stevenson said, carefully closing the front door against the heat. "I looked in on her less than an hour ago, thinking that she might be ready for some supper. But she was asleep, finally. You can imagine how loath I am to wake her." He bent down and deposited the dog on the floor. It wagged the end that I assumed was the tail and then scampered out of sight, leaving a single high-pitched bark behind as a warning.

"Perhaps you'd check for us," I said.

Stevenson stood perfectly still, his hands at his sides, regarding me. "If there's some news that Grace needs to know, perhaps you could tell me, and when she wakes—"

"I wish we could do that," I said. "But there's a few things that need to be cleared up. It shouldn't take long. If Grace is sleeping, maybe we can talk to the kids first. That'll give her some more time."

"OK, now, Mom took Melissa and Todd with her to El Paso. They're picking up Marjorie at the airport. She's flying in from San Diego this evening. She's Jim and Gracie's oldest, you know. Marjorie is, that is."

"So both Jennifer and Grace are here now?" I said gently.

Mel Stevenson was about to reply when a voice barked from the back of the house, "Dad, who is it?" I had only met Grace Sisson a time or two, but I recognized her voice immediately.

"It's Sheriff Gastner, honey," Stevenson called back. "From Posadas."

There was a pause and then, not quite so loudly, "Well, tell him to go away."

Stevenson grimaced and ducked his head with embarrassment. "Give me a moment, will you please?" he whispered.

"Sure," I said. "Take your time."

He left the room and I looked at Linda. "'Tell him to go away,'" I said softly, and grinned. "There are a lot of folks who'd like to tell us that and have it work, I'm sure."

"Does she have to talk to us?" Linda asked.

"No," I said. "But it would be nice."

While we waited, I stepped over to the bookcase and let my eyes roam over the volumes. Rev. Melvin Stevenson wasn't a fan of reprints of the classics with fancy fake leather bindings in neat gold-leafed trophy sets. His were the real thing, and I whistled softly. Several appeared to be in German, their leather spines worn soft and smooth by many hands over many years.

"A scholar," I mused. I was a fan of military history, with a library that eased my mind on frequent occasions when the country was quiet and insomnia reared its ugly head. I was no theologian, but the fact that I recognized many of the authors whose work resided on the pastor's shelves didn't surprise me. Religion and politics had often been a volatile mix over the centuries, with some of the nastiest wars a natural result.

"This doesn't look like a household that's used to having teen-agers around for extended periods of time," Linda observed. She had moved to the edge of the foyer tile and stopped, the toes of her shoes touching the posh beige carpet.

Reverend Stevenson reappeared. "She'll be out in a minute," he said, and his tone was neutral. "Come on in and have a seat. Can I get you something? Tea? Coffee? Beer? Ice water?"

"No thanks," I said. "I appreciate the thought, though. Deputy Real might want something."

Linda declined and remained a pace or two in from the door. I selected a straight chair near the television that looked as if it might take my weight without protest, but before I had a chance to settle and before Mel Stevenson faced the task of making conversation with us, Grace Stevenson Sisson appeared. She was rubbing her forehead and squinting, and she looked across the room at me with obvious irritation.

"Yes?" she said. She ignored Linda Real, and the single word served as all the greeting we were going to get.

Taking into account that Grace had had better days, I walked across the living room until I was close enough to smell the alcohol on her breath. She looked up at me and squinted, hand still massaging her forehead.

"Mrs. Sisson, I know that the deputies talked with you some yesterday, but there are some things that I need to go over with you. And I'd like to talk with the children, too."

"Well, so..." she said, and shrugged. She made no move to settle in the living room, content to stand on the cool tile of the foyer.

"You want to come in and sit?" her father asked as he drifted over toward the fireplace, but Grace shook her head.

"No. I don't want to sit." She looked up at me again. "I don't know what you want," she said. "What am I supposed to tell you that we don't already know?"

"How about telling me what happened Tuesday night, as best you can?" I said, trying my best grandfatherly tone.

"I already did that," she said. "What was his name? Mears? I talked to him."

"That's the way these things go, Mrs. Sisson. We need to know if you remember seeing or hearing anything Tuesday night before your husband's death. Or after, for that matter."

"No. I was inside. The television was on. That's what I told Mears."

"No one came over earlier in the evening?"

She finished massaging her forehead with an irritated flourish and walked quickly past me into the living room. She plopped down in her father's chair, and I settled for the nearest wingback, sitting forward on the edge, elbows on my knees.

"No," she said. "You mean someone to see my husband? No, not that I know of."

"Was Jim in the habit of working so late?"

"He worked all the time," she said with considerable bitterness.

"Do you know what he was doing out there Tuesday night?"

"The new front loader had a flat tire."

"How'd that happen?"

Grace sighed hugely and looked up at the ceiling. If she'd spent the day wracked with grief, she certainly had recovered nicely, slipping instead into a fine case of petulance. Talking slowly, she said, "He backed over a stake earlier in the day. Over at Bucky Randall's place. He was mad because it ruined the tire."

"What was he doing for Randall, do you know?"

"Of course I know. They were putting in new leach lines for the motel."

"And he decided to trailer the machine back to the shop, instead of just making repairs there? At Randall's?"

"Yes." She said it as if I were just too dense for words.

"Is that particularly unusual for him to work out back during the evening? Does he do that a lot?"

"Yes, I said. Those goddam machines just about eat us out of house and home. We just got done putting a thirty-four-hundred-dollar transmission in the one, and then he buys the new machine and, just about the first time out, ruins a tire."

"The price of doing business, I suppose." That drew a dismissive sniff from Grace. I stopped and pulled a small notebook out of my pocket. "Mrs. Sisson, on Tuesday, Undersheriff Torrez was called to your place on three separate occasions, all three times by neighbors."

"Well, duh," she said, and rolled her eyes heavenward. "I wish they'd mind their own business."

"I'm sure they meant well," the Reverend Stevenson said.

"Oh, right," Grace retorted. "We should have built the fence about twelve feet tall."

"What were the disputes about?" I asked.

Grace Sisson hesitated, then said, "Why should I answer that?"

I looked at her with curiosity. "Because it makes sense to answer it, Mrs. Sisson. An officer visited your home three times on the same day as your husband's death, responding to a domestic dispute complaint. Knowing what went on would help us establish something about your husband's frame of mind."

"His frame of mind was that he was pissed, Sheriff. He was mad at the damn tractor; he was mad at Bucky Randall for having junk all over his yard; he was mad at me because...well, maybe because the hamburgers were overdone. I don't know. I don't think that's anybody's business but Jim's and mine. We fight a lot, but that's our business. Nobody else's. That's what I told Torrez, or whatever his name is, too. I never asked him to come over."

"Did your neighbors have reason to think that the arguments you and Jim had would turn into something else?"

"What do you mean?"

"Turn physical? Violent?"

"Why would they think that?"

"Because they called the sheriff's office. Three times."

Grace Sisson turned a bit in the chair so that she was looking directly at me. She wasn't a bad-looking woman, just a bit on the heavy side, with frosted hair that she kept cut short, layered over the ears.

"What difference does it make, anyway?" she said finally. "Jim's dead. What they thought or didn't think doesn't make a bit of difference to me. I don't know how he managed to drop that stupid tire on himself, but he did. Now what are we going to do? As if there weren't problems enough already."

She said it as if Jim Sisson's death were just another unexpected monthly bill.

SEVENTEEN

"MRS. SISSON, I can appreciate how difficult this is for you and your family," I said, "but there are a couple of things I need to ask you that Deputy Mears didn't." I flipped a page in the notebook and stared down at the blank lined page.

"The arguments that you had with your husband on Tuesday...did they concern your daughter Jennifer?"

The question fell on silence and stayed there for about the count of ten, and then Grace snapped, "My God, where the hell do you get off?"

"Now, Gracie," her father said. He'd been leaning against the fireplace, one elbow on the mantle, both hands clasped as if he were deep in prayer. Maybe he was.

"No, really," Grace Sisson said, getting to her feet. "Now listen, just in case you're stupid, Mr. Gastner—"

"I'm not."

"Whatever. I already told you that what my husband and I argued about is no one's business but our own. Period. End of story."

She stepped onto the foyer tile with a sideways glance at Linda. I don't know what kind of expression Grace expected Linda Real to wear in response to the woman's performance, but Linda looked studiously unimpressed. Who knew—maybe Linda thought I was stupid, too.

Grace would have left the room without another word, I'm sure, but her daughter appeared around the corner, hesitating when she saw the look on her mother's face. Jennifer Sisson was a cute kid, fifteen years old going on twenty-eight or so. She was barefoot, wearing a white halter top that advertised the considerable extent of her charms and a pair of white shorts that must have chafed like hell in hot weather. Her tanned midriff sported a little roll of fat, and her face was round and full.

"And none of this concerns you," Grace snapped at her daughter. She took the girl's elbow and started to turn her around but stopped and looked back at me. "I assume that we're finished?"

"You assume wrong," I said.

Grace Sisson didn't exactly fit the mold of a widow trying to comfort her children from recent heartache, and I wondered what argument had led the pastor's wife to flee the house with the other two youngsters.

"We're all under a great deal of strain," Stevenson said, and he pushed himself away from the fireplace. "Gracie, I really think you should just sit down here for a minute and hear the sheriff out. It won't hurt to answer a question or two."

"I've answered everything I need to answer," Grace said. "A stupid accident killed my husband." She glared at me. "And if you can figure out how to wave a magic wand to pay the mortgage, the car payments, the dental bills, machinery loans, and the God knows what all else, then maybe we've got something to talk about. Otherwise, I'm tired."

"Now that's interesting," I said, and grinned a little. I took another step toward Grace and her daughter, thrust my hands in my pockets, and looked at them both over the tops of my glasses.

Grace managed about a three-second scrutiny before she snapped, "What's interesting?"

I took my time, watching Grace closely, assessing. The woman favored blunt, so that was the way I decided to play it. "Mrs. Sisson, we're investigating your husband's death as a homicide."

The sound of that last word had the desired effect—as if the woman had been struck between the eyes with a ball-peen hammer. Her eyes widened with the initial shock, then narrowed with disbelief. "Now where...now where did this fairy tale come from?" she asked.

"It's pretty simple, really," I said gently. "Someone came onto your property Tuesday night while Jim was working out back. The report from the medical examiner isn't finished yet, but we have every reason to believe that your husband was crushed under that tire intentionally. Someone was there. And someone probably knows who."

Mel Stevenson strode swiftly across the room and reached out to take his daughter by each arm. He leaned forward and looked hard into her eyes. "Grace," he managed, and then choked. He cleared his throat. "Sheriff, are you certain of all this?"

"Reasonably so, yes."

"My God."

"Mrs. Sisson, you can see why we need to know some basic information. Any detail, regardless of how trivial it may seem to you, might help us find your husband's killer."

It was a standard spiel, and I said it in place of what I really wanted to say—something simple like, *"Mrs. Sisson, do you know how to operate a backhoe?"* But there would be time for that later.

"You honestly think that someone came into our yard and killed my husband?" she asked. "While the three children and I were in the house?"

"Yes."

"That's impossible."

"Why is it impossible?" I asked. "You said yourself that you weren't aware of what was going on outside."

"I said I didn't hear anything. That's different."

I shrugged and glanced at my watch. "Mrs. Sisson, we're pressed for time. Given the nature of the case, my best advice to you would be to stay available." I smiled helpfully. "The district attorney will probably want to talk to you about what you remember...or don't."

Grace Sisson shook off her father's hands. "I need to talk with my own lawyer," she said. "I'm going home."

She turned and marched out of the room, daughter in tow.

"Grace, I think it's time. We're not gaining anything this way," her father called after her.

The woman turned at the sound of her father's voice, and I was taken aback at the venom. "Now that's enough," she said, and her voice had sunk to a whisper. "I'm going home."

Mel Stevenson turned away from the hall, and his eyes were pleading. "I guess it would be easier if I just said this was none of my business," he said. "But it is my business. Grace is my daughter, and I don't want to see her hurt. Or the children, either."

The man was obviously working up to something, and I said, "Sir, the more we know, the easier it will be for everyone."

Stevenson sighed and held his hand to his forehead. "This is easy when it's someone else."

"Sure."

With a final rub of his head, he stepped up close and reached out a hand, letting it rest on my right shoulder. "You have children, don't you?"

"Yes."

"Any teens?"

I smiled. "Grandchildren. My oldest daughter is forty-seven next month."

"Then you understand just a little of all this." He dropped his hand. "My granddaughter is pregnant, Sheriff." He held up a hand when he saw the puzzled look on my face. "I know, I know. In this day and age, it happens all the time. But that doesn't make it any less crushing. It's always easy to tsk-tsk when it's someone else's youngster—because obviously *they* didn't do an adequate job as parents." He smiled thinly. "So there you are. That's what Jim and Grace were arguing about. I'm sure it was quite a war. I'm glad I didn't have to hear it."

He walked off into the middle of the living room and stopped, facing the fireplace. "I really liked Jim Sisson," he said softly. "He was always such a gentleman around the wife and me."

I glanced at Linda and nodded at the door. She reached out for the door handle, and the sound of the latch brought Stevenson back to the present. "Do me a favor," I said. "Do what you can to keep Grace here. She's talking about going back to Posadas, and she's in no mental condition to be doing that. If she takes off anyway, give me a call right away." I pulled a business card out of my shirt pocket and extended it to him. "That way, we can have an officer keep her in sight. Keep her out of trouble, maybe."

He nodded and took the card. "What a mess," he muttered.

"And it wouldn't hurt if she did give her family lawyer a call, Reverend. She's going to be needing legal advice about a whole slew of things anyway."

Stevenson frowned and looked sideways at me. "Do you believe she's involved in some way, Sheriff?"

"I don't know," I replied, and it was obvious that wasn't the answer Stevenson wanted to hear.

He followed me out the door. The evening was still hot, even with the sun ducking behind the houses across the street.

I stopped at the edge of the lawn, looking at the Sisson's Suburban. "Did you drive up to Posadas to pick up Grace and the kids, or did she drive them down?"

Stevenson shook his head. "One of the neighbors brought them down. I believe one of them drove the Suburban and the other followed in their own car. I appreciated what they did, but I don't even remember who it was now. Things were so..." He twisted his hand in a whirlwind motion.

"For sure," I said. "Reverend, thanks a lot. You call me, now, if she does something foolish."

He nodded wearily and went back inside.

"Wow," Linda Real said as we settled into 310. I lowered the window while the air conditioning spooled into action. "Wow," she said again.

"Such fun, eh?" I said.

"She is a real first-class, certified A-number-one witch." Linda looked over at me in amazement.

"And a great job you did at keeping a straight face," I added, and pulled 310 into gear.

"Do you think she's going to drive back?"

"Yes. For one thing, it's going to take her about fifty years to forgive her father for spilling the beans."

I drove round the block, took the next two intersections to the left, and pulled up beside the marked Las Cruces police cruiser parked at 2190 Vista del Campo. An officer who made Thomas Pasquale look like a middle-aged veteran peered across at me.

"Officer, I'm Sheriff Gastner from Posadas."

"Yes, sir," he said eagerly. "I called in when you arrived, and the sergeant said that you and the detective were here."

I nodded and gestured at the Suburban down the block. "We've got a distraught woman, Officer. She says that she's going to drive back to Posadas tonight, and she's about the last person who should be on the highway. The whole mess is a real time bomb. Maybe they'll sort it all out, I don't know. Just keep a close watch. If she takes off, I'd appreciate knowing it. And I'd appreciate it if you'd give her a close escort and then hand her over to the state police. Make sure that she can see you. Maybe that will help her pay attention.''

"Yes, sir.''

I nodded. "Good man. And, Officer…kid gloves, all right? That's a pretty bruised family.''

"Yes, sir.''

I gave him an informal salute and we drove up the street. We passed 2121, and I was glad that I wasn't spending my evening in that place.

"It'll be interesting to know who drove her down here,'' Linda Real murmured as we drove by the house, and I looked at her in surprise. "She was certainly ready to tell all the neighbors to go to hell. But obviously there's someone looking out for her.''

I grinned. "The officer was right about you,'' I said.

"Sir?'' Linda said, but I decided to let her wonder about it.

EIGHTEEN

WHILE LINDA AND I drove back toward Posadas, Grace Sisson's Suburban didn't move from her father's driveway in Las Cruces. I could imagine the storm clouds that hung inside that house—and I was sure that matters wouldn't improve when Marjorie, the eldest daughter, arrived home. The raw wounds would be scratched again, with another dose of advice and another round of slammed doors and things said that would be regretted later.

For now, Grace Sisson's problems with her wayward daughter weren't my concern—except that it didn't take a Ph.D. in family counseling to imagine what spark had touched off the day-long war at the Sisson household. I guessed that Jim Sisson had been the last to find out about Jennifer, and when he had, he'd blown his top.

"No wonder Jim wasn't paying attention where he drove that front loader," I said to Linda. "If he was fuming all day long about Jennifer, it's anybody's guess what kind of plumbing job Bucky Randall was getting."

Linda was driving—for one thing, she talked a little less when she was behind the wheel. But more important, even with just one eye, her night vision was a thousand percent better than mine, especially when the headlights bounced off the intermittent sheen of water left on the asphalt by the storm.

"Maybe Jennifer's boyfriend," Linda mused.

"Maybe her boyfriend what?"

"Maybe he came over to talk with Jim Sisson and the two of them argued."

"I find that hard to imagine," I said. "First of all, the usual behavior of the young male is to either deny responsibility or run and hide. No kid is going to seek out an enraged dad late at night to try and smooth things over."

"Assuming it was a kid," Linda said.

"Assuming that, yes. And assuming that Jim's death was linked to his daughter's entanglements in the first place. I can imagine him wanting to thrash the kid involved with his daughter, and maybe he did take a swing. And maybe the kid swung back. Who the hell knows? But the events that followed don't fit that picture." I sighed.

"What a goddam mess. What keeps me thinking that Jim Sisson's death is somehow linked to his daughter's love life is Grace Sisson's attitude. If she's heartbroken about losing her husband, the heartbreak hasn't bubbled to the surface yet. She's clearly in a rage about her pregnant daughter. That's all she's thinking about."

Linda shrugged. "But isn't that sort of thing always supposed to happen to someone else's kid, not your own? I can imagine that when Jennifer popped the news, it stopped the Sissons' world from turning for a while." She glanced over at me. "I'm surprised that the girl even said anything, knowing what her mom's reaction was bound to be."

I frowned. "I hadn't thought of that. But maybe she didn't see much of an alternative."

"And maybe it was the boy's father who tangled with Jim," Linda said.

"Maybe, maybe." I sighed. "What I'd give for a single clear fingerprint right now."

We started down the interstate exit ramp toward the village of Posadas, the headlights picking up large puddles standing on the uneven pavement of Grande Avenue.

I leaned forward, turned on the police radio, and was greeted by silence. "Either it's a quiet evening or lightning blew out the transmitter again," I said. "Go ahead and swing by your house. I'll take the car back. I'll be at the office for a while if you think of something I missed in our conversation with Mrs. Congeniality."

The car was rolling to a halt in the middle of a fair-sized lake on 3rd Street when the cell phone chirped.

"Gastner."

"Sir," Ernie Wheeler said, "Las Cruces PD called. Mrs. Sisson and one child left the Vista del Campo address and are headed westbound on the interstate. State police are keeping an eye on her for us.''

''All right. Make sure a deputy is clear to take the handoff. And, Ernie...as long as Grace Sisson behaves herself, there's to be no intercept. Just keep an eye on her. Make sure the deputy understands that. When she's home safe, we'll figure out what we want to do.''

''Yes, sir. And you have two other calls. Estelle Reyes-Guzman would like you to get back to her this evening. She said it didn't matter how late.''

I grinned when I heard that. I had four children, all long grown and gone. I cheerfully counted Estelle as a fifth, and her two little monsters were closer to grandchildren than the godchildren that they actually were. ''Who else?''

''Leona Spears spent an hour or two in the office earlier this evening, then left. She said that when you got back, she wanted to talk to you. She left a number.''

''I'll be in the office in a few minutes.''

''Yes, sir.''

I clicked off the phone and tossed it on the seat. Linda was already out of the car, stepping carefully to avoid being sucked into the morass of the front yard. I got out, navigating around the lake that Linda had chosen as a parking spot. The air smelled good, heavy with a thousand desert fragrances turned loose by the pummeling rain.

''Linda,'' I called, ''thanks for riding along. We'll see you after a bit.''

I had slid halfway into the car when I saw her standing on the small front step, keys in hand, frowning.

''What's the matter?''

She turned to look at me. ''The key doesn't work.''

''Try the right one.''

''I did.'' She bent down, peering at the lock. If she'd left the porch light on, that would have helped. The nearest streetlight was fifty yards away, providing not much more than shadows.

I picked up my flashlight and walked across the yard, grimacing at the squelching sound of mud under my feet. ''Have some light,''

I said. She held up the small collection of keys—no more than half a dozen at most.

"This is the house key," she said, and held it up. She turned and tried to thrust it in the front door slot. "No dice. It doesn't even go in."

"Let me see," I said. The key included a large stamped *M* design on the flat just under the ring hole. I bent down and peered at the front door lock. "Bates," I said.

"That's not the one that was there before," Linda said.

I straightened up. "Someone changed the lock?" I turned and looked at Linda Real. "Was Tom going to do that?"

"If he was, he didn't say anything to me," she said. "And even if he was, he wouldn't bother do to it right in the middle of his work shift." She took the keys from my hand and held up the Martin key. "This one worked when you and I left."

I chuckled weakly. "Ah."

"What, sir?"

"I would guess that Carla Champlin has the answer."

"She can't do that, can she?" Linda rattled the doorknob. "She can't just change the locks, can she?"

"Apparently she did just that," I said. "Did you try the back door?"

"This place doesn't have a back door."

"Or a window?"

With a disgusted mutter, Linda made her way around the house. I followed with the flashlight. Sure enough, one of the west windows was open, the curtain hanging sodden and limp.

"Looks like a little rain got in," I observed, and that prompted another mutter from Linda.

"I forgot to close it when we left," she said. She pushed the flimsy aluminum window fully open and, with a youthful agility that I could only dream about, clambered inside. The physical therapists had evidently done a fine job on her injured shoulder. In a moment, light flooded the room.

"Yuck," I heard her say.

"What's the matter?"

"It really did rain," she said. "What a mess."

I refrained from sticking my head through the window to marvel at Linda's problem. Instead, I rapped the flashlight lightly on the windowsill. "I'll be at the office if you need anything." I didn't offer to call Carla Champlin for her—that was an experience the kids needed to enjoy themselves.

NINETEEN

WHEN I ARRIVED at the Public Safety Building, the good news was that the fancy new roof installed the previous fall hadn't leaked too badly. One of the prisoner trustees—at that moment the only resident in the county lockup—was mopping along the baseboard just beyond the main entrance.

Water had first soaked an area of the ceiling's acoustical tile, then run down the wall, tracing stained fingers behind several of the framed portraits of former sheriffs of Posadas County, and then puddled on the floor.

Lance Smith paused in midmop and gazed at me with amusement. "Real good roofing job," he said.

I stopped and regarded the mess. "Is that tile going to fall on someone's head?"

Lance looked up and shrugged, then gently nudged one of the sodden ceiling tiles with the tip of the mop handle. The tile didn't move, but the handle pressed a dent into the tile like a finger pushed into the crown of an undone cake. "If it does, that's what the county attorney is for."

I laughed. "You're a practical soul, Lance. But thanks for your help. I'll call someone from Maintenance over here in the morning."

"Hey, what the hell, it's probably not going to rain again today," he said. "I got nothing better to do, anyway." Even so, he was in no hurry to restart the mop. I left him regarding the water stain patterns on the wall. In Dispatch, Ernie Wheeler was on the telephone, and he held up a forefinger as I approached.

"He just walked in, Mrs. Spears. Hang on." Ernie turned and held out the receiver. "Leona Spears, sir."

I sighed and trudged to my office. It felt good to sink into the old leather chair. I glanced at my watch and realized with a start just how many hours this day had racked up. The light on the phone continued to blink, and I picked up the receiver. "Gastner."

"Sheriff, this is Leona. I've been trying to track you down all evening. I know it's late, but do you have a few minutes?"

"Sure."

"You sound tired," she said, leaving an opening for me to tell her, without being asked, how I'd spent my time. I declined the offer.

"I am." I tried not to sound too abrupt.

"It's been a busy couple of days." Again the pause, that silent fishing line cast out in the hopes of a nibble.

"Yes, it has," I said.

"Sheriff, the reason I called..." She paused and I could hear the sound of paper rustling near the receiver and then a sort of *poit* sound—the noise a bar of soap might make when knocked into the water. "The reason I called is about this puzzling note I received. It was stuck behind my screen door when I got home...the darnedest thing. I think you'd be interested."

"I'm sure I would," I said, realizing that I should have said something like, *"A note? What kind of note?"* But I could guess what she was talking about and greeted the news with considerable relief. If the note Leona Spears had been favored with was the same as the others, Thomas Pasquale was off the hook. Leona was the most vocal candidate running for sheriff, a staunch Democrat. Someone was playing politics.

"I'm in my office right now," I said. "Why don't you come on down and we'll talk about it?"

"Let me read it to you."

"Leona," I interrupted, "I don't want to talk about this on the phone. I really don't. Come on down and I'll buy you a cup of coffee."

"Well, now...maybe it could wait until morning."

"If something's on your mind, let's get it cleared up," I said pleasantly, and then I heard the unmistakable sound of water sloshing as a body changed position. The woman was lying in the goddamn bathtub, talking to me. "I'll throw in a doughnut with the coffee. Or I can run over there, if you like. It's about a minute away."

"Not...just...now," she said, and I could hear the smile. "Tell you what. Give me half an hour. I'll be down."

"And I'll be here," I said, and hung up. "Christ," I muttered. Leona Spears was an engineer in the state highway department's district office, and how she'd managed to wrangle the Democratic Party's endorsement for the third time to run in the sheriff's race I didn't know.

Before that she'd unsuccessfully chased a county commissioner's spot a couple of times and before that had lost a narrow race for a seat on the village council. Mixed in with all those disappointing election nights was an attempt or two at the school board. I wasn't sure what the voters didn't like about her, but evidently there was something. We had damn good highways, though.

And whoever was writing the notes about Thomas Pasquale considered her a candidate serious enough to be included in the little game. One thing I did know about Leona Spears—and maybe the author of the notes did, too—she was a regular contributor to the *"Letters to the Editor"* column in the *Posadas Register,* eager to vent her opinions on everything from child care to foreign policy.

I glanced at my watch again, hesitated, and dialed long-distance. It was almost 11:00 p.m. in Minnesota, but both Estelle and her physician husband were night owls. The phone rang five times with no response from either human or answering machine, and I was beginning to imagine the young couple sitting out in the backyard of their neat two-story house in Westridge, watching the display of northern lights while their two kids snoozed in the upstairs garret, their bedroom curtains hanging limp in the humid air.

What Estelle and Francis probably didn't need just then was an interruption from New Mexico or anywhere else, and on the seventh ring I had started to put the receiver back in the cradle when I heard the familiar voice, clipped and efficient as always.

"Hello."

"Francis, this is Bill Gastner."

"Hey, hey, *padrino*," Francis Guzman said, and then I could hear a hand muffle the receiver as he turned and shouted, "Estelle...it's Bill!" The hand was removed, and he added, "It's good to hear your voice, you know that?"

"Thanks. I hope I didn't haul you out of bed, but I was returning Estelle's call. How are you folks doing?"

"Well... OK, all things considered. It's been hot and muggy. I'm not sure we're used to the muggy part yet. I keep checking to make sure I don't have mold growing in my armpits."

"Green chili is the cure for everything, Doctor. That's a scientific fact."

"Yep, I suppose. And by the way, that last CARE package you sent was appreciated." I heard the mumble of another voice, and Francis said, "You been all right?"

"Well, as you say...all things considered, which I'd rather not do at this point."

"No sleep, too much food from the Don Juan, and lots of stress. Is that about right?"

I laughed. "Close enough, Doctor. It seems to be the magic combination for me."

"We should fly you up here so folks at the clinic can study you," Francis said. "Find out how you do it."

"I'll pass, thanks."

There was more mumbling in the background that brought a chuckle from Francis. "Here's Estelle. She keeps trying to pull the receiver out of my hand. Take care of yourself, Bill."

"You, too." I leaned back in the chair, making myself comfortable.

"Sir." Estelle's voice was soft and alto. "I hope things are going better for you than what Ernie Wheeler described."

"They're not. In fact, probably a good deal worse. But what else is new, sweetheart? How are you doing? How's your mother?"

Estelle laughed, and I found that was the easiest expression of hers to bring to mind—the way her face lit up around those enormous dark eyes. "*Remarkable* might be the best word," she said. "She's not using the walker anymore. And the humidity doesn't seem to bother her as much as the rest of us. Who knows why?"

"Maybe she got so desiccated living those eighty years in the Mexican desert that she can soak up more humidity than the ordinary person," I said.

"Now that's an interesting theory."

"My only one. But let me get right to the 'it's none of my business' part. I noticed the sign was down over on Twelfth Street. Maggie Payson tells me that you guys took it off the market."

"Yes." The one word carried more than just a simple nod of the head, and I got the sense that Estelle was weighing carefully just what she wanted to say. "We did that last week, sir."

"You're keeping an old man in suspense, Estelle."

"How so?"

"Well, my razor-sharp detective's mind leaps to a logical conclusion. If a family doesn't want to sell their house, maybe it means that they want to live in it. Again. Sometime."

Estelle sounded amused. "Or that they have a poor relative who wants to use it. Or they want to use it for rental property."

"You don't have any relatives in this neck of the woods, poor or rich. And owning a single-family rental from two thousand miles away doesn't make any sense, either, unless someone else is going to manage it for you. What's up?"

"Nothing yet, sir. Really. We're just not sure right now. It's going to take some time. Maybe in a month or two, we'll know more."

I frowned, not liking the sound of that. "Cheer up," I said. "In four months, the snow will be stacked up so deep around your front door that you'll long for some Posadas dust. That'll make up your mind for you."

"It's not really that, sir."

"Then what is it?" I said with a trace of impatience. "You sound like something's wrong."

There was a short silence, and I could hear Estelle take a deep breath—more of a sigh of resignation. "I guess in part it depends on how Francis's hand heals up, but in the past few days we've been thinking that isn't it, either, really."

"His hand?"

"I guess I didn't tell you, sir."

"No, I guess you didn't."

"Francis has been riding his bike to work. He enjoys that. Some klutz driving a van cut him a little close and smacked him in the shoulder with the wing mirror."

"Ouch."

"He lost his balance and crashed into a parked car. His left hand got cut up pretty badly. There was some tendon damage."

"For God's sakes. Permanent, you mean?"

"We don't know for sure yet. The clinic has been wonderful, as you can imagine." She made a little sound that was half laugh, half hum of reminiscence. "But what got us talking was something *Mama* said one evening, not too many days after the accident. We were talking about just the sheer number of people in a place like this. We're six miles from where Francis works and our house here would probably be considered rural by most eastern standards, but there are always people. People, people, people. At any intersection it seems like there's always a car or two, you know what I mean? And of course, downtown Rochester is a different universe altogether."

"Like Posadas on a busy Friday night," I said.

Estelle laughed. "Oh, sure."

"What did your mother say?" I pictured the tiny, ancient woman, dark eyes darting this way and that, not missing a thing.

"It was more just a passing remark when one of us said something about the opportunities for Francis here. I think the way she put it was, *'Es posible quemarse en su propia salsa dondequiera.'*"

"That's helpful," I said.

"It translates roughly as something like, 'You can stew in your own juice just about anywhere.'"

"And that means what? Did she elaborate?"

"Of course not," Estelle laughed. "We just got *the look,* as the kids call it. You know, one eyebrow up a little bit, just a hint of disapproval. Anyway, we got to talking, and decided not to limit our options. To make a long story short, we took the Twelfth Street house off the market. And it felt like the right thing to do."

"That's good news," I said.

"Well, I talked with *Mama* a lot after that. She's pretty sharp. She's enjoying the experience up here, but she's afraid Francis is going to take his talents where the rich folks live." Estelle did a fair imitation of her mother's dry, cracked voice. "'*And then you'll be just like them, hija.*'" She laughed. "That's her greatest fear, I guess."

"She's accepted the fact that she can't take care of herself anymore? That she's not going back to Tres Marias?"

"Oh sure. She's a remarkable woman, sir. She's very at ease with herself."

"About the house here," I said. "I can think of a couple renters, but I'm not sure I'd want to inflict them on your property, as nice as it is."

"Who's that?"

"Tom Pasquale and Linda Real. They're having landlord trouble."

"They? They're living together now?"

"Ah...I'm glad to hear that someone else is out of the loop besides me," I said. "I didn't know until yesterday."

I told her about Carla Champlin's tiff, and Estelle said, "Let's hold off on anything like that for a bit. Give us some time to decide what we want to do. In another couple of months we'll know if Francis is going to recover some of the fine motor skills in his hand. If not, then he's going to have to rethink a little."

"That's too bad," I said. "I hope everything works out for him."

"We'll just have to see."

"And you? What are you doing?"

"Well," she said, "I don't know just yet. I have to admit, I've enjoyed just being a mom the past couple of months. There's a lot to do around here. The kids love it."

"I bet they do."

"I think I'll just putter along until Francis makes up his mind. And speaking of people making up their minds, how's the campaigning coming along? That's what I wanted to ask you."

"Bob is his usual taciturn self," I said. "He's making the Republicans and Democrats nervous." I told Estelle about the Pasquale letters that I'd been handed and added, "Leona Spears is due here any minute. She's the latest on the hit list."

"Leona again, eh?" Estelle said. "That just about guarantees that the letters are a political stunt, then, sir. Somebody figures she'll take the idea and run with it."

"That's what I thought. Tom's not taking it all too well, though."

"I would think not. The Sisson thing is interesting, by the way. Ernie brought me up to speed on that."

"You have any suggestions or intuitions?" I asked.

"From fifteen hundred miles away? I don't think so, sir. If it's not money, it's passion—that's what the statistics say. Who's Grace or Jim having an affair with these days?"

"I didn't know that either of them was."

"Well, sir, you know that the daughter was busy. That's a start. Now it's just a matter of figuring out what would make someone angry enough at Jim Sisson that they'd want to kill him."

"You see? The folks around here need Francis Guzman's medical expertise, and we need you. I'd love to see Sam Carter's face when I told him that Estelle Reyes-Guzman was coming back as Bob Torrez's undersheriff. He'd have a stroke."

Estelle laughed. "Hang in there, sir. And when you see Leona Spears, give her my regards. That should be safe enough, from half a continent away."

"I'll do that," I said. "Although she'll probably find something in our conversation that will serve as fuel for a scathing letter to the editor. About the community driving away its best and brightest. Something like that."

We talked for a few more minutes about inconsequential things, and when I realized I was just jabbering away to keep from hanging up the phone, I said, "Give the *keeeds* a kick for me, will you?"

"They talk about you a lot, sir. Maybe you'd think about a Christmas visit."

"Me visiting there or you visiting here?" I chuckled.

"We'll talk about it," Estelle said.

"Do that. And take care of yourself."

I put the receiver back in the cradle. Christmas was almost six months away. That seemed like a couple of lifetimes.

TWENTY

LIKE MOST OF US, I suppose, Leona Spears had a variety of guises—but I wasn't prepared for the one that walked into the Public Safety Building at 10:33 that Wednesday night.

I had just gotten a cup of fresh coffee and was headed back to my office when she appeared through the front door, sweeping down the short hallway toward Dispatch. Had the puddles still been standing on the tile, the hem of her garden dress would have soaked them up.

Pausing with cup in hand, I smiled at her as if she really were welcome. "Coffee?" I said.

"No thank you. Not at this hour," she replied as she rolled her eyes and frowned, making it clear that she thought I shouldn't be drinking the brew late at night, either. She was probably right, but what the hell.

"Nice outfit," I said. The dress was bright yellow with large orange sunflowers, low at the neck, and long enough to hide whatever it was that she had on her feet. She darted a squint my way, as if unsure of my remark's intent.

"You don't like it?"

"I like it just fine," I said, gesturing toward the door of my office. "Around here, we get so used to the dull utilitarian look that a burst of color is a nice change. Come on in."

Leona was a heavy woman about my height. She was no stranger to dull utilitarian, either. I'd seen her often enough on various highway department job sites, clipboard in hand, hard hat firmly in place. I guess I had expected the same khaki or blue jeans that she had worn on the job.

Her long blond hair, streaked by too much time out in the sun, was braided Heidi-fashion into a generous single braid on each side of her head. The two braids were drawn back and then arranged in a bun at the back. As she flowed past me into my office with a cloud of fragrance from her bubble bath following, I wondered how long the hairdo took her to construct.

"So," I said, walking around behind my desk. "How's politics?" I indicated one of the chairs. "Make yourself comfortable." She was carrying a slim leather attaché case, and she swung it into her lap as she settled.

"Politics is as usual, Sheriff," she said. "As usual." She lifted the leather case and set it on edge, as if she were about to open it. She paused. "So bring me up to speed on this Sisson mess," she said.

I took my time sitting down, moving as if something might break if I landed too hard. "Bring you up to speed?"

"Yes. What's with the investigation?"

I grinned, probably the wrong thing to do with Leona, since she would think I was grinning at *her*—which was correct in this case. "Leona, we generally don't make the details of an ongoing homicide investigation public."

"I'm not the public. I'm a candidate for sheriff. As such, I should be brought up to speed on current issues or concerns affecting the department." She fired that out without a pause. Maybe she'd memorized it for just this occasion. I had a mental image of her lying in the tub, a great mound under the soap foam, practicing that very line until she had it just right. I was pleased I'd given her the opportunity.

"Well, I tell you what, Leona. As we get closer to the election, if I think there's a need I'll have both you and Mike Rhodes in for a familiarization session. Right now, the Sisson case is not open for discussion."

Leona's eyes narrowed again, this time at the sound of her Republican opponent's name. She regarded me for a few seconds, no doubt assessing where my weaknesses lay. I'm sure that I had a sufficient number of those that the search wouldn't take long.

"Robert Torrez is conducting the investigation?"

I nodded but said nothing.

"So one candidate has full information and the other two are left out in the cold."

"Leona, don't be ridiculous." It was the wrong thing to say, of course, but I just added it to my string. Leona bristled. For the first time, it began to dawn on me just how stupid this woman really was. I leaned forward and put on my most serious gunnery sergeant's face. "Bob Torrez is undersheriff of Posadas County, Leona. That happens to be his job at the moment—what the taxpayers pay him for. He isn't actively campaigning, and it wouldn't make any difference if he were. The investigation is a team effort, and he's one of the leaders of that team. In fact, he is *the* leader."

I sat back. "If and when you win the election on November seventh, Leona, I'll be happy to open our files to you on November eighth. One hundred percent. If you so choose, you'll walk into this office in January knowing every dark nook and corner, all the dark and dirty little secrets. But until then, the way we run an investigation isn't for public consumption."

She pressed on doggedly. "So how close are you?"

"To what?"

With a grimace of impatience, she snapped, "To finding out who killed Jim Sisson."

"I think the appropriate phrase that we give to the newspapers is that 'investigation is continuing.'" I smiled helpfully.

"Isn't it true that you're basing your guess that Jim Sisson's death was a homicide on some photographs taken by Linda Real?"

"No, that's not true, Leona. Where did you hear that zinger?"

"I have my sources, too." Smug wasn't one of her more attractive expressions, since it scrunched up her plump cheeks and made her otherwise attractive blue eyes small and piggy.

"Well, trade 'em in for new ones."

"You're saying Linda Real didn't take pictures?"

I sighed, trying to hold my temper. "I don't think you heard me say that," I said. "You asked me if we had based our decisions on Deputy Real's photographs. I said we hadn't. Deputy Real recorded evidence photographically. Any decisions we make are based, hopefully, on evidence."

"Well, it's the same thing," Leona replied.

"No, it's not," I said gently, but it wasn't a discussion I wished to pursue. "So...what did you bring to show me? A nice letter from a citizen concerned with the welfare of visiting travelers from south of the border?'' I nodded at her attaché case.

I might as well have struck her between the eyes with a hammer. She paused with her thumb on the closure of the leather case, not wanting to take her eyes off me.

"Well?" I asked.

"Yes, as a matter of fact. That's exactly what I brought. You've already heard about it?"

"Let's see what you've got," I said, and she reluctantly opened the case and withdrew the now-familiar piece of folded white typing paper. Without a word, she handed it across to me. With the exception of the *Dear Miss Spears* at the top, it was identical to those received by Sam Carter and Dr. Arnold Gray.

I let the letter fall on the desk blotter, and I sat with one forearm resting on each side of it, regarding the damn thing.

"Blah, blah, blah," I said as I finished reading it. "Yes, I've seen this before." I looked up at Leona Spears. "How was it delivered?"

"Stuck in the screen door of my house."

"Huh. When you got home from work? What, about five, five-thirty?"

"About then."

"May I have this?"

"No," she said instantly. "It was written to me."

Trying my best to keep the exasperation out of my voice, I said, "I'm sure you can appreciate that this could be evidentiary material." I don't know why I didn't simply take the note as evidence, regardless of what this woman thought or wanted, but I suppose I was still trying, however ineffectually, to remain civil.

"Yes, I know that. That's why I don't want it to go missing."

"Missing? Now that's interesting. Why would it go missing?"

"Really, Sheriff," she said, favoring me with one of those skeptical sideways looks that's supposed to say it all.

"Really what? I'm going to steal this? And do what with it?" I took a deep breath. "Do you mind if I make a copy of it?"

She nodded. "You can go ahead and do that."

"Excuse me for a minute, then," I said.

Ernie Wheeler cheerfully took the letter and went to sweet-talk the aging copier.

I returned to my office and Leona Spears. "It'll be just a minute. Deputy Wheeler has to wait for the stupid copier to warm up. About three minutes." I sat down again. "So..."

"So? What is the department doing about this? I assume that this Pasquale person—I don't think I've ever met him—I assume he's been placed on administrative leave?"

"No."

"Why ever not?"

Choosing my words carefully, I said, "There is no reason to place Deputy Pasquale on administrative leave, Ms. Spears. The only intimations of any wrongdoing come in these anonymous letters." I hesitated, glaring at Leona Spears without blinking. "That's not reason enough to ruin a young man's reputation, or his career."

"But you're going to look into it?"

"Of course."

"Why would anyone do this sort of thing if it weren't true?"

"Oh, please, ma'am. I don't mean to be evasive, Ms. Spears, but why would someone write those letters if the allegations *were* true? You express considerable interest in law enforcement procedures. If you had concrete evidence of wrongdoing on the part of an officer, would it make sense to write these cute little letters to various politicians?" I could see Leona rolling that one around in her thick skull, and I felt a surge of optimism. "Remember that it's an election year," I added.

Ernie Wheeler rapped on the door, then stepped in and handed me the papers. I started to hand the original back to Leona, but she waved it off.

"Oh, keep it," she said.

"Thanks. I look at it this way: Somebody knows you pretty well. You receive this letter, and you then write a scathing letter to the editor, making it public. The publicity doesn't do us any good, that's for sure. Undersheriff Torrez will pay the price, that's for double sure. Unless, of course, it becomes clear that the letters are a sham and that you were taken for a ride. Then it's you who will be made to look foolish." I shrugged and held up my hands helplessly. "Either way, someone gains."

"Mike Rhodes."

"Maybe."

"It has to be him."

"No, Leona, it doesn't. Sam Carter, Mike's brother-in-law and a longtime Republican, also got the letter." I shrugged again. "I don't know. I'd appreciate it if you'd just let it ride for the time being and let us sort it out. I'll give you a receipt for this, and Deputy Wheeler witnessed the fact that you turned it over to our department. It's not going to go missing or be ignored, I assure you."

"All right," Leona said, and patted her attaché case as if it still contained more good stuff. She stood up and looked at her watch. "God," she muttered. "And I have to get up in the morning and go to El Paso."

"Drive carefully," I said. "And thanks for stopping by."

As the two of us left my office, Ernie Wheeler rose, waited for Leona Spears to walk out of earshot, and then said, "Sir, Grace Sisson just pulled into her driveway."

"Good. Who's on tonight?"

"Pasquale and Abeyta. Bob's on, too, but he asked not to be called unless there was an emergency. He was going to track something down...he didn't say what."

"Ah," I said. Bob Torrez would pad around his curiosities like a big, methodical cat until the variables were sorted out to his satisfaction. "Did he already arrange to have someone stay in the Sissons' neighborhood for a while to make sure we know about it if either Grace goes somewhere or someone drops by to see her?"

"Yes, sir. He's got Tony Abeyta parked over there."

"That's good," I said. "Maybe they'll get some rest for a bit."

It would be better, in the last few hours of her privacy, for Grace Sisson to think that the world was going to leave her alone.

I walked back into my office and closed the door. Leona Spears's fragrance lingered in the room, and I walked to the desk, flipping through the Rolodex pages until I found the entry for Officer Michael Rhodes.

TWENTY-ONE

THE BLACK New Mexico State Police cruiser crunched to a stop beside 310. Behind us loomed the enormous pile of crusher fines that the state highway department was accumulating in anticipation of rejuvenating State Road 56 from Posadas to Regal. I could see the single dim light that marked the parking lot of Victor Sanchez's Broken Spur Saloon a quarter-mile to the northeast.

Rhodes rested his arm on the window sill. He regarded me soberly. "Nice night."

And it was, the air softened and cooled by the storm earlier, the prairie fragrant. Rhodes lit a cigarette, and even the smoke from that smelled pretty good. A pair of headlights appeared to the south as a faint dot, and we sat and watched them bloom until the car, a light-colored Ford Taurus with out-of-state plates, flashed past, headed toward Posadas.

"I talked with Leona Spears a bit ago," I said.

"Better you than me," Rhodes said, and chuckled. He let his head sag back against the headrest. "I try to stay on the opposite side of the district from that woman. What'd she have to say for herself?"

"Among other things, she wanted to give me this." I handed the photocopy of Leona's letter across. "Actually," I added as Rhodes took the letter, "she didn't want to give it to me at all, since she's sure it'll conveniently get lost."

The trooper snapped on a small flashlight and spread the letter out on his clipboard. "Well, I'll be damned," Rhodes said as he read the brief message. "This is pretty dumb." He snapped off the light and looked over at me. "Someone with too much free time, Sheriff."

"That's one way to look at it."

"What'd Tom Pasquale have to say about it? Did you talk to him yet?"

"He's pissed," I said. "But this isn't the first. Your esteemed brother-in-law got one just like it. So did Arnie Gray and Frank Dayan."

Rhodes sucked on his cigarette thoughtfully. "And that's it?"

"So far. Sam didn't say anything about it to you?"

Mike Rhodes grinned. "No," he said, but didn't elaborate. "You didn't receive one?"

"Nope."

"Or Jaramillo either?"

I shook my head. "That I don't know. I haven't mentioned it to Jaramillo yet, or to anyone else in the DA's office, or to Judge Hobart. And none of them has called me. And I think Don Jaramillo would have. Things like this make him nervous. I thought I'd wait a few hours and see what develops."

Rhodes laughed. "Jaramillo is too stupid to get nervous, Bill. And if Leona Spears had this, then you can guarantee that something will develop."

"She said she'd hold off."

"Oh, sure. The word of most politicians, I've come to discover, is about equal to dog shit." He blew smoke with a hiss of exasperation. "Did you come up with any prints?"

"The originals are being processed now. And just to make sure, to keep things out in the open, I asked the lab in Las Cruces to do the analysis. Not one of our own deputies."

"Ohhh," Rhodes said, "the big irons." He ground out the cigarette in the car's ashtray. "So what's the deal with Jimmy Sisson? He cut the wrong person's water line or what?"

"We don't know yet. Something stinks, that's for sure. Mama and the three kids went to Cruces, the oldest flew in from college, and then Mama and Jennifer skedaddled back here. I don't know what's going on. She had a row with her parents, that was pretty obvious."

"What'd she say when you talked to her?"

"Not much...a lot like talking to a rattlesnake. I guess I thought that grief might temper her a little, and I even took Linda Real with me. She's about the most upbeat person I know, and I guess

I thought some of it might rub off on Grace. No such luck. Then her father, the good reverend, spilled the beans that Jennifer is pregnant, and that sent Mama into orbit again. I don't know.''

''Jennifer's pregnant?''

''That's what Pastor Stevenson says. And Grace didn't deny it. And that appears to be a more important issue to her right now than a dead husband.''

''Well, I'll be damned.''

It was more than just casual amazement in Mike Rhodes's tone, and I reached out and switched off 310. Rhodes did the same, and the silence sank down around us. The trooper reached across the seat, picked up his thermos of coffee, and thoughtfully unscrewed the steel top.

''Want some?''

''No, thanks.'' I waited for him to finish his housekeeping.

''You know,'' he said, and took a moment to light another cigarette. ''You know who Jennifer Sisson hangs out a lot with, don't you?''

''Who's that?''

''My nephew. Nephew-in-law, that is, if there is such a thing.''

''Huh,'' I said. ''You're talking about Kenneth Carter, Sam's youngest?''

''The one and only. Actually, I shouldn't say 'hangs out with,' because I don't know how far it goes. But I've seen them together a time or two.'' He sipped the coffee thoughtfully. ''I know Sam's had his hands full with Kenny, but my wife's always been able to talk to him. The understanding aunt thing, you know.''

''Maybe things went a little too far, is how far they went,'' I said, and Mike Rhodes laughed.

''That's possible. I've seen Jennifer Sisson only a time or two, but the impression I got was that she'd be happier out of her clothes than in.''

I hesitated. ''Mike, has Sam said anything to you about any of this?''

The trooper chuckled at some private joke. ''Sheriff, you need to understand something. Old Sammy and I don't talk much.'' He looked across at me. ''Or to be more exact, I don't talk to *him* much. Now, I'll be the first one to admit that he's the one who talked me into running for sheriff, and the wife and I talked it over and agreed that Posadas might be a pretty comfortable place to live. MaryBeth would like to be a little closer to her sister, and I think that I can do a pretty fair job as sheriff. But that's it.'' He took a deep drag of the cigarette, then blew the smoke across the coffee cup before sipping.

"Sam Carter is one of those old-time politicians who's into it for the sport of it, Sheriff. Everything he does is wheel-deal, you know what I mean? Hell, you have to work with him—you should know what I mean.''

"Yes.''

"Well, that's not my style. My name's on the ticket, I'll put up some signs, I might talk to a Rotary Club meeting. But I won't make any promises to my brother-in-law or to anyone else.''

"When's your official date?''

He knew exactly what I meant and replied like a man who was counting the days, hours, and minutes. "September first.'' He sighed. "Twenty years on September first.''

"And you'll be ready,'' I said.

"Bet your ass, I'll be ready. There's politics in this business, too, you know.''

"I'm sure there is.''

He leaned toward me and lowered his voice so the bunchgrass wouldn't hear. "Just between you and me...'' He paused and I nodded. "The first thing I'm going to do if I win is ask Bobby Torrez to be undersheriff. Two reasons. First is that he's the best one for the job. Hell, he probably ought to be sheriff. Second is that it'll tweak my old brother-in-law so bad that he won't speak to me for a month.''

"That wouldn't be such a bad thing,'' I said, laughing.

"Nope, it wouldn't. By the way, do you have someone checking the insurance angle?''

"Sisson's, you mean?''

He nodded. "Life insurance policies are pretty handy things. It's happened before.''

"Sure it has,'' I agreed. "Anything like that is going to come out sooner or later.''

Rhodes nodded, screwed the cap back on his coffee, and started the patrol car. "Let me know what I can do for you, Bill. And be careful of Her Highness."

"Leona, you mean?"

"*Miss Spears,* as my brother-in-law always calls her. He can't ever get past the fact that the woman never married and refuses to stay home, barefoot and pregnant. But I don't trust her, either. She lives in some sort of weird parallel universe, that's for sure. Everything is an issue with that woman."

"I'll be careful."

He reached up and pulled the transmission into drive. "And for what it's worth," he said as he let the patrol car inch forward, "I've seen Tom Pasquale working down here as often as anyone. I've backed him up on routine stops a couple dozen times over the years. He's a straight arrow, Sheriff."

I lifted a hand in salute and watched the black Crown Victoria idle out onto the asphalt of State 56 and then accelerate toward Regal. I started 310 and then just sat, listening to the burble of the exhausts.

The copy of Leona Spears's letter was still lying on my lap, and I started to fold it up but then stopped and picked up my flashlight. The beam was harsh, but bright enough that my bifocals work. "Huh," I muttered, and then twisted around to look off to the west. The taillights of Mike Rhodes's car had disappeared around the twisting bends that snaked up to the pass outside Regal.

"Neatly done, Officer Rhodes," I said. "You aren't such a bad politician yourself." I pulled 310 out onto the highway and headed back toward Posadas.

TWENTY-TWO

BY THE TIME I pulled into my driveway, it was 1:15 in the morning. The thermometer that hung by the garage door read sixty-one degrees, the air cooled as it swept down from the rumbling thunderheads over the San Cristobals. That was the only benefit we were going to get, other than an occasional display of pyrotechnics as lightning lit the tops of the clouds.

I went inside, and it was only as I was shouldering the massive carved front door closed that the wave of exhaustion rolled over me. I sat down on the Mexican *banco* and leaned my back against the cool adobe wall, hat held in both hands in my lap, both feet flat on the Saltillo tile of the foyer. I closed my eyes.

The comfort of a pot of fresh coffee was out in the kitchen, a mere two dozen paces away. Perhaps better yet, my tomb-quiet bedroom was just around a couple of rounded adobe corners. That presented a choice, though, and choices took energy. So I just sat, letting the peace and quiet of the night and my home seep into my tired joints.

That was the worst decision of all, since I promptly dozed off. I started awake and would have sat bolt upright on the bench if I could, but every joint felt as if some sadist were tapping the bone with a sharp-pointed hammer.

I pushed myself away from the wall and squinted at my watch, too tired even to curse my string of bad habits. The watch said 2:55. "The hell with it," I said to the house, and struggled upright. My feet knew every wrinkle and hump in the tile, and without turning on any lights, I let them shuffle me to the bedroom. As I entered, I could smell the fresh linen. That meant that the day previous had been Wednesday, sure enough, and Jamie, my patient housekeeper, had been hard at work.

I sat down on the edge of the bed, tossed my hat toward the large wingback chair that I knew waited in the corner, swung my feet up and lay back, and prepared to let the cool fragrance play its magic.

That's all it took to complete the wake-up process. The weights slid off my eyelids and I lay staring at the spot in the darkness where the ceiling should be. As a last effort, I took off my glasses and laid them on the nightstand. All that accomplished was to turn the crisp three-inch numerals of the digital clock into an amorphous red fuzz.

I knew exactly what was going to happen. I'd lie there, wide awake, initially taking some comfort in just stretching out. Eventually, some bone or muscle would twinge, and I'd shift position, beginning the endless flip-flopping that would finish with me rearing out of bed in disgust.

That cycle hadn't started yet, and I lay still, enjoying the silence. The longer I lay there, the more alert I became. In the narrow confines overhead, between the original dirt roof and the new composition structure added years later, some small animal scuttled back and forth. The beast didn't have the nimble, delicate toe dance of a mouse but was more determined and draggy. I imagined it to be a skink, and every time the small lizard stopped, I tried to predict his course for the next move. I was wrong half the time.

Over to the left, a cricket announced himself, and I waited for the skink's course to change in pursuit. The two creatures seemed oblivious of each other.

"Ah, well," I muttered, and reached out to turn on the light. I found my glasses and swung off the bed, determined that if I couldn't sleep, at least there were better things to do than listen to a lizard draw trails in the dust.

In her own sweet way, Jamie had left other traces of her weekly visit. The coffeemaker in the kitchen fairly sparkled, and a fresh filter rested in place. I set the machine to doing its job while I showered and shaved.

At 3:45 with a full, steaming mug of coffee in hand, I stepped out of the house into the black velvet of the predawn.

Traffic on the interstate was light, with just a few truckers pounding some night miles into their logbooks. By the time I'd driven north under the exchange and idled into the village proper, even those sounds had faded to a distant hiss of tires and thump of diesel engines. I turned onto MacArthur and let 310 slow to an idle with the headlights off.

I sipped the coffee as I inched along, looking at each house in turn. I knew most of the residents and found it hard to believe that not one of them, on that quiet July night two days before, had heard anything unusual as up at the end of the street the life was crushed out of Jim Sisson.

As I continued around the long, gentle bend that took the street due north toward its intersection with Bustos, I saw the county patrol unit parked two blocks south of Sisson's place on the opposite side of the street. I let my car roll up behind it, drifting to a stop with just the faintest murmur of tires on curb grit.

I could just make out the silhouette of Deputy Jacqueline Taber's head, but the streetlight was too far away for more than that. I got out of 310, and even the sound of the door latch was loud.

As I walked along the left rear flank of the Bronco, I saw Taber's head move ever so slightly, and then an elbow appeared on the doorsill.

"Good morning, sir," she said.

"Yes, it is." I looked inside and saw that she had what appeared to be a book or magazine propped up against the steering wheel. The only light inside the vehicle was the single tiny amber power indicator on the police radio, and she wouldn't have been able to read anything by that even if it were held right up against the page.

"Any activity at all?"

"No, sir. Not for a couple of hours. Not even a stray dog since..." She stopped, then clicked on a small flashlight, with most of the beam blocked by her hand. "About two-oh-five." Before she snapped the light out, I saw that it had been a sketch pad that she'd been holding. "That was about an hour and forty-five minutes after I parked here, sir. After that, no traffic, no pedestrians, no nothing."

"Well, I suppose that's good news. I don't know. Has anyone been by to give you a break?"

"No, sir."

"Well, then, here I am." I patted the door. "Go get yourself some breakfast or something." I pointed toward the pad. "What are you drawing?"

"Oh, just sketches," she said. "It's a habit of mine." She picked up the pad and handed it to me.

"In this light, I'll have to take your word for it," I said. I turned the pad to catch what illumination there was from the streetlight and still saw a meaningless jumble of lines and shadows. I pulled the small penlight out of my shirt pocket and snapped it on. "Wow," I murmured. Her "sketch" was a fantastically detailed, shaded rendering of what she was looking at through the windshield—the end of MacArthur Avenue and its intersection with Bustos, all drawn in careful perspective, as if the viewer were floating about twenty feet above the street.

"Amazing," I said. Deputy Taber had caught the silence and cover of night in her artwork, complete with what might have been a furtive figure lurking beside the Sissons' fence. "Who's this?"

The deputy shrugged and smiled. "When I saw the pedestrian come around the corner from Bustos, she and her dog just sort of walked into the picture." I looked closer. Sure enough, a hair-thin pencil line connected the human to the shadow of a dog.

I snapped the light off and handed the pad back to her. "Hidden talents," I said. "I'd like to see this in decent light. How the hell can you tell what you're drawing in the dark?"

"Actually, once your eyes adjust, there's really quite a bit of light, sir. Enough for this, anyway."

Oh, sure, I thought. "Do you do people, too? Faces and such, I mean?"

"Yes."

"That's nice to know." I regarded Taber for a moment. She'd joined our department as a transplant from Las Cruces six months before, one of the last people that Martin Holman had hired before he'd been killed in a plane crash in April. I also imagined her as the sort of gal who would have come off a farm in Nebraska somewhere...square through the shoulders with about as much taper to the waist as a refrigerator, hair no-nonsense short, a plain, round face that could split open with a fetching grin. Whatever the urban social scene of the city had been, it hadn't agreed with her.

Something about Posadas did, though, and she seemed to take

quiet satisfaction in working the graveyard shift. As far as I knew, she hadn't taken much ribbing from the other deputies about being the only female patrol officer on the force—partly because she did such a damn good job and partly because Estelle Reyes-Guzman had broken that particular ice for our department long ago.

She started the Bronco and I stepped away. "Who was the pedestrian, by the way? Did you recognize him?" I asked.

Deputy Taber paused with her hand on the gearshift. "It was a woman, sir. She lives right there," she said, twisting and pointing over her shoulder. "Number Five Twelve. Tabitha Hines. I believe that she works at the grocery store. I didn't see her come out of the house, so I assume she walked the dog up the roadway behind the houses, then returned on the street."

"Ah, Taffy," I said and nodded. "She'd have to be a fellow charter member of the Insomniacs Club of America. What kind of dog was it, not that it matters?" I laughed. "This is all a test of your keen artist's eye, Jackie."

"It appeared to be a chow, sir. The light's not the best, but it was either a chow or husky. Short, blocky, tail over the back. I couldn't be sure of the color."

"From this distance, I couldn't have been sure it was a dog," I chuckled, then added, "or a person, either, for that matter. What time is it now, by the way?"

"Four-oh-one, sir."

"She'll be heading off to work in a little bit."

The deputy didn't respond to that earth-shaking information, and I patted the side of the Bronco. "I'll holler at you if I need anything. You might take a swing down Fifty-six if nothing better crops up. I assume you know about our friendly letter writer."

"The letters about Tom Pasquale? Yes, sir, Undersheriff Torrez told me. He said you were taking care of it, but he suggested the same thing."

"Keep an eye out," I said. "I don't think there's anything to it, but you never know."

She nodded and pulled the Bronco into gear, then U-turned in the street, letting the truck's quiet idle pull it away. I stood on the sidewalk for a while, listening to the neighborhood as the sound of Taber's unit faded.

After a moment, I returned to my car and got the larger flashlight so that I'd have a fighting chance to miss stepping in the piles left by Taffy's chow.

TWENTY-THREE

THERE ARE FOLKS who are built for nighttime stealth, those fortunate souls with vision like owls and balance like cats. I wasn't one of them. I was blessed with patience, though, and had no trouble standing still long enough so that I was sure of my next footing.

Exactly what I thought I would accomplish was anyone's guess, but my curiosity was aroused. As long as I didn't step on a rattlesnake or trip over a skunk, it would be a pleasant night for a stroll.

I took the large flashlight and crossed MacArthur south of Taffy Hines's residence. The houses that graced the east side of MacArthur were Posadas civilization, as far as it went. Behind Taffy's lot and that of her neighbors was open junk-strewn bunchgrass prairie, the land cut by tracks of four-wheelers and motorcycles.

As I walked along the side of her yard, I kept the flashlight off, making my way by what light filtered through from the street behind me and the single sodium vapor light behind the McKuens' house, two doors south. I expected the chow to burst out of a doghouse at any moment, teeth flashing. The place was silent.

Many of the yards were neatly fenced, but Taffy's wasn't. The grass of the backyard ended at the lane that served as a back property boundary for all the properties on that section of MacArthur.

I reached the lane without falling on my face and stopped, listening. In the distance, a trucker rode his Jake brake as he headed off the interstate for breakfast at the AMERICAN OWNED AND OPERATED POSADAS INN, home of the worst food in Posadas, but conveniently located at the bottom of the exit ramp.

After a moment, I turned on the flashlight and played it back and forth on the ground. The lane was what most back alleys are in towns and cities...a welter of broken glass, paper, pet manure, and the occasional automobile muffler or oil filter. The recent thundershower had turned it all into a dark soup.

Taffy Hines had kept to the high ground along the side of the lane, but her chow hadn't. His big feet had planted tracks that crisscrossed the lane, and he hadn't been all that interested in missing puddles. I'm sure he was a delight to have inside the house once back home. Perhaps that explained why Taffy had elected to walk back on the clean sidewalk, giving pooch a chance to shake off some of the mud.

With an occasional night thing clicking, buzzing, or peeping out in the prairie to my right, I passed behind seven houses before the stout six-foot board fence that marked the Sissons' property came into view.

The gate was wide and cumbersome, big enough that when Jim drove into the yard with one of his machines in tow, he could just head out the back without having to turn the Lo-Boy trailer around or back out past the house. The gate was ajar a couple of inches, and I played my light around it. Apparently a trusting soul, Jim Sisson hadn't included any way to lock the gate when he'd hung it.

It moved easily on the large barn door hinges, and I opened it enough that I could have passed through. The chow's prints grazed a puddle just inside the gate, headed westward into Sisson's property. I stood for several minutes, looking down at the tracks.

Taffy Hines, in the wee hours of the morning, had walked her dog up the back-lot lane and stopped to visit Grace Sisson. As careful as Taffy had been, I could see a couple of shoe prints that were fresh and clear and about the right size for a woman. The soles were a neat, shallow waffle pattern that would track mud into the house almost as well as the mutt would.

Other than the hour, the visit wasn't surprising. Of course Taffy Hines knew the Sissons. Everyone who lived on MacArthur, and a host of others, did, too. That they were close enough friends for a drop-in visit wasn't surprising, either, although the pleasant, almost dreamy Taffy didn't seem like a natural match for friendship with the fiery Grace Sisson.

I stopped short, my memory finally kicking into gear. The chow. I remembered his big, flat face thrust against the back door of the

Sissons' house that first night, beady little eyes watching us, a low chesty *hooof* of doggy puzzlement now and then.

Taffy Hines either owned a similar dog or was canine-sitting for the Sissons during their upset. I pulled the gate closed and continued up the lane toward Bustos. There were no sidewalks on Bustos until the intersection with MacArthur. East of that point, basically for the depth of Sisson's lot, Taffy Hines would have had to walk on the curbing or in the street—not that traffic would have been a concern.

If Deputy Taber's observation had been correct, and I had no reason to doubt it, Taffy Hines had continued her nocturnal stroll back around the long block, walking down the sidewalk on MacArthur, past the front of all her neighbors' homes, including the Sissons'.

I stood on the corner of Bustos and MacArthur, looking down the long, straight, empty four-lane street that cut east-west through the heart of Posadas, wondering if Taffy's nocturnal strolls were a habit. The supermarket where she was the senior cashier opened at 6:00 a.m., so she had another hour or so before facing the public.

I crossed the intersection and strolled down the west side of MacArthur, inspecting each quiet house in turn, recalling to mind who the occupants were and what they did for a living. Nothing was out of place, nothing amiss. I'd walked almost a block before I glanced down the street toward 310.

A lone figure was standing beside the patrol car, leaning against the front fender. I'd walked to within a dozen feet before I recognized the plump, short figure.

"Well, good morning, Ms. Hines," I said, and my voice sounded unnaturally loud after the long moments of dark silence.

"Hello yourself, Sheriff. What in heaven's name are you looking for?" She said it with good humor, the same tone she might use when she said, "Here, let me get that for you," to a customer at the store who wanted to make an exchange after reaching the checkout with the wrong brand of soap.

"Just enjoying a beautiful night, ma'am," I said.

She laughed a sort of oddly sad little chuckle and rested a little more weight on the Ford's fender. "Oh, sure. Word around is that Jim Sisson's death was a homicide, after all."

"Word around, eh?" I said.

"Well, otherwise you people wouldn't be tying up Sisson's property and your detectives scouring everything, looking for who knows what."

"That's our job, Taffy. I'd say you're not such a bad observer yourself."

"I happened to be looking out the window when you drove up to chat with Jackie a little bit ago, that's all. And then you walked around back, and up the lane."

"Like I said, you're observant, Taffy."

"Well, it's a neighborhood, you know. Lots of us nosy folks like to know what's going on. Especially after such an awful thing happens."

"And yet..." I paused.

"And yet what?"

"And yet none of you, not one, saw or heard anything when Jim Sisson was killed. No one saw anyone unusual drive up, no one heard Jim arguing, no one heard a scream or a shout, no one heard a vehicle leave or the sounds of a person fleeing on foot."

"That's not surprising," Taffy Hines said.

"Tell me why it's not," I replied. "When I arrived just now, my headlights were off, and I made a point to tiptoe." I swung the flashlight up and tucked it under my left arm and thrust my hands in my pockets. "And you heard me."

"I just happened to look out," she said.

"Uh-huh." I took a deep breath and pivoted at the waist a few degrees each way, scanning the neighborhood. "Listen."

We stood in companionable silence for a few heartbeats before Taffy said, "It's my favorite time of day."

"Quiet, isn't it?"

"Sure."

"I think I could hear a dime drop up on Bustos right now."

Taffy Hines shook her head with impatience. "And so you imagine that half the neighborhood would hear the ruckus up at the Sissons'?"

"That's what bothers me."

"Well, from what I'm told, it happened in the evening, not a whole long while after dark. Folks are still up, televisions are on, kids are playing...all that stuff. This is a whole different world, right now.''

"I guess," I said. "Is that your dog?"

She turned quickly, looking down the street in the general direction of my gaze. "What dog?"

"No, no. The one you were walking earlier this morning. At about two or so. I think he's a chow."

Taffy Hines crossed her arms over her ample chest. "My goodness," she said with more good humor than I would have been able to summon had I been in her shoes, "such efficient surveillance. You people must know all my dark secrets by now."

"Please, Taffy. Give us a break. You make it sound like Jackie Taber and I are members of the secret police from some third world country with this 'you people' nonsense. There's been a questionable death, as you apparently already know. What do you want us to do, sit in our offices and hope that someone comes in and confesses out of a sense of good citizenship?"

"Sheriff," she said, and her tone softened, "I'm sorry. That's not what I meant. In fact, I almost came out to offer Jackie a cup of coffee. But I didn't, you know, because I wasn't sure just what she was doing and I didn't want to interfere."

"To pass the time and stay alert, she was drawing pictures," I said, then added, "in her most creative secret police style. That's how I knew about the dog. She saw you, obviously, and included you and pooch in the drawing she was doing."

"I'd like to see that," Taffy said. "And the dog's name is Rufus, by the way. He's one of the sweetest dogs on the planet." She laughed. "And probably one of the dumbest, too."

"Is he yours?"

"No. He belongs to the Sissons. I've been taking care of him. I asked Gracie just a bit ago if they're ready to take him back, but..." She shook her head. "That poor family."

"Did Deputy Mears, or any of the others, talk to you Tuesday night?"

"No," she said. "Nobody came by."

I turned and calculated the distance. Taffy Hines lived eight houses south of the Sisson property, hardly close enough to be considered an immediate neighbor.

"When did you hear about Jim's death?"

"Gracie called me early yesterday morning, just before I was going to work. She could hardly speak, poor thing. She asked if I could drive her to her parents' house in Las Cruces."

"And did you?"

"No. She drove herself. I was all ready to go, though. I'd called Sam at the store and told him that I wouldn't be in until probably midmorning sometime, and he said that was fine, to go ahead and take my time. But then Gracie called back and said she'd be fine, that she was going to drive herself and the kids. That the kids would keep an eye on her."

"So she drove herself."

"Yes."

"The deputies understood that a friend had taken them."

"That was the plan originally. But as far as I know, she drove herself. Now I could be wrong."

"Huh."

"Whoever killed Jim could have parked in the lane behind the Sisson property, you know," Taffy said. "No one would see or hear anything if they did that."

"We've considered that. We hoped for some tire tracks, but the rain took care of everything except some fresh dog tracks, compliments of Rufus."

"Yuck," Taffy said. "He loves to be out, but what a mess he can make of everything." She stood on her tiptoes, stretching. "You want a cup of coffee or something? I've got some cinnamon rolls that are out of this world."

"That would be delightful," I said. As we strolled across the street to her house, I wondered how many sets of eyes were peering out around curtains, watching yet another episode that would be instantly forgotten should the wrong person ask.

TWENTY-FOUR

TAFFY HINES WAS RIGHT. The cinnamon rolls were outstanding, their aroma graced by freshly ground coffee far better than any I ever made.

"Do you start every day like this?" I asked around a mouthful of melted butter and roll.

"I try to," she said, and pointed at the small framed motto on the wall next to the refrigerator. "If that's right—if each day is a gift—then I think it's nice to mark it in some way. This is the best time of day to do that, before it's spoiled somehow after the sun comes up and people start moving around."

Her kitchen was a pleasant place to be, even at that early-morning hour. Splashes of color marked the painted cabinets, with artfully rendered vines and flowers running up the doors, the painted tendrils laced around hinges and handles.

I bent over and regarded the floor, a swirl of color and pattern that threatened to induce vertigo. The floor vinyl was an impressionist's blurred idea of a flower garden, the vibrant colors spotted here and there with shiny black insects that crawled between the washes of flower petals.

"I've never seen anything quite like this," I said.

"Neat, huh?" Taffy said.

A light, tentative scratch on the door by the kitchen range turned my head. "Rufus?"

She nodded. "He smells the rolls. But it's a dog's life. He doesn't get any. He's fat enough."

"Me, too," I said, and sighed. I watched as she refilled my cup. "Thanks. So tell me," I said, and waited for her to return to her chair. "Do things get a little hectic around the store as Election Day rears its ugly head?"

Taffy Hines coughed a sharp burst of laughter and pushed the pack of cigarettes and the lighter that rested on the table in front of her another few inches away. She hadn't lit up yet, and I was just as glad not to have to endure yet another temptation heaped on top of the rich food and wonderful coffee.

"Most of the time, Sam behaves himself," she said. "Most of the time. I guess I kind of like all the political hubbub. It gives him something to think about. Keeps him out of my hair."

"How long have you worked for him?"

"This will be my nineteenth year."

"I knew it had been a long time."

"Sometimes too long. But you know all about that, I suppose." I nodded. "I'm sort of surprised that you've stayed on."

"So am I, sometimes," she said, but she managed to say it with a smile. "I like the store, I like the customers." She sipped the coffee. "I like knowing people, you know what I mean?"

"Sure."

"I see the same faces, week in, week out. The same faces, buying the same things. It's comfortable. Live alone like I do, and it's important." She paused and shrugged. "At least to me it is."

"Not that it's any of my business," I said, "but what do you think about Leona Spears? What's your prediction there?"

"If she's going to win the election, you mean?" Taffy chuckled. "What a kook."

"That means 'no,' I take it."

Taffy frowned and gazed down at the flower garden linoleum. "I don't know why she's even interested in your job, Sheriff. I mean," and she held up both hands, "what qualifications does she have?"

"Interest, I suppose."

"Sam goes on and on about her."

"Does he."

"Sure. You'd think by the way he talks that if someone other than his brother-in-law wins the election, the whole county is going to go to hell, pardon my French."

"Well, we're on the way, it seems sometimes," I said.

"Well..." Taffy started, then bit off the words as she changed her mind.

With my finger I drew designs on the place mat for a moment, then looked up to regard Taffy Hines. "Has he been minding his own business lately?" I saw her eyebrows knit together and, so she wouldn't misunderstand me, added, "About you, I mean. Has he been leaving you alone? No more calls?"

She waved a hand in dismissal. "I'm just a piece of the store furniture to him now," she said. "And I guess that's better than being pawed or panted over." She looked hard at me. "He's a foolish old man, Sheriff. Well, not so old, either, I guess. I'm surprised that his wife hasn't either left him or shot him long before this." She managed a tired laugh. "I just don't know."

"It's his life to ruin as he chooses," I said as I admired the last bite of the last cinnamon roll that I planned to allow myself.

"He seems to like to include others in his misery," Taffy said, then shrugged as if to dismiss the whole subject.

"Did Sam happen to mention to you anything about a letter that he received?" I wasn't sure what prompted me to ask Taffy about the Pasquale letters, except that I agreed with her—Sam Carter wasn't the soul of discretion, and it was hard to believe he'd be able to keep such a juicy tidbit close to the vest...especially when he might stand to gain more than he'd lose if the letter's contents went public.

"Which letter might that be?" Taffy asked. She wasn't playing coy—or if she was, she would have made a wonderful poker player.

"Sam showed me a note that indicated one of the deputies might be involved in some shady dealings—"

She interrupted me with a loud laugh. "Oh, God...that thing. The one that says Tommy Pasquale is stopping Mexicans and extorting money from them?"

"That's the one."

"I told Sam that if he was going to send some piece of trash like that, he'd better get himself a damn good lawyer."

"You what?"

She shrugged. "When he showed it to me, my very first thought was that he was *going* to send the letter. That he'd written it himself. Then he set me straight, told me that he'd gotten it in the mail." She made a face.

"You don't think he did?"

"Maybe, maybe not. I get the mail most mornings, and I even slit open each envelope so His Highness doesn't have to. But I don't look inside. Maybe it was there, maybe not. If there's something that looks really personal, I don't even open the envelope."

"So you still think that Sam might have circulated the letter himself?"

Taffy Hines reached across and pointed at my cup. "Some more?"

"No thanks."

She picked up the cup, rose, and walked to the sink. "He's capable of it. But so are a lot of other people. He made it sound like he didn't want the story to get out until you'd had a chance to do something about it." She turned away from the sink and looked at me. "And I remember thinking that if he was so all-fired concerned about spreading rumors, then he shouldn't have shown the letter to me in the first place."

I sighed and pushed myself to my feet. "Taffy, thanks a million for the breakfast." I glanced at my watch.

She smiled. "Give you a break from the Don Juan," she said.

"Ah, another of my secrets shattered," I chuckled.

"It's a small town, Sheriff. There aren't too many secrets left."

I grimaced. "Just a few little naggy ones," I said.

As I collected my hat and started to move toward the door, Taffy held out a hand, stopping just short of touching my arm. "You're doing the right thing," she said.

"How so?"

"Keeping a discreet eye on Grace," Taffy said. "She told me last night about your visit with her down in Las Cruces and how the cops had followed her all the way home. She was pretty steamed."

"Yes, she was."

"Well, I told her it was for her own good. We've been friends for years, and there's nothing I'd say about her behind her back that I wouldn't say to her face. She's had her share of troubles and heartache, and I think she's going to need some time before she's thinking straight. There's just no telling right now what she'll do from one minute to the next."

We were close enough that by lifting my head I could focus

Taffy Hines's face in my bifocals, and I regarded her with interest. "What are you telling me, Taffy?"

She didn't flinch or backpedal. "I'm not telling you anything that you don't already know, Sheriff."

"You've known Grace Sisson all this time," I said. "Was there some family trouble that might be behind Jim's death? Something with the kids, or some affair Grace was having behind Jim's back that he found out about? Or vice versa? Something like that?"

A ghost of a smile creased Taffy Hines's face. "Let's not ruin such a beautiful morning by going down that road, Sheriff. Like I said, Grace might have her faults, but she's a dear friend."

I nodded, wondering how one went about becoming a "dear friend" with someone who flailed with a barbed-wire tongue.

"Can I ask one more favor of you?" I asked.

"Maybe." She grinned.

"This letter business has been bothering me, and if I get the time, I'm going to do my best to track it down. I have Sam's copy of the letter, the one that he handed you. Since he did that, I assume your fingerprints are on it."

"I would think so."

"Would you stop by the office sometime today if you get a chance and have Gayle fill out a print card on you, so we can eliminate your prints from any others?"

She shrugged. "Sure. Why not? Will I have black fingers for the rest of the day?"

"Probably. But I'd appreciate it."

"No problem," she said.

At ten minutes after five that Thursday morning, feeling just a tad bloated from one too many cinnamon rolls, I settled back into the patrol car and rummaged for the cell phone.

Deputy Thomas Pasquale picked up on the second ring. He'd been off-duty for five hours but managed to sound alert.

"Thomas, this is Gastner," I said. "Sorry to bother you at home. Have you got a few minutes?"

"Yes, sir."

I glanced at my watch again. "Can you meet me at Sam Carter's place at five-thirty? You know where he lives?"

"Yes, sir. I can do that."

"In uniform, Tom. A chance for a little overtime."

"Yes, sir."

I redialed and listened to half a ring before the phone was snatched up by an eager Brent Sutherland. He'd hit the flattest part of the shift, and I could imagine his youthful desperation.

Less than three minutes after my call, Deputy Jacqueline Taber's patrol unit slid into place behind mine. I raised a hand out the window in salute, tapped the mike transmit key twice, then pulled 310 away from the curb, leaving the deputy to draw more neat pictures as the neighborhood came to life.

A single car passed eastbound on Bustos, and I recognized Cal Wheeler on the first leg of his commute to his job at the truck stop west of Las Cruces on the interstate.

If my timing was right, Sam Carter would be just about half-shaved, ready to sit down to the morning paper from Albuquerque and his first cup of coffee. Thus prepped, he'd walk into the su-permarket shortly after six, and by then Taffy Hines would have the place up and running. The teenagers who worked as stockers would have the first round of cartons filling the aisles as bottles and cans clanked onto the shelves.

I didn't much like interrupting someone's comfortable routine, but Sam Carter had lied to me. That made him fair game.

TWENTY-FIVE

SOMETIMES APPEARANCES send a powerful message, and that's what I was hoping would happen when we showed up on Sam Carter's doorstep. I'd known Sam for years....I'd never liked him, and he probably had reciprocated.

He'd been a county commissioner for more than fifteen years, and during the countless meetings where I'd watched him in action I'd developed some assumptions about his character—or lack thereof. I knew, for instance, that when he thought he had the power on his side, he could be a bully, sometimes rude to citizens during public meetings who tried to speak counter to his views. He knew how to pinch pennies, stretching the budget further than it needed to be stretched just on general principles.

He could glad-hand with the best and knew how to pin someone in a corner for a nice, personal chat. I'd been in one of those corners on various occasions, and I'd learned just to let Sam Carter rattle on. He was one of those curious souls who figured that if you didn't say anything, then you agreed with him.

I also had developed the impression that, when forced to stand alone, Sam Carter was probably pretty much a coward.

What Sam Carter had told me about his receiving the letter was so counter to Taffy Hines's version that alarm bells were ringing in my head far louder than the normal tinnitus.

The early-morning hours are a good time to pay house calls. People tend to be vulnerable then. They haven't had hours to plan their day or time to brace themselves against the outrages, large or small, that will drift their way.

Shortly after 5:30, I rolled 310 to a stop in front of Sam Carter's home on Ridgeway Avenue, one block off North 10th Street. I parked facing eastbound on the wrong side of the street, so that my driver's side window opened to Sam's manicured front lawn.

Deputy Pasquale arrived a minute later from the east and parked his unit nose-to-nose with mine.

I got out with a folder in hand that contained photocopies of all the letters, Carter's included.

"Sorry to haul you out again," I said to Pasquale as he approached. "I've got me a little experiment going here, and I need your backup."

"Yes, sir," Pasquale said, glancing at Carter's house and then at the ones on either side. "What's up?"

"There are a couple questions I want to ask Sam Carter about these letters." I tapped the folder and lowered my voice. "I thought it might unsettle him just a bit if you're standing right in his face." I grinned, and Pasquale looked puzzled. "I'll explain later, Thomas. Right now I'm going to ask that you let me do the talking. If Carter asks you a specific question, just answer truthfully, yes or no. No elaboration. Just yes or no. All right?"

"Yes, sir."

I nodded. "Good man."

Together we walked up the narrow sidewalk between the displays of various cacti. Carter's house didn't try to look southwestern, didn't try to complement the cacti. The place would have looked at home on a side street in Columbus, Ohio. The white clapboard siding was evidently vinyl, and the finish was trying hard not to turn to powder under the blast furnace of the New Mexico sun.

I touched the doorbell but didn't hear anything and after a couple of seconds rapped on the door frame. In a moment the door opened and MaryBeth Carter peered out. She recognized me and smiled. "Well," she said. "Good morning. You gents are up bright and early." She turned on the porch light to give a boost to the slow dawn.

"Early, anyway," I said.

Sam Carter's wife was short and plump, the perfect picture of someone's favorite aunt or even grandmother. She wore a fluffy robe cinched tightly around her middle, with a pair of equally fluffy slippers. But my attention was drawn to her eyeglasses, a spectacularly awful design with molded curlicues and flowers in the outer corners where the bows joined the frames. They would have looked wonderful at a pet show back in 1956.

"We need to chat with Sam, MaryBeth," I said. "We'll just be a minute, if he's home."

"I think he just stepped into the shower," she said.

"We'll wait out here," I replied.

"Oh, don't be silly. Come on in."

"This is fine, ma'am," I said. "If you'd just tell him we're here."

She turned away, and I said quietly to Tom, "Have you ever been able to climb leisurely out of a shower when someone's waiting at the door?"

Pasquale grinned, no doubt thinking that, hell, it might be fun to piss off the chairman of the county commission as long as it was the old sheriff's neck that was on the block, not his.

In due course, Sam Carter appeared, hair wet and curling away from the bald spot that he took pains to cover. He wore a white terry-cloth robe, was barefoot, and had a towel in hand. He draped the towel around his neck as he swung open the door.

"Christ, what's going on?" he asked. "Is the town burning down or what?"

"Nothing like that," I said. "I had a couple of questions that I'd like to shoot your way, and from the way the day's shaping up, I thought this might be my best chance."

"Christ, it's five-thirty in the morning, for God's sakes." His tone softened a bit. "And questions about what?" he asked. If he'd had the chance to do it all over again, he might have taken pains to make his tone a little less guarded.

I moved closer to the light and opened the folder. "These letters still puzzle me, Sam."

"Letters?" He shot a glance sideways at Tom Pasquale but then concentrated his frown at me.

"Yes. Your copy of the letter about Deputy Pasquale, here, and the similar ones received by Dr. Gray, Leona Spears, Frank Dayan, and I assume other folks we haven't heard from yet."

"What about it? What did you find out?"

"Well, for one thing, we're going to get back a pretty comprehensive fingerprint analysis from the state crime lab. They're awfully good at what they do." I smiled helpfully. "That ought to come sometime today. If we're lucky, someone might have been just a tad careless."

"All right. But I'm sure you didn't come over here at five-thirty to tell me that."

"No, actually, I didn't." I leafed through the letters as if I were reading them, which in that dim light would have been a real trick. "You told me earlier that you received yours in the mail, is that right?"

"That's right."

"Well, that in itself is interesting, since of the folks who have brought this letter to my attention, you're the only one whose copy was mailed."

"What's that mean?"

"I don't know, Sam. But you also told me that you didn't show the letter to anyone at the time. I think the expression you used, if I remember correctly, was something like, 'If this got out, it'd be a real mess,' or words to that effect. Do you remember saying that?"

"Well, I guess so. I don't remember everything I say in the course of a busy day."

"Few of us do, I suppose," I said. "But in this case, you made a considerable effort to find me and talk with me in private, as I recall."

Carter lifted the towel and dabbed at his left ear and again shot a glance at the silent figure of Thomas Pasquale. "What's your point?" Carter asked, and he didn't bother trying to soften the question.

"My point, Sam, is that you specifically told me that you didn't show the letter to anyone else."

"And I didn't," he said, then retreated a bit and tacked on, "not that I recall, anyway."

"Do you recall showing the letter to Taffy Hines?"

"Taffy Hines?"

"Yes."

His pause was just a shade too long, a pause of calculation rather than simple recollection. "I...I might have, now that you mention it."

"So, despite your concern, the first person you showed the letter to was not me, but your head cashier. A woman who spends her day talking with half the town."

"Now wait a minute," Carter flared, and he grabbed the ends of his robe belt and jerked them tight. "I did show it to her, yes I remember that now. But I told her to keep quiet about it until I talked to you. Did she tell you that, too, the town blabbermouth?"

"Yes, she told me that. She also told me that her first reaction was to think that you'd written it."

"Now wait a minute," he blustered, and he took a step toward me, which by coincidence happened to be a step away from Tom Pasquale.

Before Sam could splutter out anything else, I said, "I didn't come here to upset you, or make waves. What I really need is the envelope, Sam. I understand that Taffy often opens the mail for the store, but that she doesn't remember seeing anything that might be a match. Since there might be prints on the envelope, it's important. Or a postmark. Any number of things."

"I don't think I still have the envelope," Carter said. "And now that I think about it, I'm not absolutely certain it came in the mail. *With* the mail, maybe. I'm just not sure."

"Why wouldn't you keep it?" I asked. "Something as important as that? Wouldn't you be curious about the return address, if there was one, or the postmark?"

He shook his head. "I didn't save it. I guess I should have. I...I didn't think. And you didn't ask me for it." He stopped abruptly.

"Yes, I did," I said. "You said you'd look for it, as I recall."

"And I didn't," Carter said. "I'm sorry."

"It's only been a couple of days. Is there a possibility that it's still in the trash can in your office?"

He shook his head without hesitation. "No, no. That's emptied as a matter of course every day."

"When's the Dumpster pickup? That's not until this afternoon, is it? This is Thursday?" I turned to Pasquale. "We can put a couple of deputies on that this morning. Turn the damn thing upside down. If the letter's there, it'll turn up."

"I just don't understand," Carter snapped. "Hines holds a king-sized grudge against me, and I can understand why she'd say just about anything, but you sound as if you think I wrote the damn note, too. Is that what you both think?"

"I don't know what to think," I said. "What I'm doing is trying my best to clear up the discrepancies."

"Let me tell you what's most likely, Sheriff. And I don't say this out of spite. I just don't trust the woman—"

"What woman is that? Taffy?"

"No. Leona Spears. This is just the sort of thing that Leona Spears is good at. You see all the letters to the editors that she writes? God's sakes, the woman has an answer for everything. This is just the sort of thing that Miss Spears would do." He spit out the *Miss* as if the one word included everything anyone needed to know about Leona Spears's private life and predilections.

I smiled. "Maybe so, Sam. Maybe so. Whoever wrote the letter to *Miss* Spears agrees with you, that's for sure."

He didn't ask what I meant but nodded vigorously. "Well, you just check it out," he said testily. He glanced at his wrist where a watch should have been and settled for rubbing the spot with the towel.

"We won't take any more of your time, Sam. I just wanted to check and get some clarification, that's all. We'll get the print analysis today and, with any luck, the analysis of the paper and the machine that did the printing. Maybe something will show up."

Sam Carter's reaction didn't tell me if he thought that was a good idea or a world-class waste of time.

We made our way back to the vehicles, and I turned to Pasquale. "What do you think?"

"I think he's a lying son of a bitch."

"Well, maybe."

"I think it's interesting that he never bothered to ask me if I did what that letter says I did."

"Uh-huh." I nodded. "That's because in an election year, what actually happened isn't too important to folks like Sam Carter. Give him a little time, and best of all maybe an audience, and you'd be surprised how tough Sam Carter can be."

"Five minutes alone with him might be the answer," Pasquale muttered.

"I don't think so, Thomas. Just be patient." That was easily said, of course. But I knew perfectly well that patience wasn't young Thomas Pasquale's strong suit.

TWENTY-SIX

THE STATE'S REGIONAL crime lab in Las Cruces was efficient and dedicated, but they couldn't create what didn't exist.

On the original letters, the fingerprints were easy to match. The addressee's prints were clear in each case, and in one instance where I'd been careless with Dr. Gray's copy, one of my own thumbs had left a record. Sam Carter's letter bore several prints, both his and an unidentified second party's.

Taffy Hines had been true to her word. She stopped by the Sheriff's Department on her way to work and allowed Brent Sutherland to lift a set of prints. He managed the task in the sort of self-conscious, clumsy way that rookies do until they've processed about a hundred sets. I looked at the card when he'd finished, pretended that I could see all the little swirls, gigs, and arches, and nodded approval.

Deputy Mears was our resident fingerprint expert, and he'd do a formal comparison when he came in at 4:00. But my eyes were good enough to convince me that the unidentified prints were Taffy's. That made perfect sense and supported her contention that she'd handled the letter when it was offered to her by Sam Carter.

Other than that, nothing. Whoever had sent the letters, or dropped them off, had been careful...very careful. And that in itself answered some questions. Whoever had sent the sorry little notes had been just as concerned that he or she not be caught as with having the notes read by all the right people.

Even before the morning sun had a chance to heat up the garbage and flies in the alley behind Carter's Family SuperMarket, Deputies Richard Johnson and Sutherland, who claimed to have nothing better to do once Gayle Sedillos took day dispatch, were sifting methodically through the Dumpster, looking for a plain, white number 10 envelope.

I was willing to bet a month's pay that no postmarked envelope existed. What was the point, I reasoned, in hand-delivering all but Sam Carter's copy, trusting only that one to the postal service? All of the notes had arrived at their destinations in plain white envelopes, unsealed, unstamped, unpostmarked. I had no reason to suspect that Sam's would be different.

The garbage excavation was probably a massive waste of time, considering the other drains on our resources at that moment. But I had my reasons. Bob Torrez was heading the investigation into the death of Jim Sisson, and when he needed me to do something specific for him, he'd say so.

Much of my interest in the Pasquale notes, I cheerfully admitted, was ego. I wasn't about to let someone smear a department, of which I was justifiably proud, during the final months of my tenure—and I wasn't about to let someone ruin the career of a young man who'd done nothing wrong, beyond having his name come to mind.

If we found the plain envelope, with no evidence of its having been mailed, I knew damn well what Sam Carter would say: *"Sorry, boys. My mistake. I guess it wasn't mailed, after all. But it came into my office with the mail, heh, heh, so I guess that's what I meant."*

And if we found nothing at all? *"Well, gosh, boys, I know it was there. You must have just missed it."* At least the three of us provided some comic relief for folks driving to work who glanced toward the rear of the supermarket and saw me standing beside the Dumpster, directing the efforts of the two dump rats inside.

We were lucky—or rather the deputies were lucky, since they were the ones who climbed inside to smell the roses. The Dumpsters held primarily commercial waste—crushed boxes and the like, with a few little soggy, smelly, rotting surprises.

By 9:15, we'd—they'd—reached the bottom of all three units. Sam Carter had the grace not to come outside to say, *"Well, you must have just missed it."*

Brent was exploring one last corner when the undersheriff's patrol car idled to a stop beside mine. Bob Torrez got out, a slow grin spreading across his face. "Now, this is interesting," he said, and I shrugged.

"You never know where your next meal comes from, Robert," I said.

"Oh, yes, I do," he said, and he didn't have to elaborate. I knew that Gayle Torrez could manufacture her own brand of magic in the kitchen, and I was surprised that the undersheriff's waistline hadn't started to spread after even a short period of marital bliss. "Any luck?" Bob added.

"No."

"Do you think Sam Carter is lying?"

"Yes."

"Any ideas why?"

"Other than the obvious political ones, no. Except it might just be in his nature. I think he's embarrassed that he got caught being indiscreet."

Torrez leaned against the front fender of his car and folded his arms across his chest. "Speaking of being indiscreet, I've got a couple of things that I need to run by you, when you have a chance."

I grinned at him and stepped away from the Dumpster, trying without success to avoid the greasy chocolate puddle strategically placed in front of it. I swore and stamped some of the muck off my shoes.

"What did you find out?"

He turned and reached inside the car for one of his black vinyl notepads. "First of all, I swung by Vicente Garcia's, just on the off-chance that he might talk to me, and on the off-chance that the Sissons had some other insurance with State Mutual besides their auto policies."

"Why shouldn't Garcia talk to you?" I chuckled. "He's your cousin."

"Well, but professional ethics, you know. Vicente did ask me if I was going to get a court order if he didn't answer my questions, and I told him that either I would or the district attorney would. I told him I'd go get one right then, if it'd make him feel better. I guess that was good enough for him. Besides, it turns out it might be in his company's best interests."

"Let me guess," I said, half-turned to watch Brent Sutherland vault out of the Dumpster. "There's some life insurance."

"Yep. State Mutual holds the Sissons' auto, home, business, and life. The whole package."

"How much life insurance?"

"Not all that big a deal. One hundred thousand is the limit on either spouse." He flipped open the notebook and scanned his figures. "No double indemnity or anything fancy like that."

"But still a nice, round figure," I said. "How old is the policy?"

"They took it out eight years ago."

I frowned. "Huh. Nothing recent, then."

"No, sir. They took it out four years after their youngest kid was born. Vicente Garcia said that the kid needed some expensive corrective orthopedic surgery on one leg, and Jim and Grace took out the policy then, in case something should happen to one or both of them. The kid's needs would be provided for, no matter what."

"Smart planning," I said. "If either of them dies, the surviving spouse gets a hundred grand. They had health insurance?"

"Yes, but not with State Mutual. It's that HMO that the chamber of commerce sponsors."

"Makes sense. So they were well insured, from A to Z. Someone knew how to plan. Grace and the kids are provided for...at least for the near future. A hundred thousand is no fortune, but it'll stretch quite a ways, if you do it carefully."

"Right. Unless there's a crime involved. Vicente said his company is holding off until we're finished with our investigation. If it's murder, then Grace's only recourse is a civil action against the killer's estate."

I nodded. "Interesting. What else?"

Before he could answer, Sutherland and Johnson appeared at my elbow after heaving the last of the boxes back into the Dumpsters. I held up my hands helplessly. "Thanks, gentlemen. Sorry it didn't pay off."

With exquisite timing, the solid back door of the supermarket opened as the two deputies were driving off in Johnson's patrol car. Sam Carter raised a finger in salute and minced around the puddles toward Torrez and me.

"So," he said, "nothing?" He managed to sound disappointed.

"Nothing, Sam. But, as I said before, no big deal. I'm not going to lose any sleep over it."

"Well, if it turns up..." he said, and let the thought drift off. "Robert, how are you?" He stretched out his hand, and Torrez gave it a brief, polite pump, letting a nod suffice as an answer.

"Is Kenny still living at home?" the undersheriff asked, and the question was such an abrupt change of subject that for a few heartbeats Sam Carter went blank.

"Kenneth?"

"Yes. Your son."

The grocer's mental gears meshed and he nodded. "Oh, yeah. Well...I should say most of the time. When there's laundry for his mother to do, and when he gets hungry." Carter smiled lamely. "You know how they are. Why? I mean, why do you ask?"

Torrez tossed the black notebook back on the front seat of his car and then straightened up. He was a full head taller than Sam Carter, and he leaned his elbow on the roof of the patrol car and regarded the chairman of the county commission for a moment.

"He was spending quite a bit of time with Jennifer Sisson. I'd like to talk with him, see if I can clear up a few things."

Carter's head jerked with disapproval. "I guess there are probably a lot of girls that he spends time with, and as far as I know, the Sisson girl might well be one of them. I don't know. But what did you need to clear up? What kinds of things?"

"One of the deputies saw your son that night and Jennifer Sisson as well. There's a chance that they spent some time together. If there's even a remote possibility that Kenny knows something or heard something, then I need to talk to him."

Carter grimaced. "Yeah, yeah," he said. "You guys are really on a wild-goose chase with this one."

Torrez and I both looked at Carter with renewed interest.

"And now why is that, Sam?" I said.

"Well, Christ, the man got careless and dropped a big tire on himself. Everybody says that's what happened. Stupid thing to do, working late like that, bad light. Somebody told me they'd been arguing all day, so Jim's upset. Hell, I can see that. Stupid, stupid, stupid."

"Maybe so," I mused. "But until we clear up all the inconsistencies, then we're just going to plod along."

Sam Carter, chairman of the county commission and successful supermarket owner, drew himself up to his full five feet, eight inches and painted on his best sanctimonious face, the one he used in commission meetings when some worthy agency was asking for a budget increase. "Just remember, Sheriff, that you've got a widow and four children sitting at home. Don't plod too slowly."

"I'm sure they'll be well taken care of," I said.

Carter nodded slowly. "I'm asking the Posadas State Bank to initiate an account for them, so we have someplace to put donations."

"That's good." I didn't bother to add that it was going to be interesting to see just how much sympathy and goodwill Grace Sisson's acid tongue would reap. "She's got some close friends, I'm sure." I knew of one, but Taffy Hines didn't fit my description of a deep-pocketed financial benefactor.

"Where's Kenny working this summer? Out of town somewhere?" Bob Torrez asked.

"Yes, he is," Sam said. "He's got just a few weeks left until he goes back to school. He's working with LaCrosse, over in Deming."

"Then maybe I'll swing by this afternoon, when he gets home. You might tell him I need to talk with him." Torrez reached into his shirt pocket and pulled out a business card, handing it to Carter. "If I haven't seen him by the time you do, have him give me a call."

Carter nodded. "OK. I don't know what he can tell you, but I'll mention it to him."

When Carter had gone back inside, Torrez looked at me and grinned. "You want odds that Kenny Carter knocked up the Sisson kid?"

"No," I said. "And I wonder if Sam Carter knows."

"Probably not."

"Parents are usually the last ones to hear the joyous news," I said. "And I can't imagine that Kenny would have gone over to confront Jim Sisson, either. That doesn't fit what kids do."

"It's interesting that he works for LaCrosse, though."

"Which LaCrosse are you talking about?"

"LaCrosse Construction, over in Deming. Lots of heavy equipment." He smiled and opened the door of his car. "Good place for a little experience. Maybe the kid's got some talent with a backhoe that LaCrosse doesn't know about."

TWENTY-SEVEN

WE DIDN'T WAIT for the afternoon. Fifteen minutes after we left Sam Carter and his Dumpsters, we were headed up the ramp to the eastbound interstate and the thirty-minute jog to Deming.

It wasn't that Kenny Carter had jumped to the top of any suspect list we wished that we had. But trouble in the Sisson household either centered around or was at least exacerbated by daughter Jennifer. She was their own little tropical depression, waiting to blossom. Kenny Carter was right smack in the eye of Jennifer.

Years before—hell, decades and decades before—I had been half of the team that coped with four teenagers, including two daughters. And I suppose there had been times when I viewed any teenage boys other than my own who roamed near our home as potential predators who had my daughters' virtue in their sights.

Those days had passed, and both daughters had managed to survive adolescence, early loves and breakups, the stresses of college, and, finally, the early years of their own marriages without putting the family through seven versions of hell.

The Sissons hadn't been so lucky, if luck was what it took. The script for *Life with Jennifer* might have been enough to drive Jim out into the dark solitude of the backyard, where he could take his fury out on something that didn't talk back.

I could well imagine that if Jim Sisson had suspicions about Kenny Carter's relations with Jennifer and if young Kenny had wandered into the yard that night wanting to talk to his girlfriend's old man, then fireworks could well have followed.

If that scenario was true, one thing was certain: The boy hadn't hung around the Sisson premises afterward, holding the grieving Jennifer's hand. I couldn't remember the last time I'd actually seen Kenny Carter—and I certainly hadn't caught sight of him that night when we'd responded to the domestic dispute call. If he'd been there, the Sisson women, Jennifer included, were keeping mum. And that in itself was excuse enough for a chat with the lad.

I didn't know Kenneth Carter well. I could pick him out of a crowd of teens, but that was about all. I didn't know his habits. But he was a connection, tenuous as it might be. State Trooper Mike Rhodes knew a little of the relationship between his nephew and Jennifer, had seen them together enough that it had lodged in his memory. Sam Carter, the ever patient father, would probably be the last one to know—especially since he impressed me as the kind of father who wore pretty solid blinders when it came to his own kid.

"It's interesting," I said to Bob Torrez as we hurtled toward Deming, "that Kenny Carter didn't work for Sisson."

Torrez frowned. "Jim had two employees," he said. "And bank records show that he was overextended. So I don't know. One more wage, even at minimum, might have been more than he could take."

"How much extended?"

"For this last financial quarter he had to take out a small loan just to meet the payroll obligations...let alone anything else."

"You haven't wasted any time," I said.

"Judge Hobart was cooperative, as usual." Torrez grinned. "And so was Penny Arguile, at the bank, once the court order was processed that allowed us in to look at the records."

"Any big creditors knocking at the door?"

Torrez shook his head. "It seems to me more like a gradual buildup. Sort of like a rockslide. First a pebble or two, then some bigger, then bigger, then bigger. Pretty soon Jim's got the whole hillside crashing down on top of him." He glanced over at me. "With some help, of course."

"Grace Sisson was concerned about that," I said. "That new front loader was one of the first things she mentioned when we talked to her this afternoon in Cruces. I would guess the damn thing was a bone of contention between Jim and her."

"A twenty-seven-thousand-dollar bone," Torrez agreed. "God knows what a new machine that size would cost, but a used one is bad enough. The bank records show it's an '82 model. Twenty-

seven grand for a piece of machinery that's eighteen years old."
He shook his head in wonder.

"Did you talk with Penny about that loan in particular?"

"She said the bank floated the paper with 'some misgivings.'
They let Jim sign a five-year note, and she said that was longer
than the bank likes to go. He asked for ten, but they refused."

"So on top of everything else, on top of all his other debts, on
top of his payroll, he's paying out a chunk of money every month
for that loan."

"Five hundred and twenty-eight dollars and eleven cents, give
or take. That's at nine point seven five percent interest."

"Jesus. He must have been planning to move a lot of dirt to pay
for that."

"Among other things, he was one of the bidders on the village's
project to extend the water line back behind your place, over on
Escondido."

"That's nickel-dime stuff, though. A single ditch, maybe a mile
of pipe at the most. A few trees to knock over, a little arroyo to
fill. That's if he won the bid in the first place. The profit from the
whole job wouldn't pay for one year's payments on that machine."

Torrez shrugged. "Maybe he was one of those folks who just
loved machines."

I shifted against the seat belt so I could rest my right elbow on
the windowsill. "And young Kenny? What do we know about
him?"

"We know that if he's very lucky, he might graduate next year.
He's about a year behind, give or take."

I looked at Torrez with surprise. "I didn't know that."

"An active social calendar." Torrez grinned. "According to the
principal, the kid has taken about all the vocational courses the
school has to offer."

"Which isn't much."

"No. But that means Kenny's stuck with taking stuff like history
and English and science if he wants to graduate."

"Well, gee, what a shame," I said. "And probably math...and
stuff. How unfair can you get. He can't just weld himself out of
high school. At least he's stuck with it so far. He hasn't dropped
out."

"So far."

"And Jennifer Sisson is going to be a sophomore."

Torrez nodded. "If she stays in school."

"They'll be a cute couple along about February," I said. "What other names do we have?"

"Jim Sisson's two employees. Aurelio Baca has been with him for almost ten years and Rudy Alvaro is going on three. Both good, steady men. I don't know too much about Baca except that he's on a green card and lives just across the border, in Palomas. He's got his own small plumbing business that he runs down there, on the side."

"And Rudy?"

"He used to work for the village before he went over to Sisson's. He's one of my wife's cousins."

"Why doesn't that surprise me," I said. "Did both men work Tuesday?"

Torrez nodded. "Baca left for Palomas at about ten after five. Rudy was still finishing up a few things over at the Randall job at six. He went straight home from there. He helped Jim trailer the front loader."

"Did he come back to the yard to help him take it off?"

"He told me that Jim said he didn't need to come back to the yard, that Jim thought that he could do it just fine by himself."

"So nothing about either Baca or Alvaro piques your curiosity," I said. "No loose ends?"

Torrez shook his head. "Not a thing."

"Had Jim ever missed a payroll?"

"Nope. The Sissons have been rotating their utilities for a while—make the phone wait a month, then make the electric stand in line—but they've paid both Baca and Alvaro each week."

"Huh." I let my head slump back against the headrest. In the distance I could see the flat spread of buildings that marked Deming. "You think we're wrong about this?"

"About Sisson's death not being an accident, you mean? Not a chance, sir. Not a chance." He glanced in the mirror and let the car drift into the right lane.

"People have been crushed accidentally by things like that before."

"Yes, sir, I'm sure they have. Heavy equipment thinks up all kinds of neat ways to kill the operator. And if Jim had been found right close to the machine, maybe crushed up against the axle or something, I might have believed it. But not this way. The distances don't make sense for it to have happened solo. My gut feeling is that someone took an opportunity, figuring that any investigation would just take the easy route. Big machine, dangerous wheel and tire combination, careless chain hookup. A dozen ways an accident could happen. But..." He stopped and thumped the rim of the steering wheel with the heel of his hand. "If I'm wrong, you can let Leona Spears have the job in November."

"Don't say that, even in jest," I said.

TWENTY-EIGHT

LaCrosse Construction was as large and evidently successful as Jim Sisson's firm was small and struggling. The LaCrosse headquarters was a low, white stucco building about the same size as Sam Carter's supermarket, a stone's throw from the railroad track on the east edge of town.

Behind the building loomed the stone crusher tower where LaCrosse brewed its own batches of concrete. Dotted around the crusher like small mountain ranges were enormous piles of sand, gravel, crusher fines, even shiny black asphalt. Off to the west were thousands of railroad ties, neatly bundled, the old creosote fragrant in the hot sun.

Four concrete delivery trucks, their huge revolving drums sparkling clean and white, were parked fender-to-fender, with room for another half-dozen in the row.

"Some bucks here," I observed. "LaCrosse probably does more miles of highway each year than any five of his competitors." I cranked my neck around, surveying the huge yard behind the office building. "Not a soul here, either."

We parked in front of a windowless white doorway, immediately behind a late-model white Ford three-quarter-ton truck with the blue oval logo of LaCrosse Construction Company on its doors.

The sun bounced off the white building as I stepped onto the sidewalk, a solid blast of heat and light that made me gasp. I opened the door to a second blast, this one straight from the Arctic. LaCrosse hadn't wasted time or space with foyers or receptionists sitting prettily at desks. Instead, we entered the building and found ourselves in a hallway with offices to either side, all but one of the doors closed.

The door had no sooner thudded closed behind us, locking in

the frigid air, than a chunky woman appeared from the first door on the left.

"Hi, guys," she said, and grinned as if we'd just made her whole day. "Don'tcha wish we'd get some warm weather soon, eh?"

I smiled. "Nice in here, though." I stepped forward and extended my hand. "I'm Sheriff Bill Gastner from Posadas County. This is Undersheriff Robert Torrez."

She pumped first my hand and then Bob's. "And I'm EllenFae LaCrosse. What can we do for you?" She had that air of bustle and self-confidence that went with the name. A door opened farther down the hall, and two men wearing hard hats appeared and then walked away from us down the hall without a backward glance.

"Mrs. LaCrosse, we need to visit with Kenny Carter, if that's possible. We won't take much of his time."

"Kenny?" She looked down at the floor for a moment, hands on her hips. She was short and stubby, maybe on the downside of fifty, with smooth, creamy, flawless skin that hadn't been baked to leather from a lifetime of sitting outdoors on machinery.

"Kenny Carter," I said. "He's one of your summer kids."

She looked up, grinning. "Oh, for sure I know who he is. God, we've known his family forever. No, I'm just trying to remember where he was working today. I think he's over on Route Eleven." She reached out a hand as if I were drifting away and she needed to reel me back in. "Let me go double-check."

"We'd appreciate it," I said.

She turned and bustled off, disappearing through the same doorway the men had used a moment before. She was gone not more than twenty seconds before reappearing and beckoning us into the inner sanctum.

The office was a sea of desks, computers, and drafting tables. Two men were in conference at one of the tables, and they glanced up at us with mild curiosity.

EllenFae LaCrosse led us to a large map of Luna County that was spread out on one of the tables. "The crew he's with is right here," she said, and with a shapely finger traced New Mexico 11 south out of Deming. "Just a couple miles the other side of Sunshine," she said, and grinned again. "They're putting in a road off to the east, up to that fancy horse barn that the Gunderson group is building.''

''That should be easy to find,'' I said.

She rolled up the map efficiently and thrust it in a boot on the side of one of the tables. ''We like to keep the high school kids a little closer to home,'' she said. ''That way there's not so much travel time for 'em.''

''I'm sure they appreciate that,'' I said.

''Well, it works for us,'' Mrs. LaCrosse said. ''He's a nice boy, and a hard worker, if that's the sort of information you're looking for.''

I nodded. ''We appreciate that,'' I said, and Bob Torrez and I followed her out of the room. More as an attempt to forestall the blast furnace outside for a few more seconds, I stopped with my hand on the knob and turned to EllenFae LaCrosse. ''How many kids do you folks hire during the summer season?''

Without hesitation, she said, ''Right now, we have eight kiddos working for us. And that's a full contingent. They're good workers, but you know the labor laws. We're so restricted by insurance and what all about what we can use them for that we have to be kind of careful.'' She smiled again. ''I know that a lot of the guys like Kenny. He's a quick study. I know that Pete's made him an offer to go full-time just as soon as he graduates.''

''Great opportunity,'' I said.

She nodded. ''We're always on the lookout for the good ones,'' she said. ''And we've known Kenny for years, of course.'' Her brow furrowed slightly. ''It's none of my business, I know. But I hope he's not in trouble of some sort.''

''We just need to chat with him, ma'am. He might be a possible witness to an incident that needs to be cleared up, is all.''

''Well, that's good.'' She nodded vigorously.

I started to turn the knob. The polished stainless steel was warm to the touch, passing the heat through from the outside. ''How did Kenny happen to come to work for you folks? It's a good commute from Posadas over here every day.''

''Oh, we've known the Carters for light-years,'' she said. ''Sam and Pete go way back.''

''I didn't know that.''

She nodded. "Back in the stone ages, Sam and Pete were part-ners, up in Albuquerque. And then things got so expensive, with so much competition, that they moved out of that rat race and came south." She grinned and leaned closer. "Sam got smart and took up another line of work. Pete stayed out in the sun, sniffing those diesel fumes."

I laughed, trying to keep the surprise off my face. "He hasn't done so badly," I said. "Thanks for your help."

THE VINYL CAR SEATS were damn near molten, and Bob switched the air conditioner to high with all four windows down to purge the heat.

"New and interesting," I said.

"Sir?"

"I've lived in Posadas for damn near thirty years, and I never knew that Sam Carter had been in the construction business before he started to sell milk, butter, and eggs."

"I can't imagine him wanting to get his hands dirty," Torrez said. "He doesn't seem like the contractor type."

"At least not anymore."

We reached the intersection with New Mexico 11 and turned south, the country flat, hot, and bleak ahead of us. "Maybe he just ran the books," I added, and took a deep breath. "I get the feeling we're on a giant lizard chase, Robert." I held up my hands in frustration. "If Sam Carter knew that his kid had knocked up Jen-nifer Sisson, I just can't picture him taking the initiative to visit Jim and have a parent-to-parent discussion. I can see Jim driving over to Carter's and busting him in the chops, but not vice versa. And I don't see the son stepping forward. So what's left?"

Torrez shrugged.

"We're missing something, somewhere." I watched the heat-tortured shrubs glide by outside the window of the car.

"Something simple," Torrez said after a moment. "That's what it seems to always be. Something simple."

TWENTY-NINE

AFTER A MOMENT, I could look beyond a slight bend in the highway—perhaps put there by the builder for artistic reasons—and see in the distance a collection of machinery and trucks parked near a dirt road that took off to the east. From what I could make out, the entire desert was crisscrossed with dirt roads, a grid that looked like some optimistic soul expected a sea of houses to sprout out of the sand someday.

As we drew closer, I could see a large yellow backhoe working, a section of shiny metal culvert suspended from its bucket with a length of chain. A worker walked with the machine and its load, one hand on the end of the culvert so that it wouldn't pendulum.

"I don't see the kid," I said as we slowed to a crawl.

"Nope," Torrez said. He swung the car onto the shoulder of the road and stopped. One of the workers waved instructions at the other men, then headed toward us. Torrez ignored him and instead twisted around with an old pair of military binoculars in his hand, looking off to the west. I saw a faint smile twitch the corners of his mouth.

"Help you fellas?" the man said, and leaned down, putting both hands on the driver's side door.

Torrez turned, dropped the binoculars on the seat, and lounged one wrist over the steering wheel as if he had all the time in the world. "The home office tells us that Kenny Carter is working out here," he said.

The man nodded. "Was." His eyes flicked over to me and then back to the undersheriff.

Torrez looked on down the road toward Columbus and then Palomas, across the Mexican border. "But he's done for the day or what?"

The man straightened up and hitched his trousers a little closer to his impressive belly. "He told me he had a family emergency," the man said.

Bob turned and looked at him. He could read the name over the man's pocket better than I could. "Well, Paul..."

"Paul Turner."

"Paul, what time was this family emergency? They must have called him from the Deming office, unless he walks around with his own cell phone in his jeans."

Paul looked a touch uncomfortable, having been trapped into implicating his boss. He settled for vague. "Well, I guess they did. He left some time ago."

"Going home to Posadas?"

"He didn't say."

The man stepped back and looked down at the decal on the door of the patrol car, realizing for the first time that we weren't locals. He was about to say something when I leaned over and asked, "Mrs. LaCrosse told us that the kid was out here. You have the office number handy?"

I had the cell phone in my hand, and Paul Turner obviously didn't like being caught in the middle. He pulled a business card out of his pocket and handed it across to me. "Number's on there."

"Dandy," I said, and punched it in. After four or five rings, a pleasant voice announced that I'd reached LaCrosse Construction. "EllenFae LaCrosse, please," I said. "Sheriff Bill Gastner calling. We were there just a few minutes ago."

In a moment, Mrs. LaCrosse came on the line. "Yes, Sheriff?"

"Mrs. LaCrosse, is Kenny Carter in the office?"

There was a pause, and then she said, "Well, no, he's not. Are you calling from the job site?"

"Yes. And he's not here. Apparently after you called out here, he took off. I just thought he might have headed back to the office."

"No, he didn't do that."

"Mrs. LaCrosse, let me ask you something." I glanced over at Paul Turner. He was leaning on the car, head down, looking studiously at the gravel at his feet. "Why did you bother to call out here before we had a chance to talk with the kid?"

"Well, I...well, I thought that if the boys knew you were going to drive all the way out there, they wouldn't send Kenny off on some errand so you'd run the risk of missing him. After driving all that way, I mean.''

I chuckled. ''Slick, ma'am. Thanks for your help.''

She'd started to say something else when I hung up. ''Let's go.''

Bob smiled pleasantly at Paul Turner. ''Where's that road go?''

The man glanced up briefly. ''Oh, just on over to the other side of the block. This whole area's gridded.''

''So if I went that way, I'd hit a road that would take me back to Deming?''

The man nodded, noncommittal. ''Faster, easier just to go back the way you come. On the pavement.''

Torrez nodded. ''Sure enough.'' He pulled the car into gear. ''Thanks.''

The man waved a couple of fingers and trudged back to the ditch and the new culvert.

Torrez turned the car around and accelerated hard, heading back north on the paved highway. After a minute, he said, ''Nobody passed us coming out.''

''What's the kid driving, do you know?''

''He's got a red '97 Jeep Wrangler,'' Torrez said, and pointed off to the west. ''I can't tell if that one's red or not, but I'm willing to bet.''

I squinted, trying hard, and saw a lot of blue sky, roiling white clouds building heavenward, and tan prairie. If I let my imagination play, I could pretend that I saw a thin, wispy vapor trail of dust kicked up by a speeding vehicle. ''You think he cut back on one of the side roads?''

''Yes, I do. I don't think he wants to talk to us much, and I don't think he's going to show up this afternoon at the office.'' He turned and grinned at me. ''Mama LaCrosse back in Deming must have called the instant we stepped out the door.''

''If that's the case, turning tail isn't the smartest stunt that kid's ever pulled. She should know that.''

''We'll see,'' Torrez murmured. I glanced over at him and saw the intent hunter's expression that meant Bob Torrez was having his own version of fun. ''It won't be hard to catch up with him once he's on the interstate.''

We entered the southern outskirts of Deming and in a couple minutes saw that fun wasn't in the cards for Kenny Carter. We turned onto the main drag and immediately saw the winking lights of a Deming patrol car up ahead a couple of blocks, snugged into the curb behind a red Jeep. Bob had plenty of time and eased over to the curb well back, out of view.

"You sure that's him?" I asked. "There are a lot of red Jeeps in this world."

"I'd be willing to bet," Torrez said, and he slid the cellular phone out of its boot on the dash. "I'd be just as happy if he didn't know we were here just yet." It took a moment for Information to find the Deming PD's nonemergency number, and Torrez dialed. I listened with amusement as he then said, "Jerry?... Hey, glad you're workin' today. This is Bob Torrez... Yeah. Hey, one of your units just stopped a red Jeep Wrangler west of the intersection with Route Eleven. Who do you show that vehicle registered to?"

He paused and listened and turned toward me, grinning. "That's what I thought." He shook his head. "No, just curious, is all. We're following him on in to Posadas on another deal. We don't want to talk to him, and he doesn't need to know that we're here."

He listened again and laughed. "Hell no, don't let him off. Give the little son of a bitch a ticket." I could hear chatter on the other end, and Torrez looked heavenward. "Thanks, guy. You and Sadie come over one of these days. Bring Lolo with you."

He switched off and racked the phone. "It's him."

"So I gathered. It's handy, being related to half of the Southwest," I said. "Who's Jerry?"

"Jerry Pellitier. I knew he worked days on Dispatch, but it was just luck he was on today."

"A cousin?"

"No relation."

"That's amazing in itself."

Torrez shrugged, eyes locked on the blinking lights ahead. "His wife is Sadie, formerly Sadie Quintana."

"Ah," I said. "The wife's a relative. Let me guess—a cousin."

"Nope. Sadie is actually some distant relation to my wife, but I don't know what. They lived in Posadas for a few months, and Gayle's sister—Irma?—she did some day care for them when she wasn't busy with the Guzmans. Their kid, Lolo, is about three or so."

After a few minutes, we saw the Deming officer climb back out of the patrol car, ticket book in hand. He handed the ticket to Kenny Carter and pointed on down the road, no doubt telling the kid to keep a lid on it. Even as the cop was walking back toward the patrol car, the Jeep pulled away from the curb without signaling and accelerated away.

Torrez let him have a thousand-yard head start, then pulled out into traffic. With his head buried in paperwork, the Deming cop didn't notice us as we slid by.

For the rest of the trip to Posadas, Kenny Carter kept the Jeep just a shade over eighty—close enough to the interstate speed limit that a trooper wasn't apt to bother him but fast enough to say, *"So there, a ticket don't matter to me."*

We stayed far enough back that he wouldn't recognize the vehicle in his jiggling rearview mirror, and more than once I had the uneasy feeling that we should stop playing cat and mouse and just stop Carter so that we could talk. About ten miles east of Posadas, I said as much to Torrez.

"The trouble is," I said, "we haven't talked to this kid yet—not since Jim Sisson's death. In fact, not at all, before or after. We don't know what's on his mind. He might be innocent as the driven snow."

Torrez shot a glance at me as if to say, *"You know better than that,"* but instead settled for, "That's a fact, sir."

"We don't know for sure if he's the father of Jennifer Sisson's child."

"No, we don't. But he's a place to start. He's been seen with her, and Mike Rhodes says they've spent some time together."

"He's a place to start, sure enough. I'm just not sure deliberately spooking him like this is going to be productive."

"I don't think he knows we're here, sir."

"How could he not?"

"No, I mean he doesn't know that we're sitting here, a quarter of a mile behind him, watching. He thinks he's given us the slip. As long as that's the case, I think we've got something to gain by just being patient, seeing where he's headed in such a hurry."

"Straight home to Daddy is my guess," I said.

"You think Sam would cover for him?"

"Of course he'd cover for him, Robert. Get a grip."

"That's going to make it interesting," Torrez muttered.

"Doubly so if Taffy Hines's intuition is correct."

"Taffy Hines? About what?"

"Carter couldn't keep the Pasquale letter to himself. He showed it to Taffy, at the store. She said her first thought was that Sam wrote it himself. She told him so. Needless to say, he said he hadn't. He blames Leona Spears."

"Leona never wrote an unsigned letter in her sorry life," Torrez said. He let the car coast as we approached the Posadas exit. "Old Sam keeps it up, he's going to have a full menu."

THIRTY

KENNY CARTER'S JEEP left the interstate and headed up Posadas's Grande Avenue. I half-expected to see the kid turn on MacArthur, aiming for his sweetheart's, but apparently the love of his life—if we were right about the kids—wasn't the first thing on his mind. The Jeep pulled up into the parking lot of the Family SuperMarket. We drove by just in time to see the Jeep swing around back, into the alley.

"You want to give them some time?" Bob Torrez asked.

"No, I don't," I said. "What I want is some answers."

Torrez parked the patrol car on the north side of the store, next to Sam Carter's black Explorer.

As the automatic doors swung open to greet us, Taffy Hines looked up from register one, black marker in hand. She had what looked like a proof of the weekly full-page grocery ad spread out on the conveyor. A weekday midmorning obviously wasn't hustle time for shoppers.

With a slight smile, she pointed over her shoulder with the marker. "His Nibs is in the office," she said. "I assume that's who you want to see, unless you're here to actually buy something." She grinned good-naturedly.

"Thanks," I said. "We need to see Sam." I stepped close to her and paused. "I'm sorry if you're getting sucked into this mess."

Taffy straightened up, marker poised. "Sheriff," she said, voice even and low, "I could really care less. You just do what you have to do."

"I appreciate that," I said, reaching out to touch her lightly on the forearm. If he bothered to look, Sam Carter could see us through his mirrored observation window, so I didn't bother with subtlety, didn't bother trying to make the visit look as if we'd just dropped by to pass the time of day or to check bargains on cookies.

As I opened the swinging door with the EMPLOYEES ONLY sign, Kenny Carter was coming down the back stairs from the office. He saw Torrez and me and stopped on the bottom step. His shoulders sagged just a touch, and he leaned against the wall.

"How you doin', Kenny," I said. He straightened up and glanced toward the exit door at the rear of the building. "Nobody's going to bother your Jeep, son. Can we talk for a minute or two?"

Sam Carter emerged from the office door and stood on the narrow landing at the top of the steps.

"What have you got to tell me?" he said.

I shrugged. "I think it's time we had a little chat, Sam." I stepped forward toward the stairs, giving Kenny the choice of blocking my path, trying to bolt past me, or retreating uphill. The stairs were too narrow for both of us. He retreated, and Torrez and I trudged up the stairway behind him.

"Come on in," Carter muttered. "I've got a lot of things I need to be doing, so I hope this won't take too long."

He sat down in his chair by the idling computer and waved a hand toward a single straight-backed chair over by the bookcase. The row of catalogs and binders threatened to explode off the shelf, and I pulled the chair out so I wouldn't be caught in the avalanche.

Kenny stood by the corner of his father's desk, trying his best to look unflustered. He wasn't very good at it. He toyed with a can of soda that I guessed he'd brought up from the Jeep, took a perfunctory sip or two, and then set the can on the narrow windowsill. Maybe it was Bob Torrez's towering presence that made Kenny nervous. If he wanted to bolt out the door, he'd have to go through the undersheriff, and that clearly wasn't going to work.

"Let's just cut right to it, Sam." I shifted on the chair, trying to avoid the crack in the wooden seat.

"I'd welcome that," he said, and I knew he didn't mean it.

"Kenny here knows the Sisson family, and he had contact with them recently."

"Now how do we know that?" Carter snapped.

I sighed. "Sam, I think now is the time to stop playing the games, all right? We're not all blind and deaf. We talk to people.

We know that Jennifer Sisson is pregnant, and we know that particular situation has to be partly responsible for some of the hell that family has been through recently.''

Carter started to shift in his chair, and I leaned forward, watching his face closely.

"And it's no secret that Kenny here has been keeping company with the young lady," I added, turning to Kenny. "Am I right?"

He bit his lip and took a bit too long to nod agreement, as if he needed the time to calculate his odds. He was a pretty good-looking kid, lanky and tough, with a bit more height and weight than his father and some of his mother's darker complexion.

"So then. It doesn't take a rocket scientist to put it together." I leaned back, regarding Kenny. "More than one person assumes that you're the father of Jennifer Sisson's child. What do you say?"

"Now who says she's pregnant?" Sam Carter barked, the first to be about two steps behind.

"You're going to tell us that she's not?" Bob Torrez said quietly.

Sam jerked around as if he'd been touched with a cattle prod, and he glared at Torrez.

"Well..."

"And it really doesn't matter who told us, does it?"

"Of course it matters," Carter exploded. "Jesus, you can't just go around spreading rumors like that, getting people all worked up."

"Yes, she's pregnant," Kenny Carter said before his father had a chance to take another breath. "So what."

"Listen, Son—" Sam started, but Bob cut him off.

"The fact that Jennifer is or isn't pregnant doesn't matter, Kenny. At least not to us. At least not yet. What matters is that we find the person who killed James Sisson."

"What, and you think that my son knows something about that? Don't be ridiculous. And for one thing, nobody's even proved it to be murder yet. It's just all theory on your part. Lots of publicity."

Torrez pushed himself away from the door and walked to the desk. His head was a scant inch below the ceiling fixture. "Earlier this morning, Kenny, we drove to your job site south of Deming, as you well know. When Mrs. LaCrosse called out there and tipped you off, you ran back here as fast as your little Jeep could go, short of getting a second traffic ticket.'' He stopped and grinned at the expression on Kenny Carter's face.

"Yeah," Torrez added, "it's a small world. But for starters, let's establish some relationships. Jennifer Sisson is pregnant—everyone seems to agree on that. Are you the father?"

"Now listen," Sam Carter said, but Torrez held up a hand.

"No, I'm not," Kenny said from between clenched teeth. "I don't know who knocked her up, but it wasn't me."

"All right." Torrez nodded pleasantly. "Fair enough. How do you know it wasn't you?"

"Oh, for Christ's sakes," Sam said, and he managed to find a small clear area in the landfill that was his desk so that he could slap the desktop with the flat of his hand. "What the hell does it matter, anyway? Whether the boy is or isn't?" A vein pulsed on the side of his neck, and he was red enough to have spent the whole day out in the sun. "Hell, Kenny, tell 'em the truth, if that's what they want to hear."

"I told them the truth."

"And on Tuesday night, did you have occasion to go over to the Sissons' place?" I asked.

"No."

"You didn't go over and talk to Jim Sisson?"

"No."

"Did you know whether or not Jim knew that his daughter was pregnant?"

"I wouldn't know. But I don't see how he couldn't know."

"Did you know what Jim's reaction to that news might be?"

"How could I know that? If I was him, I'd be pissed. She's only fifteen, or something. What do you expect?"

"Would he blame you, do you think?"

"Yes. And that's what a couple of the guys told me. Jennifer was telling her friends that it was me. Like she was proud of getting knocked up, or something. But I don't know for sure. I haven't talked to him in a while. If he was all mad at me, that's the last place I wanted to go."

"Were you on friendly-enough terms with him before?"

"I guess."

"You guess," I said. "When was the last time you talked with Jim Sisson?"

He frowned. For once Sam Carter kept his mouth shut. He gazed at his son, face flushed with anger. "Last week, maybe."

"That recently?"

"Something like that. Jennifer and me had an argument and broke up. At least we hadn't talked in a while. I was figuring that maybe we could get back together, you know? I mean...you know. I like her. I'd see her out on the street, but she wasn't about to talk to me. I saw Jim comin' out of the auto parts place one day last week, when I was goin' in. I think it was Saturday, maybe. He was like, 'I haven't seen you around in a while,' and I said, 'No, I think Jenny's mad at me for something,' and he was all, 'Well, that's how women are,' and then he asked me where I was workin', and I told him LaCrosse's, and he said that was good. And that was it."

"So he knew that you'd been going out with Jennifer?" I asked.

"Sure, he knew."

"And that was the last time you saw him alive? Last Saturday?"

Kenny Carter nodded.

Torrez rested his hands on his utility belt. "And at that time did you know that Jennifer was pregnant?"

"Nope. And I don't think Mr. Sisson did, either. If he had, he wouldn't have been all calm and everything."

"When did you hear that she was pregnant?"

"A friend of mine that talked to a friend of hers called me and told me."

"When was that?"

Kenny Carter shrugged. "I don't know. A day or so before her dad—"

"Maybe Sunday then? Maybe Saturday? It was after you saw Jim coming out of the store?"

"Yeah...it was after that."

Torrez shook his head slowly. "Kenny, if we drove over to the Sissons' right now and asked Jennifer who the father of her child was, what do you think she'd say?"

The kid's expression was bleak. "I don't know what she'd say," he said. "I just know it wasn't me. And I don't know why she'd blame me, neither."

"Give me a reason to believe that," I said.

He looked at me for a long time, longer than most kids his age bother to think about anything. "Jennifer and me...well, the last time we...were together was early June. Like about the fifth or so. I remember 'cause I started with LaCrosse the next day, and Jennifer was sore 'cause I was going to be workin' out of town."

"And that's the better part of seven weeks ago," I said.

Kenny almost smiled. "And knowin' Jenny, the second she knew she was pregnant, she'd blab it to her friends. That's the way she is. Got to have something to talk about. Nothin' much embarrasses her. And I know she wouldn't wait for no two months to go by before she said something."

"Maybe she wasn't sure at the time," I said.

Kenny glanced at me sideways. "Yeah," he said, but didn't elaborate.

"But she never actually called you, is that right?" Torrez asked.

"Nope. I ain't talked to her in probably three weeks."

I pushed myself to my feet. "Interesting," I said, and reached across the desk to the windowsill. I picked up Kenny Carter's soda can by the bottom rim. "Mind?"

He shook his head.

"Kenny, I want you to understand the serious nature of all this," I said, and held up the can. "You can cooperate with us or not, just as you see fit. But a simple DNA test can establish whether or not you're the father of that child. That way, we know that we have the story straight." I didn't bother to tell the kid that a DNA test was neither simple nor even a remote possibility.

"I'm telling you the truth," he said. "I don't know what an empty can of Coke is going to tell you, but I ain't lying."

"So that's where we stand at the moment," I said, nodding. "You want to tell us why you took off when you heard we were driving out?"

Kenny shot a quick glance over at his father, then at me. "I don't know. I guess I just panicked, is all."

"Just because we wanted to talk to you is cause to panic?"

"Well, I figured it was something serious, with you driving all the way down to Deming to see me."

I turned and said to Sam, "Anything else you want to tell us, Sam?"

He got to his feet, careful not to kick the overloaded trash can. "The sooner this ridiculous cat-and-mouse game is over, the happier I'll be. I still say it was an accident that killed Jim Sisson, nothing else."

"Maybe so, Sam, maybe so."

Bob Torrez hadn't finished, though. He reached across the desk and picked a cigarette butt out of the ashtray, holding it by the crushed, burned end. "You mind?"

"There's fresh ones you could buy down by the registers," Sam Carter said.

"No thanks. But as long as we're running DNA tests on lip cells, we might as well cover all the bases." Sam's eyes narrowed, and any goodwill he might have harbored for Robert Torrez vanished. And he didn't rise to the bait.

I smiled. "Thanks for your time."

I took my time heading down the stairs, trying to keep the damn treads in focus around the bifocals. Out at the car, Bob Torrez dug a couple of plastic bags out of his briefcase and sacked the can in one and the cigarette butt in the other.

"Sam was pissed," he said.

"Sure enough," I replied. "If it turns out that the kid's lying, he's going to be more than pissed. Why the butt?"

I damn near fell into the passenger seat, always surprised when my insomnia-driven body decided it was time to poop out. Torrez stowed the two evidence bags carefully in his briefcase and snapped the lid shut.

"I guess I did that just to tweak Sam a little more, give him something else to think about," he said. "Ah, I probably shouldn't have." He grimaced. "It's the idea of the thing, see. If I was to mention to someone that we were running a paternity test on Sam Carter, well..."

I grinned at Bob and he shrugged and added, "Imagine the political miles that kind of rumor is worth. I wouldn't do it, of course, but Sam doesn't know that. A little worry is good for him."

"I never thought of you as devious before, Robert," I said.

"Me, neither."

THIRTY-ONE

I THOUGHT WE'D MADE some progress with our fishing. For one thing, my large gut's feeling was that Kenny Carter was lying. He was just too goddamn earnest and believable to be believed. And Bob Torrez agreed.

But since neither Jennifer Sisson nor her mother was protesting Kenny's suspected paternity up and down the street, the kid had good reason to stonewall us until we could sledgehammer some holes in his defenses. The trouble was, I didn't have a clue about how we might do that.

If he was lying about fathering Jennifer's child, then there was a good chance some connection existed between him and Jim Sisson that Kenny didn't want us sniffing into, and that idea intrigued me.

All of this seemed a profitable avenue to explore, if we could find a way, especially since we didn't appear to have any others.

Bob Torrez dropped me off at the office, remarking that after a quick errand or two, he wanted to head south toward the little village of Regal and "check my freezer." I knew what that meant. We all had our worry sites—I suppose my personal favorite was the booth at the Don Juan de Oñate Restaurant. Robert, the unrelenting hunter, liked to cruise the boonies, watching the game animals that he would hunt come fall. I could imagine that as he sat on some knoll with binoculars glued to his eyes watching the phantoms of antelope or elk in the distance the problems of the day might sift into some perspective.

As I walked into the office, I toyed with my own important decision—lunch or a nap. I checked my mailbox and found the ubiquitous Post-it note, this time telling me that Judge Lester Hobart had called. His office was no more than a hundred yards from mine, over in the new east wing of the Public Safety Building. But with the good judge's gout, a walk of even a few yards was torture for him. I crumpled up the note, wondering if the judge had received his own version of the Pasquale letter, and went to return the call.

Violet Davies, the court administrator, answered the phone.

"Violet," I said, "this is Gastner. What's new in your life?" I could picture her pretty face framed with all the tight blond curls, breaking into the easy, bright smile that made nasty court appearances just a touch more pleasant for so many people.

"You wouldn't believe it if I told you," she giggled. "Ah, well..." She let that thought drift off.

"Just one of those days?" I could hear a voice or two in the background. Her office was sort of like a nurses' station in the hospital, open to the hallway that led to the courtroom's back door, the judge's chambers, and the other county offices beyond, but partially corralled by a low counter where she met the public.

"Well, we've had company most of the morning. Really interesting company. You got the judge's note?"

"Yes."

"He'd like to meet you for lunch, if that's possible."

"Sure enough possible. Will you join us?"

She laughed. "No, thanks. I'll keep Carla company."

"I beg your pardon?"

Her voice dropped a bit. "Carla Champlin's been sitting out in the hall all morning. She said she's going to sit there until the judge signs a court order evicting one of her tenants."

"Lucky you," I said. "She bent my ear a day or so ago, but I guess that didn't do any good. Did you tell her to bring a pillow? My guess is that it's going to be a long wait."

"Oh, sure," Violet said. "You come over and tell her that."

"Nope. Did the judge say where he wanted to escape to?"

"He asked that you meet him at the country club at twelve-thirty, if that's going to be possible for you."

"I can do that," I said, and groaned inwardly.

"He said it was his treat," Violet added, and I grinned. After nearly thirty years, the judge knew my habits, even if he didn't share my enthusiasm for Mexican food.

"Well, tell His Honor to sneak out the back door. I'm on my way."

"I'll do that," she said. "And so will he."

I could picture Carla Champlin, ramrod straight, jaw thrust out pugnaciously, sitting on the blond oak bench under the display of western paintings by various county artists. Maybe after a few more hours her bony butt would hurt enough that she'd go away. Or maybe she'd overheard Violet and even at that moment was planning to join the judge and me for lunch.

I suppose I was a touch annoyed with Carla, too. I'd told her that I would talk to Pasquale, and I had. She wasn't allowing much time for success before badgering someone else. But if she wanted to sit in the courthouse hallway, that was her call. She could talk to the potted plants. I'd rather have a conversation with a good green chili burrito.

The Posadas Country Club was less than two years old, and despite the grand implications of its name, it was no more than a nine-hole patch of irrigated sand, rattlesnakes, and Bermuda grass. The club sported a restaurant—Vic's Place—in what long ago had been one of the county's maintenance barns. Renovated and painted with a jazzy new hung ceiling, the clubhouse and restaurant still smelled vaguely of old hydraulic fluid and rubber.

Shortly after its grand opening, I'd eaten the worst chicken salad of my life at Vic's Place—cold, slimy, and reptilian. I was no golfer, so it wasn't hard to avoid a repeat of that culinary adventure. As far as I could tell, the quality of the restaurant matched that of the rest of the club.

The wind usually blew so hard that I guessed it was possible to tee off from the first launch pad and whack the ball all the way across nine holes to the parking lot of Posadas High School on South Pershing Street.

But golfers were ecstatic to have a spot closer than Deming to play, and they took the snakes, goat heads, and wind in stride. When Vic's Place had somehow managed to find a brand-new liquor license, the restaurant with the awful chicken salad had become a sort of watering hole for "who's who" in Posadas—or for who wanted to be who. It was an out-of-the-way spot for Judge Hobart to feed his gout.

I drove down Grande to Country Club Road and turned right past a short block of apartments and then the sprawl of Posadas High School. What had once been a gently rolling short-grass prairie was now a nine-holer, watered just enough that the grass on the putting greens remained an alkali-bleached, sickly ochre.

I parked beside the judge's white minivan and noticed the assistant district attorney's Corvette nestled off in the corner in the shade of a single valiant elm tree.

Inside Vic's Place, the air conditioning was cranked to maximum. As my eyes adjusted, I could see Judge Hobart across the dining room, seated with Don Jaramillo under the display of historic golf clubs.

"Afternoon, gentlemen," I said.

With a glass in one hand, the judge waved at the chair beside Jaramillo.

"Seat yourself," the judge said, and reached out a hand. I shook, and felt joints older and more arthritic than my own. I braced myself for Jaramillo's knuckle-duster, but he was surprisingly gentle this time. Maybe he knew he was in the company of duffers.

One of Vic's waitresses, a young gal whom I didn't recognize, appeared at my elbow with a mug of coffee. While she was setting the cup on the table, I shifted my bifocals so I could see her name tag.

"Mr. Palacek said you'd want coffee," she said brightly. "Do you use cream?"

"Everything, thanks, Tamara," I said. The judge and the ADA watched as I emptied two packets of cream and two of sugar into the coffee.

"I remembered that you drank coffee black," the judge said after the waitress had left.

"I do. This isn't coffee." And it wasn't. Even with the additives, it tasted like a quarter-teaspoon of instant coffee dissolved in dishwater. I took a sip, grimaced, and pushed it aside.

"I ordered the chicken salad, and Don here is having the halibut."

He pushed a menu across toward me. The print was so fuzzy that even with my bifocals I couldn't read the grim details.

"They don't have enchiladas," the judge added helpfully. "But the whiskey sours aren't bad."

The waitress appeared at my elbow and I looked up into her sober face. "I guess I'd like a ham and cheese, hold the cheese," I said. She nodded and turned away, laboriously writing something far more complete than the word *ham* on the ticket.

"Bob tells me that you and he talked to the Carters," Don Jaramillo said. He was a pudgy man, with a good set of jowls forming despite not yet having reached his fortieth birthday. His shirt looked as if he'd slept in it, tucked carelessly into jeans—the Jaramillo uniform when not in court. I somehow always expected him to blurt out, "I'm not really a lawyer, really, I'm not." He eyed me sideways, which was pretty direct for him.

"We did that." I nodded.

Bob Torrez had dropped me off at my office not many moments ago, but he hadn't mentioned that the assistant district attorney had been one of his "errands."

"What's he have to say?" Jaramillo asked.

"Who?"

"Sam. Sam Carter."

"Oh, I thought you said you just talked to Bob. I figured he'd tell you."

"Well, no," Jaramillo fussed. "We just crossed paths, so to speak. We didn't have time…"

I put his floundering out of its misery. "Kenny Carter says he had no conversation with Jim Sisson beyond a chance encounter— a friendly encounter, he claims—last Saturday, three days before Sisson's death."

"And the chairman of the county commission? What's he got to say for himself?" Judge Hobart asked.

"Sam blustered, as always. My guess is that he doesn't know what his son's doing most of the time. Par for that course."

"Bob says that he thinks Kenny Carter is the father of Jennifer Sisson's child," Jaramillo said.

"So do I."

Judge Hobart frowned. "She's a tad young, isn't she?"

"Sure."

"But the boy denies it?"

"That's correct, Judge. Sincerely denies it, too. With a good, level, unblinking gaze," I said. "In the best *'I am offended you should think such a thing'* tradition."

Jaramillo leaned forward and glanced across the empty dining room. Apparently other folks shared my opinion of the food. He lowered his voice. "The undersheriff thinks it might be profitable to order a paternity test. That's why he stopped by a bit ago, to see what I thought."

Judge Hobart toyed with his whiskey sour but didn't take a sip. I watched him thinking and was surprised how much he'd aged in the past year or so. The New Mexico sun had reduced the skin of his cheeks to a blotched parchment, with a particularly nasty patch in front of his right ear. His hand drifted up toward the blemish, then hesitated at the last instant, leaving it alone.

"And what do you think?" the judge said finally to Jaramillo.

"Well," he shrugged, "I don't know. I guess I'm of mixed minds about it, without some rock hard evidence to back it up."

"Don't be ridiculous," I snapped. "Last time I looked, Hitler and his gang were dead. I don't think any court in the state is going to let us run around sticking needles in the bellies of pregnant women to suck out DNA samples. And if we had rock hard evidence, it'd be doubly pointless."

"Well—" Jaramillo started, but I interrupted him.

"Forget it, Don. Unless Jennifer requests the test herself, with the mother's written consent, forget it. I'm surprised that Torrez brought it up."

Judge Hobart almost smiled and gestured toward the waitress, arriving with our food. My ham sandwich was recognizable, a slice of ham on white bread with eight potato chips on the side. Jaramillo looked with something akin to alarm at the thing that was touted to be a fish fillet, floating in a sea of yellow curdled sauce. The judge's chicken salad looked exactly as I had remembered it.

"What if Kenny Carter is lying, though?" Jaramillo said, tapping the lump of fish tentatively with his fork. "If he knocked up Jennifer, then there's every reason to think that Jim Sisson would go ballistic when he found out. If the two of them had a confrontation—"

"That doesn't matter," I said flatly. "If we can't solve this thing some way short of the sort of intrusive procedure that I understand amniocentesis to be, then forget it. Jim's ghost can come back from the grave someday and whisper who did it in our ear. And this is the goddamned worst chunk of ham I've ever tasted.'' I looked at Jaramillo. "And if that stuff doesn't kill you, I'll be surprised."

"It's not that bad," Jaramillo said lamely.

"Jennifer Sisson and the food aside," Judge Hobart said around a mouthful of chicken salad that clung to his dentures like wallpaper paste, "Bill, we need to decide what to do about Carla Champlin."

"I'm not sure there's a whole lot *to* do, Judge. Except maybe find someone who can make her understand what her legal options are. If she wants Tom Pasquale evicted, then I suppose there's a process she can follow, isn't there?"

"Well of course there is," he said testily. "Damn woman won't, though." He put down his fork. "Look—all she needs to do is go see her goddamn lawyer, whoever that is, and have him look over the rental agreement. If there's something in the lease that Pasquale has screwed up, then she can ask that the lease be canceled, in an appropriate manner. But Jesus, she can't just go yowling around the neighborhood, changing locks willy-nilly, and yelling threats."

"You heard about the locks, eh?" I asked.

"Course I heard about it. And I heard about the open bedroom window, and about the kid changing the oil on his goddamn motorcycle in the back bedroom, and on, and and on." He jabbed at the salad. "Christ, she spent nearly the whole morning camped out on the hallway bench in the county building, yammering." Hobart glanced up at me and grinned. "I should have sent her on over to your office."

"Thanks. I already talked to her. Apparently it didn't do any good."

"Hell, why should you be any different? You know, I always used to wonder about her, just a little. Back when she was running the post office. Licked one too many stamps."

"I'll try to talk with her again," I said. "I don't promise much."

"Better still, why don't you just tell that young deputy to move the hell out and save us all a headache. Before she shoots him or does something equally nuts."

I swallowed the last of the ham and tongued the slab of white bread paste off the roof of my mouth. "I'm not sure I want to arbitrate housing disputes for my deputies, Judge. They're all consenting adults, perfectly capable of running their own lives."

Hobart laughed, a barking rasp that threatened to spray chicken salad across the table. "Don't be so modest. You're their goddamn father confessor, and you know it." He frowned at Jaramillo. "Torrez asked you what you thought about the paternity thing?"

"Yeah, well," Jaramillo said, "I think Bill's probably right. We'd be apt to get ourselves in a royal mess, one way or another."

"Us being in a mess wasn't what I was worried about," I said, and looked at the sludge in the bottom of my cup. "And let me talk with Carla again, Judge, and see what I can do." I pushed myself away from the table and stood up. "No promises." I glanced at my watch. "I really need to be on the road, gents. Thanks for the company."

"Bill..." Judge Hobart said, and then finished the thought with just a nod, as if he was sure I could read his mind.

"We'll keep you posted," I said to Jaramillo, and tossed a couple bucks on the table for Tamara, who thoughtfully hadn't tried to inflict any more of the awful coffee on me.

Outside in the sunshine, I looked at my watch again. The Don Juan wouldn't be crowded, and a fast burrito would settle my writhing stomach. I managed to drive within a hundred feet of the restaurant's parking lot on Twelfth Street before the telephone rang.

THIRTY-TWO

I CLEARED the intersection of Hutton and North Twelfth Street and a quarter of a mile further on managed to turn into Judge Lester Hobart's driveway without sliding into the bar-ditch.

The judge's rambling home, one of the first frame houses in the county, had been built in the late 1800s by one of the Bennett brothers...two aging cattlemen who had seen some future for the place that others didn't understand.

The graveled driveway wound through a collection of old, rusting farm machinery, none of which had been capable of finding much wealth in the raw Posadas soil. The high-wheeled rake and sickle-bar mower, the baler, and a 1927 Ford AA truck without wheels, axles, or bed sank into the desert along with a half-dozen other relics.

If attention was what she was after, Carla Champlin had hit upon a surefire strategy. The blue-and-white RV looked bigger than it had when parked in the grape arbor behind Carla's house. She's driven up the driveway and onto the judge's yard, parked squarely with the vehicle's big picture window staring into the judge's front door. One of the vehicle's front tires had crushed a small cactus planter near the pebbled walkway.

Even as I pulled 310 to a stop, Undersheriff Robert Torrez arrived. As we got out and advanced toward the RV, the judge's niece stepped out of the house and walked toward us, her hands in the hip pockets of her jeans. A scrawny gal maybe forty years old, she'd inherited the Hobart genes that gave her a face full of angles and planes, with high cheekbones and full eyebrows. I didn't know Lucy Hobart well but got the impression that she didn't smile much.

"Lester is on his way," she said, and stopped a couple of paces from the back of the RV, surveying the towering aluminum sides with distaste.

"Miss Champlin is inside, you say?" I asked, and Lucy nodded.

"I asked her to come on in for coffee, but she refuses to talk to anyone but Lester. That's one crazy lady in there."

I turned and looked at Bob Torrez, who shrugged helplessly. He leaned against the fender of 310, crossed his arms over his chest, and appeared to be ready to wait for Christmas.

"Christ," I muttered, "why us, why now," and walked to the door of the RV. It was locked. I rapped it with my knuckle and waited. "Carla?" No response. "Carla? It's Bill Gastner. Let me in."

I rested my hand on the door frame and felt the slight motion of the RV as something inside shifted.

"Carla, it's hot out here. Give me a break." Carla wasn't about to give anyone a break. "What did she say to you?" I asked Lucy.

"That she wasn't coming out or moving," Lucy said.

"Until what?"

Lucy took a few steps and peered at the crushed cactus under the RV's front tire. "She didn't say until what."

I banged on the door so hard that the flimsy aluminum shook in the door frame. "Carla! Open the door. Don't be ridiculous."

"Not until I talk to the judge." The voice was small but determined.

"That's what telephones are for, Carla," I said, and when she didn't respond added, "You can't just camp out here."

"Oh, yes, I can," Carla Champlin said.

"Can you believe this?" I said to Torrez, who grinned.

"I can just pop the door open," he offered.

"No, don't do that," I said. "Carla, open the damn door,. You're going to roast in there. And I'm going to roast out here." There was no answer, but I detected more shifting. "Carla," I added, "come on. I'm dying out here." I hoped the feeble attempt at humor might loosen her tongue, but she didn't say a word. "For Christ's sakes, Carla, I've known you for twenty years. Talk to me."

"I talked to you before, and you didn't do anything. Now I'll talk to Judge Hobart," she said. "And that's that."

"I thought you already talked to him. Earlier this morning."

"He wouldn't listen to me," Carla said sweetly. "Now maybe he will." I could imagine her nodding her head with satisfaction.

"Carla..."

"I said I'm not going to talk to you. Now just go away."

"Ma'am, I can't just go away. What you're doing is illegal. Not to mention silly."

She didn't reply and I took a deep breath. "Suit yourself," I said and walked back to 310. I settled into the seat, found the phone, and called the office. "Gayle," I said when her calm voice answered, "we're going to need a matron out here. If Linda's handy, send her on over."

"She and Tom are downstairs, sir. In the darkroom. I'll buzz her up."

I hesitated. "Well, on second thought, let's wait on that. Tell her to sit Dispatch for a bit, and you come on over."

"Yes, sir."

"And tell Thomas that I don't want him anywhere near this place, all right? If Carla catches sight of him, she'll go ballistic."

"Yes, sir. I don't think he's going to stray far. Howard Bishop found a little blood smear on the underside of the grab rail of the backhoe. Linda took close-up photos, and they've been processing the prints. The lab's got the blood sample."

"Outstanding. We'll be out here just a few minutes."

"Is Miss Champlin all right?"

"Well, that's a hard question to answer just now. The sooner you can get here, the better."

I twisted around at the sound of tires crunching on gravel. Judge Hobart's minivan drifted to a stop. He didn't get out immediately but sat with both forearms resting on the top of the steering wheel, gazing at the new addition to his landscape.

"Carla Champlin's inside," I said when I reached the door of his vehicle. "She refuses to move or even to talk with anyone but you."

"She does, does she," the judge said in a tone that promised a sentence of twenty years to life. "Damn crazy woman spent all morning down at the county building. Looked like a goddamn old bag lady camped out in the hallway. I told her once what she should do, but I guess that wasn't good enough.'' Hobart popped the door and got out, moving slowly.

He took his time making his way along the flank of the RV until he reached the door. The tinted glass made it impossible to see inside.

"Miss Champlin?" he said, keeping his tone conversational and light. "It's Lester Hobart. You've got to move this damn thing out of my yard."

"Not until you sign an eviction order I won't."

The judge looked at me and then rolled his eyes heavenward. "Carla, look.... I told you earlier what you have to do. It isn't all that complicated."

"Well, apparently it is, since you won't sign an order."

Judge Hobart frowned, and I could see the color creeping up his neck. "Miss Champlin, I won't be threatened or coerced. Get this damn thing out of my yard, then go and talk to your lawyer, and we'll take it from there. That's what I told you this morning."

"I know you did."

"Well, nothing's changed. This is nonsense."

Carla Champlin's tone reminded me of a starched elementary school teacher. "Well, nonsense or not, this is the way it's going to be. I've got rights, just like anybody else. Everybody thinks they can just ignore me, but well...you sign that eviction order, and I'll just trot on."

Hobart thrust his hands in his pockets and regarded the pebbles by his feet. Perhaps he was counting to ten. Finally he looked up at me and said, "Goddamn woman is nuts."

"I heard that," Carla Champlin barked, and I saw Bob Torrez grin.

"I bet you did," the judge muttered. He turned and walked toward the house, stopping as he passed me. "Goddamn woman deserves to be committed," he said between his teeth.

"You want to bother with a formal trespass complaint?" I asked.

Hobart looked pained. "Don't be ridiculous, Bill. Just get her the hell out of my yard without killing anybody."

He nodded curtly at Robert and strode into the house.

"You guys want anything?" Lucy Hobart asked without enthusiasm.

"No thanks," I said. "Gayle Sedillos will be here in a few minutes. Then we'll see what we can do."

I stepped up to the side of the RV. "Carla? Did you hear the judge?" She didn't answer. "He's not going to negotiate with you, sweetheart. It's time to pack up and move this beast out."

"I told you what I was going to do," Carla said.

"Carla," I said patiently, "you can't stay here. Either you move the bus or we're going to come in there and move it for you."

"Don't you threaten me."

"I'm not. It's just the way things are. If I have to bust the door, I will." I reached out and ran a hand down the polished aluminum frame. "And it's a pretty nice door, too."

"Go away. If you cause any damage, I'll sue you, too."

I glanced over at Bob Torrez. "what's your suggestion?" I said. "She's a voter, remember."

Torrez grinned. "When Gayle gets here, pop the door, remove Miss Champlin from the vehicle, let Gayle drive the RV back to Miss Champlin's house, and you can take the woman in your car. Maybe by then she'll be settled down."

"Oh, sure. And I notice that you're conspicuously absent from that formula." I walked away from the RV and took up the number-two position against the fender of the car. "And by the way, Bishop found a small blood smear on the underside of one of the grab rails of the backhoe. They're processing it now. Prints, photos, the whole nine yards."

Torrez straightened up, his face coming alive with interest. "I better get back there, then. You're on top of this?"

"Does it look like I'm on top of it?" I chuckled. "But go ahead. But the time Gayle gets here, Carla might have reconsidered."

Gayle Torrez arrived two minutes after her husband left, and in that time Carla Champlin did not reconsider. The afternoon sky didn't help me any—blank blue without a trace of clouds. No afternoon thundershowers were going to cool things off. I could feel the sun that bounced off the patrol car baking the underside of my chin, and just when I was beginning to feel a touch sorry for Carla Champlin simmering inside her tin can, the RV's engine burst into life, and the air-conditioning unit on top kicked in. She was probably enjoying a glass of iced tea, content to let us broil outside.

Gayle stepped out of the car with Linda Real in tow. "Tom's sitting the desk," Gayle said, and I nodded.

"This is the deal," I said. "Carla Champlin is inside that thing, and she says that she won't come out until the judge signs an eviction order against your friend and mine, Tom Pasquale."

"She's never even talked to us, face-to-face," Linda said with wonder. "I told Tom that he should just find someplace else, but he doesn't see why he should have to move for no reason. I guess he's talked to her a couple of times, but she won't listen to anything he says."

"Well, no reason or not, that would be the simple solution," I said. "Otherwise, we're going to have to go in there and physically remove her...which is why I asked you-all to come over. To act as a matron."

Linda regarded the RV for a moment, eyes squinted against the sun. "This is silly," she said. "Tell her we'll be out of her house by the weekend."

"Tom will agree to that?"

"I think so."

I nodded with satisfaction. "All right. Hell, you can use one of the empty guest rooms at my house for a night or two if you need it." I stepped up to the RV's door.

"Carla, Linda says that they'll be moved out by the weekend."

There was a pause. "Linda who?"

"Linda Real. Tom Pasquale's...ah...friend," I said.

"Fiancée" Linda said, and I looked at her in surprise and then turned back to the RV.

"The deputy's fiancée. They'll be out of the house by the weekend. How's that?"

"I don't know who she is."

"So what? What difference does it make whether you know her or not? You've got my word."

"You just show me that order signed by the judge, and we'll talk business."

"Carla..."

"I've made up my mind, and that's that."

"Who the hell put this foolish idea in your head anyway, Carla? You can't just force a judge to issue a court order."

"We'll see."

"Carla," I said, standing close to the door and dropping my voice, "you heard him. He already gave an order, and that was to move you out of here."

"Don't you even think about interfering, Mr. Gastner. You just go away and let me wait. He'll change his mind; you'll see."

"For one thing, you're blocking his niece's car. She can't get out to go to work."

"Isn't that just too bad, though."

I looked at Gayle and Linda and held up my hands in resignation. "Suggestions?" Both shook their heads.

"Carla," I said, "what more do you want? The kids said that they'd move out. That's what you wanted. That's what you've got. What's the big deal?"

"You know as well as I do what will happen," she said primly. "I'll give in, and they won't move, and I'll be right back where I started, with everybody just laughing at me. Foolish old lady. Well, I won't have it."

I took hold of the doorknob and levered it this way and that, judging the fit of the door against the trim.

"You leave my camper alone," Carla snapped. "It's locked, and it will stay that way."

"I don't think so, Carla. It's hot out here, and I'm just about out of patience." I turned to Gayle. "See if there's a tire iron in the trunk of my car. Something I can pry with."

She returned in a moment with the folding jack handle, a neat gadget with a hooklike flange on one end for popping wheel covers. The flange slid under the lip of the door, and I moved it so that it was directly opposite the lock. With a hard thrust, the door popped open. I could feel the rush of cool air from inside. I handed the jack handle to Gayle and pushed open the door.

The two stairs up to the driver's seat were nicely carpeted, and I stepped carefully, one hand on the chrome railing for balance.

"Oh, no, you don't," Carla Champlin shrieked. "Now you get out of here," and I looked up into the muted light of the camper's interior. The shades were drawn, but it wasn't so dark that I couldn't clearly see the crazy woman standing beside her dinette table, holding what appeared to be a shotgun with its muzzle pointed squarely at my face.

THIRTY-THREE

FOR WHAT SEEMED LIKE hours, all manner of bizarre thoughts ranged through my mind. None of them were as practical as a simple inner command to duck or dive for cover...to jump down the three steps and cower behind the wafer-thin wall of aluminum that wouldn't stop a single pellet.

Instead, they were really helpful thoughts, like a review of the FBI's statistics about how dangerous domestic disturbances were for responding law enforcement officers, or a brief instant when I wondered what Frank Dayan, the *Posadas Register*'s publisher, would put in the headline if Carla's finger cramped or slipped.

It wasn't that I was brave or even foolhardy. I just didn't have the energy to move, and I couldn't bring myself to believe that Carla Champlin would really shoot me. Maybe her goal was to force me to shoot her...and if that was the case, she was wasting her time.

"Carla," I said slowly, searching for just the right words and just the right tone of voice, "what's that supposed to accomplish?"

"You just get on out of my trailer."

"Nope."

She frowned. I looked more closely at the shotgun. She was holding it by the fore-end and by the wrist just behind the trigger guard, her hands clamped around it like a pair of old vises. No finger was near the trigger or even the trigger guard, and the single hammer of the old break-open was down. My heart settled down a bit.

"Carla," I said, "these tinted windows make it kinda nice. No one outside can see how silly you're being."

"It's not silly."

"Oh, yes, it is. What's the old shotgun going to accomplish? Do you think we're all just going to go away? If you made the mistake of shooting me, what do you think the two deputies outside would do...in the short blink of an eye and long before you could reload that thing?" She frowned again. The blinds were drawn, so she couldn't see that my two "deputies" were a couple of nervous young gals, neither of whom was armed.

"Look," I continued, and took a half-step forward so I could lean against the fake wood of the bulkhead. "Here's the deal. Put that thing down, and you and I will be the only ones who ever know about it. Put it down, crank this buggy up, and go home. Water your plants. Your tenants will be out of the house on Third Street by nightfall. Guaranteed."

"How can you guarantee that?" she snapped, and the shotgun didn't waver.

"Because they said they would be. I told 'em they could use my guest room for a while, if it came to that." I spread my hands. "Anything to make you happy."

"What about all the damage?"

I shrugged. "What about it? Hell, I don't know. Keep their deposit. I assume they paid one. It's some dead grass and some ruts. That's not the end of the world."

"Oh, it's more than grass and ruts," she said. "And what about the oil on the floor inside?"

I took a deep breath and glanced at my watch. "I don't know about the oil on the floor inside," I said. "I guess you can always take them to small-claims court and settle up there." I took another step, running a finger along the bottom lip of one of the cabinet doors. "You've really got two choices." I held up the finger. "One, you can refuse to put down that damn gun, and you'll end up facing a charge of threatening a police officer at the very least, or maybe assault, or reckless endangerment, or a whole bunch of other ugly things. That's the good news. That's if the gun doesn't go off. Of course," I shrugged, "if it goes off, then I'm going to be pissed, and your problems will be over. You won't have to worry about tending plants in the state pen."

I smiled at her without much humor. "How about that, eh? Not much of a choice. The other sounds better. Stash that old piece of junk, go home, be patient, let the kids get their act together. I'm

sure that you know that I've got better things to be doing just now.
So do you.''

I heard a vehicle drive up outside, recognizing both the sound
of its exhausts and the manner of its approach. I reached out and
tipped the blind to one side. Bob Torrez was out of the car, face
grim, and was striding toward Gayle Sedillos, who stood by the
open front door of 310.

"Oh, dear,'' I said. "You don't have a whole lot of time left to
decide, sweetheart.''

I let the blind fall back and looked at Carla Champlin. Her hands
hadn't moved on the shotgun. The end of the barrel was within a
stretch, and I took a quick step and swept it to one side, being just
as gentle as I could be while still accomplishing the job. The bead
front sight whacked into the door of the cabinet. With my other
hand I clamped down on the receiver, my palm over the hammer.
I didn't twist or yank but just held it while Carla decided what she
wanted to do.

She didn't bother to struggle but released the shotgun. I pushed
the lever behind the hammer and broke it open. The old 20-gauge
wasn't loaded.

"Whose is this, anyway?'' I asked.

"I got it for skunks, years ago,'' Carla said, still perky and on
the offensive.

"Well, I'm not a skunk,'' I said and stepped past her. I tossed
the gun on the bed behind the first partition.

"Now what if I refuse to move this?'' Carla said. "You can't
force me to drive this away.''

Undersheriff Torrez appeared in the doorway, and by the set of
his shoulders I knew that his right hand was on the butt of his
service automatic.

"Everything all right?'' he asked.

"Fine, Robert, fine,'' I said. "You might as well call the wrecker
and have them come hook up.'' I turned to Carla. "And if you
force us to do that, the tow charge is going to be a hundred bucks
or so. Guess who's going to pay that.''

She took a deep breath and made a petulant face. "Oh, all right.''
She made sweeping motions with both hands. "Just both of you
get out and leave me alone. I'll be on my way.''

"We'll help you maneuver out of the judge's driveway," I said. "It's kind of narrow. We don't want any plants damaged."

"I'm perfectly capable."

"I'm sure you are, Miss Champlin."

She shook an admonishing finger at me. "And remember what you promised. This evening, at the latest."

"Absolutely," I said.

Torrez stepped down out of the RV, still eyeing Carla Champlin, who settled into the driver's seat, muttering to herself.

I stepped down from the RV and felt the blast of hot air. Even with the air conditioning in the RV, I was glad the confrontation was over.

"Gayle said she had a gun," the undersheriff said quietly when I was a pace or two away from the doorway of the massive vehicle.

"Broomstick," I said. "She was going to attack me with a broomstick. I talked her out of it."

THIRTY-FOUR

I SPENT A COUPLE of minutes following the RV as Carla Champlin trundled it home. She drove it reasonably straight and true, signaling and stopping at all the right places. Pausing 310 at the curb in front of her house, I watched her wedge the big machine back into its place in the grape arbor. She glanced my way as she darted inside the house, and I waved a hand. She didn't acknowledge.

But that was ok. I didn't have time just then for tea and crumpets, or whatever she might serve, even if she had showed signs of wanting to continue her conversation with me. Maybe a little conversation was just what she needed. Maybe Carla Champlin had started her long slide downhill toward the loony bin, and this was the one day that fate had given her to teeter on the edge. She could be hauled back to the world of the reasonable or pushed on over. But I didn't feel that I had time to stand on the edge with her just then. She was going to have to depend on her own sense of balance.

Instead, I drove directly to the Public Safety Building and discovered I was just about the last one at the party. In the few moments that I'd been following Carla Champlin, Gayle had taken up Dispatch again, and when she saw me she motioned toward the basement door.

"They're all down there, sir," she said.

The "they" were far too many large people for the small space outside the darkroom. On the utility table photographic enlargements were lined up in neat rows, and as I walked down the stairs Linda Real was bending over one of the prints, guiding one of those little photo gadgets used to check the focus of a print. The aroma of chemicals from the darkroom was strong enough to make my eyes burn.

At her elbow on one side was Tom Pasquale, with Bob Torrez

on the other. Both were trying their best not to knock heads on the spiderweb of plumbing and electrical pipes.

Howard Bishop sat at the end of the table, his considerable bulk balanced on an absurdly small stool.

The only fan was the exhaust unit in the darkroom behind them, and with so many large individuals so long from a shower on a hot day, I was surprised Linda hadn't keeled over from the rich locker-room effluvia.

"We've got a nice conference room upstairs," I said by way of greeting. But they were too excited to bother with amenities. "What have you got?" I asked, and Linda glanced up from the lens.

"Sir, Sergeant Bishop lifted a neat set of latents from the cabin frame on the backhoe," she said. "I had just finished processing the initial prints when we got called over to Judge Hobart's." She swept a hand to include the dozen or so prints. "They're pretty clear."

Bob Torrez braced both hands on the table and scanned the photos. The dusted fingerprints, little more than dark ghosts against the lighter steel, showed clearly enough in one of the photos that I could actually see them, with the tractor's sunshade in the background blanking out the bright sky.

"It looks like somebody grabbed real low on the frame and hit a sharp spur on the weld joint," he said. "And then the blood smeared on the metal, maybe when he was getting off."

"He's going to grab it in the same place each time?" I asked.

"If it's a habit," Bishop said without shifting the position of his chin on his hands. "It wouldn't start bleedin' fast enough to smear like that the instant he cut it gettin' on."

"Huh," I said, and pondered the picture. It didn't mean much to me. "Good enough," I said. "But I guess I need to see it for real. Anything on the blood type yet?"

"Mears is at the hospital now," Torrez replied.

"Then let's ride out and take a look at this thing. Maybe whoever left this," I tapped the photo, "got careless and dribbled somewhere else."

"I've been over that machine ten times," Bishop said, and heaved himself to his feet. "Course, we found this on about round nine, so another good look wouldn't hurt."

"Who's out there now?" I asked.

"Taber's taking the afternoon," Torrez said, and I grimaced. Jackie Taber normally worked midnight to eight. Like everyone else, her eight-hour workday had gone extinct.

The hot, windless afternoon air was a relief after the basement. The machinery in Jim Sisson's backyard rested silently, circled by a yellow ribbon. Deputy Taber had parked in the Sissons' driveway, well back so that she could watch the back and front at the same time.

If Grace Sisson and her daughter objected to the surveillance, they hadn't told us. Neither had been outside since returning home, at least that we knew of. And friends weren't exactly standing in line to visit. Maybe the neighborhood assumed the Sissons were still at Grace's parents' place in Las Cruces.

I walked up to the backhoe, and Linda Real pointed at the steel frame just above the outriggers. Originally, the backhoe had sported a nifty enclosed cab. Over time, it had shed various parts, with most of the glass or Plexiglas or whatever it was going first. The remaining cage had plenty of sharp spots that an operator would avoid out of habit.

"Under there, sir," she said, and I cranked my neck around so I could see under one of the braces. The smear was a light brown against the machine's yellow paint.

Reaching out my hand as if to grab the bar, I said, "So he grabs hold to pull himself up. He cuts himself on the weld somehow."

"There's a spur there, if you look close," Bishop said. "Linda got a good photo of it."

"I'll take your word," I said. "So he grabs here, cuts himself, and then on the way down grabs again and leaves blood." I shrugged. "Possible. If he got on this side, he's got a cut on his left hand somewhere." I held my hand near the bar. "If he grabbed it in the usual fashion, it would nick him right about between the first and second knuckle. If he got on the other side, he'd grab the bar with his right hand."

"But he wouldn't leave blood here if he got on the other side," Torrez said.

I turned to Bishop. "You were on and off this machine a number of times yourself," I said.

He stepped up close and reached out a hand. "And my prints are right about here," he said. "I kinda reach on over a ways."

"Or it could be Jim's blood," Torrez said. "I asked Alan Perrone to double-check for minor injuries that would be consistent with this. But that's going to be a tough call."

"Impossible," I said. "What about on the operating levers themselves?" I peered close at the black rubber handles. "Anything there?"

"No," Bishop said. "We'd expect a pretty good collection there, too. We dusted before I touched them, so at the very least we should have Jim Sisson's and maybe the killer's. But they're clean."

"Wiped, then. Very clever. Just the sort of thing a person committing suicide would do."

Bishop actually came close to laughing. "They always slip up somewheres, if you look close enough," he observed. "Whoever bled on this thing didn't take the time to wear gloves."

"If the levers hadn't been wiped clean, the most logical guess would be that the blood is Sisson's himself," I said. "Maybe. So look, we'll get a blood type, and that's a start. We've got some good prints off the bar, and that's another plus. Maybe the blood's enough for a DNA match, if it comes to that. What I want you to do now is go over these machines, this entire area, for the ten dozenth time. Slow, careful, methodical...every square inch of the machines, the tire, the wheel, hell, even the shop itself. I want to make sure that we looked at everything, too many times."

I turned to Bob Torrez. "And before we get busy, I need to ask you something." I pointed at Tom Pasquale. "And you stay close. I need to talk to you in just a minute."

Pasquale hadn't said a word in the darkroom, and he'd been a shadow while we discussed the machine. When I spoke to him, he nodded as if he'd been waiting for the ax to fall.

Torrez accompanied me back to the front curb where 310 was parked. "I talked to Judge Hobart and Don Jaramillo at lunch today," I said.

"Jaramillo's not being much help with any of this," Torrez said. "I'd expect him to be doggin' every step of this investigation, but he's been staying about as far away as he can get."

"I can think of all sorts of reasons for that," I said, "but that's not what interests me just now. He's just an assistant DA with politics on his mind, and nobody's going to be very popular with this case, no matter what happens. We can cut around him if we have to, go straight to Schroeder. But what did surprise me is that he mentioned something about asking for a court order to run a DNA test on Jennifer Sisson's unborn child."

Torrez frowned and leaned toward me as if he hadn't heard right. "On the kid? The fetus, you mean?"

"That's what he said."

"That's not going to happen," Torrez said. "I know I said that to Sam, back there in his office, but that was just to jerk his chain a little bit...make him nervous."

"I understand that. And I knew that's what you were doing," I said. "But did you bring up the idea to him? To Jaramillo?" Torrez's eyebrow cocked at me in surprise, but he didn't reply. "Don Jaramillo told Judge Hobart and me that you had suggested to him a paternity test on Jennifer Sisson might not be such a bad idea."

"Jaramillo's a liar," Torrez said matter-of-factly. "As simple as that. I never suggested that to him. Like I said, you were there and heard what I said to Sam Carter. That's it. I haven't mentioned the idea to anyone else." He looked hard at me. "I don't think we're going to go around sticking needles in the bellies of teenage girls. If Jaramillo thinks Hobart's going to go for that, he's more of a jerk than I think he is. And unless he came up with the idea himself, there's only one place he could have gotten it—and that's from Carter himself."

"That was the conclusion I'd reached," I said. "If Carter thinks you're actually going to do a test, he might well start to panic, afraid of what would happen if it ever leaked out...and all it takes is one blabby nurse or lab tech."

Torrez hitched up his gun belt, his face twisted with annoyance. "Maybe I'm wrong, but knowing exactly who's the father of Jennifer Sisson's child doesn't tell me who pushed the levers on that backhoe over there."

"It might give a suggestion of who might want to," I said.

"Not even that. If Kenny Carter is the father, why should he want to kill his future father-in-law?"

"Self-defense springs to mind, Roberto."

"That murder wasn't self-defense, sir," he said. "You don't drop a tire on someone in self-defense and then squash it flat with a backhoe in self-defense. It's a murder carried out by someone who thought he was goddamn clever, is what it is."

"What do you want to do, then?"

Torrez gazed off down the street. "I want a few answers from the lab first," he said. "And then I think it's time we haul Grace Sisson into custody and put her under the lights. The one thing I'm sure of is that she knows a hell of a lot more than she's letting on. She's good. She sits still and watches us watching her. That all by itself makes me nervous. If she wanted to find out who killed her husband, she'd be cooperating with us. Or at least going through the motions."

He turned and nodded at the house. "I'd like to give her one more night to think about it. Tomorrow morning, we'll pick her up."

"And we have nothing to hold her on," I reminded him. "One phone call, and at the most one quick preliminary hearing, and she walks. You'll be lucky to hold her for an hour."

"Sure. But she doesn't have to know that. She doesn't know what we've found in that backyard. Or not found."

I shook my head in frustration. "I don't know. Go with the prints off the bar first and the blood sample. Maybe we'll get lucky."

Deputy Pasquale appeared in the driveway, and I beckoned him over.

"Keep me posted," I said to Torrez, and watched him amble off, head down, deep in thought. I leaned on the fender of the car and crossed my arms.

Tom Pasquale stopped two paces away. "Sir?"

"Thomas," I said, "did Linda get a chance to talk with you?"

"Just a little. She said that Miss Champlin pulled a gun on you."

"Well, strictly speaking, I suppose that's true. It turned out to be an old unloaded shotgun, more of a stage prop than anything else. But for a few seconds there, it was a magic moment." I grinned. "I need to ask you to do me a favor."

"Sure."

I held up a hand, interrupting myself. "And first, I know just as goddamn well as you do that none of this is any of my business. But chalk it up to me being a little worried about an old friend, OK? Here's what I'd like. I'd like you and Linda to take the rest of the afternoon off, starting five minutes ago, and get yourselves moved out of that place on Third Street. Can you do that?"

He hesitated. "Well, sure, I guess, but—"

I shook my head. "At this point, it has nothing to do with right or wrong, or tenant rights, landlord rights, leases, ruts in the yard, motorcycle oil on the floor, or any other goddamn thing, Thomas. It has to do with you doing me a favor."

"Well, I don't see, then—"

I cut him off again. "I want you out of Carla Champlin's way, Thomas. And not for your sake, either. For hers."

"Is she nuts or what?"

"Well, some of both, probably. Or headed that way. I want to defuse this thing, today. And tomorrow, I'm going to ask that one of the home health workers from Social Services stop by and chat with her. In the meantime, let's get you and Linda out of the line of fire, all right? I told her that you two can camp out in one of the guest rooms at my place, if you need to."

"Thanks, sir, but that won't be necessary. I've got a cousin who said he's got a place he'd rent us. Maybe for a few bucks less than what I'm paying now, too."

"Then go for it. Tonight. All right? And I'm serious. Not in the morning, not tomorrow afternoon. This very evening."

Tom looked like he wanted to say something else but swallowed and settled for, "Yes, sir."

"Good." I turned to get into the car. "That's one thing out of the way." I stopped abruptly and glared at the young deputy. "Linda used the word *fiancée*. Is that right?"

He ducked his head and actually blushed. "We hadn't told anybody yet."

"Secrets around here seem to be department policy," I said wryly. "Well, congratulations. You take good care of her." He stammered something in return, but I didn't hear it. I slid into 310, wincing as the hot vinyl seat scorched my backside.

THIRTY-FIVE

TIME HUNG HEAVILY that afternoon. I was too tired to sleep, too confused to relax, too hot and sweaty to socialize.

My musty adobe house on Guadalupe Terrace was just the burrow I needed, and I headed there after leaving Tom Pasquale standing on the hot sidewalk in front of the Sissons'.

Even without an air conditioner, the temperature differential was enough to prompt a groan of relief when I stepped inside and shut the heavy carved door behind me. After a shower and change of clothes, I settled in the kitchen, made a pot of coffee, and then sat, staring into the swirls of steam coming out of my cup.

I hadn't taken a sip, and I have no idea how long I sat there, mesmerized, trying to think about absolutely nothing. I must have succeeded, because the phone's first ring practically sent me into orbit.

I answered a little more gruffly than I meant to, and a moment's silence on the other end prompted me to repeat myself. Finally a small voice said, "Bill?"

"Yes?"

"This is Carla. Carla Champlin."

I took a deep breath and moved my right hand away from the coffee cup so I wouldn't spill it—just in case there were more surprises.

"How are you doing?" I said, trying not to sound as if I was talking to someone who'd just stuck a shotgun in my face.

"I...well, I...better," she said, and then some of the old brusque postmistress efficiency came back into her voice. "The dispatcher said that you'd be home, and I just called to tell you that I'm really terribly sorry about what happened this afternoon," she said.

"That's all right."

"Well, no, it isn't. It most certainly isn't."

"These things happen," I said.

She hesitated, then said, "I'm just awfully glad that it was you in the RV, not someone else."

Of course if I'd had a coronary and dropped dead on her mobile carpeting, she wouldn't have been so glad, but I didn't say that. "Carla, let's just forget it happened, all right? I haven't given it a second thought. You shouldn't, either."

"I just hate being an old fool, that's all," she said. "I can't even imagine what that young couple must think. Or Judge Hobart, either, for that matter. Honestly. I don't know what came over me."

I didn't see any bombshells on the horizon, so I risked taking a sip of coffee. "Tom and Linda will be out of the house this evening. They've found another place, and just between you and me, I bet they'll take a little better care of it. I think you taught them a good lesson."

"Um, well," she said, not ready to be placated, "none of it was necessary. Especially with all of you people being as busy as you are right now."

"Carla," I said, not needing to be reminded that I *should* have been busy just then, "I appreciate your thoughts. We all do. Just give me a buzz if you need anything."

She sounded a little miffed that she was being cut off and took the offensive. "All right then," she said and hung up.

I chuckled and put the phone down and immediately thought about Grace Sisson. If Carla Champlin, a half-crackers old lady with steel rebar for a backbone, could apologize for being ridiculous, perhaps we could expect a miracle from Grace, too. I contemplated making a casual, only half-official visit with the woman and her daughter but then rejected that idea as unlikely to produce anything except another vitriolic eruption.

Bob Torrez's strategy was probably sound. Let the woman stew overnight without knowing what the deputies had found in the backyard and then put the pressure on in the morning—perhaps after someone other than myself had had a sleepless night.

I refilled my coffee, shut off the machine, and left the house, heading for Bucky Randall's construction site just north of the Posadas Inn on Grande Avenue. He'd been Jim Sisson's last customer, and although any connection between that job and Jim's murder was pretty dubious, it was worth the shot. At least one of the deputies had already touched bases with Bucky, but another perspective wouldn't hurt. Normally people didn't kill each other over flat tires or some other construction glitch, but it was a crazy world.

I had heard various rumors about what kind of motel-restaurant combination was going in at the Randall location, from steak house to seafood joint to saloon. At the moment, the property was flat and dusty with a touch of white alkali frosting the soil, not a tree or shrub or cactus in sight.

Machinery—presumably Jim Sisson's big new front loader—had taken a chunk out of a small dune, leveling it away from the highway. Various ditches mapped the property as the contractors piped and wired.

Several vehicles were gathered around one corner where a crew worked with a transit, shooting across to an array of plumbing near the access hole for the village water meter. I stopped 310 beside one of the trucks, a red Dodge with a T. C. RANDALL CONSTRUCTION, LORDSBURG, NM logo on the cab.

I swung open the door and started to pull myself out just as one of the young men near the transit headed my way. At the same time, my cell phone chirped, and I slid back into the seat, both feet outside the car.

I found the phone and flipped it open. "Gastner," I said, and glanced at my watch. It was ten minutes before six—the construction crews were on overtime.

"Sir, this is Ernie Wheeler. Mrs. Sisson just called and said she needs to see you. She said it's an emergency."

I swung my feet inside the car, shook my head at the young construction foreman, and said into the phone, "Is Torrez still over there?"

"Yes, sir. But she insists that she talk to you."

"I'll be there in a couple of minutes."

"I'll tell her, sir. She's still on the line."

Without explaining to the puzzled contractor, I backed clear of the trucks, then headed north on Grande toward MacArthur. By the time I'd reached the Sisson address, I'd run every scenario I could imagine through my head, right down to the pipe dream where

Grace Sisson stretched out both wrists toward me, ready for the handcuffs, and said, *"Take me. I did it."*

Torrez's patrol car was still in the driveway, parked behind the Blazer that Howard Bishop favored. The Sissons' Suburban was parked at the curb, and I pulled in behind it. I slid the cellular phone into one pocket, then snapped open my briefcase and rummaged for the tiny microcassette recorder. The gadget was smaller than a pack of cigarettes. I could count on one hand the number of times I'd used the recorder even after Estelle Reyes-Guzman had convinced me of its value. The tapes were so dinky that my fat fingers fumbled them all over the place, and the control buttons were worse.

I squinted at the thing and saw that it was loaded. I pushed the record button and dropped the recorder into my shirt pocket.

Bob Torrez and the deputies were still out back, and I wondered if Grace Sisson had mentioned a word to them. The undersheriff appeared before I reached the steps to the front door, and I stopped.

"She asked me where you were," he said. "I suggested she call Dispatch if it wasn't something I could help her with."

I nodded and then shrugged. Grace Sisson jerked open the front door between my first and second knock.

"Come in," she said, and held the door at the ready, the way a person does when a rambunctious mud-covered pet is about to barge in on the heels of polite company.

"What can I do for you, Mrs. Sisson?" I asked.

She shut the door solidly behind me, then stood with her arms crossed, regarding me. "Do you have any idea why I asked that you come over here?"

"None whatsoever," I said. "All I'm told is that you wanted to talk to me and that you didn't want to speak with one of the deputies or with the undersheriff." I shrugged. "So...here I am."

"My daughter is gone," she said abruptly.

Fatigue and an almost endless list of other excuses had deadened my brain, and it took a few seconds for that to sink in.

"Did you hear me?" Grace snapped.

"Yes, as a matter of fact, I did."

"Well?"

"What time did she leave?"

With a grimace of impatience, Grace Sisson rolled her eyes. "Who's got cops crawling all over my property all day long, watching every minute? Ask one of them."

"That's helpful, Mrs. Sisson." I stepped toward the door.

"Where are you going?"

I stopped and turned slowly. "I tell you what. When you're ready to be civil and tell us what we need to know, then give me a buzz. If your daughter's missing, I'm sorry. If you want to report her as a missing person after she's been gone twenty-four hours, feel free. You're the parent here. We're just the cops. You might check with her friends. That would be my suggestion. If we find her on the street after ten p.m., we'll bring her home. No charge."

I reached for the doorknob, and Grace Sisson held out a hand. "No, wait."

That's as far as she got, since she had enough brains to know that if she fired any more shells at me, I'd be out the door. But anything less was difficult for her.

"Ma'am, I know you don't want to talk to us. I know you've got a world of problems right now. But if you've got something to say to me, just take the easy road. Spit it out and get it over with so I can get to work."

She took a deep breath and said, "Jennifer wanted something from the place across the street. I told her I didn't know if we could do that or not."

"You mean because of the deputies?" She nodded. "Mrs. Sisson, this property is under surveillance. So are you. The reason for that is that you've decided we aren't worth talking to, and so we have to dig for the answers to all our questions without your help. But you're not under house arrest. You can go anywhere you like. Any time you like. And we'll follow along."

Grace accepted that without a snide retort, and I chalked it up to slow progress. "So did she go over there? Across the street?"

"Yes."

"What time?"

She turned and glanced at a small wall clock in the kitchen. "About twenty minutes ago."

"About five-thirty or so, then. Give or take."

"Yes. And she didn't come back."

I raised an eyebrow at Grace. "So let me ask a foolish question. Did you walk over there? It's maybe a hundred yards, at most. Or call?"

"I called. She isn't there. They told me that she had been there for a while but left."

"And you have no idea where she might have gone?"

Grace shook her head. "I'm just afraid..."

"Of what?"

By this time, I could see the misting in the woman's eyes and realized that Grace Sisson was wrestling with a fair-sized dragon. "Grace," I said quietly, "it's just you and me. If there's something I need to know, then now's the time."

She turned and walked into the living room, plopping down on the burgundy corduroy sofa. She clasped her hands between her knees and nodded at the overstuffed chair opposite. From the faint, cloying smell of oil mixed with cigarette smoke, I knew it was Jim's television chair. I sat down, rested my forearms on my knees, clasped my hands together, and regarded Grace with sympathy. The broken mirror still hung on the wall behind her chair.

"So tell me," I said.

"We've been arguing all day," she said. "Jennifer and I. All day long, back and forth. If she doesn't keep that baby, it's going to kill her grandparents. First Jim dying, and now this. It'll be something she'll regret until the day she dies."

I frowned. "Was Jennifer raped, Mrs. Sisson?"

She looked as if I'd slapped her.

"No, she wasn't raped," she snapped. "My God, what do you think? If she was *raped,* then you'd have heard from me long before this."

"Then I'm not sure any of this is our concern."

"It is if he takes her somewhere for an illegal abortion. She's only fifteen years old, Sheriff. Do you understand that? Fifteen years old."

"I understand that perfectly well, Mrs. Sisson. And you think that's what she's doing? Looking for a quick way out?"

Grace Sisson nodded. "Of course that's what she's doing. That's what we argued about all day." She pulled a folded piece of paper out of her pocket and held it out to me. It was just a piece of school kids' notebook paper, with large loopy handwriting at the top. "Mom," I read. "I need some time to think. I'll be ok. Jennifer."

I looked up at Grace. "She left this when she was supposedly going across to the burger place?" Grace nodded, and I added, "Maybe she means what she wrote."

"Jennifer doesn't *think* about anything, Sheriff. That's why she got pregnant in the first place. She's not into introspection."

"Who's the father?"

"I assume that it's Kenny Carter."

"But you're not sure."

"No, I'm not sure."

"Do you have any ideas who else it might be?"

She was too long answering. "No."

"Was Kenny over here Tuesday night?"

This time, she looked at me steadily, with no petulance, no evasion, no rudeness. When she spoke, it was as if each word were timed with a metronome. "I...really...don't...know." She took a breath and added, "I really don't know who killed Jim."

Every instinct told me that she was telling the truth. I said, "We'll find out who killed your husband, Mrs. Sisson. And we'll find your daughter for you."

Undersheriff Robert Torrez was waiting by 310 when I came out of the house. "You survived Grace," he said.

"Two wackos in one day, Roberto. It's got to be something in the village water."

He laughed. "No more prints, by the way," he added.

"I didn't think we'd be that lucky."

"So what now?"

I straightened up, stretching my shoulders, the early-evening sun feeling good after the refrigerated air in the Sissons' house. "I guess I'll get me a burger. Want to come?"

He glanced across at the Burger Heaven and made a face. "I don't think so," he said. "Gayle's got something. Why don't you come over? She'd like that."

I reached out and patted him on the arm. "Some other time. I appreciate the offer and I know what I'm missing, but I need to check out one little thing. And you might stay close to the radio. I've got a feeling that it's going to be a busy night."

THIRTY-SIX

BENNY FERNANDEZ had opened Burger Heaven seventeen years before, and for a few years the business had blossomed into one of the most successful teen hangouts in Posadas. Benny had understood some basics about a kid business: give 'em lots of food for not very much money and free refills on the watery fountain drinks, and don't harass 'em when they get so noisy that they drive out the adults. That was his policy.

When Benny died in 1991, his wife had tried to carry on, but she had mistakenly believed that high school kids could be prim and proper, quiet, and well behaved. She'd raised prices and improved food quality, cleaned the place up, and restored order—and lost business. Five years later, she'd sold the place to Nick Chavez's nephew.

Nick owned the Chevy-Olds dealership across the street, and if nothing else, Buddy Chavez could count on his Uncle Nick to send the salesmen and service crew across at lunchtime. But Buddy Chavez was also smart. He turned up the music, piled on the fries, used humongous cups, and brought back free refills. He didn't care if kids were rowdy, and he kept the place open at night until the Posadas police cruiser drove by to remind him about the curfew.

I stepped into Burger Heaven and sucked in my gut, remembering with a pang of longing just how good all that stuff with quadruple-digit cholesterol tasted. The smell of deep-frier grease three days past its prime hung heavy in the air.

For a summer weekday dinner hour, the place was busy. Two brave tourists—white-maned, with white pasty northern skin, she in an orange jumpsuit and he in white seersucker trousers and a golf shirt—were the only folks I didn't know.

Buddy Chavez saw me, gave the table he was wiping a final

negligent swipe with the cloth, and headed my way, pausing just long enough to twirl the soggy cloth into a snap for one of the three kids sitting near the jukebox.

"Hey, Sheriff," he said, and the elderly tourists heard him and gave me the once-over. I sort of wished that I had been wearing spurs or something equally authentic.

"Buddy, let's talk," I said, and took him by the elbow, gently steering him toward the small office off the kitchen. He shouted something to one of the counter kids about the air bottle in the diet Coke dispenser and then shrugged at me.

"You got to keep after 'em every minute," he said. The office door had sagged enough that it wouldn't latch, but Buddy banged it into the jamb so it stayed closed. He motioned me toward a chair.

"No, I won't be a minute. I need to know something about Jennifer Sisson, Buddy."

"Jeez, wasn't that an awful thing, though," Buddy said. He was carrying fifty pounds too many, and he dabbed at the sweat on his neck. The closed door shut off the icy cold air from the restaurant, and the west side wall of his office was radiating heat into the room like a sauna.

"Jennifer came in here earlier. In fact, just a few minutes ago."

Buddy frowned. "She did?"

I smiled at him. "You've been here all afternoon?"

"Sure. Since ten this morning."

"Then you know she was here."

"Well, okay. I saw her. Sure."

"Who did she leave with?"

"Hey now, I don't keep track—"

I cut him off. "Buddy, look. It's no big deal. You told deputies a couple of days ago that you didn't hear or see anything across at the Sissons', and I believe that. Hell, it was dark, and whatever happened over there took place in the backyard, out of sight. But Jennifer Sisson came in here today, sometime around five-thirty."

He nodded vigorously, and the fat under his chin shook. "She was here, Sheriff. Honest to God." He held up his hands plaintively, as if he wished the one answer might end the conversation and let him off the hook.

"I know that," I said patiently. "I asked who she left with."

"Why would I know that?"

"Because you do, Buddy. You're being evasive, and you're sweating like you're standing out in the sun." I smiled pleasantly at him again. "And in a minute, I'm going to start wondering why."

Buddy Chavez leaned against the door. "Look, Sheriff. I don't want to start anything. I really don't. Just ask the girl who she was with. That makes more sense. Or Jennifer."

"It might make sense," I said, "if I can find her. If some helpful soul hasn't dumped her in a ditch somewhere."

Buddy's eyes opened wide and he paled a shade or two. "You're kidding."

"I'm too tired to kid anyone," I said. "Who was she with?"

He gulped a time or two and then managed to say, "I think it was Sam Carter." He could see the surprise on my face, I'm sure.

"You think? You *think* that it was Sam Carter?"

"Well, he didn't actually come in. I was cleaning off a table, and I saw him pull into the parking lot, over there by the light pole. At first I didn't recognize him.... Well, I mean I didn't recognize the vehicle. Well, I mean I did, but I thought it was somebody else's. His kid's maybe. That red Jeep Wrangler that Kenny Carter drives all the time. I thought it was probably Kenny. But then he opened the door just a bit, and he kinda waved, like this." He held out his hand, palm up, and flexed the fingers rapidly.

"And at that point you recognized the person as Sam Carter?"

Buddy nodded. "Sure. Jennifer had picked up her order and was sitting with a group of kids over on that six top," and he motioned toward a table at the east end of the restaurant "over by the door. She got up and left, and I saw her get in the car."

"Why were you watching her, in particular?"

Buddy Chavez looked embarrassed. "Hell of a body, you know?"

"And fifteen years old, Buddy."

He shrugged.

"You're sure about the car."

He nodded.

"And you're sure it was Sam Carter. Not Kenny."

He nodded, pursing his lips as if he knew something else juicy. "Oh, I'm sure."

"You didn't hear her say, 'Here's my ride,' or something like that?"

"No. She just got up and I heard her say, 'I gotta go. My mom's waiting.' And then she skipped out."

"But her mom wasn't in the car."

"No."

"You didn't see anyone else in that Jeep with Sam? Maybe someone else sitting on the passenger side?"

"He was by himself. The back window on that rig was unzipped. You know the way they drive around with it out. I could see plain enough."

"And when Grace Sisson called over here, were you the one who answered the phone?"

Buddy took a little bit too long answering but finally nodded and said, "Yeah, I guess I was."

"And you told her that Jennifer had left."

"Yep."

"But you didn't tell her with whom?"

He shook his head. "Nope. I didn't figure it was any of my business."

"And Grace didn't ask?"

"Well...no, she didn't."

"So you didn't tell her that you'd seen her daughter drive off with Sam Carter? Didn't let his name slip, even casual-like?"

"Nope, I didn't tell her."

I had moved to the door, and Buddy stepped aside. I rested my hand on the worn brass knob. "That sort of puzzles me, Buddy."

He peered out through the dirty window of the door, still leaning hard against it. "It ain't any of my responsibility," he said, and glanced at me quickly to see if I'd agree. But then he added, "Besides, I figured she knew."

I regarded Buddy with interest. "Now why would you figure that, as disinterested as you are in the whole mess?"

"Well, she sees Sam Carter often enough. She can take care of her own business. It's not any of my concern."

My hand froze on the knob. "She sees Sam Carter 'often

enough.' What does that mean? And who do you mean? Grace or Jennifer?'' I had the nagging feeling that I knew exactly where the conversation was headed.

Buddy grimaced. "Come on, Sheriff. Please." I ignored his entreaty and just glared at him. "Shit, they meet here all the time."

"They who, Buddy?"

"Sam and Grace. I mean, she walks over to pick up some lunch, and Sam, he's usually waiting out in the car, out in the lot. He never comes in or nothing. Just kind of casual, you know. She gets her lunch, then moseys on out. And ends up in his car. And then they drive off. Or once in a while just sit and talk, I guess. I don't know."

I grinned. "It would appear you see quite a bit. How often does this happen?"

He shrugged. "I don't keep count. Once, twice a week, maybe. Well," he said, and inadvertently started to look a little pleased with himself. "You know how it is. Like a couple of school kids. They're tryin' to be so clever and end up being more obvious than not."

"And how long's this been going on?"

"Couple of months."

I reached out and took Buddy by the shoulder, digging my thumb in by his collarbone just enough that it got his attention. "Thanks, Buddy. And this is between you and me, all right? You don't tell anybody else."

"Wouldn't think of it."

"That's good." I gave his shoulder a parting shake. "That's good. Hell, for all we know, the county commission chairman is just helping out with a little baby-sitting."

"Oh, yeah," Buddy said, and managed a weak laugh.

Back outside in 310, I turned the air conditioning full up and sat for a minute, staring out across the parking lot. "Sam, you goddamn old fool," I murmured.

THIRTY-SEVEN

I HAD LITTLE DESIRE to make a bigger fool of myself than I assumed Sam Carter to be, so when I left Burger Heaven I dipped across the street to Grace Sisson's. I left 310 idling in the driveway, and Grace had the front door open before I'd crossed the sidewalk.

"What did you find out?" she barked.

I wasn't about to shout across the front yard. She might have been rude, contrary, and stubborn, but Grace Sisson was not stupid. Her puffy eyes narrowed as she watched me silently approaching, and she could see damn well that I had news...none of it good.

"We need to talk," I said, and for once Grace didn't argue. She turned on her heel and retreated into the house. I closed the door behind me, took off my hat, and wiped the sweat from my forehead with my shirtsleeve.

"Grace," I said, "there are some things you need to explain to me."

"What are you talking about? Where's Jennifer?"

"I don't know. But I'm pretty certain about *who* she's with. And I think you are, too."

She wasn't ready yet. I saw the lines of her jaw harden, and her eyes grew resentful and wary. "I don't know what you're talking about."

"Yeah, you do," I said. "Tell me about Sam Carter."

The house was absolutely silent for about the count of ten. The tinnitus in my ears was cranked up as loud as it would go, and I listened to that symphony while Grace made up her mind.

She surprised me. "What do you want to know?"

"Why would he pick up Jennifer across the street?"

If Grace had a ready answer, she wasn't prepared to share it. She turned, arms crossed tightly across her chest, and walked slowly across the length of the living room. At the far wall, she leaned against the doorjamb, her back to me. Her shoulders jerked every so often, and then she tipped her head until it was leaning against the doorjamb, too, and I knew she was crying.

She wasn't the sort who invited a warm arm around the shoulders, and I stood silently in the foyer, hat in hand, waiting.

"He and I have been seeing each other," she said after a few minutes, voice husky.

"All right," I said, trying to keep my tone neutral.

"No, it's not all right," Grace snapped, and she had the old nasty twang back. "It's not anywhere near all right."

"Did Jim know?"

She turned to face me, making no effort to wipe her face. "I don't think so." She shrugged. "But who knows, in a town this small? If he did, he never said anything." She stepped across and wrenched a fistful of tissues out of the box on top of the television.

"And Jennifer?"

"Sam saw her all the time in the store. Sometimes we'd be in there together, Jennifer and me. Sam would flirt with her." She turned away again. "I guess I thought it was cute. And then a time or two over here, just in the past few months. And then last week, he offered her a job at the store." She hauled out more tissue, and her face was flushed red. "That slimy son of a bitch," she muttered.

"You don't think the baby is Kenny's, then, do you?"

"The kids broke up in early June. Jennifer never mentioned Kenny after that. So no...I don't think so."

"Sam picked Jennifer up at the burger joint a few minutes ago," I said. "Any idea where they're headed?"

"Oh, God," Grace said, and sagged onto the sofa. She dabbed at her face, but no amount of dabbing was going to do any good. "Jenny doesn't want to carry the baby. That's what we were arguing about. My folks and Jim—and he assumed that the baby was Kenny's, of course—they all see it as some kind of goddamned deadly sin that she might try to get rid of it." She heaved a deep sigh. "That's what Jim told her at lunch on Tuesday, in between screaming matches. That it was just bad judgment that she got pregnant...that she wasn't going to compound that with murder." She shook her head. "She's scared, Sheriff."

"Was Sam Carter over here Tuesday night?"

Grace shook her head wearily. "I just don't know. I don't know why he would be. The last person he'd want to cross would be Jim. I think he was afraid of my husband. He always acted like it, so supercautious and all."

I pictured the wiry, sun-browned Jim Sisson, arm muscles like steel cables, lifting the balding, potbellied Sam Carter off the ground by the scruff of the neck.

"Were you and Jim going to get a divorce?"

"We hadn't discussed it."

"Did you discussed it with Sam?"

"He told me that I should leave Jim. That he'd take better care of me."

"Of course, he didn't say anything about leaving *his* wife, did he," I said, and Grace shot me a dark, venomous look. "Where would they go? Jennifer and Carter. Any ideas?"

Grace balled the tissue up into a tight little wad and chucked it into the wicker wastepaper basket by the end table. "Maybe he knows somebody," she said. "A little money to the right doctor." She shrugged. "Obviously, he wouldn't want Jennifer to have the child any more than she does."

"You'll sign a complaint against him? Not that we'll need it if we catch them together. But if you'll sign a criminal complaint, and if you'll testify, then that puts the ball in our court. That gives us all the leverage we need."

She almost smiled. "With pleasure. I hope you find him before I do."

"There's no question that we'll find him, Mrs. Sisson. It's out of your hands now, though. You let us handle it."

"He has my daughter, Sheriff. And while we're standing here talking there's nothing but harm that can come to her."

"Stay by the phone," I said. "I need to know that I can reach you at a moment's notice. You'll do that for me?"

She nodded and reached for more tissue. I left the house by the back door, ready to give the troops something more interesting to do than lifting faded prints off hot metal.

THIRTY-EIGHT

SAM CARTER MIGHT have been an old fool, but he made a pretty good stab at being clever. It didn't take us long to find the red Jeep, since it was parked squarely in Sam's driveway on Ridgeway. I could think of a couple of reasons why Sam would borrow his son's distinctive vehicle, only one of them innocent.

I pulled in close beside the little Jeep and got out. Unless it was inside the garage, Sam's Explorer was gone. Bob Torrez drove on up the street to the dead end and turned around, idling his patrol car to a stop by the curb just as I reached the front door of Carter's house.

I could hear a television inside, and when I rang the doorbell a dog started yapping. I heard Kenny Carter's voice over the din, and the dog shut up just as the front door was pulled open.

The youngster took a step backward when he saw me, and then he ducked his head sideways, looking past me to catch a glimpse of the two patrol cars out in the street.

"How you doin', Kenny," I said. "I need to speak with your dad."

"He's not here."

"Your mom?"

"She's got Thursday night bowling. She'll be home about nine or ten."

And what a homecoming that will be, I thought. "I see. Well, say, do you happen to know where your dad went? You think he might be down at the store?" Tom Mears had headed directly for the Family SuperMarket, and when he called in momentarily it wouldn't matter much what Kenny said.

Kenny glanced at his wristwatch. "That's where he said he was headed. His car's on the fritz and he was hunting around for some part. He borrowed my Jeep to run a couple of errands."

"And then he came back and got his own car?"

Kenny nodded and shrugged. "I guess he found what he needed."

"I guess he did," I said. "We'll check there," I added, and started to turn away.

"Store's closed now, though. At six," Kenny offered. "That's why he was going to do some work. After-hours. He kinda likes to do that, especially when Mom's out."

"I see," I said, and regarded Kenny for a moment. If he was lying, if he actually knew what his father was up to, he deserved an Academy Award. "Thanks."

The undersheriff and I met in the middle of the street.

"Kenny said his father was heading for the store."

"The store's locked up," Torrez said. "Mears is keeping an eye on it, but Sam's car isn't there. No sign of anyone inside."

"What did Howard find out at the Posadas Inn?"

"He hasn't called in," Torrez said. He opened his cell phone, clicked it on, and waited while the circuits did their thing.

"Any luck?" Bob said, and then frowned while he waited. I could imagine Howard Bishop's slow, measured tones, never too excited about anything. "You're sure," Bob said and nodded as if the sergeant could hear the head motion, then added, "Probably you ought to stay down at that end." He snapped the phone shut. "Nothing."

"He could have used another name," I said. "He's well known, all right, but if the right kid was working the registration desk, he wouldn't know Sam from Adam."

"Howard said he's going to go through the register one name at a time and check the vehicle registrations. Maybe he'll turn up something."

"So," I said, hands on hips and standing squarely in the middle of Ridgeway, "where the hell did he go? If he wants to be home by the time his wife is finished with her bowling, then he's got until about nine o'clock." I glanced at my watch. "Two hours and fifteen minutes. If he was taking the girl out of town, that's not enough time."

"No, it's not."

"Maybe he's got a friend somewhere," I said. "If Sam wanted to be discreet and rent a room, then the Posadas Inn is just about it...the only game in town. If it's somewhere private, who the hell knows. Put out a bulletin for the vehicle. He doesn't have much of a head start if he was heading out of town."

"Been there, done that," Torrez said. "He's not going to go anywhere on the interstate or the major state highways."

"And if he's smart, he's kicking dust somewhere on a dirt road," I said.

"To where?"

I grinned. "Hell of a good question." Torrez's cell phone chirped again and he had it out and to his ear before I could tell him the damn thing was ringing.

"Yo," he said, and listened intently. I saw a grin starting to spread across his face. "Outstanding," he said, turning toward his vehicle. "We'll be there in about two minutes. Wait for us. And make sure Gayle is there."

Torrez was yanking open the door of his car even as he said over his shoulder to me, "He didn't reserve a room today, sir." He grinned. "It was yesterday evening. The night auditor remembers the call."

Two minutes was an exaggeration. We hit the parking lot of the Posadas Inn so fast we practically went airborne. Sgt. Howard Bishop was standing on the concrete skirt that wrapped around the building. As I got out of the car, he held up a key.

"Room two-oh-seven. The night auditor said that Sam Carter reserved the room for two days for his brother and sister-in-law."

I heard another engine and turned in time to see Tom Pasquale pull in beside 310, with Gayle Torrez riding shotgun. "Let's go visit this brother and sister-in-law," I said. As Tom fell in step beside me, I said, "I thought you were supposed to be moving."

"We are, sir. But I checked in with Dispatch and there was so much going on that I figured I'd better get in on it." He grinned.

We found the outside stairway, tucked in beside the soda and ice machines, and Torrez and Pasquale were up the stairs and padding down the hallway before I'd taken five steps. Room 215 sat on the corner by the stairs, with 207 just about halfway down the hall.

A DO NOT DISTURB sign was hooked over the doorknob.

Bishop had the key in hand, but I held up a hand. "Why don't we just knock?" I said.

Out of the corner of my eye, I saw Tom Pasquale drift off to one side, and his hand was on the butt of his service automatic. If he drew the damn thing, I didn't want him standing behind me.

I rapped on the door just loud enough that the occupant, if there was one, would hear it even if in the bathroom. There was no response, and I knocked again. This time, a small voice said, "Who is it?" The three words were enough. I could picture the kid standing on the other side of the heavy door, scared and alone. It sure as hell wasn't Carter's sister-in-law.

I glanced at Gayle and she nodded. "Jennifer? It's Sheriff Gastner." That brought no response, and I added, "We met down at your grandpa's place. Remember? Yesterday, or whenever it was?" I tried to imagine what the girl was doing while the crowd of law enforcement types stood outside her door. Unless she wanted to climb out the window, this was her only exit.

"Jennifer? Are you all right? You need to open the door."

She didn't answer, and Howard reached out with the key. I didn't know why, but at the moment it seemed important to me that Jennifer open the door herself, if she could. I waved Bishop off and said, "Jennifer, it's over. Nobody else is coming. It's just us. Your mother's waiting for you."

I tipped my head, listening hard. I thought I could hear the padding of feet coming across the carpet. Sure enough, the dead bolt snicked back and the door opened an couple of inches against the security chain. Jennifer Sisson's round face peered out, and I felt such a surge of relief that an audible groan escaped from me.

"You OK?" I said. How any scared kid stuck by herself in a motel room could be OK looking out into a hallful of sober-faced strangers was beyond me. She managed a small nod. "Gayle and I want to come in, all right?"

Jennifer pushed the door shut, slipped the chain, and then pulled it open. I stepped into the room, and Gayle slipped in and wrapped an arm protectively around the girl. "Did Sam say that he was coming back in a little bit?" I asked.

"Sam who?" She was a rotten liar. "I don't know any Sam." She retreated back to one of the black vinyl chairs tucked under the window table.

"Sam Carter picked you up at the burger place across the street from your house. He reserved this room yesterday, sweetheart. So yes. You know Sam Carter. When's he coming back? Tonight sometime?"

"Yes." I saw the blush spread up her neck, turning her plump cheeks crimson. "He said he'd be right back."

"Did he tell you who he was going to get?"

Jennifer shook her head.

"And then what? Where were you going after that?"

"Nowhere," Jennifer said, almost inaudibly. "Just home. I told Mom I'd be out for a while. I figured she wouldn't care all that much."

"Well, she does. She cares about you and she cares about the baby. I wonder..." Jennifer didn't have a chance to learn what I wondered. The small handheld radio on my belt barked loudly, "Three ten, three oh seven on channel three."

I pulled the radio off the clip and keyed the mike. "Go ahead, three oh seven."

"Three ten, be advised that a black Ford Explorer, license three-seven-three Victor Charlie Kilo, is parked on Rincon Avenue, just behind the *Register*."

"That's a just a block north of the supermarket," I said to no one in particular. "Three oh seven, are there any occupants?"

"Negative, three ten. The back door of the store is unlatched, though."

"Stay put. We'll be there in about a minute and a half. If the owner of the vehicle shows up, take him into custody."

"Ten-four."

I pulled the door open and beckoned to Tom Pasquale. "Thomas, you and Gayle take Miss Sisson home. Gayle, you stay at the Sissons' until you hear from me. I don't care what Mrs. Sisson does or doesn't say. And, Thomas, as soon as you've dropped them off and you've made sure that Deputy Taber is with them, post yourself over at the Carters' place on Ridgeway. I don't want Kenny going anywhere until this mess is sorted out. If he argues, take him into custody.''

"Yes, sir.''

I turned to Bishop. "Howard, you need to stay here in case someone shows up. Who the hell knows. Whoever it is, take 'em into custody, too, and charge 'em with conspiracy for starters. Hell, we might as well just round up the whole goddamn town.'' I took Torrez by the elbow. "Let's see what Carter's up to.''

THIRTY-NINE

WE DIDN'T WASTE any time. At thirty-two minutes after six, I pulled into the empty parking lot of Sam Carter's supermarket. Monday through Thursday, the place opened at 6:00 a.m. and closed twelve hours later. On Friday and Saturday, the store stayed open until 8:00. It was probably one of the few supermarkets left in the world that was closed all day on Sunday.

By driving around behind the building, I could look up the alley that ran behind the supermarket and Tommy's Diner, then crossed Rincon to pass behind the large metal building that housed the *Posadas Register*. I caught a glimpse first of the big white-on-blue lettering on the side of the newspaper building and thought with grim amusement that if Frank Dayan was working late the day before publication, it would pay him to step out his own back door to catch the scoop of the year.

Tom Mears's Bronco sat squarely in the middle of the alley beside the Dumpsters. From that point, he could watch the back door of the supermarket and the black Explorer parked on Rincon just west of the alley. He couldn't see the front doors of the grocery store but had wisely chosen the two targets most removed from casual view by passersby.

He got out of the Bronco and met Torrez and me as we approached the back door of the store.

"I walked around," he said in a husky whisper. "The front doors are the kind that you have to open with a key, even if you're inside. There's no push bar."

"All right. And this one is open?" I stepped to the back door and could see for myself. The door may have been locked, but it was ajar about a quarter of an inch.

I stood at the door, my ear to the metal. "Nothing? Did you hear anyone?"

"No, sir. Not since I drove up. I tried the front door and then came around here. I could see that the door might be open, so I didn't touch it. And then I caught a glimpse of the Explorer."

I stepped away from the building and looked down the alley. "Someone just driving by on Grande wouldn't be apt to notice his vehicle, parked off to the side like that. And if they did, there's no reason to think anything about it." I turned to Bob. "What do you think?"

He pulled a hefty pocketknife out of his pocket and reached up high on the door, within an inch of the top corner. He inserted the blade and gently twisted. The door moved a fraction, held tightly in the jamb. It hadn't been slammed quite hard enough to catch the bolt in the striker plate. Torrez slid the knife down a bit and twisted again. The door moved a bit more. He knelt and repeated the maneuver down at the bottom, and at the fourth twist, the steel door popped open.

"Uh-oh," he whispered and grinned. Using the point of the knife, he tipped the door open far enough that we could enter without touching it.

No sooner had he done that than he held up a hand sharply, gesturing upward. Looking past him, I could see the lights on in Sam Carter's upstairs office. The three of us stood in the door, listening. The outer door of Carter's office, positioned right at the top of the short stairway, was open. If he was in there, even talking quietly on the phone, we'd hear him.

"I'll check," Mears said, and he moved across the concrete floor to the stairway, then ascended two or three at a time. He stopped in the office doorway, turned, and shrugged.

"Nobody," he said.

I moved to the bottom of the stairs.

"He might be planning to come back," Torrez said quietly.

"Maybe," I said. "Or maybe he just didn't pay attention when he closed the door."

"Sir," Mears said, reappearing in the open office doorway, and this time there was some urgency in his voice. "You might want to look at this."

I made my way up the stairway, with Torrez patiently following, Mears waiting until I'd reached the landing, then stepped into the office, moving quickly to the one-way glass that overlooked the store. He pointed. Over to the left, near one of the glass cases that held the refrigerated beverages, was a considerable pool of liquid on the floor—perhaps water, maybe soda pop or beer.

"The glass in the cooler door is broken, too," the deputy said, but I had to take his word for it. It looked fine to me.

I took a moment and scanned the rest of the store. Everything appeared in place.

"Take a look," I said. "I'll be down in a minute."

The papers on top of Carter's desk interested me, and I took out my pen and used it as a probe to move things slightly, looking at this and that, being careful not to start a landslide. There were order forms, inventory, correspondence with vendors, time sheets...all the sorts of things one would expect to find on a store manager's desk. Sam would have been delighted to see me rummaging, I'm sure.

After no more than thirty seconds, my radio startled me as Mears's disembodied voice broadcast in a harsh whisper, "Sheriff."

I moved my pen and let an invoice from Royalty Line Food Specialties drop back in place, then stepped to the window and looked down. Mears and Torrez stood at the near end of aisle 12, and I could tell by their posture that they weren't looking at a puddle of spilled mountain spring water.

Despite a hammering pulse, I took my time negotiating the steep stairway. I turned into the store and came up behind Mears, who looked as if he'd been flash-frozen in place. Torrez turned to me, one eyebrow raised. Sprawled on the floor with his blood mixing with whatever liquid was running out of the drink cooler was Posadas County Commission Chairman Sam Carter.

"Oh, for God's sakes," was about all I managed to say. Mears lifted a foot to move closer and Torrez snapped, "Watch your step." By moving along the opposite side of the aisle, staying close to the shelves of pretzels and chips, Torrez avoided the puddle. He knelt near Sam's head and reached out to check the carotid pulse.

"He's dead," Torrez said. He regarded the blood under Carter's head. "Hasn't been long, though." Remaining on his haunches,

Torrez pivoted slowly, scrutinizing the area around the body. "It looks like he took one in the back of the head, kind of a grazing shot. That would do it."

"And look at this," Tom Mears said, pointing at the cooler door. "Ricochet, maybe. Or maybe the one that killed him. It isn't a clean hole in the glass. Whatever it was exploded a couple quart bottles of beer."

"Christ," I said, "I can still smell the gunpowder." I looked at Torrez. "You smell it?"

He nodded. "Look over in the corner there." I did so and saw the blue plastic bank money pouch, zipper gaping wide open. "Somebody came in right at closing, maybe." He made a hammer-and-trigger motion with his right hand. "*Pop*. Take the money and run." He stood up with a loud crack of the knees. "Or at least that's what we're supposed to think." He backed away from the body.

"Explain the door to me, for instance," I said.

Torrez nodded. "The cooler door is closed. The broken bottles are behind it. So how does the beer spill so far across the aisle if the door is closed, with only a little bullet hole through it?"

"Unless Carter grabbed it when he fell," Mears said. "Maybe pulled it open some, then the door closes after he tumbles away."

"Could be," Torres said. "Could be." He was gazing at the floor, and held up both hands as if he were blocking traffic. "Stay put," he said, and brushed past me, staying close to the racks.

"Christ, Sam," I muttered, "what the hell have you gotten yourself into?"

In a few moments, Torrez returned with his flashlight. The evening sunshine was still bright outside, streaming in through the advertisement-plastered store windows. The specialty stock, piled high in pyramids at the end of each row, bounced and shadowed the slanting sunlight so that most of the cavernous store, especially the rear portion where we were standing with its high fluorescent lights turned off, was gloomy.

"Just a thought," Torrez said. "The killer didn't run out the front door, unless he had Carter's keys...and he's not likely to spend time fumbling there and risk being seen. And we found the back door ajar. That's what makes sense to me. You've got to really give that door a good hard push to make sure it latches securely. So if whoever it was goes out the back way after tussling with Carter, he either goes down this same aisle, maybe even having to step over the body, or goes up front, cuts across, and then down another aisle.''

"We don't know if there was a struggle or not," I said. "And we don't know how Sam was standing when he was shot."

"No, but we've got a trajectory in the cooler there, from door to bottle. That's a start."

"We've got to take this one step at a time now," I said, apprehensive that the undersheriff was just eagerly charging ahead without any clear notion of what he was looking for. "We need to call Perrone over here," I said to Mears. Trying to reach conclusions without even preliminary findings from the medical examiner always made me nervous.

Sam's corpse hadn't been touched yet. I looked down at him, wondering if his keys were in his pocket, wondering if he'd had a weapon when he came down the stairs to confront the killer, wondering who the hell had pulled the trigger, wondering all kinds of things in a confusing blizzard of questions.

Moving methodically, Bob Torrez crouched down, snapped on the flashlight, and laid it on the polished tile floor. "Some things we don't want to have slip away," he mused. "I don't think we want to wait on this one." The beam shot down the aisle toward the back wall, a parabola of white light harsh on the white-and-gray-flecked tile. He rolled the flashlight slowly across the tile, using just the tip of his index finger.

None of us were breathing. I bent down with my hands on my knees as the light stopped, and even I could see what had to be shoe prints.

"Bingo," Torrez whispered. "Somebody got careless."

"Well, I'll be goddamned," I said.

"We need Linda here with the camera," he said to Mears. "And Perrone, and the whole crew. But stay off the radio. Use the phone."

Mears backpedaled down the aisle, following Torrez's example by keeping his steps immediately beside the shelving...an awkward and difficult place for anyone to walk and the least likely place for us to plant our size twelves on important evidence.

I knelt down while Torrez held the light motionless. "See 'em?"

"I see something," I said. "I'd hate to be the one to have to swear what they are."

He reached out his left hand toward the ghostly patterns. "Not much," he said, "but something." With his index finger, he traced the print's outline in the air just above it. "It looks like whoever it was just sort of grazed the puddle here, enough to leave about a quarter of a print, a slice lengthwise from toe to heel. If we're lucky, we can even measure a size."

"What's it look like to you?"

"It ain't very big. Teenager, woman, small man."

"You think it'll show up in a photo?"

"If it can be done, Linda can do it," Torrez said. "If we can bounce the light just right, I don't see why not. If we can see them clearly with the flashlight, there's no reason the film shouldn't be able to see 'em, too."

I remained kneeling, gazing at the prints—or at least at the spot where Bob Torrez said they were. "Shit," I said, and shook my head. It was more than just a comment on the current state of affairs, particularly those that included the dead Sam Carter. Torrez caught the inflection and looked sharply at me.

"What?"

I took a deep breath and then pushed myself to my feet. "It was no casual robbery. Not shooting him in the back of the head like that. And unless Sam's lying right on top of it, I don't see a weapon, either. Nothing left behind."

Torrez looked sideways at me. He held out a thumb. "Kenny Carter is home, under surveillance. Sam's wife could have done it, but she's bowling. I already verified that with a phone call after we stopped by there and saw Kenny. Grace Sisson is home, and has been ever since she came back from Las Cruces. Jennifer was locked in a motel room, waiting for her sugar daddy, here." He gazed down at the corpse and then back at me. "So who does that leave?"

"I don't know," I said. "I wish to hell I did." I looked down the aisle. "Tell you what. You don't need me here. While you're working this, I'm going to go back upstairs and turn that office upside down. I gave it a once-over, but now..." I hesitated. "And don't forget to have Gayle, or someone else who's good at that sort of thing, break the news to MaryBeth Carter." I turned to go, then stopped. "And make sure you give our brilliant assistant DA a call. He should be in on this. If you don't, you'll be on his shit list for life. And he's too stupid to have as an enemy."

I looked down at the remains of Sam Carter. As bad as I felt about not being able to save Sam Carter from his own foolishness, some ideas were beginning to coalesce in my mind that were making me feel a whole lot worse.

FORTY

I SAT DOWN in Sam Carter's chair and looked out across the sea of papers on his desk. If there was some kind of order there, it escaped me. The Mexican brass trash can under the left desk wing was packed to the brim, just as it had been when Torrez and I had visited not too many hours before. If possible, more stuff had been piled on top until it looked like some crazy artist's mixed-media bouquet.

The computer near my elbow was the same model as those in the county building, and I pushed the corner key, rewarded by the symphony of start-up chimes. Sam Carter might have been working after-hours, but it hadn't been on the computer—unless when he'd been interrupted he'd taken time to shut down the system first.

While I waited for all the bells and whistles to do their thing, I opened one desk drawer at a time. Guessing what might have been out of place was impossible, since nothing appeared to be *in* any particular place. Sam Carter had been a fan of landfill filing—the most recent junk on top.

In the right-hand drawer, hidden under a pile of old-fashioned receipt books, was a small nickel-plated pistol, one of those cheap imported things that are supposed to make you feel safe until you actually have to use them. With the tip of my pen I lifted it out by the trigger guard. The clip was missing, and it hadn't been fired. I put it back.

Turning to the computer, I looked at the list of the most recent files that had been accessed and clicked on the top of the list. After a few seconds a letter to QuadState Distributors appeared on the screen blistering them about dairy product expiration dates—perhaps a subject near and dear to Sam Carter's heart. An irate milk distributor might have shot Sam Carter, but it seemed unlikely.

I heard voices downstairs as the party got under way. If they needed anything from me, the undersheriff knew where I was.

The bulk of the files were spreadsheet types of things, either inventory or ordering files or pay and time sheets—endless rows of numbers. What correspondence there was appeared to be Sam Carter taking various people to task—usually errant distributors but also a series of letters to his insurance company about their subpar performance when he had asked for a new section of ceiling damaged by a leaking sprinkler pipe.

I ducked out of the files and sat back, thinking. In the lower right-hand corner, the little trash-can icon bulged, and I grinned. It looked just like the real trash can under the desk. A click of the mouse brought up the trash file—unemptied for a significant number of bits, or bites, or whatever counted for trash to a computer.

I didn't know much about computers, but Estelle Reyes-Guzman had once shown me that the trash can could be emptied, just like its real-life counterpart. That and the off-on switch accounted for at least half of what I knew about the electronic world.

The file names didn't mean much, except for one titled *"commissioner: you."* I selected it, and in an instant the pathetic little note aimed at smearing Tom Pasquale's name—and the Sheriff's Department's reputation—appeared on the screen.

"Well, I'll be damned," I said, and sat back.

Sam had let the computer program name the document for him but then had trashed the file, covering his tracks. Except he'd forgotten to take out the garbage, leaving it to ripen in its little electronic trash bag.

While I waited for the printer to warm up, I retraced my tracks and pulled up the letter of reprimand Sam had written to the distributors. "Sure enough," I muttered, and sent that, the trash file, and the trash index to the printer.

I heard steps behind me, and Tom Mears appeared in the door. "Sir, they're going to remove the body now."

"All right. Any other wounds?"

"No, sir. Just the one in the back of the head."

"How about a cut on the finger?"

"The undersheriff asked Perrone to check on that first thing," Mears said.

"And no weapon?"

"No, sir."

"I'll be down in a minute. Is Linda here yet?"

"Yes, sir. She and Bob are doing some measurements. Did you find anything up here?"

The printer started its whine, and I nodded. "I think so. Give me a minute."

I sat silently, watching the pages ooze out of the little laser printer. I wanted the souvenirs for Tom Pasquale's benefit as much as anything else. Now that I'd found the original home of the smear letters, Tom was going to feel a lot better. And when he compared the phrase *"in five instances that we have documented"* that appeared in his note with the phrase *"in several instances that we have documented"* that graced the letter to the dairy products distributor, he would feel confident that not only had the letters come from Sam's computer, but Sam himself had written them.

My hunch was that Taffy Hines was correct: Sam Carter had been too proud of his little libel scam not to show the draft to Taffy and then had let his tendency to be a slob trip up any effort he might have made to cover his tracks. He had miscalculated in thinking that folks would be more interested in the rumor itself, rather than wondering where the note might have originated.

I turned off the printer. They'd be bundling Sam's corpse up, and nothing I'd found pointed to his killer. Maybe he had interrupted a two-bit money snatch.... That was the simplest scenario.

Even as I was pushing myself out of Sam's comfortable chair, I heard steps coming up to the office. Don Jaramillo appeared, face flushed. Behind him were Tom Pasquale and Frank Dayan.

"My God," Jaramillo said, "what kind of mess is this?"

"Are you talking about the office here, or downstairs, or the world in general, Counselor?" I asked, and cocked my head in Dayan's direction. "And who called you? And better yet, who the hell let you in the door?"

"I told him that if he walked right behind me, he could come as far as here," Deputy Pasquale said.

"If you want me out, I'll go," Dayan said. "I happened to see all the cars and lights and came on down. But I'll stay out of the way. I'm holding my front page. It's really Sam Carter?"

"What's left of him, yes," I said. "Sam's got you on a deadline. He would have liked that."

"So what the hell happened?" the assistant district attorney asked.

"I don't know," I said. "Beyond what's obvious."

"And what's that?"

"You haven't been in the store yet?"

"Well, yes, I was in the store. Torrez is busy mucking around trying to establish the trajectory of the bullet that broke the beer bottles."

"Mucking around?" I looked at Jaramillo, trying to keep the expression on my face pleasant.

"Well..."

I stepped up close to Jaramillo and lowered my voice. "I think in a murder investigation it's interesting to know where the bullet might have come from and where it went, don't you?"

"Well, of course." His eyes darted around the office, and then he lit on a new topic. "The money bag didn't contain any cash...just checks and stuff. So it looks like robbery. We have no way of knowing how much they got unless Carter had the deposit slip already filled out."

"Did you check for that?"

Jaramillo frowned as if the thought of him actually doing some of the fieldwork was a foreign idea. Perhaps that was just as well for us. "No," he said. "I think Tom Mears was working that angle."

"That's good," I said, wanting to add, *"Now you just stay out of the way."*

To Dayan, I said, "You know about as much as we do, Frank. The deputies arrived after-hours to discuss certain other matters with Sam Carter and discovered his body down in the store, lying on the floor by one of the beer coolers. He'd been shot once in the back of the head. Money is apparently missing from the bank bag. Whether Sam was carrying the bag or not we don't know. It would appear that the shooting happened very close to closing time. Deputies will be interviewing the store employees to determine who might have been the last one to see Sam alive."

Dayan had a small recorder in his hand. "Any other leads? Suspects, that sort of thing?"

I exaggerated my enunciation, eyes locked on the recorder: "In-ves-ti-ga-tion is con-tin-u-ing, Frank. Period, thirty."

Dayan hesitated. "And what was going on down at the motel a little bit ago? Was that a related incident? Someone said that every cop car in the county was there."

"That would be about three units," I said. "No big convention. We had a tip that a minor who had been reported missing might be holed up there. She was. End of story."

"Who was it?"

I grinned at Dayan and motioned him back out of the doorway so I could pass. "You know I'm not going to tell you that, Frank. The key word is *minor*."

"And was, is, there any relationship between that incident and this shooting here?"

I stopped on the top step. "Frank, I'll make you this promise. I'll let you know the minute we have something significant. All right?" He was smart enough to notice that I'd ignored his last question and in so doing had supplied an answer of sorts. "The big scoop." I thumped the railing for emphasis. "What's your absolute deadline?"

"I'll hold," he said with a shrug. "The big morning dailies aren't going to get anything this late, so I've got some time."

I nodded. "Fair enough." I glanced at my watch. "Hunt me down around midnight. That gives us five hours. I think we'll have something by then."

"Now what direction are we going with this?" Jaramillo asked, and he pulled a slender fancy leather memo book from his suit coat pocket.

"Give us until midnight," I said again.

Annoyance flashed across Jaramillo's pudgy face. Midnight would also give me plenty of time to find Daniel Schroeder, the district attorney. His office was in Deming, and I considered it a cruel twist of fate that most of the time we had to deal with his assistant rather than him.

"None of this can be published yet," Jaramillo said to Dayan. "This is an ongoing investigation."

"Indeed," I said as I let them go past me on the stairs. I started down after them, saying, "And the sheriff just gave a statement to the press. Use your own judgment, Frank."

Tom Pasquale closed the office door, and I turned and handed him the printer pages. As Dayan and Jaramillo continued on out of earshot, I said quietly, "You might read those and see if you see any similarities." He took the papers, and before he had a chance to read more than a couple words I added, "Both were on Carter's computer. He could have taken the file on a disk to any printer, I suppose, but I doubt that he was smart enough to do that." I reached out and punched Pasquale lightly on the arm. "Did you get more than two lamps and a bookcase moved?"

He grinned, more with relief at seeing the documents than at the question.

"No, sir. But we'll get to it."

"Other things take precedence right now, Thomas. I'm sure Carla Champlin will understand." I pointed at the documents. "Don't lose those. Put 'em in your briefcase. When you get a moment, start a file. I'll write a formal deposition about where I obtained them...all that sort of thing. As soon as he gets breathing space, I'll get Tony Abeyta to come up and make a copy of that computer's hard drive, just to be double sure. I would think he can do that. If he can't, some computer guru can tell him how. Just in case at some later date someone wants to make an issue out of all this."

"Yes, sir." He folded the papers and glanced at the doorway leading to the crime scene. "It's all too bad, though."

"Yes, it is."

"Any ideas about who might have done this?"

"Yes," I said. Frank Dayan was headed out the back door, stepping carefully around Howard Bishop and Tony Abeyta, who were working prints. Don Jaramillo followed, apparently preferring the fresh air outside to the smell of spilled beer and blood.

FORTY-ONE

COUNTY COMMISSION chairman Sam Carter would have cringed at the rate at which we emptied the county's coffers during the next several hours, but he would have swelled at the attention. Of our dozen or so Sheriff's Department employees, ten were on duty that evening.

Deputy Taber got to shake out the kinks when she drove to Las Cruces, hand-delivering a briefcase full of evidence for processing by the state's regional crime lab. Among other things, we had requested a DNA test that would compare the blood from the metal brace on the backhoe with a sample from Sam Carter. I didn't bother to voice my skepticism about that sort of high-tech testing: Maybe it would produce results, maybe not. But if it could weld a direct link to Sam Carter's presence in Jim Sisson's back yard, that was a major step.

If that was Sam's blood on the machine, what would still be missing is the *when*—the smear could have been made anytime, even out on the job site before Jim brought the beast home.

Part-timer Brent Sutherland took over the odious, deadly boring job of keeping an eye on the Sisson household from a new position a block farther down the street. I wasn't ready to cancel the surveillance, as unproductive as it had proved so far, but I wanted a wider view—all of the neighbors included.

Sam and Grace had been hip-deep in an affair, and people had been murdered for a lot less than a hundred-thousand-dollar life insurance policy. Whether or not Grace Sisson was a coconspirator was one of our large, neon, nagging questions. I couldn't believe that Sam's dalliance with Grace had been so discreet that it had been witnessed only by Buddy Chavez, the nosy manager of Burger Heaven across MacArthur.

And who the hell knew what little Jennifer was capable of in her own darker, introspective moments—if, in fact, she had such.

Four deputies were down at the store with Bob Torrez, meticulously combing the crime scene and trying to reconstruct exactly what had happened. By 8:00 p.m., we knew that Sam Carter had most likely spun around after the impact of the fatal bullet through the base of his skull. His hand had spasmed and grabbed one of the polished chrome door handles of the glass cooler. The door had swung open as he fell away, allowing the ruptured beer bottles to foam and spit across the smooth tile floor.

A .38-caliber half-jacketed hollow-point bullet was recovered from the insulated wall of the cooler, stopped dead by the appliance's outside metal casing. The slug was mushroomed and missing fragments of lead, but there was plenty of rifling visible and what must have been bits of Sam's brain stem and skull embedded in the hollow-point tip. All of that went to Las Cruces as well.

Torrez could now establish a trajectory, lining up the hole in the door with the hole in the cooler's cabinetry. The distance between the two was less than eighteen inches, but that was enough.

The entry wound in Sam's skull was on the left side, and the trajectory of the bullet was consistent with his facing the back of the store, the beer coolers on his right and the killer behind him and to his left.

The complete lack of any other evidence suggested to us that Sam hadn't been caught in a struggle. Shoe soles would scuff that polished tile floor easily, and any flailing of arms would scatter chips and canned dip off the shelves opposite the glass coolers.

The zippered bank bag produced lots of prints, and sorting those out became Tom Mear's task.

If Jennifer Sisson hadn't been Sam Carter's major concern just then, the robbery scenario made sense. I could picture Sam Carter walking toward the back of the store, away from the cash registers up front, bank bag in hand, full of the afternoon's receipts. The killer could have entered the store through the back door if it had been unlocked at the time, or he could have been waiting anywhere in the store at closing time. As Sam walked down the aisle, the killer came up behind him, and that was that. One bullet, down goes Sam, grab the bank bag, stop to remove the cash, fling down the useless paperwork, and it's over.

A simple script, and not remotely close to what must have happened. Sam Carter was in the process of arranging some specialized medical treatment for his fifteen-year-old girlfriend. He'd taken the time to reserve a room for her, doing so the day before. He'd picked her up at Burger Heaven when she'd slipped out of the house, heading supposedly for a simple hamburger and some quiet time-out from her mother. Sam had been slick. He knew his wife was busy chasing bowling pins, and he used his son's Jeep—a nice touch by a caring father.

After making Jennifer comfortable in the motel room, he'd headed back to the store. And that's where the puzzle remained. Why he hadn't used the telephone at the motel maybe only Sam knew. It could have been as simple as where he'd placed—or misplaced—the note with the proper telephone number. The puzzling half hour included Sam leaving the motel and arriving back at the store to close up—and keep his appointment with a .38-caliber slug.

Shortly before 9:00 p.m., Linda Real handed me what I wanted to see. I took the eight-by-ten glossies from her and settled back in my chair. She came around the desk to narrate over my shoulder.

"Nicely done," I said.

In good light, with my bifocals held just so, I could see the distinct shoe sole patterns in the thin film of liquid coating the tiles.

"There are just four of them that were still damp enough to photograph," Linda said. She looked tired, the dark circles under her eyes pronounced. "But the first two are really clear."

"Clear enough to match for size, I suspect," I said. "And an interesting tread pattern. A woman's shoe."

"I think you're right, sir. That's a utility tread with the diagonal cleats," Linda said. "More like something a nurse would wear. Not so much a child's shoe."

I leafed through the set until the background changed. "And these are the others that I asked you to take."

"Yes, sir. It's been a day or two, and there have been people walking through the area, but it wasn't hard to find a couple that matched what you wanted."

I took a deep breath and sighed. The dried mud had locked in two sets of prints—the prints of the big, flabby-footed chow, so eager for some exercise and not minding a romp in the fragrant mud after a summer shower, and the shoe prints of the chow's escort. Taffy Hines had been much more careful than the dog about where she'd stepped. The mild waffle soles of her shoes had left distinctive prints, captured easily on the film.

"No match, sir," Linda said. "Not even close."

I got up, tapping the pile of prints into order. "No, the pattern's not even close." I slid out one copy of each shoe print and handed the remaining pile back to Linda. "Outstanding work, Linda. Thanks. I'd appreciate it if you'd stay close, in case someone needs your help."

I found Robert Torrez in the small room that we used as a lab, in close conversation with Tom Mears.

"Can you break away for a bit?" I asked, and Torrez nodded.

"So far, a good set of Sam's prints from the bank bag. We're workin' on the others. But it's going to be almost any store employee, first of all."

"Yep," I said. "If you've got a few minutes, I'd like you and Gayle to take a ride with me." The undersheriff looked at me sharply, and I nodded. "We need to make a stop at Judge Hobart's. I'll fill you in on the way."

FORTY-TWO

TAFFY HINES OPENED the door on the second knock, and if she was surprised to see the three of us on her doorstep, it didn't show.

"Well, now," she said, holding open the door. "Party time! Come on in." She was wearing a loose flannel jogging suit that looked more like pajamas. The outfit was complemented by a pair of rabbit-headed slippers. "And I don't know you, I guess," she said to Gayle.

"Gayle Torrez. I'm the undersheriff's wife."

"Ah," Taffy said. She clasped her hands together, and I saw the tremor there. She looked expectantly at me. "So. What can I do for you-all?"

"I think you know why we're here," I said.

"Well, I know that Jennifer Sisson is home with her mother, and I'm glad about that."

"You were at the store all day?"

"Sure."

"But you heard about Jennifer's little trip nonetheless?"

"Sure." She smiled, but there was another little quiver at the corners of her mouth, and her eyes were sad. "Let's sit. I'm tired." She led us into the kitchen. The table was clean, no cinnamon rolls this time. The coffeepot was clean and dry, sitting under the drip unit. The kitchen counters were bare, polished dry. The place looked as though the owner was making preparations for a long trip.

Gayle and I sat down with Taffy. Bob Torrez remained in the doorway between kitchen and living room, hands hooked in his belt.

"You heard about Sam," I said. "Or maybe 'heard' is the wrong way to put it."

She laughed a quick, nervous little laugh. "Listen," she said, and closed her eyes for just a moment. "This is going to be hard, isn't it?" she said.

"Yes." I reached across and patted the back of her hand.

"You want me to make some coffee or something?" She started to get up.

"No. Thanks."

"Let me tell you why," she said, and then watched as I pulled the small recorder out of my pocket and set it on the table.

"Before you say anything, Taffy, let's get the formalities out of the way," Torrez said, and the undersheriff opened his black vinyl clipboard and extended a form to Taffy, along with a ballpoint pen.

"Mrs. Hines," he said, and she looked up, grinned a brave little smile at his formality, and corrected him.

"Miss Hines," she said. "Or Taffy is just fine. It's actually Tabitha, but heavens, who wants to manage that?"

"Miss Hines," Bob said, "you have the right to remain silent. If you understand that right, would you please say so for the sake of the recording, and then initial in the space provided after the statement I have just read to you. That's number one."

She did so, and Bob continued, "Do you understand that anything you say can and will be used against you in a court of law? If you understand that, initial after number two."

"Heavens," she said. "I thought this was the sort of thing you just mumbled off a little card and that was that."

"In some cases," I said.

"But not this time, eh?" she replied. "How times are changing."

Bob continued on, leading Taffy Hines through each statement, finishing with her signature at the end.

I nudged the small tape recorder. "Now, we're formal, Taffy."

"Am I actually charged with anything?"

"You're about to be."

She shrugged helplessly. "Where would you like to start?"

"First things first. Where's the weapon?"

She started to rise, but I held out a hand. "Just tell us."

"In the bowling bag by the front door."

Torrez turned and left the kitchen, returning with a gold-and-blue vinyl carryall. He hooked the tip of his pen in the zipper latch and pulled it open, then reached in and hooked the pen through the trigger guard of the snub-nosed revolver. He held it up.

"That little thing was my father's," Taffy said. Torrez sniffed the barrel and raised an eyebrow. "Oh yes, it's been fired. But it's not loaded now. I took the shells out. They're in the bottom of the bag, too."

"Taffy, what happened?"

"Grace called me at the store. Normally Sam closes on the slow days and I close up on the weekends. But he asked earlier today if I'd mind closing. I said, 'Sure.' What's it to me? Grace called just about six, to tell me that Jennifer was missing and that Sam had taken her, and that you folks were looking for her. You could have knocked me over with a feather. I mean, you know, she and I had talked and talked over the past month or so about Jim, and about her, and about the affair she was having with Sam. But you know..." she said, and stopped.

"Know what?" I prompted.

"Well, I've had my share of trouble with Sam's hormones. As you know perfectly well." She smiled and looked heavenward. "I just had this nasty feeling that Sam Carter was the one who killed Jim Sisson."

"What made you think that?"

"People are creatures of habit," Taffy said. "That's what I figure. Sam is one—was one—of the world's biggest gossips. He's forever talking about what's going on in the town. But the morning after Jim Sisson was found dead? Wednesday, I guess it was? Sam spent most of it in the office. I asked him if he'd heard anything, and all he said was, *'Well, the village and the county are working on it, and between the two of 'em, they'll botch things up just fine.'* " She glanced over at Torrez.

"That seemed a typically ugly Sam Carter thing to say, even for an election year. And then I wondered afterward why he'd say that at all about something that everyone said was just a careless accident. I mean, unless he already knew otherwise, what would there be to botch up? Even if you did, which obviously you didn't." She laughed. "If you follow."

"What reason would Sam have to kill Jim Sisson?" I asked. "That's a hell of a risk."

She ticked off on her fingers. "Get Jim out of the way. If Jim's got insurance and it looked like an accident, then that's a plus. Maybe it's even double indemnity, or whatever you call it, for accidents. I don't know. And Jennifer is pregnant, and Sam knows he can't get close to do anything about that if Jim is alive. If he tried and Jim found out, that would be the end of old Sam, for sure. Oh, I can think of all kinds of reasons. We could even go to fantasyland and imagine that Sam Carter went over to have it out with Jim, to say, 'Look, I'm taking your wife, so deal with it.' But Sam going face-to-face is probably the least likely."

I frowned. "Then tell me something, Taffy. If that's the fantasy, why would he bother to go over there at all that night? Face-to-face with Jim? For what reason?"

"That's typical, crafty Sam," Taffy said. "Why did he use his son's Jeep a couple of hours ago? Same crafty reason."

I regarded her in silence.

"I can choreograph the scene just fine." She affected her version of Sam Carter's West Texas twang. " 'My boy done wrong, Jimbo, and I'm here to see just what we can do about it.' " She leaned her head on one hand and closed her eyes. "And how's poor Kenny going to deny it so that anyone believes him?"

"And Jim Sisson goes ballistic," I said. "Maybe he takes a swing at Sam, or threatens him. When his back is turned, some hard object comes to hand and then clever Sam has a real problem on his hands and has to cover his tracks. The backhoe is idling with the massive tire hanging by a chain."

"Maybe that's the way it happened," Taffy said. "Remember when we talked last?"

"Sure."

"And I asked you to be mindful of Grace? I was sure, just sure in my heart of hearts, that she had nothing to do with Jim's death, other than in weak, confused moments maybe wishing it might happen. I just thought that if you kept her in sight all the time, then Sam would trip up somehow. And if you were watching her, then she'd be in the clear."

"You knew Jennifer was pregnant?"

"Sure. Grace told me that some time ago, and that she didn't know what to do."

"Did she think that Kenny was to blame?"

"At first. At least that's what she wanted to believe. But, Sheriff, when she called me at the store and told me that Sam had taken Jennifer somewhere, I was just in such a state. I wanted to do something but didn't know where or how.

"Anyway, it was a few minutes after six. I had locked up, just in a swivet about what I should do—what I could do—and I was taking the day's receipts out of the last register when I heard Sam going up the stairs in the back. At least, I assumed it was Sam. Fast-like. Now maybe it wasn't any of my business, but...well, yes, it was my business." She dipped her head in emphasis. "It was my business. I went to the back, and the door to his upstairs office was open. I could hear him talking on the phone. What I heard him say was that the girl was at the motel, and he gave the room number, two-oh-seven, and that everything was all set."

"Do you know who he was talking to?" Torrez asked.

"No, sir, I don't. But Sam did ask whoever it was if he thought that there would be any complications, and he used the phrase 'with it being so early on, and all.' I distinctly heard him say that, and I knew damn well, excuse my French, that he was talking about an abortion for that poor child."

"And then what?"

"And then he said something like 'well, that's good.' And then I made a mistake, maybe. I saw red. I admit it. I went charging up the last two steps and I heard Sam say, real quick-like, 'Wait a minute. I'll call you back. Just hang on.' When I walked into his office, he was just putting the phone into the cradle. And boy, did we have a go-around."

"Physically, you mean?"

"No. But I called him every name in the book, and told him that by the time I was through with him, he'd be in the state pen for a hundred years for statutory rape and murder, and anything else I could think of. He got all blustery and said I didn't know what I was talking about. I said, 'We'll see about that,' and went back down the stairs. He followed me, the both of us shouting at each other. What a scene that would have made, if we'd had an audience." She grinned apologetically.

"How did it end up in a shooting?" I asked.

"I was halfway up the side aisle there by the drink coolers. I don't know where I was going, except maybe to the telephone by the checkout. I wasn't thinking straight, I was so angry. Too angry to be scared, and I guess with him, if I'd had any common sense, I'd have been petrified."

"Why didn't you just run straight up the first aisle you came to, the one directly opposite the door?" Torrez asked.

"Who knows?" Taffy said. "He's following me, shouting, and I guess ducking and dodging some just comes natural when you're being chased. He's shouting all of a sudden about how I live all alone and did I think anyone was going to miss me. That little shit. Excuse me again. All of a sudden, he's threatening *me*, for crying out loud. After all he's done. But he knew damn well I'd do something. I mean, after all, I filed a complaint against him last year with you folks, didn't I?"

"And what did you do then?" I asked when her torrent of words subsided.

"Then I lost my temper altogether. I still had the dumb money bag in my hand, and it's my habit to carry that little gun when I have to go make bank deposits. Just habit all these years. Anyway, I turned on him before he had a chance to grab me, and pulled that out, and it was worth the price of admission to see his eyes. Big as cheap pizzas. He kind of backpedaled, and turned, and I didn't know what he was going to do. But the gun went off just then. I don't know if I meant to pull the trigger or not. I really don't. The thing was just clenched in my hand, and *bang*. Down he went, and what a mess. I just stood there for the longest time, sure I was going to faint."

"And then you left."

She nodded. "That's not what I should have done, of course. I should have just gone to the phone and called you, shouldn't I?"

"Yes. But instead you decided to make it look like a robbery."

"The receipts are in the bowling bag, too," she said, and Torrez nodded. "It was just a dumb idea."

I sat back. "Taffy, these photos," and I opened the manila envelope that had been lying on the table at my elbow, "show your shoe prints, where you stepped in the beer."

She leaned forward with interest, and I handed the photo to her.

"We have a warrant from Judge Hobart. We'd like to see those shoes."

"For heaven's sakes. I didn't even think about that. I didn't know you people could even do such things."

"We people can," I said gently.

"They're in the hall closet," she said. "First pair on the left. And I have to apologize, Bill. In the past few hours, I came to the conclusion that I could live pretty easily with what I did, if your department could never solve Sam's death. I mean, he was a real first-class skunk. And he threatened me. If I'd just blabbed it all out a day or two ago, when you were sitting right there eating cinnamon rolls, then Sam might still be alive." She tried a grin. "Not that that's necessarily such a good thing. But I could have saved you some time and work."

I shrugged. "Saving us work isn't what's important," I said.

"So," Torrez said. "Let me make sure I understand all this. You felt, number one, that Sam Carter may have been responsible for Jim Sisson's death?"

"Yes, I did."

"But you didn't have any certain proof of that. Nothing he said, or anything like that."

"No."

"And number two, you had information that led you to believe that Sam Carter was in the process of arranging for an illegal abortion for Jennifer Sisson, a minor well known to you?"

"Yes."

"And number three, you felt that Sam Carter had threatened you? In fact, threatened your life?"

"Yes."

"And that had he continued in his pursuit of you, you might have been in physical danger?"

"Yes."

"Miss Hines, are you in the regular habit of carrying a loaded weapon when you carry the store's receipts at night?"

"Yes."

"Did you realize that carrying a concealed loaded weapon is against the law in the state of New Mexico?"

"No, I didn't know that. Or care, I guess, would be more like it."

"Did anyone else know that you carried a weapon in that bag as a matter of habit?"

"Sure. Even Sam Carter knew that. He thought it was funny."

Torrez turned to me and shrugged. "Seems to me that we have a civilian who interrupted a person in commission of a felony, sir. And in so doing, she put herself in jeopardy, and then defended herself with the only means at her disposal."

I reached out and snapped off the recorder. The room was quiet for a long time. Finally, I said, "Taffy, we'll want to talk again in the morning. My first inclination is to agree with the undersheriff, but ultimately it's the decision of the district attorney. He'll want to make sure that all the evidence we have corroborates what you say. He'll be in town either later tonight or first thing tomorrow, and we'll get together with him and his assistants."

"What should I do?" she asked plaintively.

"Try to get some rest. I'd prefer that you didn't discuss the matter with anybody—Grace Sisson included. If you'd just sort of turn off the world until tomorrow, I'd be grateful."

"I'll unplug my phone."

I laughed. "OK. One of my deputies is going to be staying with you, right here in the house." I shrugged. "It's either that or you stay at the Public Safety Building for the night."

"In jail, you mean," Taffy said, and I nodded. "I'll take my own bed, thanks just the same."

Taffy Hines came around the table and put an arm around me. Both of us were on the fat side, so it was like a couple of bumper cars hugging. "Thanks so much."

"We'll see, Taffy. It's not over yet. But you try and get some rest."

I followed Bob Torrez and his wife out the door, and as they stepped out into the soft evening, I saw Gayle Torrez reach out and give Bob a gentle, wifely tweak of approval on the back of his arm.

FORTY-THREE

BY MIDNIGHT, the list of what we knew for certain was almost as long as the collection of questions.

Sam Carter's fingerprints were etched in blood on the backhoe, and the blood was consistent with his blood type. Since about a billion people around the world shared that blood type, we were going to have to wait for a DNA comparison from the state lab, and who the hell knew how long that was going to take?

Dr. Perrone found a small cut on the underside of Sam's left middle finger, but there were small nicks and cuts in several other places on Sam's hands, too—the sort of little inconsequential wounds that could be caused by something no more sinister than being careless while opening a cardboard box.

But since Sam had already stood a brief trial, it didn't matter much. He'd been on board the machine when he had no reason to be, and there was plenty of motive.

We had witnesses that he'd reserved a room in his brother's name when he, in fact, had no brother and another witness who'd seen him pick up Jennifer Sisson at Burger Heaven.

Jennifer acknowledged that the child she was carrying was probably fathered by Sam Carter and that if she could find a way, she'd lose it—but that particular snarl was well beyond our province. We left it for Grace Sisson to solve.

Whether Grace Sisson had conspired with Sam Carter to murder her husband was a question that four of us argued and debated for more than an hour in my office. By 1:00 a.m., Bob Torrez, District Attorney Daniel Schroeder, Assistant DA Don Jaramillo, and I reached consensus—we had no evidence that suggested a conspiracy to commit murder.

Crushing someone with a weighted tractor tire was one of those "moment of opportunity" crimes that would be impossible to plan accurately ahead of time. Sam had taken the opportunity, and most likely Taffy's version of events was correct.

At 2:30 a.m., I called a groggy Frank Dayan and gave the newspaper publisher an abridged version of events as we understood them.

"Good grief," Dayan whispered when I'd finished.

"And I don't envy you the job of trying to make sense of all that," I said.

"It's one of those stories that has *'officials said,'* or some other attribution, after about every other sentence so someone doesn't file eighty-five lawsuits against us," Dayan muttered. "I think we'll be using a lot of *'investigation is continuing'* jargon. That'll let people fill in their own holes."

"That's more entertaining, anyway," I said. "Best of luck."

"Sam didn't exactly accomplish what he wanted, did he?"

"Nope."

"And by the way, I never asked you.... What did you find out about those little notes about Tom Pasquale?"

"The original was in the trash in Sam Carter's computer. Evidently he didn't realize he had to empty the can. I had no idea someone existed in the world who knew less about computers than I do."

"You want me to print something about that?"

"I'd rather you let it stay in the trash, Frank. We've got a file here, should anyone ever try to make something more out of it. Let it lie."

"All right. And by the way... I was over at the sheriff's office earlier this afternoon, or yesterday, or whenever the hell it was, and saw a report about Carla Champlin parking her RV on Judge Lester Hobart's front lawn. What the hell was that all about?"

"Ah, she just took a wrong turn."

"No, seriously. What was she doing?"

"I *am* serious, Frank. That's about all there was to it."

"Assault with a broomstick?"

I laughed so loud it probably hurt Frank Dayan's ears.

"Great headline, Frank. Go ahead and print that. I dare you. About now, the county needs a good chuckle."

"So what now?"

"I'm going home to bed, if I can remember where I live."

And for the first time in a long, long time, I did just that.

CHANGELINGS

JO BANNISTER
A CASTLEMERE MYSTERY

It begins with contaminated yogurt in a
supermarket. Next, the tampering of
showers in a girls' locker room. Caustic
soda in baby powder. Cholera in cough
medicine. An anonymous note promises
much more—unless the town of
Castlemere pays a ransom of one
million pounds.

Superintendent Frank Shapiro, recovering from a bullet
wound, has been cleared for desk duty. But with Sergeant
Cal Donovan on holiday cruising the Castlemere Canal,
he must rely on Inspector Liz Graham as hysteria rises.

The situation worsens when the detectives learn Donovan's
abandoned boat has been found—and that the volatile
sergeant is believed dead by the hand of the blackmailer....

Available February 2002 at your favorite retail outlet.

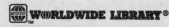

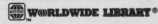

Take 2 books and a surprise gift FREE!

SPECIAL LIMITED-TIME OFFER

Mail to: The Mystery Library™
3010 Walden Ave.
P.O. Box 1867
Buffalo, N.Y. 14240-1867

YES! Please send me **2 free books** from the Mystery Library™ and my free surprise gift. After receiving them, if I don't wish to receive anymore, I can return the shipping statement marked cancel. If I don't cancel, I will receive 3 brand-new novels every month, before they're available in stores! Bill me at the bargain price of $4.69 per book plus 25¢ shipping and handlng and applicable sales tax, if any*. That's the complete price and a savings of over 15% off the cover price—what a great deal! There is no minimum number of books I must purchase. I can always return a shipment at your expense and cancel my subscription. Even if I never buy another book from the Mystery Library™, **the 2 free books and surprise gift are mine to keep forever.**

415 WEN DFNF

Name _____ (PLEASE PRINT)

Address _____ Apt. No. _____

City _____ State _____ Zip _____

* Terms and prices subject to change without notice. N.Y. residents add
  applicable sales tax. This offer is limited to one order per household and not
  valid to present Mystery Library™ subscribers. All orders subject to approval.
© 1990 Worldwide Library
™ are registered trademarks of Harlequin Enterprises Limited

MYS01-R

THE PUMPKIN SEED MASSACRE

Native American psychologist Ben Pecos has returned to New Mexico as an intern with the Indian Health Service. Still struggling with the demons of his past, he is plunged into the nightmare rampage of a mysterious virus that is killing the residents of the pueblo, including his own grandmother.

One of the victims, the powerful tribal governor, opposed the construction of a proposed gambling casino on pueblo land. Ben suspects his murder was premeditated—but that doesn't explain the insidious killer now stalking the innocent.

"...great plot...a gripping novel."
—Tony Hillerman

Available February 2002 at your favorite retail outlet.

SUSAN SLATER
A BEN PECOS MYSTERY